Tarod alone knew the nature of the supernatural force locked within his soul – and he
knew that it must be thwarted, no matter what
the sacrifice. Denounced by his fellow Adepts
as a demon, betrayed even by those he loved, he
had unleashed a power that twisted the fabric of
time, to put himself beyond the reach of that
monstrous force and avert the pandemonium
that threatened the world.

He thought that nothing could break through
the barrier he had created.

He was wrong . . .

By the same author
The Initiate – Book 1 of the Time Master trilogy

THE
OUTCAST

BOOK 2 OF THE
TIME MASTER TRILOGY

LOUISE COOPER

London
UNWIN PAPERBACKS
Boston   Sydney

First published by Unwin Paperbacks 1986
Reprinted 1986, 1987

UNWIN HYMAN LIMITED
Denmark House
37–39 Queen Elizabeth Street
LONDON SE1 2QB
and
40 Museum Street, LONDON WC1A 1LU

Allen & Unwin Australia Pty Ltd
8 Napier Street, North Sydney, NSW 2060, Australia

Unwin Paperbacks with Port Nicholson Press
60 Cambridge Terrace, Wellington, New Zealand

British Library Cataloguing in Publication Data

Cooper, Louise
  The outcast.—(The Time master trilogy;
  bk2)—(Unicorn)
I. Title   II. Series
  823′.914[F]   PR6053.05/
ISBN 0–04–823299–8

Typeset by Computerised Typesetting Services Ltd, London N12
Printed in Great Britain by Cox & Wyman Ltd, Reading

THE OUTCAST

Chapter 1

'I'm telling you, you won't find better foodstuffs anywhere in Shu, or Prospect or Han for that matter!' The market trader thrust a handful of dark pinkish-purple roots under his customer's nose and brandished them almost threateningly. 'And I've better things to do on a market day than waste my time with an outland slut who probably hasn't even got a coin to her name – so make your mind up now, before I set my dog on you!'

The mangy cross-breed hound that was sprawled inelegantly under the rickety stall glowered jaundicedly at his master, and the girl the trader had addressed stared back coldly, unimpressed. She was too experienced a haggler these days to pay any attention to threats or insults; she had judged the quality of the fruit and vegetables on offer and made her own decision as to their worth. She thrust a dirty hand into her belt-pouch and pulled out a tarnished brass coin.

'I said a quarter-gravine and I meant a quarter. Take it or leave it.'

For a moment the man glared at her, resenting her manner, the fact that she refused to be intimidated, the ignominy of having to barter with a woman – and a low-class of woman – in the first place. But it was obvious she didn't intend to give way, and a sale was a sale . . . Winter business was slack at the best of times.

He snatched the money ungraciously and dumped the roots into the hemp bag she held out.

'And the fruit,' she said.

Resentfully he threw six shrivelled pears in after the vegetables, then spat on the ground at her feet. 'There! And may cats eat your carcass!'

1

Quickly, reflexively, the girl made a gesture before her own face intended to ward off curses and negate the evil eye, and for a moment the look in her peculiar amber eyes made the trader feel distinctly uncomfortable. Something about her had raised his hackles; she was a coastal Easterner to judge by her accent, and they weren't noted for feyness . . . but as she made that sign he'd felt as if the venom in his own words was being palpably turned back on him.

Ah, damn the woman. Nothing but a peasant girl in handed-down men's clothes . . . he had her money in his pocket, and that was what counted. Nonetheless, he watched her surreptitiously as she walked away, and the unease only left him when she had finally merged with the crowd and vanished from sight.

Cyllan Anassan swallowed her anger as she headed back through the market square towards her uncle's pitch on the outskirts of the clusters of stalls. She should be accustomed, by now, to the attitude of such men, especially here in the more affluent South – they expected a girl of her age and lowly status to be at best a simpleton; and when they failed to palm her off with the dregs of their produce at extortionate prices, they resorted to abuse. Admittedly Shu-Nhadek – province capital of Shu – was an improvement on many towns she had visited, but the cavalier treatment still rankled. And when all was said and done, she had come away with substandard foodstuffs that would take twice the cooking to make them palatable.

She would have liked to linger at the better end of the market and choose from the succulent vegetables on sale there – and, she admitted to herself, have had the secret pleasure of mingling with the high-clan folk who graced those stalls with their custom – but the thought of her uncle's rage at such profligacy had deterred her. If he was sober she'd feel the buckle of his belt across her back; if he was drunk he would probably kick her from one end of the square to the other.

Unconsciously goaded by that thought, she quickened

her steps, muttering an apology as she bumped against a group of well-dressed women who were gossiping beside a stand selling sweetmeats and wine, and tried to make haste through the crowd. But now that she had left the cheaper and less well-patronised section of the market behind, haste was impossible; the press of people had simply become too great. And the temptation to dawdle was irresistible; this was her first visit to Shu-Nhadek, and there was so much to see and take in. All around her the huge market square was filled with colour and move-ment; in the distance the jumbled rooftops and pastel-washed walls of the tall old buildings rose to frame the picture, and further away still, if she craned her neck to look, the slender masts of ships riding at anchor in the harbour were just visible. Shu-Nhadek was the largest and oldest sea-port in the entire land; sheltered in the South-facing Bay of Illusions and served by the kindly currents of the Summerisle Straits, it was a perfect year-round haven for traders and travellers alike. Most of the major drove-roads terminated at the town, and its prox-imity to the Summer Isle, home of the High Margrave himself, lent it a status no other province capital could hope to match. People from every walk of life imagin-able could be found here; wealthy merchants, crafts-men, farmers, drovers like her uncle's band, white-robed Sisters of Aeoris, even men and women from the Summer Isle taking a respite from the formalities of court life. And on the two days of the monthly market, the town's population increased fivefold. Cyllan could have simply stood by and watched the bustle from dawn to dusk without ever growing bored.

At last though, she was forced to stop altogether to allow a groom with several Southern blood-horses to lead his charges across her path. Waiting, Cyllan stared enviously at the tall, elegant animals – a far cry from the stocky and evil-tempered little pony she herself rode when she travelled with Kand Brialen and his drovers – and abruptly, unbidden, the colour and bustle and sheer exuberant life of the market brought back a memory that she had been trying for months to quell. A memory of another place, another festive occasion . . . and one beside which the grand market of Shu-Nhadek suddenly shrank to a pale echo. A spectacle that probably wouldn't be repeated in her lifetime – the inaugural celebrations for the new High Initiate, at the Castle of the Star Peninsula on its remote stack far away in the North. It had been late Summer then, even the Northern climate kindly, and images of the ceremony and panoply, the unimaginably ancient Castle decorated with streamers and pennants, the long processions of nobility, the bonfires, the music, the dancing flashed through her inner vision as clearly as though she were seeing them again with her physical senses. She had even glimpsed the new High Initiate himself, Keridil Toln, young, assured and resplendent in his ceremonial robes, when his procession emerged through the Castle gates to give Aeoris's blessing to the vast crowd.

It had been an unforgettable experience . . . but the memory which had caused her both joy and pain over the last months stood apart from the glory of the celebrations. A man; tall, black-haired, pale-skinned, with a haunted disquiet in his green eyes; a sorcerer and high Adept of the Circle. They had met once before, by chance, and against all likelihood he had remembered her. She had been drinking some vile brew which she had bought with her last coin from a wine stall; he had tipped the cup's contents on to the grass, given the stall-holder a tongue-lashing and replaced the wine with a high quality vintage. And Cyllan, overcome by shyness and by an acute sense of her own lowliness, had made a feeble excuse and run away as soon as she prudently could. Since then she had regretted her cowardice a thousand times; yearned for another chance . . . but the chance hadn't come her way. And later that same night, her psychic senses had told her that her dreams could have borne no fruit when she had conjured a vision of him in his private rooms, with a graceful, patrician girl, and had known that she was already forgotten . . .

The horses had cleared the square now and the crowd moved forward again. Passing a stall that sold ornaments of fashioned metal and enamel, Cyllan paused suddenly as something, half hidden among the piled wares, caught her eye. She moved closer, peering, then looked guiltily towards the stallholder, expecting to be driven away. This trader, however, knew from experience that good customers often appeared in the most unlikely guises, and courteously nodded for her to continue. Encouraged, Cyllan took out the object which had intrigued her and held it up. It was a necklace; a finely wrought chain of copper from which depended three beaten copper discs. On the centremost and largest, a skilled craftsman had worked a filigree design in silver and blue enamel – a lightning-flash bisected by a single eye.

The lightning-flash . . . symbol of an Adept . . . Cyllan bit her lip as memory surged again, and wondered how much the necklace might cost. She wouldn't dare to haggle at a stall of this nature; and besides, she knew nothing of metal values. But she had a little money – a very little; one or two gravines she had managed to scrimp for herself over the months. And it would be so gratifying to own just one beautiful thing; one artefact to remind her . . .

'Derret Morsyth's one of the finest craftsmen in the province,' the stallholder said suddenly. Cyllan started, then looked up at the man's face. He had moved to stand opposite her, and there was no hostility in his eyes.

'It's . . . beautiful,' she said.

'Certainly. Mind you, he tends only to work with the lesser metals, and there's some who'll dismiss him because he doesn't bedeck his pieces with gold and gems. But to my way of thinking, there can be as much beauty in a piece of copper or pewter as in any number of emeralds. It's the hand and the eye that count, not the materials.'

Cyllan nodded emphatically, and the man gestured to the necklace. 'Try it on.'

'No, I – I couldn't . . .'

He laughed. 'You don't know the price yet, girl! Derret Morsyth doesn't overcharge, and neither do I. Try it – the copper almost matches your pretty eyes!'

Cheeks reddened by the unaccustomed compliment, Cyllan hesitantly held the necklace up to her throat. The metal felt cool and heavy against her skin; it had a substantial feel to it . . . Half turning, she was about to let the stallholder fasten it for her when she glimpsed her own reflection in a polished bronze mirror, and what she saw destroyed her eagerness instantly.

Pretty eyes, the stallholder had said . . . gods, she wasn't pretty! Face plain, too tight and pinched, mouth too wide, and her amber eyes weren't beautiful, merely peculiar. Her hair – so pale that it was almost white – hung in tatty strands round her shoulders; she'd made an effort this morning, for practicality's sake, to tie it into a bunch at the nape of her neck, but now half of it had worked free and she looked like a scarecrow. Dirty old shirt, jerkin and trousers, handed on from a man in her uncle's droving crew. And there on her breast hung the necklace she had coveted. It had been fashioned for a lady, not a down-at-heel urchin, and on her it became a grotesque parody.

Quickly she looked away from the awful revelation, and put up a hand to stop the trader who was about to fasten the necklace's clasp.

'No. I – I'm sorry, but I can't. Thank you, but I don't want to buy it.'

He was nonplussed. 'It's not expensive, girl. And any young woman surely deserves –'

The attempt at kind persuasion was like a knife-thrust to Cyllan, and she shook her head violently. 'No, please! I – haven't got any money anyway. Not even a half-gravine. I'm sorry to have wasted your time . . . thank you.' And before he could say another word she almost ran from the stall.

The baffled trader stared after her until a new voice drew his attention back to his business. 'Trader Rishak?'

Collecting himself, Rishak looked at his customer, and recognised the eldest son of Shu's Provincial Margrave.

'Oh – forgive me, sir! I didn't see you – I had my mind on that young woman there. An odd one if you please!'

Drachea Rannak raised his eyebrows enquiringly. 'Odd!'

Rishak snorted, wryly amused. 'First she shows great interest in one of Morsyth's pieces – on the verge of buying it, mind you – then suddenly she's changed her mind and bolted before I can say a word!'

The young man smiled. 'They say it's a woman's privilege to be contrary.'

'So they do . . . ah well, if I was a married man maybe I'd understand 'em better. Now, sir; what can I show you today?'

'I'm looking for a gift for my mother. It's her birth-anniversary in three days, and I'd like something special . . . and a little personal.'

'For the Lady Margravine? Well, please give her my most respectful congratulations for the day! And I think I have just the thing for her good taste right here . . .'

Only when she was well clear of the trinkets stall did Cyllan finally stop and get her breath. She was furious with herself, both for her initial vanity and for her foolish behaviour when she realised her mistake. What use would a necklace have been to her? Something to wear at her next social occasion, perhaps on her next visit to the Castle of the Star Peninsula? She almost laughed aloud. Something to get in her way when she was trying to stew her third-rate vegetables into edibility, more like! Or for her uncle to find and sell, and pocket the proceeds . . .

Her heart was still thumping painfully with the ignominy of the experience, and she had an illogical conviction that everyone around her knew of her humiliation and was secretly laughing at her. She had finally halted near the door of a tavern at the square's edge, and in a desultory attempt to cheer herself she pushed through the crowd and bought a mug of herb beer and a chunk of bread spread with milk-cheese. The tavern room was stiflingly overcrowded, so she found a quiet bench outside and watched the market shoppers go by while she slowly ate and drank.

After a little while, a steadily droning voice from a booth next to the tavern caught her attention. The boothman was a fortune-teller, and was regaling his current customer with a long tale of great fortune and fame. Intrigued despite her mood, Cyllan edged closer until she could peer across and observe the proceedings – and her pulse quickened.

The fortune-teller had cast six stones on to his table, and was apparently reading his client's future from the pattern they formed. Geomancy was one of the most ancient techniques known in Cyllan's Eastern homeland, and quickly she looked at the clairvoyant's face, searching for the pale skin and distinctive features of a Flatlands native. But whatever else the man might be, he was no Easterner. And the stones . . . there should have been many of them, not merely six. And sand on which to cast them. And the pattern they formed was nothing but meaningless gibberish . . .

Inwardly, Cyllan seethed. The fortune-teller was a charlatan, trading on superstition and on a psychic skill that was long dead but for a few secret practitioners. In the Great Eastern Flatlands, anyone with the fey touch was little better than a pariah now; she herself had learned at an early age to keep her innate and developing skills a secret from all but the old woman who had quietly tutored her in reading the stones, and even her uncle knew nothing of the precious collection of pebbles, worn smooth by the sea, which lodged in her belt-pouch. An apprentice drover, lowliest of the low, would never broadcast such a talent if she knew what was good for her . . . But Cyllan's talent was real, unlike the trumpery lies of this trickster, playing on his client's mixture of fear and gullible fascination.

She should have been in a Sisterhood Cot. Suddenly she heard the words in her head as clearly as if the tall, dark Adept had been standing before her and speaking them aloud once more. He had recognised her skill, and he had paid her that compliment. *She should have been admitted to that august body of women, servants of the gods, and her talents fostered and nurtured* . . . But the Sisterhood had no time for the likes of a peasant drover. She had no money, no sponsor . . . and so, instead of wearing the white robe, she sat on a tavern bench and listened to a charlatan prostituting a seer's skills, and had no authority to intervene.

The fortune-teller's monologue finished and his client rose to leave, flushed and thanking him profusely. Cyllan saw a five-gravine piece change hands, and was disgusted, but if the fake seer felt anything of her fury he didn't show it. He was counting his afternoon's takings when a slight, brown-haired young man paused by his booth. The newcomer's gaze flicked from the fortune-teller to Cyllan and lingered a moment as though in recognition; then, glancing surreptitiously over his shoulder, he slid into the empty chair opposite the boothman.

The charlatan made a great show of welcoming his visitor; so much so that Cyllan realised he must be the favoured son of an out-of-the-ordinary – and wealthy – local clan. But whatever his status, the young man was clearly no less gullible or superstitious than any peasant. His manner, the way he sat attentively forward, his whispered questions, all betrayed a naïve eagerness which the fortune-teller was quick to exploit. Cyllan watched as the six stones were produced and meaningless signs and passes made over them, before the fake seer began his monologue.

'I see great good fortune for you, young sir. Good fortune indeed; for within the year you will wed. A love match, if I may venture to say so – a lady whose beauty will be unequalled among her peers – and many fine children. And I see, too . . . ' Here he paused dramatically, as though waiting for divine inspiration to touch his tongue, while the young man stared fixedly at the stones, ' . . . yes! High office, young sir; great power and renown. I see you standing in a great hall, a resplendent hall, dispensing justice and judgement. A long life, sir; a good life and a happy one.'

The young man's eyes were alight. Breathless, and completely enamoured of the charlatan's pronouncement, he murmured a question which Cyllan didn't catch, and suddenly, watching him, she found herself unconsciously adjusting her vision so that the two figures at the cloth-covered table faded out of focus. On rare occasions, she had discovered, she could make predictions in a small way, or divine a stranger's character or background, without the need for her stones. It was a sporadic talent, unpredictable at the best of times; but now she felt that her psychic touch was sure . . . Closing her eyes she concentrated harder and a vague mental impression began to form, growing clearer until at last, satisfied, she opened her eyes again.

The fortune-teller had done, and the young man was getting up to leave. Coins changed hands, thanks were given and obsequious bows received in exchange; then the boothman dodged behind his curtain and out of sight.

The young man was about to pass by Cyllan's bench, and she knew suddenly that she couldn't keep silent. Little good it might do her, but her sense of justice rebelled at the thought of letting such chicanery go unremarked. As the young man reached her she stood up.

'Excuse me, sir . . . '

He started, turned, then frowned, clearly unused to being so directly addressed by a low-class stranger. Anxious that he shouldn't think she was importuning him, Cyllan spoke quickly and softly.

'The fortune-teller is a charlatan, sir. I thought you should know.'

He was surprised. A fresh, smooth face, she thought; he'd never known hardship, never wanted for anything – and probably that explained his naïvety in the face of the seer's blandishments. Now, collecting himself, he strolled closer to where she sat.

'A charlatan?' His smile was faintly patronising. 'What makes you so sure?'

Obviously he suspected her of harbouring some personal motive for attempting to discredit the man. Cyllan met his gaze steadily. 'I was born and brought up in the Great Eastern Flatlands. Reading the stones is an ancient skill there . . . and therefore I know a faker when I see one.'

The young man clasped his hands together and stared

thoughtfully at an expensive ring on one finger. 'He is a stranger to Shu-Nhadek – as, it seems, are you – and yet he divined a good deal about my position. Doesn't that speak in his favour?'

Cyllan decided to gamble that her flash of clairvoyance had been accurate, and smiled. 'It takes small seer's skills, sir, to recognise and acknowledge the son and heir to the Margrave of Shu Province.'

She had been right . . . he raised his eyebrows and stared at her with a newly dawning interest. '*You* are a seer?'

'A stone-reader, and of small talent,' Cyllan said, ignoring the insult – no doubt unintentional – that his surprise implied. 'I don't ply my skill, nor do I seek to profit from it; I'm not trying to steal the boothman's trade. But it offends me to see tricksters preying on innocent victims.'

The idea that he was one such innocent victim clearly didn't appeal to the Margrave's son and for a moment she wondered if she had been too blunt, and affronted him. But after a brief hesitation he nodded curtly.

'Then I'm indebted to you. I'll have the charlatan run out of the province before the day's over!' His eyes narrowed suddenly and he studied her face more closely. 'And if you are what you say you are, I shall be interested to see if you can succeed where the charlatan failed!'

He wanted her to read the stones for him, and Cyllan was alarmed. Her uncle, who like most of his peers was deeply superstitious and regarded psychic talents as the rightful province only of the privileged – and officially sanctioned – few, would kill her if he ever found out that she had been using her skills. And to read for the son of the Province Margrave . . . she couldn't do it – she didn't dare.

'I'm sorry,' she said indistinctly, 'I can't.'

'Can't?' He was suddenly angry. 'What d'you mean, *can't?* You say you're a seer – I ask you to prove it!'

'I mean, sir, that I daren't.' She could do nothing

other than be honest. 'I'm apprenticed to my uncle, and he disapproves strongly of such things. If he were ever to find out – '

'What is your uncle's name?'

'He is – ' She looked at the young man's face, swallowed. 'Kand Brialen. A drover.'

'A drover who doesn't exploit a profitable enterprise right under his nose? I find that hard to believe!'

'Please!' Cyllan entreated him anxiously. 'If he were ever to know –'

'Oh, by the gods I've got better things to do with my time than run tattling tales to peasants!' the young man retorted petulantly. 'And if you won't read for me, you won't. But I'll remember the name. Kand Brialen – I'll remember it!' And before Cyllan could say anything more, he turned on his heel and walked away.

Slowly, she sat down again. Her heart was thumping and she wished that she hadn't been so foolhardy as to interfere. Now, if the whim took him, the Margrave's son might find some excuse to seek out her uncle and, if he was sufficiently offended by her refusal, let slip enough about their encounter to ensure that she'd suffer for it. He wasn't used to having his wishes thwarted; he was obviously spoilt and might choose to be spiteful. And if –

She checked the train of thought suddenly, and sighed. Whatever the Margrave's son did or did not do, she couldn't change matters. She had survived Kand Brialen's rage before now, and could survive it again. Best to finish her beer, return and face whatever had to be faced.

The tavern potboy emerged to take her mug and ask if she'd like more. Cyllan shook her head and reluctantly rose from the bench, heading away towards the side of the market place where the crowds began to thin out. Here, stalls and booths gave way to the thatch-roofed livestock pens, where herds of dull-eyed animals milled and complained and awaited their fate. Kand Brialen and his drovers had pitched their tents to one side of the largest pen, and throughout the day trade had been brisk; they had a hundred cattle, driven in from Han, to sell, together with four good work-horses which Kand had bought for a disgracefully low sum after a good deal of barter in Prospect. And with Spring and the breeding season almost in sight they were fetching good prices.

Cyllan had long ago learned not to think too often about her own future with Kand Brialen and his drovers. Four years ago, when her mother – Kand's sister – and father had been lost with their fishing boat in the treacherous Whiteshoals Sound, her uncle had taken on responsibility for her, but from the beginning he'd made no effort to disguise his resentment of the duty. As far as he was concerned Cyllan was an unwanted liability; he had no use for women other than the occasional whore when the mood took him, and had made it clear that if his orphaned niece expected him to provide for her, she must repay him by working as hard as any of the men in his band. And so for four years Cyllan had dressed like a drover, worked like a drover and coped, too, with all the 'women's work' demanded of her. Admittedly, she had also travelled widely and seen a good deal of the world; something unheard of for any girl in the Eastern Flatlands. But it was a life that gave her little to look forward to.

Back at home – although it was becoming harder every season to think of anywhere as home – she would doubtless by now have been matched with the second or third son of another local fishing family in a pragmatic clan alliance. Hardly a great achievement, but it would have been better, surely, than this harsh nomadic existence. As it was, her future stretched endlessly ahead; work, travel, sleep when she could snatch it, until the Northern winds and Southern Sun withered her before her time . . .

She shook the unhappy thought off as she glimpsed her uncle's burly figure moving among the lines of horses tethered near the pens. He was accompanied by a tall and slightly stooping middle-aged man who, to judge from his fur-trimmed coat and Kand's obsequiousness, was a wealthy potential customer. Cyllan tried to make herself as inconspicuous as possible as she headed towards their pitch, anxious not to disturb her uncle while he was trading. She had almost reached the tents when a voice spoke softly but with satisfaction behind her.

'Ah – so there you are!'

Startled, she turned to find herself facing the Margrave's son. He was grinning conspiratorially, and gestured in the direction of the two men.

'Kand Brialen – I remembered. And when I saw that he had good livestock for sale, I insisted that my father should see for himself!'

So that was the Margrave of Shu . . . Cyllan realised suddenly that she was staring like a Moonstruck yokel, and hastily looked away.

'You and I,' the Margrave's son said, 'have some unfinished business. And I think my father and your uncle will be quite a time in making their bargain, so your secret's safe enough. Come with me!'

He was obviously not about to be argued with, so Cyllan made no attempt to protest as he took her arm and hurried her away from the pens. They entered a narrow street which led off the market square to the harbour, and the young man indicated an ill-kept building with a sign over the door depicting a crudely painted white ship on an unnaturally blue sea.

'The White Barque Tavern,' he said as he led the way through into the dark interior. 'It's used by sailors and traders, mostly – we're unlikely to be seen by anyone who might know me.'

Cyllan wryly shrugged aside the implied insult – after all, he was in his terms lowering himself by appearing publicly in her company – and tried to assess her first impressions of her companion. She had noted an almost feverish look in his eyes when he demanded that she should read her stones for him, and his determination to get his own way said far more about his personality than any words. She had met such people before; those who, preoccupied with the occult, defied the conventions which barred the subject to all but the Circle and the Sisterhood of Aeoris, and all too often their fascination bordered on obsession. Cyllan had recognised the trait immediately in the Margrave's son, and was wary of it; it was a tendency that could, if she wasn't careful, lead her into trouble.

But otherwise, the young man seemed unremarkable enough. He had the typical good looks of a Shu Province native; abundant warm brown hair which curled about his head in the short style currently fashionable in the South, fine skin with an olive tinge that disguised a tendency to floridity, and expressive dark eyes with unusually long lashes. He was quite tall for a Southerner, and although in later years he would probably run to fat, there was no sign of it as yet.

Now he pulled out a stool at an empty table in the corner of the tavern, and snapped his fingers to attract a potboy. Cyllan slid silently into the seat opposite and waited while he ordered wine for them both, and a slice of beef on black bread for himself. He didn't ask if Cyllan was hungry. The wine and food were brought and unceremoniously dumped on the table; the potboy gave the well-to-do customer a withering look as he stalked away.

'Now,' said the Margrave's son, 'let's deal with first things first. Tell me your name.'

'Cyllan Anassan. Apprentice drover, from Kennet Head on the Great Eastern Flatlands.' She introduced herself in the customary formal way by placing her hand palm down on the table.

He laid his over it, but very briefly. 'Drachea Rannak. Heir Margrave of Shu Province, from Shu-Nhadek.' And leaning back, he added. 'So tell me, Cyllan Anassan, what brings you to be a drover, of all the unlikely occupations for a female?'

Her story was brief and dreary; she told it in as few words as possible, and he regarded her with curious interest.

'And yet you're a seer? I'd have thought the Sisterhood would have been of more interest to you than droving.'

She smiled thinly. In his world, a girl who wanted to join the Sisterhood of Aeoris merely said so and it was done, and she doubted if he could envisage matters any other way.

'Let's just say that the – opportunity – eluded me,' she replied. 'Besides, I doubt if I'm what the Sisters would call a seer.'

Drachea pushed the slab of black bread around his plate with distaste. 'Maybe so – but you should have pursued it.' He looked up. 'As a matter of fact, were it not for my position here in Shu I might well have thought along similar lines and presented myself as a candidate for the Circle.'

'The Circle . . . ?' Her response was immediate and her eyes narrowed. Drachea shrugged carelessly. 'As it is, of course, such a thing isn't possible unless I were to stand down in favour of my younger brother, and there'd be all manner of complications.' He paused, then: 'You've obviously travelled a great deal. Have you ever seen the Star Peninsula?'

Cyllan was beginning to understand what lay behind his fascination with arcane matters. 'Yes,' she told him. 'We were there last Summer, when the new High Initiate was inaugurated.'

'You were?' Drachea leaned forward, his condescension abruptly forgotten. 'And did you see Keridil Toln in person?'

'From a distance only. He came out of the Castle to speak and give Aeoris's blessing to the crowd.'

'Gods!' Drachea took a mouthful of wine, hardly noticing what he was doing. 'And to think that I missed such an event! My parents made the journey, of course, but I was ill with a fever and had to remain at home.' He licked his lips. 'So you saw it all . . . and did you cross the causeway to the Castle itself?'

'Yes . . . for a short while.'

'Aeoris!' Drachea made a sign before his heart to show that he meant no disrespect to the highest of the gods. 'It must have been the experience of a lifetime! And what of the Initiates themselves? Doubtless you saw some of them – but I don't imagine you actually *met* any one of their number, did you?'

Cyllan's suspicions were at last confirmed. Drachea's

one burning ambition was to join the ranks of the Circle, so that he could satisfy his craving and learn the truth behind the secrets which obsessed him. And she knew, too, why he was so determined that she should read his future. He wanted to believe that his ambition would be fulfilled, and her word as a seer would be enough to fuel the fire inside him.

'Cyllan!' She was startled as he grasped her arm and shook it. 'Listen to me! I said, did you meet any of the Initiates?'

A discomforting juxtaposition of images flickered through Cyllan's mind as she stared back. Drachea's face, young, untrammelled, filled with a sense of his own importance; and another face, gaunt, self-contained, the eyes betraying knowledge and emotions far beyond physical years . . .

She said huskily, 'I met one man . . . a high Adept.'

'Then the Adepts don't keep themselves to themselves? I'd heard – ah, but rumours grow like weeds! I must go there and see for myself. I would have done long since, but it needs so much time!' He clenched his fists together in frustration, then abruptly his expression changed. 'Have you been back to the Peninsula since those celebrations?'

'No. We spent a month in Empty Province and since then have been making our way South.'

'Then you won't know the truth or otherwise of these newest rumours that are being whispered.'

'New rumours?' Cyllan was alert. 'I've heard nothing.'

'No . . . I doubt you would have. They began in West High Land and Chaun, and now they're spreading here as well. No one seems to know the facts, but they say,' and Drachea paused for emphasis, 'that there's something wrong at the Castle. No word has been received from anyone there for some while now, and no one knows anyone who has visited the Castle from outside since last Moon-conjunction.'

A peculiar sensation clutched at the pit of Cyllan's stomach. She couldn't explain the feeling or put a name to it; it was as if deep down within her some dormant, animal sense was stirring. Keeping a tight rein on herself she said again, 'I've heard nothing. What do people say might be amiss?'

'That's just it – no one knows. There was a tale from West High Land recently about some dangerous wrong-doer apprehended at the Sisterhood Cot there, and there's talk of a connection with events at the Castle, but beyond that everything's speculation. It seems that the Initiates have decided to shut themselves off altogether from the rest of the world, but no one knows why.' He clasped his hands together and frowned at them. 'I've been looking for clues and omens, but can see nothing that makes any sense. The only strange thing to have happened here is an unusual number of Warps.'

Cyllan shivered involuntarily at his mention of the word *Warp*. Every man, woman and child in the entire land was justly terrified of the weird supernatural storms that came wailing out of the North at unpredictable intervals. No one had ever dared to face the pulsating skies and demonic, shrieking voices of a Warp out in the open – the brave or crazed few who had ever done so had vanished without trace. Not even the wisest scholars knew where the Warps came from or what drove them; legend had it they were the last legacy of the forces of Chaos, left behind when the followers of Aeoris swept the Old Ones to destruction and restored the rule of Order.

But whatever the power behind the Warps might be – and it was something that sensible folk preferred not to dwell on – Drachea was right when he said that the incidence of Warps had been increasing of late. Only five days ago, crossing the fertile plains that divided Shu Province from Prospect, Kand Brialen's band had heard the most dreaded sound in the entire world – the thin, high wailing far away Northward that heralded the approach of the storm. Cyllan had had nightmares since then of the full-pelt ride to the nearest storm-haven – one of the long, narrow sheds that had been built for the safety of travellers along all the main drove roads, and of the seemingly endless torment inside that precarious shelter, lying with her face buried in her coat, blocking her ears against the howling chaos outside while the terrified livestock milled and bawled around her. It had been the third such experience since they left Empty Province . . .

Even Drachea's easy composure had been shaken by the topic, and, aware that the atmosphere was growing uncomfortable, he gestured to the flagon that stood between them on the table.

'You haven't touched your wine.'

'Oh . . . oh, yes; thank you.' Cyllan wasn't concentrating; she had shaken off the ugly recollection, but a disturbance still remained. The animal instinct was nagging at her again . . .

'As for this mystery at the Castle,' Drachea continued, 'it's my belief that the Initiates have their own reasons which others might do well not to question. Although if, when you read your stones, you should see an omen there that might tell us something . . . ?' He looked at her hopefully, and she shook her head with some vehemence.

'No! I wouldn't dare – I wouldn't presume to try to see into such things. I'll read for you, Drachea – but I'll go no further.'

He shrugged his careless shrug. 'Very well, then. Let's not waste any more time – show me what the charlatan could not!'

Cyllan felt in her belt-pouch and pulled out a handful of small, smooth stones of varying shapes. Ideally, she needed sand as a base on which to cast the pebbles, but she had worked without it before and doubtless could do so again.

Drachea leaned forward, staring intently at the stones as though trying to divine something from them without her help. And suddenly, as she gathered them in her palm ready for the first cast, Cyllan stopped. Something was tugging insistently at her mind, a warning, as clear as if it had been spoken aloud in her ear.

Whatever happened, she must not read the stones for Drachea Rannak!

'What is it?' Drachea's voice broke querulously in on

her, and she started violently, staring at him as though she had never seen him before. 'Come now, Cyllan – either you're a fortune-reader, or you're not! If you've been wasting my time – '

'I haven't!' She rose unsteadily to her feet. 'But I can't read for you, Drachea – I can't!'

He rose too, suddenly angry. 'Why not, in the name of seven hells?'

'Because I *dare* not! Oh, gods, I can't explain; it's a feeling, a fear – ' and suddenly the words were out before she could stop them. 'Because I know in my bones that something terrible is about to happen to you!'

He was stunned. Very slowly, he sat down again, and his face was ashen. ' You – *know* . . . ?'

She nodded. 'Please, don't ask me anything more. I shouldn't have spoken – doubtless I'm wrong; I have no real talent, and – '

'No.' She had been moving away from the table and suddenly his hand shot out and gripped her arm painfully. 'Sit down! If there's something afoot then by all the gods you're going to tell me what it is!'

One or two of the tavern's other customers were watching them by now, grinning with amusement and no doubt putting their own interpretation on the argument. Anxious not to draw further attention to herself, Cyllan reluctantly sat.

'Now, tell me!' Drachea commanded.

The stones felt like hot coals in her hand. Reflexively, she let them fall, and they scattered on the table in a disturbingly explicit pattern. Drachea stared at them and frowned. 'What does it mean?'

Cyllan, too, was looking at the stones and her heart thumped. She didn't know this pattern, and yet it seemed to speak to her, call to her. A faint tingling sensation assailed the nape of her neck and she shivered. 'I – don't know –' she began to say, then gasped as an image flashed across her mental vision, so quickly that she could barely grasp it. A star with seven points, radiating indescribable colours –

'No!' she heard herself hiss vehemently. 'I can't do it!
I *won't*!'

'Damn you, you *will*!' Drachea countered furiously.
'I'm not about to be made a fool of by some outland
peasant! Tell me what you see in those stones, or I'll
have you before my father for trying to hex me!'

The threat was real enough. Cyllan looked at the
stones once more, and suddenly their pattern crys-
tallised in her mind. She knew, with an unerring instinct,
what they meant – and Drachea's arguments had no
power to sway her.

Abruptly, she swept up the stones and deposited them
back in her pouch, rising to her feet again.

'You must do as you think fit,' she said quietly, and
turned to leave.

'Cyllan!' Drachea shouted after her, and when she
didn't hesitate she heard the scrape of wood on stone
and his footsteps coming after her. He caught up with
her just before she reached the door. 'Cyllan, what do
you think you're doing? I won't have this! You promised
to read for me, and – '

'Let me go!' She twisted free as he tried to catch her
arm and pull her back, but as she made for the tavern
entrance she collided with a tall, burly merchant-sailor
who was hastening in with his three companions.

'Look what you're doing!' the man snapped, pushing
her aside. She mumbled an apology and hurried on,
Drachea following, but the sailor called out again. 'Hey
– you two! Where in the name of all the devils of
darkness d'you think you're going?'

They stared uncomprehendingly at him, and he
jerked a thumb towards the door, where more people
were hurrying in. 'Haven't you got a quarter-gravine of
sense between you? There's a Warp coming! Whole
place is in an uproar – market day, and a whore-
spawned Warp decides to descend on us! As if storms in
Summerisle Straits weren't enough –' He stamped
irritably towards the counter, shouting for a drink.

Cyllan's face had drained to a grey pallor. At the
sailor's mention of the Warp she felt as if her stomach

had turned to ice inside her. A terrible fear had taken
hold of her reason and was growing with every moment
– she was safe in the tavern, but she didn't *feel* safe. And
if she had interpreted the stones' portent rightly –

Drachea, meanwhile, had moved to the door and was
looking out. Everywhere people were running for shelter; somewhere a child wailed in fright. Beyond the
crowding roofs of the houses in this narrow street the sky
was no more than a thin band of brilliance, but already
the brilliance was clouding, tarnished with sickly
shadows that marched across the blue. And over the
noise of rushing feet and shouting voices came an eerie,
thin wailing, like a chorus of hellbound souls in torment.

'Gods!' Drachea stared at the fast-changing sky with a
morbid fascination. 'Cyllan, look! Look at it!'

Their quarrel was forgotten, and Cyllan was suddenly
afraid for his safety. 'Drachea, don't! she pleaded.
'Come in! It's dangerous!'

'Not yet, it isn't. We've a few minutes more before it'll
be on us. Look – ' and then in an instant his expression
changed and his voice with it, rising in incredulous horror. 'Oh, by Aeoris, *look at that*!'

He had caught hold of her, and dragged her forward
so that she faced the door. Outside the street was deserted and shutters were being slammed at all the windows. Drachea was pointing down the length of the alley
to where it ran out into Shu-Nhadek harbour, and his
hand shook violently.

'*Look!*'

Cyllan looked, and blind terror overcame all reason.
At the end of the street a solitary figure stood like a
statue. Some shroud-like garment hid its frame, but the
cruel, fine-boned face was clear enough, and the halo of
gold hair, shot through with coruscating light. A dark,
misty aura shimmered around it, and even as she
watched it raised one long-fingered hand, and
beckoned.

She had seen that nightmare image before . . . Cyllan
tried to step back, away from the hypnotic figure and its
commanding hand, but couldn't move. Her will was

weakening; she was overcome by an insane desire to step through the tavern door, out into the street, to obey the summons. Beside her she heard Drachea whisper '*what is it?*' in the voice of a terrified child, and she shook her head, unable even to grope for an answer.

The figure beckoned again, and it was as if invisible strings pulled at Cyllan's limbs. She fought the compulsion with all her strength, but her left foot slid forward, propelling her . . .

'Cyllan, what are you doing?' Drachea cried out. 'Come back!'

She couldn't go back. The call was too strong, swamping fear and self-preservation. And from the grim apparition's heart a ghastly light flickered to life and grew, flowering into a harshly brilliant star that blotted out all but the slowly beckoning hand.

'*Cyllan!*' Drachea's voice was a scream of protest as she suddenly broke free and plunged forward, out of the tavern. Not stopping to think, he raced after her – and the shimmering apparition vanished.

Cyllan gave an animal shriek that echoed the length of the alley, and skidded to a halt so that Drachea cannoned into her. He shook her as though she was a rag doll, yelling to make her understand.

'Cyllan, the Warp! It's coming! In the name of all that's holy, *move!*' As he shouted the final words he spun her round, meaning to drag her if necessary back to the safety of the tavern before it was too late. He turned –

The wall of darkness hit them full on as it swept the length of the street with the speed and ferocity of a tidal wave. Drachea heard the voice of the Warp rise to a howling crescendo of triumph, and glimpsed a maelstrom of twisted forms and shapes that hurtled at him out of nowhere. For an instant he felt Cyllan's hand gripped in his own; then a hammer blow of agony seemed to smash every bone in his body – and with it came searing, white-hot oblivion.

Chapter 2

The shock of swallowing something that burned her throat and lungs brought Cyllan violently back to consciousness. She tried to scream, but choked as her mouth and nose filled again with the burning stuff. For a nightmarish moment she thought she was dead, plunged into some green and black hell that roared in her ears and through which her body twisted and turned helplessly – but then realisation struck her returning senses. *She was drowning!*

With a savage self-preservation instinct she jack-knifed her body and struck in the one direction from which a faint light glimmered. If she had chosen wrongly, she would be dead within minutes – but seconds later her head broke clear of the water and she was lifted on the swell of a black wave, spluttering and gasping as she dragged air into her lungs.

She was in the sea – and it was night! The insanity of the fact numbed her momentarily as she trod water, struggling to stay afloat. Overhead the sky was a vast bowl of darkness tinged with nacreous green, and around her restless waves humped threateningly, monstrous silhouettes that tossed and carried her willy-nilly on their swell. There was no land, no Moons – and no Warp.

Shocked and confused, she didn't see the breaker until it bore down on her, plunging her underwater again. Kicking out, she fought back to the surface. She *must* rally her mind to survival, or she'd drown like a rat in a bucket! But how *could* she survive? There was no shore, no direction – she had been hurled somehow through the Warp, thrown into this unimaginable nightmare –

And then she heard a cry. It was faint, but not far away, as though someone were calling from an invisible safe haven. Cyllan turned, striking out in the direction from which the sound had come and thankful for the salt water which gave her buoyancy – and a moment later she saw him.

He was clinging to a spar of wood and almost submerged by the waves that battered him relentlessly. *Drachea!* Memory of the last seconds before the Warp struck surged back – he had been trying to pull her towards the tavern; they had been hit together –

'Drachea!' Her voice was weak as she tried to cry out to him, and he didn't hear. Saving her breath for swimming she propelled herself towards him, aided by a wave that rose on a cross-current and swept her almost to his side. She caught him under the arms, holding him against the pull of the sea, and instantly he panicked and began to struggle.

'Drachea!' she screamed in his ear. 'It's Cyllan! We're alive, we're *alive!*'

He took no notice, but continued to writhe in her grip, hitting out at her with flailing hands. She had to stop him, or he'd drown them both – reaching out, she snatched the spar to which he'd been clinging. It was waterlogged, but small enough for her to heft, and clumsily she brought it down on his skull. He slumped, and Cyllan hauled with all her remaining strength as his body began to slip beneath the waves.

Turning on to her back, she dragged Drachea's inert form behind her and began to kick out. The water held her up – but she couldn't sustain this struggle for long. Like all Eastern coast-dwellers Cyllan had learned in childhood to swim like a fish, but her strength was ebbing fast; the water was ice cold, already numbing her hands and feet, and with the added burden she could make only painfully slow headway.

And if she found no landfall? a small voice whispered in her head. *What then?*

Then she and Drachea would drown, as surely as the Sun would rise tomorrow. She might increase her own chances if she let him go and preserved all her energy for herself – but she couldn't. It would be tantamount to murder; she couldn't abandon him now.

She took a firmer grip on her limp burden and struggled on, battling against the tide which, capriciously, seemed to change the direction of its pull every few moments, as though a dozen different currents battled for supremacy. The roar of the sea was a ceaseless dinning in her ears, wearing her down; the icy drag of the water seemed to grow greater with every kick and her limbs were slowly losing all sensation as the cold penetrated to her marrow. And soon the constant surge and fade of the swell, as she tried to keep a rhythm to her swimming, became dangerously hypnotic. Strange, dreamlike images flowed across her inner vision, until she thought she saw the prow of a boat looming out of the darkness towards her; she raised one arm and shouted, then her mouth and nostrils filled with stinging salt water as, losing way, she slipped under. Instantly the shock snatched her out of the dream, but it was all she could do to drag Drachea's dead weight back to the surface. She gulped air, sobbing with terror and relief in equal measure, and when her streaming eyes cleared she realised that there had been no boat, no salvation; only the delusion of an exhausted mind.

She was weakening. The mirage had almost killed her, and one more such mistake could be her last. And still there were no white crests on the waves to tell her she was nearing land; the vast, implacable ocean stretched endlessly around her and she visualised a sudden, terrible image of herself and Drachea bobbing like tiny, insignificant flotsam on a gigantic expanse of nothing. She forced the thought away, knowing that if it took hold it would sap the last of her will to survive. But that will couldn't sustain her for much longer.

Without warning, a heavy black swell borne on a vicious cross-current slapped her sideways, and this time she couldn't regain her momentum. Drachea's body was pulling her down, and her limbs were almost completely numb. In an instant of hideous clarity Cyllan faced the knowledge that she was defeated. She had tried but she had no more resources of strength, and even without her burden she'd no longer be capable of saving herself. The hungry sea had won, as part of her had known it must. She was going to die . . .

And then, in a dazed corner of her mind, she remembered the fanaani . . .

The chance was so slender that she almost abandoned it. It would be better, surely it would be better, to give herself up to the inevitable and let the cold, surging depths take her now, rather than prolong the agony with a hope that couldn't be fulfilled. But an echo of her desire to survive still remained, enough to make her failing senses fight back in a final, desperate attempt to live. She struggled to focus her mind, rally her will, feeble though it was.

Help me . . . The silent telepathic plea flowed from deep within her. *In the name of all the gods, please help me* . . .

The sea surged around her, its booming voice mocking her desperation. If her call went unheard, she'd be dead within minutes . . .

Help me . . . *please help me* . . .

Suddenly she felt it – the first faint stirring of another presence in her mind, a detached curiosity as to the nature of this strange creature that struggled through the water with its unconscious burden. Cyllan redoubled her efforts to call, and the presence grew stronger, closing in.

When she heard the first bittersweet harmony of the fanaani's song she almost cried aloud with joy. The silver notes echoed against the sea's roar, rising and falling, calling to her, and a moment later she felt something sleek and alive brush by her legs.

The first one rose beside her, its blunt-nosed, catlike face only inches away from her own. The limpid brown eyes gazed sorrowfully into hers, and the fanaan – bigger than she was, brindle-furred and almost phosphorescent in the darkness – twitched its short whiskers and whiffled, blowing fishy breath into her face. Then another joined it, and from below she felt a third rising, taking Drachea's weight on its back and supporting him.

Cyllan twisted in the water and clutched at the heavily muscled shoulder of the sea-mammal beside her. The fanaan lifted its head and called in a sweet, plaintive voice, and the second creature moved in so that between them they held her, bearing her up against the swelling waves. She glimpsed Drachea being carried likewise between two more, and her exhausted mind gave silent and fervent thanks. Her last desperate plea had been answered – these strange, rare, telepathic beings had answered her call and, in their enigmatic way, had chosen to help her. They had come from the gods alone knew where, to aid an alien being in distress, and the debt she owed was one that could never be adequately repaid.

The first fanaan called again, and its companions joined in the chillingly beautiful song. Exhaustion washed over Cyllan as the creatures surged forward, and the eldritch singing of her saviours tumbled into a miasma of bizarre sea-dreams as she slid thankfully into unconsciousness.

She woke, to find herself lying face-down on shingle. The world was still again – in the background the sea still beat and boomed relentlessly, but the rocking of the cold tide had ceased. She had been brought to shore – and the fanaani were gone.

Slowly, Cyllan pulled herself up until she was kneeling on the hard shale. Water streamed from her hair and clothes, and her limbs shivered involuntarily with the saturating cold. It was still night – a white sea-mist permeated the darkness and made phantoms out of the jagged rocks that surrounded her. At her back, the shingle sloped away to a dully roaring tideline, strewn with jetsam that the sea had rejected. Before her –

Before her, a black granite wall rose sheer into the sky, reflecting no light. The shore stretched dismally away to either side, offering no sanctuary, and when she struggled to focus her eyes upward she saw only the cliff,

towering beyond the boundaries of vision. The fanaani
had brought her to land – but a cruel, harsh land that
bore no resemblance to anything she knew.

Something moved nearby, rattling the shingle, and
Cyllan turned in shock. Five paces away, Drachea Rannak sat with his back propped against the rock face. He
was staring at her, but his eyes were glazed and she was
sure he didn't recognise her. Shock . . . the ordeal had
proved too much for him . . . but at least he, too, lived.

Fighting the frozen aching in her marrow, Cyllan
crawled towards him. 'Drachea . . . Drachea, we're
alive . . . '

He continued to stare at her, looking like a puppet
whose strings had been abruptly cut. 'Alive . . . ' he
repeated.

'Yes, *alive!* The fanaani saved us – I called, and they
came, and . . . ' She shook her head, coughing. 'We're
alive.'

There was silence for a moment but for the ceaseless
noise of the sea. Then Drachea said dully, 'Where?'

'I don't know . . . ' His reason had warped, she was
certain. He was unable to face the reality of their peril
and something within him had snapped, and she only
hoped that he'd recover his wits before the cold overcame them both. Rallying herself, she added more vehemently, 'But wherever we are, Drachea, we're *safe!*
We've survived – isn't that what matters?'

'Who knows?' He smiled an oddly twisted smile with
no humour. 'Maybe we're dead, and this is the afterlife.
A shingle shore, an unending night, a cliff we can't
climb. Hell, Cyllan. Isn't that what you saw in your
stones? *Isn't it?*' Suddenly he lunged forward and
grasped her shoulders, shaking her violently. For a
moment she thought he would try to strangle her; then
abruptly his grip loosened and he turned away, pressing
his face against the cliff wall and curling up like a frightened and defiant child.

'Go away,' he said indistinctly. 'If it wasn't for you, I'd
be safe at home in Shu-Nhadek! Go away, and leave me
alone!'

If it wasn't for me, you'd be dead! Cyllan thought
savagely, then quelled the thought as uncharitable and
unworthy. Perhaps he was right – but for her, this nightmare would never have happened.

She remembered then, for the first time, the apparition which had appeared as the Warp bore down on
them in Shu-Nhadek. The hand, beckoning – a shudder
racked her. That had been far more than a portent. And
the stones . . . instinctively she put a hand to her belt-
pouch and felt the familiar bulge of the pebbles there. So
she hadn't lost them . . . although she was beginning to
wonder if they were more of a curse than a blessing.

Drachea was still hiding his face, and Cyllan realised
that, if they were ever to escape from this hellish shore,
she would have to take charge. Danger and privation
were alien concepts to the son of the Margrave of Shu;
she was better equipped to save them, if there was
salvation to be found. Turning, she gazed out to sea. The
mist had deepened, it seemed, in the few minutes since
her rude awakening; beyond the first few lapping waves
at the shingle's edge she could see nothing. She shivered
with something besides cold. What lay beyond that
mist? Familiar, known land, or . . . nothing? There
could be nowhere in the world so bleak, so barren, so
devoid of hope . . .

Nowhere, said a silent inner voice, *but for one place
. . .*

It surely wasn't possible . . . Cyllan struggled to her
feet as speculation threatened to flower into certainty,
and craned to look up at the towering cliff. Vertigo made
her feel sick; she quashed it determinedly and tried to
see to the top of the rock face, backing away down the
shingle slope until she was wading knee-deep in the sea.

There *was* an end to the monstrous granite. She could
glimpse a point where the rock abruptly cut off, and
from here the perspective of the shore had changed
enough for her to realise that the cliff was in fact a stack,
rising out of the surrounding ocean.

Her pulse quickened. If her suspicions were right,
then she should be able to see the narrow arch of the

causeway that connected this solitary stone pinnacle to
the mainland. Straining her eyes through the mist-
shrouded gloom, Cyllan stared . . .

Nothing. The fog was too dense, or she was wrong and
the nagging sense of familiarity which assailed her was a
delusion.

But whatever the truth of it, there had to be a way to
scale that daunting face. To stay on this shore would be
to give up, and, having survived this far, giving up was
something Cyllan couldn't bear to consider. There *must*
be a way – and perhaps with daylight to aid her, she
could find it.

Still unsure of herself, but a little heartened, she
trudged back to where Drachea lay. He seemed to have
fallen asleep – or lapsed back into unconsciousness –
and his skin was disturbingly cold to the touch. Cyllan
turned and began to look about her for something that
would provide warmth until dawn. Seaweed – it stank
abominably and was as wet as they were, but at least it
might protect them from the worst of the Winter night's
cold. Aware that her limbs were stiffening with fatigue
and chill, she started to gather great armfuls of the stuff
from where the sea had washed it, and soon had a pile of
green-brown strands which she heaped over Drachea's
still form. Then she lay down at his back, pressing close
against him so that their remaining body heat might not
be wasted, and, pulling some of the weed over herself,
closed her eyes.

Cyllan woke from a sleep racked with hideous nightmares, aware that something was wrong. The blanket of
seaweed had done its work well enough, and some of the
cold had eased from her bones; but when she tried to
move, her body was so agonisingly stiff that it would
barely obey her. And something was wrong . . .

She raised her head, staring into the grey-green darkness. Mist still hung like an impenetrable curtain only a
few paces away, and the sound of the sea seemed further
off than before, muffled by the dense fog. The tide had
gone out, leaving a newly washed expanse of shingle

gleaming dully at the edge of the mist, which meant that she must have slept for some hours. Even in the extremes of Winter, nights weren't eternal. The Sun should have risen by now . . . but there was no trace of the dawn.

An uneasy foreboding assailed Cyllan. There was no place in the world where the Sun didn't rise; and yet the night still held this shore fast. Everything felt too quiet, too still – as if beyond the mist there was nothing but a void . . .

Shivering, she turned back to where Drachea lay beside her, and shook him. 'Drachea! Wake up!'

He stirred reluctantly, and from the way he swore at her she realised that he believed himself in his bed at Shu-Nhadek and berating a servant for disturbing him. She shook him again.

'Drachea!'

Comprehension slowly dawned as Drachea opened his eyes. 'Cyllan?' he mumbled, then became aware of the damp shingle beneath him. 'Where are we?'

'I wish I knew!'

'What?'

'Never mind.' She hadn't the energy to spare for an argument. 'Listen to me. I've explored as best I can, and it seems that we're on an island. There's no link with the mainland that I can find, so we have to seek a way of climbing the cliff.'

Drachea struggled into a sitting position as clearer thought took over from his weariness, and pushed at the stinking heaps of seaweed that covered him. When he answered, his voice was petulant.

'It's still the middle of the night! We're not going to die in the time between now and dawn! And when the Sun comes up, we'll be found! There must be people out looking for me now – my parents will have raised the alarm. So why should I waste my strength scaling a thrice-damned cliff to no good purpose?'

Cyllan's mouth tightened angrily. Drachea, it seemed, had no true concept of the predicament they were in – accustomed to having his every wish granted, he blithely assumed that rescue was imminent. And so it might have been, were they still in the vicinity of Shu. But Cyllan knew better . . .

She tried to make him understand. 'Drachea, listen to me! The tide has gone out – that means we've been here long enough for dawn to have broken, and yet it hasn't.'

He frowned. 'What do you mean?'

'I don't know – only that something's terribly wrong here. And another thing – we're not in Shu Province, or anywhere near it.'

He tried to protest at that. 'But – '

'*Listen* to me! Don't ask how I know – I do! I can *feel* it, Drachea, as surely as I've ever felt anything!' She paused, swallowing to catch her breath. 'If we're not to rot and die here on this shore, we *must* find a way to the top!'

Drachea stared at her, unwilling to acknowledge the truth of her words. Then he said resentfully, 'I'm hungry.'

Cyllan could have strangled him. He was wilfully refusing to face harsh reality, and although part of her pitied him – he had, after all, never known such straits in his life before – another part felt only frustrated disgust.

Knowing that they could afford no more wasted time she rose and paced to the foot of the sheer cliff, laying her palms against the unyielding granite as though seeking to divine a path upwards. Luck and determination had brought them this far – unless the gods chose capriciously to abandon them now, there must be an answer. From behind her Drachea complained of stiffness and pain, and Cyllan lost her temper.

'Then move, damn you! Help me! I can't do everything alone, and you expect me to carry you as though I were your servant!'

Drachea stared back at her in angry consternation, and Cyllan felt tears prick her eyes as the pent-up fear within her threatened to break through to the surface. She forced them back ferociously and took a grip on herself. She couldn't afford to lose self-control – to weaken now would bring disaster.

'Wherever we are,' she said, clenching her teeth to stop them chattering, 'Shu Province is a world away. And we've no food and no shelter. If we stay here we'll die from cold or hunger or both.' She stared speculatively up at the forbidding mass of the cliff wall. 'We *have* to find a way up.'

Drachea hugged himself, shivering. 'If you don't know where we are, how can you be so sure that we won't be rescued?' he argued sullenly.

'I can't be sure. But I'm not about to sit here and wait until I'm too weak to look for an alternative.' Cyllan had begun to trudge away from him; now she stopped and looked back. 'I'm going to look for a path. What you choose to do is your concern.'

He gave her a withering, venomous glare and turned his back. She had walked two more paces when she heard him sigh and mutter an imprecation under his breath. Then, thrusting his pinched hands into the pockets of his jacket, he moved stiffly across the crunching shingle to join her.

It was Drachea who finally found the worn steps, carved unimaginable generations ago into the sheer rock, and winding up into the night. Centuries of erosion had worn them to a treacherous glass-like smoothness and their steepness was daunting, but Cyllan believed that, with good fortune on their side, they could make the climb without mishap.

'It should be easier the higher we go,' she told Drachea, privately praying that she was right. 'Beyond where the sea can reach there should be less erosion and our passage will be safer.'

He looked at the carved stairs dubiously. 'I can't imagine who could have carved them, or why. And they can't have been used in generations.'

'But they *have* been used – that's what counts. If others have scaled them, so can we! And it means . . . ' She looked up at the vast stack toppling out of the night towards them. 'It means that there must be something at the top. Sanctuary, Drachea . . . '

He nodded, afraid but trying not to show it. They had subsided into a slightly uneasy truce, submerging their differences in the mutual need for survival, and now Drachea gestured at the worn steps. 'You go first. I'm more likely to catch you if you fall than you'd be to catch me.'

The attempt at gallantry, gratifying though it was, was misplaced as Cyllan soon discovered. Drachea's head for heights was sound enough, but as they climbed the treacherous steps it became evident that his strength was rapidly deserting him. Shock, fatigue and hunger had taken their toll, and Cyllan – who was a good deal fitter – frequently had to pause to avoid leaving him far behind. To her, the climb was difficult but not impossibly so; she had taken equal risks in the past, scaling the giddying cliffs of the West High Land coast in the hope of glimpsing the elusive fanaani, but with Drachea toiling painfully behind her she forced herself to hold back an instinct to climb faster, to reach the top of these terrible stairs before her will or her energy gave out.

That, she thought, was the most daunting part of the climb. By now they must be at least six hundred feet above the sea, yet there was no sign of the vast cliff coming to an end. When she once dared to look up, she saw only the endless wall of granite rising beyond the limits of vision, offering no hope of reprieve.

And when – if – they finally reached the summit, what then? As the ascent continued, Cyllan had been acutely aware of an unpleasant core of fear growing within her. That same animal instinct which had assailed her in the tavern at Shu, but greatly increased. Something awaited them at the top of the cliff . . . and she was afraid to discover what that something was.

But there was no other choice. Hundreds of feet below lay a barren shore that offered no hope of rescue, and even a dreaded unknown held a better prospect than that. They must go on, and face whatever awaited them.

A fit of coughing from below halted her then, and she looked cautiously back to see Drachea doubled over, clutching at a precarious handhold. Cyllan slid carefully back a pace or two and reached down to take his hand, helping him over a place where the granite steps had crumbled away. He bit his lip, holding his breath until he was up with her, and slowly, painfully, they continued on.

Eventually, the climb dissolved into a mesmeric, waking nightmare for Cyllan. Each upward step became a torment of fierily aching muscles, each inch of progress a small triumph in itself. She might have been climbing for the whole of her life, Drachea struggling in her wake, ever onward and up with no end in view. Sometimes she almost laughed aloud at the bizarre nature of it all – the unchanging rock, the unchanging sky, the unchanging, mourning note of the wind that froze her hands and threatened to prise her stiff fingers and toes away from their insecure holds. How long had they been climbing? Minutes? Hours? Days? The sky gave her no clue; still the night hung over them with neither Moon tracking across its arc to mark the passing of time. If this was insanity, it was like nothing she had ever imagined before . . .

'Aeoris!'

The oath was out before she could stop it as, with no warning, the cliff-face ended and she sprawled on to soft, yielding turf. She had time for the shocking image of what confronted her to register in her brain before, remembering Drachea, she had turned and was reaching down to help him scramble the last few steps to safety. They lay gasping on the ground, the world seeming to swing giddily around them as both struggled for breath, and Cyllan thought she heard Drachea murmuring what sounded like a fervent prayer of thanksgiving through dry lips. At last, when she had strength enough, she roused him by taking his arm, and pointed, unable to speak.

No more than a hundred paces away, the castle rose out of the ground as though it had grown from the living rock. Blacker than anything Cyllan could imagine, it towered into the night, dominated by four titanic spires which reached skyward like accusing fingers, and it seemed to absorb what little light fell on it, swallowing and crushing it. Above the sharply defined battlements, a crimson glow tinged the air as though within the castle's precincts some vast fire burned sullenly but steadily. And although the monstrous structure seemed changed beyond recognition, Cyllan knew it . . .

Drachea's hands clawed reflexively at the turf. 'What . . . is that place?' he whispered.

Cyllan felt her pulse pounding suffocatingly in her throat, so that speaking was a great effort.

'You said that you wanted to visit the stronghold of the Circle,' she whispered harshly. 'Your wish has been granted, Drachea. That is the Castle of the Star Peninsula!'

Drachea didn't reply. He was staring at the Castle, seemingly unable to credit the sight that confronted him. At last he managed to form words.

'I didn't imagine . . . none of the stories said . . . that it would be like *this!*'

A shiver racked Cyllan, and the fear redoubled. 'It isn't,' she murmured. 'Or at least . . . it wasn't when I saw it. Something's wrong . . . '

'The rumours – ' Drachea began.

'Yes . . . if the Initiates have shut themselves away – then how is it that we've broken through the barrier?'

Unsteadily, Drachea rose to his feet. He still watched the distant Castle, as though fearing that if he dared to look away for a moment it would vanish. 'We must find out,' he said.

She didn't want to go near it . . . she was suddenly desperately afraid. But Drachea's reasoning couldn't be argued with. If they crossed the causeway, there was nothing but the Northern mountains for leagues. Two exhausted and hungry souls couldn't hope to survive the road through the pass in Winter. And even when she looked to where the causeway should have been, Cyllan could see nothing. Only the mist, hanging like a curtain, as though to mark an impassable barrier between the real world and this world of nightmare and illusion.

She got to her feet, disturbed by the thought, and moved closer to Drachea. He glanced at her and attempted to smile. 'We go forward,, or we stay here,' he said. 'Which is it to be?'

'Forward . . . ' The word formed on her lips almost without her realising it.

Slowly they began to walk towards the Castle that towered to meet them. Here even the wind was stilled, and the silence was eerie. As they approached the massive entrance, Cyllan realised that there was no sign of life in the Castle. The great gates were shut, and the dull crimson radiance from within remained unchanging. The place seemed deserted . . .

And how, she asked herself again, *had they penetrated the barrier that held the Castle aloof? How had they broken through the Maze?*

'Drachea – ' She clutched his arm and pulled, abruptly attacked by an unhealthy doubt. 'Drachea, something's terribly amiss . . . '

It was a feeble repetition of her old fear, but she could find no clearer way to give voice to her misgivings. Drachea, however, was not to be daunted. He shook her off irritably and began to walk faster, almost running down the final slope of the sward that brought him to the Castle entrance. Cyllan followed, and caught up with him as he pushed vainly at the huge gates.

'Locked!' Drachea swung breathlessly round, leaning his back against the gates and pushing, but to no avail. 'Damn them! I've not come through so much to be thwarted now!'

'Drachea, no!' Cyllan protested, but it was too late. He had turned to face the entrance once more, and hammered ferociously with clenched fists on the wood of the gates, shouting in near-hysterical fury.

'Open! Open, damn you all! Let us in!'

For a moment nothing happened. Then – as much to Drachea's astonishment as Cyllan's – the massive gates creaked. Something clicked with a hollow, echoing sound . . . and slowly, slowly, the huge wooden structures swung slowly inward, silently and smoothly, spilling out a gloomy blood-red radiance that stained the sward.

'Gods!' Drachea stepped back, staring with a mixture of awe and chagrin at the sight which the slowly swinging gates had revealed. Before them, framed by a dense black arch, lay the Castle courtyard, and they both took in the scene with disturbed amazement.

The great courtyard was empty, and as silent as the grave. In the centre, reflecting the desolation, stood a derelict and dry fountain, its carved statues leering frozenly at them. The nightmarish crimson light which had shone above the black walls was greatly magnified here, but seemed to have no source; it simply existed, with no visible origin, and when Cyllan glanced uneasily at Drachea she saw that his skin was tinged a bloody hue by the glow.

Softly, he whistled between his teeth, and Cyllan shivered. 'It feels – dead. Empty. As if there was no living soul here . . . '

'Yes . . . ' Cautiously, Drachea stepped forward, moving under the silent black arch until he emerged into the courtyard with Cyllan at his heels. He breathed in deeply. 'There can be no doubt? This is the Castle . . . ?'

'Oh, yes. There can be no doubt of it.'

He nodded. 'Then the Initiates must be here. And whatever their purpose in sealing themselves off from the rest of the world, they surely can't deny us sanctuary now!' Eagerly he started across the deserted courtyard, but not before Cyllan had seen the flash of almost feverish anticipation in his eyes. Drachea had forgotten the Warp, the sea, the grim shore at the foot of the Castle stack – all that mattered to him now was the fact that fate had brought him to the stronghold of the Circle. Why and how he had come meant nothing – the old, obsessive ambition to be a part of that revered and select few had eclipsed all other considerations.

He had already outpaced Cyllan, heading towards a flight of wide, shallow steps that led to an open set of double doors. She hastened after him, afraid of being left alone in this grim and disturbing place, and came up with him as he began to climb the flight.

'Drachea, please wait!' she pleaded. 'We can't simply walk in; there may be reasons – '

He interrupted her, dismissing her doubts impatiently. 'What would you prefer – that we should stay out here in the courtyard until someone finds us? Don't be a fool – there's nothing to be afraid of!'

But there is, an inner voice protested. Still she couldn't shake off the foreboding – it was growing by the minute and she had to fight down a desire to turn and run back towards the gates and the seeming safety of the cliff-top. Quickly she looked over her shoulder – and with a sinking sensation realised that any attempt at flight would avail her nothing.

Whatever silent, secret force had opened the gates to admit them to the Castle had now closed them again. They were trapped, like flies in a spider's web . .

Cyllan felt sick. She didn't want to venture through the doorway into the Castle, but Drachea wouldn't listen to her. He meant to investigate further whether she willed it or no – she could follow him, or remain here with only the dead, grinning gargoyles of the stilled fountain for company . . .

Turning back, she saw that Drachea had already crossed the threshold of the doorway, and was standing in a corridor. The crimson light permeated even here, like a distant hellfire, and its glow made him look unhuman. He glanced back, and snapped, 'Are you coming? Or must I seek out the Initiates alone?'

Cyllan didn't answer, but with a pounding heart hastened to join him, feeling as though she were choosing the lesser of two tangible evils. Slowly they advanced into the Castle, their footfalls echoing eerily in the profound silence. Still nothing moved, no one emerged to welcome or castigate them . . . and then Drachea stopped at another heavy door which stood partly open.

'A hall, or some such . . . ' He touched the door and it swung back easily to admit them to a huge and lofty hall. Long, scrubbed tables stretched the length of the great room, and at the far end a vast, empty hearth gaped, polished copper fire-irons gleaming bloodily in the strange light. Above the massive mantel was a balustraded gallery, all but invisible in shadow, with heavy curtains hanging motionless to either side. The place was as empty and lifeless as the courtyard had been.

'This must be where the Adepts dine . . . ' Drachea said softly, and Cyllan echoed his following, unspoken thought.

'But there's no one here . . . '

A sound, so faint it might have been imagination, flickered at the borders of awareness and was gone. A woman's distant laughter . . . Drachea paled. 'Did you hear – '

'Yes, I heard. But there's no one here!'

'There *must* be – the Castle of the Star Peninsula, abandoned and empty? It isn't possible!'

Cyllan shook her head, trying to quell the nagging little inner voice which still assailed her, and which now asked, *do you believe in ghosts . . . ?* Drachea's steps seemed obscenely loud as he approached the nearest of the tables and laid his hands on it. 'This is real enough,' he said quietly. 'Unless I'm dreaming, or dead, I – '

And he stopped as they both heard the unmistakable sound of a footfall in the gallery.

For a moment they stared transfixed at the shadowed platform above the empty hearth. The curtains didn't move, and as the small sound died there was no further sign of life. But Drachea's face was suddenly triumphant.

'You see!' he hissed. 'We're not alone – and I'm not dreaming! The Initiates *are* here, and they're aware of our presence!' He drew himself up, placing one palm to the opposite shoulder in a formal gesture, and called out loudly, 'Greetings to you! I am Drachea Rannak, Heir Margrave of Shu Province! Kindly show yourself!'

Silence answered him. No further footfall, no movement. Cyllan's skin began to crawl and she moved to

Drachea's side. The young man was frowning, non-plussed, and cleared his throat.

'I said, kindly reveal yourself! We are wet and exhausted, and we demand the hospitality due to any tired traveller! Damn it, is this the Castle of the Star Peninsula, or – '

'Drachea!' Cyllan cut in, clutching at him.

He saw it a moment after her quicker senses had discerned the first movement. A shadow, which detached itself from the deeper darkness in the gallery, moved swiftly to the head of the staircase that spiralled down into the dining-hall, and began to descend.

Drachea stepped back, bravado deserting him in the face of such a manifestation. The figure – for now it was discernible as human – reached the hall floor and stopped. Cyllan was horribly aware of its cold, impassive scrutiny, but it was still too deeply immersed in shadow for any feature to be visible. But whoever – *whatever* – it was, its appearance conjured an uneasy sense of recognition.

A hand, white and thin, flicked impatiently at the darkness surrounding the apparition, and something black shifted and rippled. Cyllan realised that the figure was wearing a dark, high-collared cloak which swept the ground at its feet. Then a voice, with an edge to it that made her shiver, snapped harshly,

'*How in the name of the Seven Hells did you break through the barrier?*'

Drachea backed away, shocked by the venom in the figure's tone. But Cyllan stood rooted by a memory that crowded back into her mind, a memory which she had been striving to blot out. Her eyes widened as the tall, dark man moved and for the first time the crimson glow fell on him, illuminating his features.

He had changed – gods, how he had changed! The flesh of his face was cadaverous, the bone-structure jagged and skeletal. But the unruly black hair that cascaded over his shoulders was the same, and the dark-lashed green eyes still held their haunted intensity –

though now they glittered with a cruel understanding that was far beyond her comprehension. He seemed more of a demon incarnate than a living man . . . but she knew him. And the momentary spark of recognition that flared in his look confirmed her certainty.

Cyllan said unsteadily, '*Tarod* . . . '

Chapter 3

Tarod stared at the two bedraggled creatures who stood before him, the first human beings he had seen in – he mentally checked himself, distantly amused by the fact that a part of his mind still insisted on thinking in terms of time. That girl – memory stirred at the sight of her pale hair and the odd amber eyes, and a name came to his mind. He had forgotten her – but against all possibility she was here in the Castle, where no foot save his own had walked since Keridil Toln's attempt to destroy him.

The shock had caught him off guard, but now he was rallying his composure – although it took considerable effort in the face of what had happened. No human being should be capable of breaking through the barrier which held this Castle frozen in a Timeless limbo. His own power, great as it was, couldn't penetrate the formless, dimensionless yet appallingly real warp of time and space that had trapped him here in his last, desperate effort to save his life and his soul; and whatever her psychic talents, Cyllan was no true sorceress. Yet she was *here*, as real as he was . . .

He stepped forward, the movement implying a threat that made Drachea back away, and his cold stare flicked from one to the other. 'How did you break the barrier?' he demanded again. 'How did you reach the Castle?'

Drachea, his confidence sapped, swallowed and made an attempt at a formal bow. 'Sir, I am Drachea Rannak, Heir Margrave of Shu Province,' he said, trying to wield the rank as a defensive weapon. 'We have been the victims of a bizarre accident which – '

'I'm not interested in your name, your title or your

circumstances!' Tarod snapped. 'Answer my question – how did you get here?'

Stunned by the fact that any man, whatever his rank, should dare to treat a Margrave's son with such open contempt, Drachea opened his mouth to make a furious retort. But before he could speak, Cyllan said quickly, 'We came from the sea.'

Tarod turned to stare at her and she looked back, not flinching. She was afraid of him, bewildered by the shocking changes which he seemed to have undergone, and aware that to anger him could be dangerous; but she wouldn't give ground. And abruptly some of the peculiar light faded from Tarod's eyes.

'From the sea?' he repeated with a gentler curiosity.

Cyllan nodded. 'It was the Warp – we were in Shu-Nhadek . . . ' She faltered, realising how impossible the story must sound even to an Initiate, and before she could stumble on Tarod forestalled her by reaching out and taking a strand of her hair. He squeezed it between his fingers; it felt stiff and sticky with salt, and the strands refused to separate.

'You're barely dried.' A small spark of charity was fighting its way through the mixture of shock, suspicion and the glimmerings of an uneasy understanding in his mind. A Warp . . . his own horrific experience as a child, which had brought him into the Castle's embrace in the first place, came sharply to memory. He, too, had survived a Warp, only to find that it had transported him halfway across the world. It was possible, surely it was possible, that if the Warps could transcend space they could also transcend time?

Suddenly, he demanded, 'What season is it?'

'Season . . . ?' Cyllan was nonplussed. 'Why – almost Spring. The Quarter-Day is in fifteen days from now.'

Winter had yet to take full hold when the changes had taken place here . . . had years passed beyond the time-barrier, or merely weeks? Tarod had no chance to speculate, for Drachea abruptly spoke up.

'Sir, I must protest! We've arrived here through no fault of our own; we are exhausted; damn it, we're lucky to be alive! We ask the simple courtesies due to anyone in distress, and you seem to consider it more important to establish the season! Surely the weather beyond these walls is quite sufficient to –

He stopped as Tarod looked at him with contemptuous hostility. Whatever he might be – Initiate or no – the man was insane; there could be no other explanation. And the thought of what an insane Adept might be capable of was daunting. Drachea swallowed and went on, trying to sound calm but uncomfortably aware of the tremor in his voice. 'I mean no offence – but if I might be granted an interview with the High Initiate – '

Tarod's answering smile was faintly ironic. 'I'm afraid that's impossible. The High Initiate isn't here.'

'Then whoever is in charge in his stead – ' Drachea persisted.

Tarod had taken an immediate dislike to the self-important youth, and the prospect of trying to explain the truth to him was one he didn't relish. Even Cyllan, with her broader perceptions, would find the facts hard to accept.

'There is no one "in charge", as you put it,' he told Drachea. 'And this isn't the moment for explanations. You've both suffered an ordeal, and your needs have been neglected – as you took pains to point out. Before anything else is considered, you should bath and rest.'

'Well . . .' Drachea was mollified. 'I'd be grateful for that! If there are servants to spare – '

Tarod shook his head. 'There are no servants, not now. I'm afraid you must make do with what I can offer.' And, seeing that the young man still didn't comprehend, he added, 'There is no one else in the Castle.'

Drachea was stunned. 'But – '

'You'll have the answers you want soon enough,' Tarod said in a voice that brooked no argument. He waited until Drachea subsided, then gestured towards the far end of the hall. 'The Castle's facilities are this way. Follow me.'

Cyllan tried to catch his eye as he led them across the room, but failed. She fell into step beside Drachea, her thoughts whirling. From two brief meetings she could hardly say that she knew the black-haired Adept well, but an unerring intuition told her that he had changed in far more ways than mere physical appearance indicated – and that was to say nothing of the changes which had apparently taken place at the Castle itself.

Where were the Circle Initiates? What had happened to this community? Questions crowded her brain, and even her wildest flights of imagination provided no answers that made any sense. She glanced at Drachea, saw his tense, troubled expression, and surreptitiously tucked her hand into his. It was something she would never have had the temerity to do under normal circumstances, but these circumstances were very far from normal. Drachea, rather than being offended, seemed to take comfort from the small contact, and squeezed her fingers in an attempt at reassurance.

Tarod led them through silent corridors that echoed hollowly to the sound of their feet. The Castle's North wing was largely devoted to both private and communal living accommodation, but there wasn't the smallest sign of life in any of the passages or rooms. No voices carried on the still air, no one emerged from a doorway to hurry by on some errand. The entire Castle was eerily, frighteningly dead.

At last their route took them down a flight of steep stairs that descended into the Castle's foundations. A pale glimmer showed from below, and they emerged suddenly on to a broad shelf overlooking a network of artificial pools. Cubicles had been constructed to provide privacy, and the entire chamber was faintly lit by softly shimmering reflections from the water.

Tarod turned to them and smiled slightly. 'Not as sophisticated as the baths of Shu Province, I'll grant, but you'll find the water warm and refreshing. When you've done, I will be in the dining-hall.'

Drachea glanced swiftly at Cyllan, then gave Tarod a curt nod and hastened away along the shelf towards one of the further cubicles, as though anxious to put as great a distance between himself and his host as possible.

Cyllan gazed at the glass-smooth surface of the water, only now fully aware of how exhausted she was in the wake of her ordeal. The thought of being clean, of being able to sleep on something other than shingle or granite, made her want to pinch herself to be sure she wasn't dreaming. She made to strip off her wet and dirty clothes, then stopped as she realised that Tarod hadn't moved, but was still standing behind her.

Slowly she turned to face him. Drachea was by now out of earshot, and there were a hundred questions she wanted to ask. But her nerve failed her, for although the tall Adept was watching her she had the discomfiting feeling that his thoughts were an unimaginable distance away. She shivered, and the movement caught his attention, seeming to bring him back to reality. He said:

'I'm sorry, Cyllan – I delay you.'

'You remember my name . . . ' She was surprised, and irrationally gratified; it was the first time he had addressed her personally.

He smiled. 'My memory hasn't failed me yet. And you – you recognised me. I was flattered.'

She flushed, sensing irony and not wanting to guess at the reason for it. 'I'm sorry.'

'Sorry? For what?'

'For intervening in something that isn't our concern. I realise we're not welcome here; that our arrival has been . . . inopportune. We won't impose on you longer than necessary.'

'Your friend Drachea might not be so obliging.'

She looked up quickly, almost angrily. 'He's not my friend.'

'A Margrave's son doesn't associate with a drover-girl from choice, is that it?' He saw her face cloud, and realised with faint surprise that she was stung by his words. The slight had been intended against Drachea, and to take the edge from the remark he added, 'Then he must be even more of a fool than he seems.'

Some of the hurt faded, but Cyllan was still defensive. 'We'll go as soon as we can,' she said. 'When we've rested.'

'Ah. As to that . . . ' Tarod sighed. 'I can't explain fully, Cyllan; not here and now.' His mouth twisted briefly as if his own words had reminded him of some private and none too pleasant joke. 'But there's one fact that in all conscience I can't keep from you.' *In all conscience? He had almost forgotten what conscience meant* . . . 'Now that you have come here,' he continued, 'you can't leave.'

She stared at him, not comprehending. 'Can't? But –'

'I mean that it isn't possible. You are, effectively, trapped here, and even I haven't the power to change matters. I'm sorry.' The last words were chilly, and Cyllan felt herself turn cold inside as the animal foreboding she had felt before awoke yet again. Something wrong . . . so hideously wrong that it was beyond her understanding . . .

Mustering all her courage, she spoke with slow deliberation. 'Tarod – if what you're saying is true, then something terrible must have happened here.' Intuition made the nape of her neck tingle, and she knew that, as happened on rare occasions, it was guiding her surely. 'Something has happened to you,' she stated.

Tarod knew that she implied far more than she was saying. For an instant his gaze filled with such venom that she recoiled. Then he took a grip on himself, and shook his head. 'You're too perceptive for your own good, girl. But if you're wise, you'll make no more presumptions. Whatever answers you think you've found, they're less than the truth!' Abruptly he turned away, and with that movement an invisible but tangible barrier seemed to descend between them.

'You'll find robes on a rack at the end of the shelf,' he said coldly. 'Make use of anything you please.'

She tried to call after him as he walked away, but the words died on her tongue. His footsteps echoed from the cavern roof, and the last she saw of him was a black shadow that moments later was swallowed by the darkness on the stairs.

She didn't understand. For a few brief moments the impassive mask had relaxed a little; then he had deliberately and almost contemptuously withdrawn, shutting her off as though she were beneath his notice.

Which perhaps she was . . . slowly, Cyllan peeled off her salt-stiffened shirt and trousers, and sat down on the edge of the shelf to let her legs dangle in the water. It was surprisingly warm, bringing a stinging, fiery ache to her bruised and lacerated feet, and she let herself gently down into the quiet depths until she was immersed to her shoulders. Her own face, pinched and pale, stared solemnly back from the mirror-like surface of the pool, and not so much as a single ripple spread out to break the calm.

She had to forget, as best she could, the confusion and fear that were trying to eat at her. She was too tired for coherent thought; Tarod's strangeness and the mystery surrounding the Castle were too much for her exhausted mind. She craved sleep, craved the relative sanity of a new day. Then, and only then, could she begin to take stock of the predicament she was in, and try as best she could to find the answers to her questions.

The water was a soothing balm to aching muscles. Cyllan took a breath, then ducked under the smooth surface, letting the warmth of the pool suffuse through flesh and bone to bring its own form of comfort.

She was lying not on familiar hard ground, but in a bed. Her head was cradled by pillows, softer than anything she'd ever experienced . . . Cyllan emerged from a chasm of sleep, and at first thought she must be dreaming one of the hurtful and unfulfillable dreams of another, better life which often plagued her in her tent. Then, gradually, memory returned . . .

She had found the rack of bathing-robes when she emerged from the pool, and had found Drachea, who was waiting for her, wrapped in a similar garment several sizes too large for him. His eyes were haunted and he had tried to launch into a flood of questions, protests, arguments; but sheer fatigue had the better of them both, and they lapsed into silence.

Ascending the stairs seemed more arduous than the long toil up the face of the stack. Twice Drachea faltered and might have slumped and slept where he stood, but for Cyllan's hand which gripped his and urged him on. She herself felt sick and feverish with exhaustion, and her perceptions sank into a nightmarish miasma, clouding awareness. She vaguely remembered seeing Tarod again – in her confusion he seemed to have taken on the air of some dusty and foreboding spirit rather than a living man – and she recalled pleading to be allowed to sleep. A hand had touched her forehead – Tarod's or Drachea's, she didn't know – then there were blurred recollections of more stairs, a long corridor, a door which seemed to open without a hand to touch it, and a high-ceilinged room furnished with dark draperies. She felt a surface that yielded beneath her, then sweet oblivion claimed her consciousness.

Now though, the tiredness had washed away, and as she opened her amber eyes she was instantly alert. The bed in which she lay occupied one corner of the room, and the gory light from the courtyard, filtering through the one window, cast a dim, blood-red sheen over the shadowed furnishings. The room's grim unfamiliarity put Cyllan on guard in spite of her physical comfort – that, and an instinct which told her she wasn't alone . . .

Very cautiously she turned her head – then uttered a sigh of relief as she saw Drachea, half hidden by shadow, sitting on the window-ledge.

'Cyllan . . . ?' He rose and came hesitantly towards her, and she saw that he had exchanged the robe for a shirt, jacket and trousers which weren't his own. 'I've been waiting for you to wake.'

She sat up, shaking off the last remnants of sleep, and looked quickly around, fearing that other presences stood silent and invisible in the bedchamber. Her senses discerned nothing untoward . . .

'Here,' Drachea said, dropping a shapeless bundle on the bed. 'I found a chest with all manner of garments in it. I brought these for you.'

'Thank you . . . ' Wondering at his disregard for what was, after all, a theft of someone else's property, she none the less shook the clothes out and fingered the material. Wool – and fine wool at that; a world away from the rough fabrics she was used to. But they had still been designed for a man . . .

Cyllan pushed down a small and foolish sense of insult, and looked at Drachea again. 'How long have I slept?' she asked, not quite knowing why she felt the need to whisper.

Drachea scowled. 'As well ask the High Margrave as ask me – I can barely remember anything since I emerged from those damned baths! I woke some while ago and came to find you. I couldn't make you stir, so I waited.' He glanced over his shoulder towards the heavily curtained window, and shivered. 'And the gods alone know how long I've been sitting here. We must have slept for hours, but – I looked outside just now. There's still not the smallest glimmer of light in the sky. Just as before; no sign of the dawn. It's as though the whole world has stopped.'

Cyllan looked in the direction of the window again. The peculiar crimson hellfire still hung beyond the glass, but there was no paler hint of daylight to redeem it.

Drachea shivered, and helped himself to one of the blankets from Cyllan's bed. The room wasn't cold, but he felt the need of it to stave off an inner chill. 'And as for our host, or whatever he chooses to style himself – ' Suddenly his voice sharpened. 'You recognised him, didn't you? And he knew your name. Who is he?'

His tone verged on the accusing, and Cyllan wondered if, in a dark recess of his imagination, Drachea suspected her of being involved in some complex plot of which he was the victim.

'His name is Tarod,' she said. 'He's the Initiate I met . . . when I was here before.'

'An *Initiate* . . . What's his status?'

'I don't know. I hardly know him, Drachea! All I remember is that he's a high Adept; seventh rank, I believe.'

Drachea was taken aback. 'That's the highest of all!' Chagrined, he remembered his own attempt to treat the Adept with disdain, and the memory made him break out into a cold sweat. If the half of what he had heard about the Circle was true, the man could have destroyed him with little more than a look. 'But – where are the rest of the Circle?' he demanded. 'All the other Castle inhabitants?'

'I don't know, any more than you! Gods, Drachea, all I *do* know – *sense* – is that something's terribly wrong! I felt it when we arrived, I tried to tell you then, but you were so intent on gaining entrance to the Castle – '

'And what would you have preferred to do? Sit outside on the stack like some importunate beggar, and wait for the wind to strip the skin from your bones? Damn you, if – ' And Drachea abruptly took a grip on himself, realising that he had been leaning over her as though about to strike out in angry frustration. His face coloured. 'I'm sorry,' he said with an effort. 'We shouldn't quarrel. It only makes matters worse.' He sat down on the end of the bed. 'Besides, our circumstances hardly give us cause for alarm. We're safe from the sea, sheltered, rested. There's sure to be an explanation for the Castle's desertion – and it can be no great distance to the nearest village. From there I can despatch a messenger to Shu-Nhadek – ' The smile that had spread across his face abruptly died as he saw Cyllan's stricken expression. 'What is it?' he demanded. 'What's wrong?'

'Tarod told me – ' She couldn't finish.

Suspicion filled Drachea's eyes, and behind it lay a dawning premonition. '*What* did he tell you?'

She couldn't hide it from him. If she didn't tell him now, Tarod soon would. 'We can't leave the Castle,' she said quietly.

'*What?*'

Afraid that this time he would be unable to control his temper, she went on hastily. 'Drachea, please don't ask me to explain, because I can't. I know only what Tarod told me – that it's impossible for us to leave. He said . . . we are trapped.'

Silence hung as sharp as a knife blade in the room, until Drachea explosively broke it.

'Damn him!' He hurled himself off the bed, paced the floor like a caged cat. 'This is insane! The Castle of the Star Peninsula – the Circle's own stronghold – empty; one Adept who claims that we're prisoners here – it's *insane!*'

Cyllan was on the verge of tears; a state that had been rare throughout her harsh life. She could understand Drachea's fury, but the instinct which had guided her with such alarming clarity thus far told her that no amount of ranting and raving would alter their predicament. And although she couldn't begin to comprehend the truth behind Tarod's cold revelation, she didn't doubt for a moment that it *was* true.

Drachea came to rest at last with his hands pressed flat against the door. He was breathing heavily, trying to control his anger.

'Where is he?' he said through clenched teeth. 'Adept or no, I'll have this out, and now! He can't treat an Heir Margrave in this careless fashion – there must be searchers looking for me, my parents will be wild with distress! He can't *do* it!' He thumped his fists impotently against the unyielding wood, then a little of the rage drained from him and he turned to look searingly at Cyllan.

'Come with me or stay as you please – I'm going to find your Initiate friend and remind him of his responsibilities!'

Despair flooded Cyllan. Drachea was reacting like a thwarted child, and in his current mood she shuddered at the thought of the conflict that might ensue. But, remembering Tarod's distant coldness, she reminded herself that, petulant or no, the Margrave's son was her only sure ally.

She slid from the bed, reached for the clothes Drachea had brought her, and hastily began to dress.

Finding Tarod proved to be less easy than they had anticipated. Drachea strode through the empty, echoing corridors of the Castle, stopping to fling open doors, twice shouting furiously in his frustration, but there was no answering footstep, no sign of movement. Cyllan caught up and followed him, trying to ignore the leaden weight that seemed to have settled in her stomach. Her unease was increasing with each moment, and she was torn between hoping that Tarod would choose to show himself before Drachea's frail hold on his temper finally snapped, and dreading what might happen once the two met face to face.

And last they found themselves at the double doors which led down the wide, sweeping steps into the courtyard. Cyllan stared at the dead scene before them, the relentless black walls tinged with a gory crimson cast from the unnatural glow that permeated everywhere – then a flicker of motion at the edge of vision alerted her.

Tarod's tall figure emerged from a doorway set into the foot of the Castle's Northernmost spire. Instinctively Cyllan looked up to where the gargantuan tower loomed into the night sky, and immediately had to fight back an attack of vertigo. Far, far above, at the spire's summit, a faint glow burned in a tiny window . . .

'Adept Tarod!' Drachea's voice brought her back to earth and she turned her head to see him swaggering down the steps to intercept Tarod's path. 'I've been looking for you!'

Tarod stopped and regarded the younger man dispassionately. 'Indeed,' he said.

This time, Drachea's anger was enough to overcome awe. He halted three steps from the bottom, so that their eyes met on an equal level, and said angrily, 'Yes, indeed! And I think that an explanation is long overdue! I have just been told that I am, effectively, a prisoner here – and I demand to know what you mean by such an impertinence!'

Tarod glanced briefly at Cyllan, who flushed. Then he folded his arms and regarded Drachea as though he were some unknown species.

'I told Cyllan nothing but the truth,' he said with cool disinterest. 'And as your uninvited presence here is none of my doing, so the fact that you must stay is something I can't influence. Believe me, you don't regret it any more than I do!'

Drachea was far from satisfied. 'This is outrageous! I'd remind you that I'm not some peasant whose absence counts for nothing! My clan will be searching for me, the militia will have been alerted – if I'm not found, then I warn you, there will be severe consequences!'

Tarod pinched the bridge of his nose between thumb and forefinger, and sighed with irritation. 'Very well. If you wish to leave – if you believe you can do so – then go. I'm not your jailer, and the gates aren't locked.'

Drachea had been on the verge of a fresh tirade, but now he stopped, nonplussed. He looked at Cyllan and frowned.

'Well?' he said, gesturing towards the Castle gates.

'No, Drachea. It's pointless.' She shook her head, knowing in her bones what would happen; knowing, too, that there was nothing to gain from trying to convince Drachea. He had to find out for himself.

He gave her a scathing glare, and strode across the courtyard. Cyllan hoped that Tarod might turn to her, say something to dismantle the icy wall that he seemed to have built around himself, but he didn't move. Drachea reached the gates and began to wrestle with them; they swung easily enough on vast, well-kept hinges, and he started out –

And stopped. Even at this distance Cyllan could share the appalled fear that swamped him as he stared out beyond the Castle, at nothing.

She could see it for herself as the great gate swung noiselessly back. Not fog, not even darkness, but a void, so unutterably empty that it made her feel sick just to look at it. Drachea uttered a single, inarticulate cry and stumbled back. As he released his hold on the gate it closed once more, of its own volition, and slammed into place with a dull boom that made Cyllan jump.

The Heir Margrave returned slowly to where they stood waiting. His face was the colour of putty, and his hands shook as though he had a fever. At last he stopped, at a safe distance from Tarod.

'*What is it?*' he grated through grey lips.

Tarod smiled with more than a trace of malice. 'Didn't you feel the inclination to step through and find out?'

'Damn you, there's nothing out there! It's like – it's like the darkness of all the Seven Hells! Not even the stack to be seen! Cyllan – ' he appealed to her. 'When we came here – there *was* a world beyond! The beach, the rock – it wasn't illusion?'

'No . . . ' *Yet there had been the mist; and the terrible feeling that the real world lay somewhere out of reach . . .*

Drachea turned again to Tarod and almost pleaded. '*What does this mean?*'

Unmoved, Tarod regarded him coldly. 'I've told you that you can't leave the Castle. Do you now believe me?'

'Yes . . . '

'And will you, then, believe that I can't change matters?'

'I – ' Drachea hesitated, then burst out, 'But you're a High Adept of the Circle!'

Tarod's eyes narrowed. 'I *was*.'

'Was? Then have you lost your power?' The words were a fear-driven challenge. Tarod didn't answer, but instead his left hand moved slightly. Cyllan was just able to glimpse something on his index finger before his form was blurred by a dark aura that seemed to flow out from within him, swallowing even the grim red light. The air turned bitterly cold as Tarod raised his hand higher, holding it, palm upward, towards Drachea.

What Drachea saw, Cyllan would never know and preferred not to speculate. But his eyes stared, starting almost from their sockets, and his jaw dropped in a rictus of sick terror. He tried to speak, but could only utter a tormented moan – then he sank to his knees on the steps, doubled over and retching with blind, helpless fear.

'Stand up.' Tarod's voice rang harshly, and the dark aura winked out of existence. Cyllan stared at the tall Adept, horrified by the sheer inhumanity of what he had done – and by the magnitude of the power he had commanded with such careless ease. Now, the only hint

of what had gone before was an echo of something
unholy in Tarod's green eyes . . . but she wouldn't
forget it easily.

Drachea staggered to his feet and turned his head
away. 'Damn you – '

Tarod interrupted him, speaking very softly. 'You
see, I have power, Drachea. But even my skills aren't
sufficient to break down the barrier and allow you your
freedom. Now do you begin to understand?'

Drachea could only nod, and Tarod inclined his head
in acknowledgement. 'Very well. Then you shall have
your explanation.' He turned to look at Cyllan. 'He'll
need help to reach the dining-hall. And perhaps you can
make him understand that I had no desire to harm him.
He simply had to be shown.'

Was he trying to justify himself, Cyllan wondered? If
he regretted his behaviour towards Drachea, his voice
showed no sign of it. She licked dry lips, nodded, then
tried to take Drachea's arm. He shook her off angrily
and turned his back, walking with rigid dignity ahead of
them towards the double doors.

The remote, dusty shadows of the Castle's great dining-
hall were beginning to grow unpleasantly familiar to
Cyllan. Entering, she had to suppress an instinctive
shiver at the sight of the long, empty tables, the gaping
fireplace, the heavy curtains that hung without a trace of
a draught to stir them. The Castle seemed to mock the
life which had once filled it.

Tarod moved to the fireplace, while Drachea stopped
at one of the tables, staring down at the wood and
seeming to find something in the grain to absorb his
interest. His face was still an unhealthy grey in the wake
of Tarod's unpleasant demonstration in the courtyard,
and his eyes smouldered with hatred. Cyllan realised
that the shock of that experience had gone deep, and she
wondered how much more he could withstand. With so
much damage already done, any further strain could
send him over the thin dividing line between sanity and
madness.

Tarod's voice cut across her thoughts. 'Sit down, Drachea. Your pride is commendable, but it seems pointless now.' Their eyes met, clashed, then Tarod added, 'Perhaps my demonstration was precipitate . . . if so, I'm sorry.'

Drachea stared back with wordless fury before abruptly subsiding on to a bench. It was on the tip of Cyllan's tongue to ask Tarod point-blank why he had chosen to demonstrate his powers with such callous disregard for the consequences; but she couldn't summon the courage. The respect and admiration which he had originally inspired in her were badly shaken by the incident in the courtyard; she was being forced to reassess the impressions of those two previous meetings, and they seemed a world away. Silently, she moved to sit beside Drachea. Under Tarod's steady, impassive gaze she had the discomfiting feeling that he and they were adversaries facing each other across a battle-line.

Tarod regarded them, reluctant as yet to speak. He needed to learn the details of whatever inexplicable twist of Fate had brought them through the barrier between Time and no-Time, in the hope that it might provide him with a desperately needed clue to his own dilemma; but in return he was bound to explain the truth of that dilemma to them. Or at least, as much of the truth as would suit his own purposes . . .

It all hinged on a question of trust. Tarod had learned, through bitter experience, that to trust even those who professed to be closest to him was a dangerous and self-destructive game. And if Cyllan and Drachea were to discover the full facts behind his story, he could rely on their enmity but on little else. Already the seeds were sown – his angry reaction to Drachea's challenge in the courtyard had been no more than a catalyst that triggered the young man's already unstable emotions, but it had spawned a fear that was fast growing into deep hatred. Drachea's good opinion was of no interest to Tarod; but it would be as well to alienate him no further.

Cyllan was another matter. Her thoughts were a

closed book to him, yet his feelings towards her were kinder. She had a rare inner strength that he could acknowledge and appreciate . . . but even she, if faced with the full truth, was unlikely to prove a willing ally. And impinging on the detached disinterest with which he viewed her opinion or her eventual fate was a worm of reluctance to take any steps which might do her harm. The old debt, which he had never repaid, seemed to call to a sense of honour and conscience that he had all but forgotten, and the sensation was uncomfortably alien.

The safest course, he felt, was to compromise – to tell them as much of the truth as they needed to know in order to be of use to him, whilst side-stepping the full story. It would be easy enough – even the arrogant young Heir Margrave would be unlikely to dare question the Circle's ways.

He spoke, so abruptly that Drachea jumped. 'I promised you an explanation, and I don't break my word. But first, I must know how you came to the Castle.'

'*Must?*' Drachea echoed. 'I think you're in no position to make demands of us! When I consider the cavalier treatment I have received since – ' And he stopped as Cyllan, who had seen the flash of irritation in Tarod's eyes, ground her heel hard against his instep.

'Drachea, I believe we owe it to Tarod to tell our story first,' she said, praying that he wouldn't be so foolish as to lose his temper. 'After all, we are the intruders here.'

Tarod glanced at her, apparently amused. 'I appreciate your consideration, Cyllan, but it's not a question of courtesy,' he said. 'Some accident brought you to the Castle, and you want to leave. I believe, as I've told you, that that's impossible – but it may be that something in your story will prove me wrong.' He looked at Drachea again. 'Does that satisfy the Heir Margrave?'

Drachea shrugged irritably. 'Very well; it's reason enough. And as Cyllan is so anxious to please you, she might as well speak for us both!'

Cyllan glanced at Tarod, who nodded encouragement. And so she began to tell of the Warp and its aftermath in as much detail as she could recall. But

trying to describe the apparition that had appeared in
the street outside the White Barque Tavern, she faltered, and Tarod frowned.

'A human figure? Did you recognise it?'

'I . . . ' She looked up at him, her eyes troubled. 'I
thought I did, but . . . now I don't know, and I can't
visualise it. It's as if the memory has been – blotted out,
somehow.' She looked to Drachea for help, but he only
shook his head.

Frustrated, Tarod gestured for her to continue, listening carefully as she explained how they had survived the
Warp only to find themselves in the middle of the Northern sea, with the day turned shockingly to night.

'I thought we'd both drown before we could reach
land,' Cyllan said, 'and so I called to the fanaani for
help.' She swallowed. 'If they hadn't answered, we
would have died then.' She looked up again, and Tarod
knew that she was remembering a Summer day in West
High Land, when she had led him down a treacherous
cliff-face to show him where the Spindrift Root could be
found. They had seen the fanaani then, heard their
bittersweet singing . . . he pushed the memory aside; it
no longer interested him.

'Go on with your story,' he said.

She bit her lip, and without any further show of emotion
recounted the rest of the tale, to the moment when she and
Drachea had finally reached the top of the stack and found
themselves facing the Castle of the Star Peninsula.

'There's no more to tell,' she said finally. 'We entered
the Castle, and we thought it deserted . . . until we met
you.'

Tarod said nothing. He seemed to be lost in thought,
and finally Drachea couldn't stand the ensuing silence.
He twisted around on the bench and brought one fist
down on the table-top.

'The Castle of the Star Peninsula, deserted!' he said
savagely. 'No Circle, no High Initiate – only one Adept
who tells us that the outside world is beyond our reach,
and gives no answers to our questions that make any
sense! A seemingly endless night, with no sign of the

dawn – it's *insanity!*' He stood up. Now that the first
words were out, they had opened a floodgate. 'I'm not
dreaming,' he went on, his voice growing harsher, 'and
I'm not dead – my heart still beats, and even the Seven
Hells can't be like this place! Besides,' he pointed at
Cyllan, 'she knew you – she recognised you. *You* live –
therefore we must be alive also.'

'Oh, yes; I live.' Tarod stared at his own left hand.
'After a fashion.'

Drachea tensed. 'What d'you mean, after a fashion?'

'I mean that I'm as alive as anything can be, in a world
where Time doesn't exist.'

Drachea had been pacing alongside the table, but
stopped in his tracks. '*What?*'

Tarod gestured towards one of the tall windows. 'As
you so astutely remarked, dawn hasn't broken. Nor will
it break. Tell me; are you hungry?'

Nonplussed by the apparently irrelevant remark,
Drachea shook his head angrily. 'No, damn it! I've got
more important matters on my mind than – '

'When did you last eat?' Tarod interrupted.

Drachea suddenly understood the implication, and
his face paled. 'In Shu-Nhadek . . . '

'Yet you feel no hunger. Hunger needs Time to
develop, and there is no Time here. No hours, no change
from day to night; nothing.'

Very slowly, as though doubting his ability to co-ordi-
nate his movements, Drachea sat down. Now his com-
plexion was ashen and he found his voice only with great
difficulty.

'You're telling me . . . seriously telling me . . . that
Time itself has ceased to exist?'

'In this Castle, yes. We are in limbo. The world outside continues, but here . . . ' He shrugged. 'You've
seen it for yourself.'

'But . . . how did it happen?' Drachea was torn
between disbelief and a terrible fascination with a mystery beyond his understanding. After the initial outburst
he had himself under control, only a faint tremor in his
voice betraying any emotion.

Tarod studied his left hand again. 'Time was banished.'

'Banished? You mean that someone – but *who*, in the name of the gods? Who could have done such a thing?'

'I did.'

There was silence. Drachea, wide-eyed, was trying to assimilate the idea of a power so titanic that it could halt Time – and the concept that a single man, however skilled, could wield it. Tarod watched him, outwardly impassive but inwardly apprehensive, waiting to see how he would finally respond – until the tension was broken by Cyllan.

She said, simply, 'Why, Tarod?'

He turned to look at her, and had the discomfiting feeling that, against his private predictions, she was prepared to believe him. Suddenly he laughed, coldly.

'You accept the word of an Initiate for something that, to any right-minded citizen, should surely seem impossible,' he said. 'Does the Circle really have so much influence?' Cyllan flushed, and the laughter faded to a humourless smile. 'I meant no slight. But I hadn't anticipated such unquestioning belief.'

A bench grated against the floor as Drachea moved to sit beside Cyllan once more. His gaze didn't leave Tarod's face, and his expression was an odd mixture of uncertainty, wariness and curiosity. When he spoke, his voice was steadier than it had been.

'Let us say, Adept Tarod, that we do accept the truth of your story – so far as it goes. I don't claim knowledge of the Circle's capabilities, and maybe an Initiate can wield a power that's capable of stopping Time. But you've not answered Cyllan's question. And besides – if you could banish Time, for whatever purpose, why can you not recall it again?'

Tarod sighed. 'There is a stone; a gem,' he said quietly. 'I used it as a focus to summon the necessary power for my work. When Time ceased to exist, I lost the stone . . . and without it I can't alter this predicament.'

'Where is the stone now?' Cyllan asked.

'In another part of the Castle – a chamber that, because of certain anomalies brought about by the changes here, I can no longer enter.'

Drachea had been fidgeting with his hands, twisting the fingers together. Without looking up, he said, 'This – work you speak of. It was a Circle matter?'

Tarod hesitated briefly, then: 'Yes.'

'Then where are your fellow Initiates now?'

'To my knowledge, they're neither in your world nor in whatever dead dimension this Castle inhabits,' Tarod told him. If Drachea chose to misinterpret what he heard, he wasn't about to correct him.

The young man nodded. 'Then this – circumstance – is the result of a Circle working which went wrong?'

Tarod resisted the temptation to smile at Drachea's further unwitting irony. 'It is.'

'Then it seems that, like it or not, we now share your predicament. And unless you can retrieve this gem you spoke of, we have no hope of reprieve.'

Tarod inclined his head, but his eyes gave away nothing.

'Yet if we have somehow managed to break through this barrier – albeit unintentionally – it surely follows that it's possible to reverse the process?' Drachea persisted.

'I wouldn't deny that. But my own efforts have thus far achieved nothing.' Tarod smiled a small, chilly smile. 'Of course, it may be that your skills can succeed where mine have failed.'

Tarod's sarcasm bit home, and Drachea gave him an angry glance. 'I wouldn't presume to suggest it, Adept. But it strikes me that we'd be better occupied in at least trying to solve this conundrum, if the only alternative is to wait apathetically for eternity!'

Tarod saw the motive behind Drachea's words, and it confirmed his belief that the young man would prove troublesome. Hiding his annoyance, he said indifferently, 'Perhaps.'

'Certainly it's worth further investigation.'

'Indeed it is.' Tarod rose. 'Then maybe you'd care to consider the problem at your leisure.' He smiled thinly.

'After all, we don't have the constraints of Time to hinder us.'

'No . . . ' Drachea's confident mask slipped and he glanced uneasily around him at the empty hall.

'And now, if you'll forgive me . . . ' Tarod looked at Cyllan, then away. 'I think there's little more we can say to each other at this stage.'

Drachea might have argued, but Cyllan gave him a warning glance and he subsided, making the best of the dismissal. 'Come, Cyllan. We've taken up too much of the Adept's time – ' he checked himself. 'A slip of the tongue – old concepts still linger.' He bowed, not entirely courteously. 'We'll take our leave of you.'

Tarod watched them go, and when they were out of sight he made a small, impatient gesture. The hall doors swung noiselessly shut, and he subsided on to the nearest bench.

Drachea's efforts to dissemble had been clumsy and amateurish; but his attitude was clear enough. The young man's suspicions were aroused, and that could prove irritating. There was little he could do to upset Tarod's plans, embryonic as they yet were, but his intrusion was an annoying complication none the less.

Tarod sighed, aware that it wasn't worth the trouble of taking any action at this stage. If Drachea proved too tiresome, dealing with him could be an enjoyable if brief diversion . . .

He rose, crossed the hall. The doors opened once more to allow him through, and he walked to the main entrance. Cyllan and Drachea were nowhere in sight, doubtless making their way to one of the Castle's empty rooms, to confer. Tarod laughed shortly and softly, and the sound gave back a peculiar echo that might almost have been another, alien voice. Then he turned out of the door and down the courtyard steps towards the Northern spire.

Chapter 4

Drachea stalked into Cyllan's chamber, leaving her to close the door behind them both. As she followed him into the room, he said, 'Well?'

Cyllan recognised the challenge in his eyes and in his voice, and turned away, torn between conflicting feelings. Every instinct warned her against trusting Tarod without question; yet she and Drachea were uneasy allies at best, and, irrationally, his attitude now put her on the defensive.

'I don't know,' she said.

'You don't *know*?' Drachea's voice was laced with incredulous contempt. 'You're not telling me that you're prepared to take the word of that – that *tyrant*?'

Cyllan's eyes flashed angrily. 'I said no such thing! But neither am I willing to condemn out of hand without more knowledge!'

'Then you're more of a fool than I thought you.' He raked her with a searing glance in which she saw the echoes of the wide gulf between them. The fact that she was unwilling to accept his judgement as superior to her own infuriated him; and he paced across the room, tension radiating from every muscle.

'First, he launches an unjustified and unprovoked attack on me – is that the behaviour of an Adept? And then he tells us a story of some Circle ritual that went wrong; as unlikely a tale as ever I've heard! He's lying to us; I'm certain of it!'

Cyllan moved to the window and stared out across the gloomy, silent courtyard. 'There's one fact we can't escape, Drachea,' she said with an edge to her voice.

'We're trapped here. Whatever your view of Tarod, you can't deny that he spoke the truth in that regard.'

'Can't I?' Drachea retorted savagely. 'For all we know, he could have his own reasons for holding us prisoner. The son of a Province Margrave would do well as a hostage, if his captor had sufficient motive – '

Cyllan swung round. 'A *hostage*?' she echoed, astonished by the conceit of the idea. 'What need would a high Adept have of a hostage?'

'Damn it, how should I know?' Drachea shouted. 'It makes as much sense as anything else here! And besides – ' His expression worked into a sneer, 'I have only his word – and yours – that he's an Adept at all.'

'That's ridiculous – '

'Is it? Or are you so jealous of your claim to comradeship with such an exalted figure that you'll hear no word against him?'

Cyllan bit back the furious retort that came to her lips as she realised, with chagrin, that Drachea had made a fair point. She was prejudiced – old memories had a hold on her still. And that could set a dangerous precedent . . .

'Think about it,' Drachea said obsessively, starting to pace again. 'The Castle of the Star Peninsula trapped in some unimaginable dimension, beyond the reach of Time. Very well, I grant the point you made; that much we can perhaps believe. The Circle gone – dead, fled, in limbo; we don't know. One man remaining, who implies – *implies*, mark you; he was careful to admit nothing directly, but allowed me to draw my own conclusions – that it's all the result of some hideous accident, and that he has no power to right matters. And we are expected to believe him?' He snorted. 'I'd as soon trust a snake!'

Cyllan's sense of justice protested at the sweeping condemnation, but she bit her tongue. 'What, then, do you think is the truth?' she asked.

Drachea shook his head. 'Aeoris alone knows the answer to that!' Reflexively he made the White God's sign as a mark of respect, then continued, 'You remember my telling you of the rumours rife in Shu? No word from the Castle, and a garbled tale of some trouble or danger in West High Land. This is the root of those rumours; it must be! There's something evil afoot – I *feel* it – and I feel, too, that it's of Tarod's making.'

Although deep down a part of her rebelled, Cyllan couldn't in all conscience argue with him. Too much of what he said rang uncomfortably true – and she, too, sensed the pervading threat of something dark and unholy that haunted the Castle. But if some black purpose lay behind Tarod's actions, she couldn't begin to imagine what that purpose might be.

Involuntarily, her gaze roamed to where old, discarded clothes lay on the window-ledge. The pouch containing her precious pebbles was among them; and it was possible, even here, that the old skills might work and allow her to uncover some clue to the mystery. But immediately, an inner voice said vehemently, *no!* She couldn't do it – a primal and irresistible fear stood in her path. She didn't have the courage, for fear of what she might see . . .

Drachea, unaware of her dilemma, was staring moodily out of the window, and suddenly he said, 'He spoke of a jewel . . . '

Cyllan looked up. 'A jewel? Yes, I recall it.'

'A focus for the power that halted Time, he said. And it's lost – or at least, wherever it is, he can't reach it. And he needs it.'

She laughed mirthlessly. 'We need it too, Drachea, if we're ever to leave this place!'

'Do we?' He hunched his shoulders like some bird of ill omen. 'Or is that, too, a lie? We don't know what that stone is or what it can do. If he retrieves it, with or without our aid, who's to say what the consequences might be? The return of Time, and with it freedom – or something else; something too hideous to imagine?' He faced her, eyes ablaze. 'Are you willing to take that risk? Because I, for one, am not!'

She didn't answer him, and he crossed the room, brushing her out of his path. 'Damn him!' he said explosively. 'If he thinks that I'll sit meekly by, awaiting my fate at his hands, he's *wrong*! The Castle might be abandoned, but its occupants haven't disappeared entirely without trace.' He indicated his own borrowed clothing. 'There must be clues – documents, records, the gods alone know what else. And I'll find them – Aeoris help me, I'll find the answers to this mystery, and I'll thwart him!' He whirled. 'Well? Are you coming with me, or d'you prefer to skulk here?'

His stare reflected the half-pitying, half-contemptuous attitude of a high-ranking citizen towards the gutter-born, and Cyllan's pride rebelled against his arrogance. 'No,' she replied with an icy edge to her voice. 'I'd prefer to skulk here, as you term it!'

'Do as you please.' Drachea strode to the door and pulled it open. On the threshold he looked back, but she had turned her head away, and he went out into the corridor, leaving the door to slam ferociously behind him.

When Drachea had gone, Cyllan shut her eyes tightly against the wave of bitter resentment that threatened to overtake every other thought. Drachea's manner towards her was an insult – and she had to admit that it also hurt. The comradeship, the sense of fighting on the same side, that she might have hoped for in these straits was absent – instead, they seemed to be constantly at loggerheads. Drachea's attitude had stung her pride to the core, and the same pride made her want to retaliate in some way; show him that she was more than an ignorant and worthless nonentity.

She opened her eyes, and looked at the pouch of stones. The clues Drachea was so confident of finding were more likely to be found through a seer's craft than through any haphazard physical exploration . . . if she could summon the courage to try.

Obscure fears crowded her brain, arguing violently against the idea; this time, Cyllan forced them firmly into submission. She had never been a coward; she wasn't hampered by the superstitious terrors of ordinary folk. What had she to be afraid of? Clenching her hands into determined fists, she moved towards the window-ledge.

Her old clothes were sticky with dried salt, the leather pouch stiff and cracking. Cyllan shook the stones out into her palm and sat cross-legged on the floor. A familiar tingling sensation assailed the nape of her neck, a sure sign that her psychic senses were awakening; and the suddenness of it took her aback. It was almost as though some outside power were pulling at her, like a strung marionette. She closed her eyes, and instantly a darkness clouded her inner vision, a dense blackness which told her that her consciousness was giving way to something far deeper. The pebbles burned like ice crystals in her cupped hands; she focused the darkness, concentrated, pushing back the wave of sick fear . . .

A tattoo of small, harsh sounds broke the silence as the stones scattered from her hands on to the floor, and Cyllan rocked back with a gasp. The psychic surge had come quickly, and its sheer strength astounded her. The room seemed to dip and recede momentarily as she opened her eyes, then her vision righted, and she looked down at the pattern the stones had formed.

The largest pebble of all lay in the pattern's exact centre. Around it, the others spiralled outwards to form seven uneven arms. The design was familiar – horribly familiar – and yet she couldn't place it, couldn't remember –

'*Cyllan.*'

She cried out with shock and almost bit through her tongue as the strange, silver-edged voice spoke her name from empty air. And at the same instant she felt a terrible premonition; the grim certainty that something stood behind her, in the room, watching . . .

Her throat was so constricted that she could barely breathe. And the room's contours were changing, losing their solidity, growing alien and fearsome . . . Odd colours flickered at the borders of her perception, and she felt a chill which pervaded the air, sank into her bones . . . Savagely, struggling against the threat of blind terror, Cyllan forced her muscles to obey her and turned her head.

The room was empty. *Too* empty . . . as though the real world had winked out of existence, stranding her in a half dimension of trickery and phantasm. And despite what her eyes told her, she could still sense the presence of another intelligence in the chamber. It watched her; she felt that it laughed at her inability to see . . . and she sensed a cold, sharp knife-edge of evil . . .

A single clap of sound, so loud that it went beyond the threshold of hearing, smashed into her head. Through a daze of pain she saw the door to her room begin to undulate, warping into impossible shapes. An aura appeared around it like some nightmarish halo, wild colours agitating furiously and all but blinding her. Something was approaching; she felt it – something that could crush her out of existence as a careless child might crush an insect underfoot.

With no warning the door disintegrated, and in its place was black light. Cyllan fought desperately against the terror of what she knew must be an appallingly powerful hallucination, but no amount of reason could combat the image of the not-quite-human figure which was slowly forming in the heart of the light, or the long, thin hand which reached out slowly, compellingly towards her.

Cyllan screamed, and knew that no sound escaped her lips. Every muscle in her body locked into a rictus, and a single, vast spasm racked her from head to foot before she fell helplessly, unconscious, to sprawl among her scattered stones on the floor.

Drachea's heart was beating uncomfortably fast as he made his way down the wide sweep of the Castle's main staircase. He was excited at the prospect before him, pleased with his decision to take positive action rather than passively awaiting developments; and yet the pleasure was heavily laced with apprehension which grew as he ventured further from the sanctuary of Cyllan's room.

Reaching the foot of the stairs he hesitated, looking carefully about to make sure there was no sign of Tarod. Beyond the half-open doors the courtyard showed dim and uninviting, the blood-red glow intensified by the contrasting blackness of walls and flagstones, and Drachea's courage began to slip. He wished – though nothing would have induced him to admit it to her – that Cyllan had accompanied him. He had dismissed her refusal carelessly, telling himself he had no need of help, but here alone in the gloomy silence the Castle felt threatening, an enemy only waiting for the right moment to strike at him.

He was also anxious above all to avoid another encounter with Tarod. No amount of bravado could eclipse his fundamental fear of the Adept, and he imagined that Tarod wouldn't look kindly on his attempt to unravel the Castle's secrets. Memory of what had happened in the courtyard turned his stomach momentarily to water; with it came a resurgence of hatred, and when the sweating terror passed Drachea felt better, buoyed up by the anger which was beginning to germinate into a desire for revenge. Damn Cyllan – if she chose to skulk in that musty room, so be it! He'd find the answers he needed, and show her that a Margrave's son had no need of a peasant-drover to champion him.

He stepped outside, and glanced up at the Northern spire, jagged against the featureless pewter sky. The light in the topmost slit of a window was no longer visible, but Drachea suspected that Tarod was up in that room. All well and good – his own destination lay elsewhere, and the thought that he was unlikely to cross the Adept's path bolstered his confidence.

To the right of the steps which led down into the courtyard was a colonnaded walk, with a door at the far end. Odd, Drachea thought, that another way in to the Castle should exist so close to the main entry . . . it suggested some ulterior purpose.

With a further, quick glance towards the spire he ran down the steps and along the walkway to the door. It opened easily when he lifted the latch, and he felt disappointed – surely, if it led somewhere significant, greater care would have been taken to protect it? Expecting perhaps nothing more than a storeroom, Drachea peered through – and saw a long, narrow corridor that led away, on a downward slope, seemingly into the bowels of the Castle. For the first twenty paces or so the crimson glow permeated, illuminating ancient stains of damp . . . then the passage was swallowed by darkness.

The thought of venturing into the black unknown beyond the door was enough, at first, to sap Drachea's resolve. If Cyllan had been with him –

No, he told himself. He had no need of her. His eyes would grow accustomed to the darkness soon enough, and if, as he suspected, this passage led him closer to some of the Castle's secrets, he might soon have a story to tell her that would open her eyes to the truth!

Taking a deep breath – and disliking the old, musty smell that hung in the air – he stepped through the door, being careful to leave it wide open at his back. The floor of the passage was even enough, and as he advanced, his vision began gradually to adjust to the dark until he could just make out the dim contours of the walls ahead. They seemed to go on forever, and always downward . . . he hesitated, then pressed on, fighting down his unease.

The soft sound of his padding footsteps became almost mesmeric as he made his way further along the corridor. Now and again some trick of acoustics almost convinced him that he heard another footfall at his back, fractionally out of synchronisation with his own. Once he stopped, quickly; thought he heard the illusory steps shuffle to a halt behind him, and sweat broke out on his forehead and neck. But when he turned, there was nothing to be seen . . .

Imagination. The mind played all manner of tricks under such circumstances as these. There could be no ghosts here . . . Drachea continued on, resisting the temptation to whistle aloud as a boost to his courage – and suddenly the passage ended at the top of a flight of steps. He paused, feeling his way cautiously on to the first tread, and again looked over his shoulder. Nothing untoward . . .

The stairs wound steeply down, and Drachea sensed that he was nearing his goal. Then he felt a surge of excitement as he saw that, ahead of him, the stairs terminated at another door.

It stood open, as though someone had walked carelessly through it only moments before, and beyond it a trace of light faintly illuminated a large, vaulted room. Eagerly Drachea hastened through, and as he entered the vault he tripped over something lying on the floor, and went sprawling. He swore aloud – his voice echoed loudly, compounding the shock, and as he sat dazedly on the hard stone he realised what had brought him down.

Books. Hundreds of them, scattered all over the flagstones. Wherever he looked, wherever he put his hands, there were tomes and manuscripts and rolled parchments, some whole, others split and separated. And in the faint glow that pervaded the room he could see shelves lining the walls, many of them broken, but a few still containing precariously balanced volumes which looked as though they might slip and crash down at the slightest provocation. It was as though some mad scholar had run riot in his own library . . .

Of course – this was the Castle's library! As the revelation struck him, Drachea immediately forgot his original intention, stunned by the awesome fact that, by sheer fortuitous accident, he had literally stumbled on the greatest storehouse of arcane knowledge in the world. He reached out and picked up the nearest of the fallen books, wincing as several damaged leaves came loose and fluttered to the floor. All the Circle's secrets, its lore, its practices, revealed to his gaze with no one to forbid him . . . It was more than he could ever have dared to dream of!

Drachea opened the book at random and pored over it. The script was closely written and hard to make out in the poor light, but he deciphered enough to set his pulse racing. Initiation rites – the formulae were all here; the prayers, the incantations – he snatched up another volume at random, turned the pages feverishly. This one was older, harder still to read . . . he put it aside, reached for one of the scrolls. Parchment, this: the ink so faded that he judged it had been written centuries ago, before the process of pulping wood to make a finer medium had been invented and had replaced the use of animal skin . . . almost reverently, Drachea placed it with the first tome, then stood up, looking wildly about him.

He could spend a lifetime here. He could study year after year, until he was grey with age, and still never slake his thirst for occult knowledge. Envy of the Initiates who had free run of this unbelievable place filled him – and then he checked himself, almost laughing at his own absurdity. *He* had the run of the library now – there was no Circle to stand in his way! Only one man, and however high an Adept he might be, there were ways and means to outwit him. Even if Tarod used the library for his own purposes, he wouldn't miss a few volumes from among the chaos. And in the sanctuary of one of the Castle's upper rooms, Drachea could absorb this fabulous knowledge at his leisure.

Cyllan was forgotten; their predicament was forgotten. Drachea began to search through the books, gathering up those which seemed to hold the most promise, until he had as many as he could carry. He straightened, face flushed with exertion and excitement – and froze as he heard the sound of footsteps from beyond the vault.

Several books fell from his arms to the floor, and the noise they made brought him out in a cold sweat. The footfalls were coming from the stairway beyond, slow, measured, echoing faintly. *Tarod* – it had to be! Drachea's triumph crumbled before the thought of what the Adept might do to him if he discovered his presence here, and frantically he looked around for a hiding place. At first the library seemed to hold no hope – then he saw a door, low and insignificant, half hidden in an alcove between two rows of shelves. The books forgotten, he ran towards it . . . and as he reached it the footsteps faded away into silence.

Drachea stopped, feeling the icy crawl of gooseflesh on his skin. Human footfalls didn't simply die away like that. Someone had been approaching, had almost reached the bottom of the stairs – they couldn't just vanish!

Eyes wide, he looked towards the stairs, dimly visible beyond the vault entrance. No shadow moved, and the silence was absolute. Fear began to flower into panic, and he found himself involuntarily backing away, until he collided with the small door. It sprang open, making him yell with shock, and he stumbled through.

He was in a long, narrow passage which sloped steeply down before him. The faint light that filtered throughout the vault was stronger, as if its source lay somewhere in that corridor, and a violent shudder racked Drachea, a twisting terror that he couldn't name, but which eclipsed all other sensation.

Something lurked at the invisible end of the passage. He felt it, a palpable presence . . . and it was slowly moving towards him. A soft sound, like an echo of not quite human laughter, seemed to reverberate in his head and he backed away, aware of bile rising in his throat and striving to force it back. He could see nothing, but he *knew* it was there . . . a presence, a monstrously evil presence . . .

The faintest of breaths brushed past his face, and Drachea's self-control snapped. Whatever might await him on the stairs, it was as nothing compared to the unknown horror beyond this door – and he ran like a hunted animal, hurling himself across the vault and through the arched doorway. On the stairs he fell, scrambled to his feet, raced on and upward, while blind panic overcame all else. Nothing stood in his way, no one appeared suddenly from the shadows to confront him, and at last he burst out into the comparative brilliance of the courtyard, collapsing with a bone-jarring momentum that scraped the skin from his knees and hands.

Drachea rolled over and staggered to his feet, leaning against one of the pillars of the colonnade for support

while he fought to get his breath back. The empty courtyard felt bleaker and more menacing than ever; shadows
beyond the reach of the blood-red glow seemed to his
overworked imagination to form lurking, threatening
shapes. He shuddered, shutting his eyes against
unwanted images, and forced himself to gulp stale air
into his lungs. His pulse began to slow, and eventually he
opened his eyes again, feeling in better control.

He'd made a fool of himself. There had been no one
on the vault stairs, and nothing in the corridor beyond
the small door. He had allowed imagination to run away
with him, and had panicked at an illusion . . . Drachea
looked over his shoulder to the entrance through which
he had come. The thought of returning didn't appeal,
despite the lure of the books; and with an angry gesture
in the door's direction he started back to the Castle's
main entrance. Inside, and halfway to the stairs, he
stopped. To return to Cyllan with nothing to report
would be to admit failure, and therefore demean himself
– something against which he rebelled violently. He
wouldn't return to the library, as yet (and he dismissed
the small inner voice which suggested he was afraid to
return there alone). The Castle must hold many more
revelations – there were other, and doubtless better,
places to search for the answers he wanted.

With a swift, furtive glance around to ensure he was
alone, Drachea hastened away along one of the Castle's
seemingly endless corridors.

It was sheer fortuitous coincidence which brought
Drachea at length to the suite of rooms on the ground
floor of the North and centremost wing. He had reached
them by a circuitous route, doubling back time and again
through the warren of passages that threaded
throughout the Castle, and he was tired, frustrated and
disheartened when he came upon the studded door with
its highly polished surface. But as soon as he lifted the
latch and looked in, he knew he'd stumbled on more
than merely another empty chamber.

The room was dominated by a large table with a

carved and padded chair set tidily behind it. A pile of papers had been neatly stacked on the table as though awaiting imminent attention; an inkstand and several pens lay beside them. And Drachea's gaze alighted on something else. A seal, half hidden behind the inkstand . . .

He closed the door softly behind him and crossed to the table. As his hand reached out towards the seal he hesitated, assailed suddenly by a feeling that he was trespassing on strictly forbidden ground. If this room was what he thought it was, then merely to touch that seal would be little short of blasphemy. Yet he had to know . . .

Mouth dry, Drachea steeled himself and snatched up the seal. The emblem on it reflected bloodily in the crimson glow, and he saw that it was a lightning-flash, bisecting a double circle.

The seal of the High Initiate himself . . . Reverently, and a little fearfully, Drachea laid it back in its place and stared about him at the room, feeling suddenly awed. This must be – or have been – Keridil Toln's study . . . he shivered. He had never seen the High Initiate, but his half-imagined ghost seemed to hover in the room, watching from whatever unimaginable limbo he now inhabited.

Slowly Drachea turned, taking in every detail of the shadowy chamber. Everything was perfectly in place, as though Keridil Toln had left his room for the last time with some premonition of what was to happen. The chill that hung in the air was more than physical . . .

He turned his back abruptly to the gaping fireplace, which for some inexplicable reason made him doubly nervous, and approached the table again. Three shallow drawers were set beneath the polished surface on one side, and tentatively Drachea tried each in turn. If records of recent events existed, this was surely where they would be lodged . . .

The first two drawers yielded nothing but sheaves of everyday records – tithe lists in the main, and of little interest. The third drawer wouldn't yield at first, and

Drachea thought it to be locked – until, abruptly, it came free with such force that it fell out of its housing, scattering its contents to the floor.

Drachea snatched up one of the papers at random – and his heart missed a beat painfully as one word, one name, caught his eye. *Tarod*.

He all but ran to the window, holding the paper up against the glass to make the best of what little light there was. The paper, he now saw, was a formal document, signed and sealed by the High Initiate and witnessed by six elders of the Council of Adepts.

It was an execution order.

Drachea put a hand to his mouth, feeling sick with a mingling of excitement and horror as the first echoes of the truth sounded in his head. His suspicions had been right . . .

He tucked the document inside his jacket and feverishly set about gathering up the other scattered papers. At last he found what he had hoped and prayed for – a report, written in the same careful and well-formed hand as the execution order; and intended solely for the eyes of senior Councillors. With it was an opened letter, and he recognised the seal of the Sisterhood of Aeoris, intertwined with the fish symbol of West High Land Province.

West High Land, where the rumours of trouble had begun . . . Drachea lowered himself into the carved chair, no longer caring whether it belonged to the High Initiate or Aeoris himself. Reading was difficult in the gloom, but he no longer trusted his legs to support him. Silently, avidly, he scanned the letter first. The Lady Kael Amion . . . she was Senior at West High Land, it seemed; the dispatch she had sent to Keridil Toln was of the utmost urgency, and concerned an Initiate and one of her own novices. Yes, it began to make sense . . . but he needed more; much more.

Drachea's hand was unsteady as he picked up the report. He read it in its entirety, only the occasional rustle of a new page breaking the room's bleak silence. And when he had finished he stood up and, with a deliberation that suggested he wasn't quite in control of his limbs, hid the papers carefully with the first document inside his coat. His face was ashen as he turned to look again at the fireplace and the flagged floor in front of the hearth. A morbid fascination urged him to go closer, to study that part of the floor for signs that would prove what he had read beyond doubt; but he couldn't. And the High Initiate's words rang too icily true for there to be any shadow of disbelief.

He had to show what he had found to Cyllan. He had to prove to her that he was right – far more right, in fact, that he had ever dreamed. And above all, he needed to share the burden of his fear.

Drachea replaced the fallen drawer, straightened the seal so that it aligned neatly once more with the pens and the inkstand on the High Initiate's table. He closed the door of the study quietly behind him and made the sign of Aeoris before his heart before turning and hurrying back towards the main stairs.

Chapter 5

Tarod's acute senses were alerted by the first inkling of something untoward that pervaded his mind. It was as though a faint breath of wind had disturbed an utterly still day, presaging some change; and it disturbed him on a deeper level than he cared to admit.

He rose from the battered, hide-covered chair where he had been sitting, and moved silently to the window which looked out from the spire's summit over the sickening drop to the courtyard. Nothing moved there; and the sky that seemed to loom so chillingly close to the window was still empty and dead. But, somewhere in the Castle, something was amiss . . .

A sudden sharp sensation in his left hand surprised him; a once familiar feeling which he had almost forgotten. He glanced at his fingers, at the ruined base of the ring which once had held his soul-stone, then flexed the hand thoughtfully. Fear was beyond him, but whatever it was that had come to disturb the Castle's deathly quiet would have struck panic into a mortal man.

Behind him on a small table, amid a clutter of books and manuscripts which he had idly gleaned from the library vault, stood a sconce containing a single, partly burned candle. Tarod moved his left hand over it and a pale, nacreous green flame sprang into being. Holding his fingers in the flame he coaxed it, drawing it upward and outward, watching it respond to his mental command until it formed a perfect if sickly halo. The light reflected on his face, highlighting gaunt shadows, and his eyes narrowed as he looked into the elemental fire and beyond it, seeking the source of the disturbance.

He found the source, and, again, it troubled him. At a

single sharp gesture the green fire vanished, and as the small room sank once more into darkness Tarod turned towards the door. A peculiar compulsion was urging him to leave the spire, where he spent so much of his existence, and seek out the root of the strange and unexpected shift. He crossed the room, ignoring the jumble of scattered artefacts that made it chaotic, and which he never took the trouble to clear. He was as indifferent to his own comfort as to anything else; but something was challenging that indifference, and his curiosity was aroused.

Beyond the door, black stone stairs spiralled down into crimson-tinged darkness. The door closed softly behind him, seemingly of its own accord; then Tarod's dark shape faded and merged with the shadows, leaving only a brief after-image.

Cyllan hadn't barred her door. Tarod's hand on the latch met with no resistance, and he let the door swing open gently and slowly. For a moment he thought the room empty; then he saw her – and an old, dead memory lurched deep within him, momentarily breaking through his guard.

Cyllan lay sprawled on the floor, her head twisted at an ugly angle and one arm flung crookedly out. She looked like a broken doll, and the image she presented was instantly superimposed in Tarod's mind by another image, another woman. Themila Gan Lin, who since childhood had been his dear friend and mentor, lying on the floor of the Council Chamber, her life bleeding away from the wound inflicted by Rhiman Han's sword . . .

It had been pure accident, a moment of hot-headed confusion which had ended in tragedy. Themila hadn't had an enemy in the world; the small, elderly historian had been like a second mother to many of the younger Initiates, and especially so to Tarod when he came, clanless and injured, to the Castle. Yet she had died – and with her death the whole savage chain of events had been unleashed. Cyllan's huddled, broken attitude recalled the dying Themila, and Tarod was shocked to realise that the memory brought back all the pain of her loss, as though from a great distance his lost humanity was striving to reassert itself.

He crossed the room, ignoring the pebbles which slipped and scattered under his feet, and knelt beside the girl. She was alive, and there was no outward sign of injury; but neither was there any clue as to what had struck her down. Tarod's immediate thought was of Drachea, but he dismissed the idea, sensing something afoot that Drachea couldn't even comprehend, let alone influence. The atmosphere of this room was subtly changed, charged . . . some power independent of his own had been at work, and he couldn't begin to guess at its source.

But the motivating force was a less urgent consideration. Tarod lifted Cyllan, surprised by her lightness, and carried her to the bed, taking care to lay her down gently. She stirred, mumbled something unintelligible then lapsed into stillness once more, and he stood back, looking at her. Something had stirred briefly within him, conjured by the juxtaposition of Cyllan and Themila in his thoughts, and now, though he tried to dismiss it as meaningless, another, older part of him was fighting back. Ghosts of the past had never troubled him before; the past was lost and could never be regained. The manner in which he had thwarted Keridil and the Circle had seen to that when it rendered him soulless and immortal . . . yet *something* stirred, and he couldn't banish it.

On impulse, he sat down on the edge of the bed and smoothed Cyllan's tangled hair away from her face. Her lip trembled in response, and her eyelids fluttered spasmodically. One hand reached up blindly and Tarod took hold of it, offering her a physical link with consciousness as she began to awake.

'Drachea . . . ?' Her voice was weak and hesitant.

'Not Drachea.'

Her eyes snapped open and she swore aloud in shock, a drover's oath that Tarod had never heard uttered in the Castle. She pulled away from him like a cornered animal, and he released her hand, the expression on his face hardening into a thin, humourless smile.

'You've suffered no ill effect from your ordeal, I see.'

'I – I'm sorry. I didn't intend . . .' She shut her eyes again, overwhelmed by confusion. *She had been trying to read the stones – something had come, something from outside; and she'd been so afraid –* Uneasily she forced herself to look at Tarod once more, her eyes hunted. She feared him too, but at least his was a physical presence, an anchor to hold her back from the edge of the nightmare.

'I was trying to read the stones . . .' She had to find an outlet for the unformed terror, but her tongue couldn't cope with more than a simple statement.

Tarod asked, more gently, 'What did you see?'

'Something came through the door . . .' she whispered. He waited, but she offered no further explanation; and the few words she had spoken disquieted him. *Something through the door . . .* Either Cyllan had hallucinated, or she had unwittingly tapped a force that shouldn't have been able to exist in the Castle, unless he himself had deliberately conjured it. Another, alien presence? It surely wasn't possible . . .

Cyllan's voice intruded abruptly on his thoughts. 'I thought,' she said slowly, deliberately, 'that you were responsible.'

Tarod's eyes lit angrily. 'You think I have nothing better to do than divert myself by frightening undefended women. I thank you for the compliment!'

She was unsure of her ground, yet now that the nightmarish memory was giving way to reason she could see no other answer. 'Who was responsible, then?' she countered. 'Drachea? I doubt it!'

Her determined aggression amused Tarod. She wasn't afraid of him, and for some inexplicable reason he found that pleasing. He laughed, and Cyllan turned away sharply.

'Mock me if it entertains you,' she said, 'but I've seen no other power here save yours. And you don't seem overly concerned how you use it!'

Tarod sighed as the momentary amusement gave way to irritation. 'Believe what you like,' he retorted coldly. 'I'm not interested in your opinion of me, and I assure you I had no hand in whatever happened to you. If I'd anything to gain from – ' And he stopped, suddenly furious as he realised what he was saying. 'Damn you, why should I justify myself in your eyes? If you choose to bring suffering on your own head by dabbling out of your depth, it's no concern of mine!'

Cyllan didn't reply, but rolled over and hid her face in the pillow, her attitude radiating mute resentment. Exasperated, Tarod reached out and took hold of her. 'Look at me, Cyllan.' She resisted and he gripped her chin, forcing her to meet his gaze. 'I said, look at me!'

She stared back, angry and hurt and defiant at once, and he said softly, venomously, 'Don't pit yourself against me. I'd take no pleasure in harming you, but whether you prosper or perish is of no moment to me whatever.' He raised his free hand, the fingers curling in a casual, graceful gesture that nonetheless chilled Cyllan to the core – then abruptly lowered it again. It would be so simple to inspire in her a terror beside which her hallucination would pale to nothing; but there seemed no point. He could sense the fear in her now, although she did her best to hide it, and suddenly he was disgusted with himself. She was irrelevant; the idea of wasting energy on her was too petty to be worth contemplating – and yet he had been on the brink of striking at her as though reacting to some personal slight.

He released her, and she drew back quickly, hunching against the wall. Irritated, Tarod rose – but before either of them could speak, the door of the bedchamber was flung open and Drachea burst in.

'Cyllan! Look what – ' And he stopped, eyes widening as he saw Tarod.

Tarod bowed slightly to him, conveying devastating contempt in the apparently careless gesture. 'Heir Margrave – I trust your explorations have proved fruitful?' His gaze alit on the heavy book Drachea carried in his hands, then moved, amused, to the young man's face.

Drachea paled, and Tarod crossed the room to lift the
volume easily from his fingers and study the cover.

'Very diverting.' He flicked a page or two, then
graciously handed the book back. 'If you have
difficulty understanding its content, I'm at your
disposal.'

Two spots of livid colour flamed into life on Drachea's
cheeks and he made as if to retort angrily; but a brief
movement of Tarod's hand triggered a force that sent
him reeling backwards. His spine connected painfully
with the wall; and by the time he regained breath and
balance, the Adept had gone.

Drachea stared speechless at the still-quivering door,
then in a violent movement swung round and hurled the
book ferociously across the room. The ancient binding
split in half and pages scattered across the floor.

'Curse him, what in the name of all the hells did he
want here?' The question was a savage demand; Tarod
had humiliated Drachea in Cyllan's presence, and he
was using her as a scapegoat for his anger. Sensing the
underlying accusation, Cyllan flared back.

'I don't *know* what he wanted – I didn't have the
chance to ask him! Something happened while you were
away; something that –'

He interrupted her, dismissing what she had been
about to tell him as of no consequence. 'Never mind
that! I've more important matters at hand.' Fumbling
inside his jacket, he brought out the bundled papers
from the High Initiate's study. 'Tarod might well sneer
at a book from the Castle library, but if he knew I was in
possession of these he'd sing to a different tune! Look –
look at them!' He thrust the sheaf towards her chal-
lengingly. 'I've learned the truth about your Adept
friend, Cyllan. Go on – read for yourself!'

Cyllan made no move to take the papers. The aftermath of shock, coupled with Drachea's disinterest in
her experience and the tension of the brush with Tarod,
had put her on a knife-edge, and she only glared at
him.

'By all that's sacred,' Drachea snapped, 'this is no

time to be childish! These documents are vital – for Aeoris's sake, will you *read* them!'

Cyllan's lips whitened and she said harshly, 'And where do you think that I learned to read?'

He stared at her nonplussed. 'You mean . . . you've had no schooling?'

'No. I can't read, and I can't write. Is that such a surprise to you? My clan didn't send me to a tutor – I was too busy learning to gut fish and herd cattle!'

She felt mortified, hating herself for having had to admit to her own failing. Drachea continued to stare at her with an expression that might have been disdain or pity; she couldn't tell which. Then he made a sharp, dismissive gesture.

'Damn it, what does it matter? If you can't read them for yourself, I'll read the documents to you – but you *must* listen!' He snatched at her arm, pulling her with him across the room. 'You've got to realise what's truly happened here – what Tarod has done, and what he is!'

The urgency in his voice made her quell her resentment. If he had discovered something vital, then any quarrels and tensions between them should be forgotten, and as he subsided on to the bed she sat beside him, peering over his shoulder at the papers.

'This,' Drachea said, brandishing what she took to be a letter, 'was written by the Lady Kael Amion, Senior of the West High Land Sisterhood Cot – and I don't believe anyone would call *her* word into doubt. Listen; she says *"My dear Keridil – I have entrusted this letter to the hand of my colleague, Sister Erminet Rowald. Your report came as a great shock to me, and I can only thank Aeoris that in His wisdom He has seen fit to thwart the fugitive Tarod, who was apprehended at my own Cot last evening. Novice Sashka Veyyil – whose circumstances you are, of course, already aware of – was blessed with the moral courage to realise her duty, and it is because of her swift action that we are able to deliver this man into your safe keeping. It is a sad day for Circle and Sisterhood alike when such evil is uncovered, but with Light and Law to guide us we shall prevail. Charity commands that*

I should pray for a condemned man's soul; I would therefore be obliged if you will apprise me of the date set for Tarod's execution –"

Cyllan interrupted, her voice low and incredulous. '*Execution . . . ?*'

Drachea laughed sharply. 'Oh, yes! And there's more; far more.' He set the letter aside, picked up another document. 'It's here – in Keridil Toln's own hand! This is the High Initiate's report of the trial and planned execution of our good friend Tarod!'

Cyllan stared at the papers, stunned. The writing was meaningless to her, and she railed against her own deficiency. Something within her protested that Drachea must be wrong; that the Circle could never have cause to condemn one of their own . . .

'But Tarod's a high Adept,' she said uneasily. 'That much we know is true.'

'Adept he may be. But what *man* is it who carries his soul in a gemstone?'

'*What?*'

'It's nothing less than the truth. Tarod's no ordinary mortal; he never has been. The High Initiate discovered his real identity.' Drachea paused for dramatic effect, then added: 'Tarod is not human!'

Cyllan felt a deep-rooted shudder rack her, as though some inexplicable and indecipherable premonition were at work. 'Then . . . what is he?'

Drachea looked nervously about the room, as though convinced that some unholy presence was watching them. The shadows were still and silent, and, before courage could fail him, he whispered, '*Chaos.*'

The word sent knives through Cyllan's nerves, and instinctively she made the sign of Aeoris before her face. Every instinct rebelled against the concept – it was an *impossibility*. And Tarod, one of Aeoris's own servants –

'Chaos is dead . . . ' She barely recognised her voice. 'It – it can't be true, Drachea. It can't!'

'When I was a child,' Drachea said, 'I once heard an Adept speak at a Summer Quarter-Day celebration. He exhorted us always to keep faith with the cause for which the gods came to this world and fought the last great battle against the Old Ones. He warned us always to be vigilant, lest Chaos should one day return. And now . . . it would seem that his exhortation was well founded.'

'But Aeoris himself banished Chaos!' Cyllan protested. 'To suggest that the dark powers might defy the gods – ' She shuddered. 'It smacks of blasphemy.'

'Then you call the High Initiate a liar?' Drachea countered. As her eyes widened, he went on, 'Keridil Toln knew. He discovered what Tarod truly is, and set out to destroy him.' Again he glanced around the room, then added darkly, 'It seems that he failed.'

Cyllan stood up and went to the window, staring out at the now disquietingly familiar vista of the hellfire-lit night. Unwillingly, she found her gaze drawn to the Northern spire. No light burned there, and she looked away.

Chaos. She couldn't make herself believe it. All that time ago on the cliffs of West High Land, she had met a man, not a demon. And yet she remembered her terror when she had woken in this room to find Tarod's hand gripping hers. He had claimed to know nothing of the nightmare which had assailed her; now though, her doubts were swelling into a fearful certainty that only he could have been responsible. An insane part of her wanted to give Tarod the benefit of the doubt; but she knew that to do so could put herself and Drachea into unimaginable danger. She couldn't take the risk.

Turning back towards the bed she said quietly, 'Read me the papers, Drachea. Please. I want – I want to know all that they say.'

And so, while she sat silent beside him, Drachea read the High Initiate's detailed report. The story began to form a frighteningly cohesive picture; Tarod's near-death from an overdose of the Spindrift narcotic, the taking of the old High Initiate, Jehrek Banamen Toln's life; the encounter with Yandros, Lord of Chaos, and the revelation that the gemstone of Tarod's ring was the repository for a life-essence created by the Chaotic powers . . . and there was far more, as Tarod and the High Initiate began to clash. But finally the document posed its own mystery, ending merely with Keridil Toln's statement, undated, that *'on this night, the being called Tarod will die'*.

There was utter silence when Drachea stopped speaking. Cyllan's finger traced the wax seal at the foot of the execution order – he had read it to her, and its stark simplicity was somehow the ugliest condemnation of all. She felt the contours of the High Initiate's symbol, the double circle with its bisecting lightning-flash, and at last said, softly,

'But he didn't die . . . '

Drachea gave her a look that was impossible to interpret. 'No . . . he thwarted them. By halting Time itself. Gods!' The thought made him shiver, then he collected himself and managed to summon a faint smile. 'But it was an empty victory, wasn't it? When the trap was sprung, he too was caught in its jaws, and now he can't escape.'

Cyllan hugged herself uneasily and said, 'Unless he should regain the stone he spoke of, and use it to call back Time.'

'Yes – and now we know the true nature of that gem! A soul, born of Chaos . . . it doesn't bear thinking about.' He stood up, strode across the room. 'Just imagine what the consequences of his retrieving that stone could be! Without it, he's powerful enough – as I can attest. The Circle have already failed to defeat him once – can you envisage what he might be capable of, if that stone were in his possession once more?'

Cyllan could, and shied away from the thought. But she couldn't escape the other consideration that haunted her, and to which she could find no answer.

She said, hesitantly, 'And yet without the stone, we are as trapped as Tarod. We can't leave, and even he hasn't the power to release us.'

'If he should choose to,' Drachea put in darkly.

Cyllan smiled with irony as she recalled Tarod's words

to her. 'Why should he not? He's not interested in us – and we're of no use to him.'

'Aren't we?'

She frowned. 'What do you mean?'

'I mean that we might be able to succeed in retrieving that gem where he has failed. There's something – some power – preventing him from getting his hands on it. But if we're not bound by that same power, then we're invaluable to Tarod.' Drachea paused, thinking. 'We broke through the barrier that separates the Castle from the rest of the world. We don't know how it happened, and neither does he – you saw how shocked he was at our arrival. If we can reach that stone, he'll use us to do so. And then . . . ' He let the sentence hang unfinished.

Cyllan looked again towards the blood-red light beyond the window. The thought of what might happen once the stone was in Tarod's possession was terrifying; yet without it, there could be no hope of escape. Eternity, spent in a world enclosed by four black walls, companioned only by Drachea and by a man who was no mortal man at all, but owed his origins to something beyond her comprehension . . . never changing, never ageing, denied even the release of death. Suddenly she smiled thinly to herself. Was that prospect so much worse than the life she had known? At least here there was no hardship, no endless toil. Here, she wanted for nothing. Except, perhaps –

Drachea broke abruptly into her reverie. 'There is a way,' he said, 'just one way to escape this place without playing into Tarod's hands. We must find the stone for ourselves, and use it.'

Cyllan turned and stared at him. 'Find and *use* it?' she echoed, incredulous. 'Drachea, this is no child's bauble! If what is in those papers is true, then that gem is a thing of *Chaos*! Are you or I such great adepts that we would *dare* to use it, even if we could?'

'We can at least try!' Drachea insisted stubbornly. 'Have you a better plan? No, I see you've not! Look – ' He darted to the bed and scooped up the scattered documents. 'The High Initiate speaks of a chamber

called the Marble Hall. It seems to be the Circle's sanctum; the place where the most sacred rites are performed and the most sacred artefacts kept.' He grinned.
'You'll recall that Tarod chose to be cryptic on the
subject of the gem's whereabouts. It's my belief that if
we can find the Marble Hall, we'll find that stone, too.'

'A place that for some reason Tarod can't enter . . .'
Cyllan mused. Drachea's theory seemed plausible.

'Or won't. It may be that it's the one thing of which
he's afraid – and that can only be to our advantage.'
Drachea was riffling through the papers. 'There must
surely be some hint here, some idea of the Marble Hall's
location . . . no, nothing!' He threw the papers aside in
frustration.

'You found these,' Cyllan said, indicating the scattered pages. 'There must surely be other documents;
something that will help us.'

'Yes . . . either in the High Initiate's study, or better
still, in the library.' Suddenly Drachea's eyes lit up.
'Gods, Cyllan, the library – it's a treasure-house of
knowledge, the arcane wisdom of centuries! I found it by
chance, and the thought that it's there, open to me
whenever and however I choose – ' He stopped as he saw
that her expression hadn't changed. 'No, well – of
course, to you it would mean little.'

'Indeed,' she said with gentle acerbity.

He had the good grace to blush. 'Naturally, I'm far
more concerned with our plight and how to resolve it
. . . but I'll wager anything that the library will provide
what we need to begin our search. There must be histor-
ical records that explain the Castle's layout.' He recalled
his previous visit to the library, and the memory unset-
tled him. Though nothing would induce him to admit to
fear, he was determined not to return there alone.

Cyllan glanced at the broken book on the floor.
'Tarod already knows of your first visit to the library,'
she reminded him. 'We must take care not to arouse his
suspicions any further.'

Drachea smiled condescendingly. 'What he doesn't
know can't trouble him. Don't concern yourself with

Tarod. He's not as invincible as he seems to think – and before long, I intend to prove that to him!'

The two figures making their way through the courtyard were all but hidden by the vast shadows of the Castle wall, but even the smallest movement amid that dark stillness was enough to attract attention. Tarod stood by the window in his unlit room at the top of the spire, his face expressionless as he watched them creep cautiously along the colonnaded walk towards the vault door, Drachea leading and stopping every few paces to make a gesture that cautioned silence. Like as not he meant to show Cyllan the treasures he had unearthed in the library; and from there it seemed logical to anticipate that they would, eventually, discover the entrance to the Marble Hall. Tarod had refused to allow himself to speculate on whether or not they would be able to enter the Hall – the force that held the Castle in limbo had, somehow, shifted the peculiar chamber a fraction out of synchronisation, and he himself was barred from it as surely as if it hadn't existed. But Cyllan and Drachea had broken through one barrier . . . it was possible that they could reach the Hall where he had failed.

And if they did? Tarod didn't know what they would find, but of one fact he was certain – the Marble Hall held the crucial key to his hope of release. It was the sole gateway back to the disturbing astral planes through which he had travelled to find and halt the Pendulum of Time; and, too, it was the place where the Chaos stone – his own soul – was trapped.

He looked out of the window again, and saw that the two distant figures had vanished, leaving the vault doorway ajar behind them. Briefly, an unaccustomed yet distantly familiar feeling assailed him; a sense of anticipation coupled with a formless pre-echo of fear. A very human sensation . . . he smiled to himself. Imagination must be getting the better of him; human feelings lay in the buried past. Or at least, he had believed so . . .

Tarod swung suddenly away from the window, disliking the unexpected turn his thoughts had taken. Since he

had left Cyllan's room, unable to control the temptation
to swat Drachea aside in the way he might swat an
irritating insect as he left, the encounter had been preying on his mind. He had little else to think of, but
nonetheless he was unused to being troubled by such
thoughts. The old memories awakened by finding Cyllan
lying senseless on the floor refused to be quieted; and
they were complicated by odd, random recollections
that flashed unbidden into his head. The lightness of the
girl when he had lifted her; the roughness of her skin
when he took her hand to help her back to reality; even
the way she had sworn like some hard-bitten merchant-
sailor at the shock of finding him at her side. Though
afraid of him, she had refused to be intimidated, and
her spirit struck a chord somewhere within him. He
had found himself wondering if, in spite of the indifference he professed to feel, he could trust her . . . and
then the thought had been abruptly curtailed as he
remembered another life, another girl in whom he'd
placed trust.

Sashka Veyyil had been everything Cyllan was not;
beautiful, educated, assured of her place in the world.
Theirs had been, he'd thought, an idyllic match – until
she had callously betrayed him to safeguard her own
standing, and advance her own cause. Sashka now languished in limbo with the Castle inhabitants; Tarod's
love for her had turned to searing contempt, and
thought of her plight gave him a malevolent satisfaction.
But, against all reason, Cyllan's presence in the Castle
had harked back to those old times, stirred up something
which should have been unable to exist.

He was suddenly angry, both with himself and with
the girl. The concern that had moved him when he found
her unconscious was ashes, and that was how it should
remain. She was nothing to him beyond a cipher that he
might, with fortune on his side, use to further his own
aims; and if she suffered in the process it was of no
moment. To put faith in her would be madness – he
would watch and wait, assess her value to him and make
use of her. Beyond that, she was nothing.

Picking up a book he had already read twice, Tarod sat down, ignoring the faint and distant voice that accused him of self-delusion. Such human failings were a thing of the past. And the past was dead.

* * * * *

Cyllan stared in amazement at the thousands of books and manuscripts that littered the vault floor and lined the row upon row of shelves. Starting to move forward she stumbled over a huge, black-bound tome and hastily sidestepped it, overawed and afraid of damaging any of the precious volumes.

Drachea had no such compunction. Now that he had a companion to bolster his courage, he had forgotten his first unnerving experience here and was rummaging among the books, picking out those which seemed to offer promise. Cyllan watched him, acutely aware of her own shortcomings – save for making some sense of a map, she had no part to play in the search for clues. Discomforted, she wandered to the far side of the vault where the light seemed a little better . . . then stopped, noticing a small, low door set deep in an alcove and invisible but from close quarters. Experimentally she touched it; it moved, a little stiffly at first, then the hinges unjammed and it swung fully open.

'Drachea . . . '

He answered with a dismissive grunt, but she persisted.

'Drachea – look! There's another passage . . . '

His head came up and he looked round – then froze. He recognised the door – it was the same one he had unwittingly and unwillingly discovered in his moment of panic here alone, and he didn't like to be reminded of that incident.

'Doubtless it's unimportant,' he said carelessly.

'I don't think so . . . ' Cyllan frowned. The narrow, palely illuminated corridor that sloped steeply away downwards intrigued her; intuition told her there was more to it than met the eye, and she took a few steps into the passage. The light increased; faint still, but unmistakably growing, as though some hidden source lay at the end of the corridor. She wanted to explore further.

'Drachea – I think we should investigate. Perhaps I'm wrong, but – I think we should.'

She heard Drachea curse impatiently under his breath, then his footsteps sounded across the flagstones and he came to join her.

'Look,' she said quietly, pointing. 'The light . . .'

He saw what she meant, and his curiosity was aroused. There was, after all, nothing to fear here – no lurking horrors, no demons, no phantoms, except those his own mind chose to create.

'Very well,' he said, brushing her aside and taking the lead. 'If you're set on it, we'll find out where it leads!'

He set off, walking fast and not waiting for her to keep up. Cyllan hurried after him – then, barely able to stop herself on the steep gradient, all but collided with him as, without any warning, he halted abruptly with an oath of surprise on his lips.

The door that confronted them was made of metal, but it was no metal that either had ever seen before. It gleamed sullenly, like old and tarnished silver, yet the glow it gave off was sufficient to light the corridor and filter into the vault beyond. A peculiar, sourceless illumination . . . something about it made Cyllan's hackles rise, and she arrested her hand midway to the door, afraid to touch it.

Drachea had forgotten his scepticism and stared at the door with burgeoning interest. 'The Marble Hall . . .' he said, half to himself.

Cyllan glanced quickly at him. 'Do you think it could be?'

'I don't know. But it would seem possible . . . even likely.' Licking dry lips, he reached out and gave the door an experimental push. A tingling sensation ran from his fingers through his hand and arm, and the door didn't move.

Drachea withdrew his hand and shook it. 'Whatever lies beyond, it must be significant. This door's either locked or magically protected.'

'There's a keyhole,' Cyllan said, indicating a small slot in one side of the silver surface.

'Yes . . . ' Drachea crouched, squinting but being careful not to touch the door again, then shook his head and stood up. 'It's impossible to see anything.' Resentment and frustration tinged his voice. 'But it *is* the Marble Hall – I feel it in my bones!'

She didn't answer, but continued to gaze at the door. Her spine was prickling in the way she knew so well; as though something that lay just beyond the borders of psychic consciousness were awakening and crawling towards the surface. Her vision distorted momentarily, so that she saw the silver door as if from a great distance; the illusion passed quickly, but when her senses righted themselves she thought – no, *imagined*, she told herself – that she felt a presence on the other side. It lived, it was aware of them; she felt it waiting and watching . . .

Perhaps Drachea, too, glimpsed something of the same sensation, for he backed away suddenly, and his face had lost its colour.

'The key,' he said. 'There must be a key.'

'You searched the High Initiate's study,' Cyllan reminded him. 'Was there nothing there that you might have overlooked?'

'I don't know . . . it's possible. Though more likely, I'd suspect, that if this door leads where we think it does, the key's in Tarod's possession.' He smiled thinly. 'After all, if you were in his place wouldn't you take that precaution against your secret being uncovered?'

It made sense, and if Drachea was right Cyllan didn't relish the thought of attempting to retrieve the key. Yet she *wanted* to open that door and see whatever lay beyond. Something about this mystery caught and pulled at her, and it had nothing to do with the enigmatic jewel. Something was calling to her, summoning her; and the desire to answer the summons was growing out of all proportion.

Alarmed by the strength of her own feelings she moved away from the door, and thought that she heard, so faintly that it might have been illusion, a soft sigh that emanated from nowhere and drifted away along the corridor. She looked back, saw nothing, then realised that Drachea was as uneasy as she.

'We should go,' she said softly.

He nodded, trying to disguise his relief. 'We'll return. We'll find the key, somehow, and we'll return.'

He took hold of her hand as they turned and made their way back towards the library, whether to reassure her or himself Cyllan didn't know. Reaching the vault, Drachea closed the small door carefully behind them, then gathered up the books he had collected.

'I don't know if Tarod ever comes here, but I wouldn't relish the prospect of meeting him face to face.' His smiled was forced. 'It might be prudent not to linger.'

What he had sensed beyond the silver door Cyllan didn't know, and doubted if he would tell her. She said nothing, only looked back once, speculatively, as they left the vault and started to climb the stairs.

Chapter 6

Gant Ambaril Rannak was trying to control his impatience and irritation, but it was a losing battle. He stood staring through the long window of his drawing-room, his mind not registering the sight of the gradually burgeoning gardens, unpleasantly aware of the sound of his wife sobbing quietly in the background. Today was her birth-anniversary, and should have been an occasion for celebration. Instead, they were in the midst of a nightmare from which there seemed to be no awakening – the mystery of their eldest son's disappearance.

There should have been news by now. The heir to a Margravate didn't simply vanish without trace. *Someone* must have seen Drachea leave the market square with that damned drover-girl, and yet although he had used all his considerable resources to the full, Gant could find not one single witness to his son's fate. He had, at first, tried to face the possibility that the Warp which had struck Shu-Nhadek on that day had taken them both, but he knew his son, and his son wasn't such a fool as to let himself be caught out in such a grisly way.

There was, of course, the theory that the drovers' leader had been behind the whole thing, setting up the girl to lure Drachea away and hold him to some form of ransom. Such crimes weren't unknown, and, with the increase in lawlessness over the past year or so, there were a good few ruffians who'd consider the prize well worth the risk. In the first throes of fury and anguish Gant had had the drover imprisoned and mercilessly interrogated, but it soon became apparent that Kand Brialen knew nothing of the affair. His horror at the occurrence was painfully genuine, and even if it stemmed solely from his fear of losing a wealthy customer rather than any concern for his own niece, Gant had grudgingly been forced to abandon his suspicions.

And so, frantic for news and frustrated at every turn, Gant had applied all his considerable resources to what had been, thus far, an utterly fruitless search. The province militia under his command had unearthed nothing; the seers of the Sisterhood had exerted their skills to no avail . . . and now it seemed that even his last hope would fail him.

He turned to where the heavily built man with the Initiate's gold insignia on his shoulder stood conferring in a lowered voice with the Lady Silve Bradow, Senior of the province's largest Sisterhood Cot. It was by sheer good fortune that Hestor Tay Armeth, a fourth-rank Adept of the Circle, had been staying at the Cot when Gant's messenger arrived to seek the Sisterhood's aid, and Lady Silve – who was newly promoted to her office and had never before had to deal personally with such a crisis – had looked immediately to Hestor for advice.

But now it appeared that the Circle's representative was powerless to help. Far from offering the solution that Gant and his family craved, Hestor had thus far done little but prevaricate. The Margrave had a suspicion that there was more behind his dissembling than met the eye, but couldn't draw him, and his patience, goaded by the worry that ate at every fibre of his being, was running out.

He turned on his heel, clearing his throat loudly to draw their attention. The Margravine sniffed and wiped her eyes, looking to her husband with tearful hope.

'Adept.' Gant spoke politely, but with an edge. 'You'll pardon my speaking bluntly, but this matter grows more urgent with every minute that passes! My son, the Heir Margrave, has disappeared, and all efforts to find him have failed. I turn to the Circle for help, as anyone might surely be entitled to do in such circumstances – and yet it seems you can offer me nothing! I ask one simple question of you – can you aid me, or can you not?'

Hestor and Lady Silve exchanged a glance, then the Sister-Senior clasped her hands and stared down at the thickly carpeted floor as Hestor replied.

'Margrave, all I have said to you is that I can make no promises. There are complexities involved which – '

Gant interrupted him. 'As I see it, sir, the only complexity is the mysterious nature of my son's disappearance! *Surely*, in this case, there's reason enough to send word to the High Initiate?' He licked his lips. 'I know Keridil Toln, as I knew his father Jehrek; and I'm certain that he would wish to be informed and to offer the Circle's resources.' Gant paused, wondering if Hestor would react to the gently implied threat; then, when the man appeared unmoved, he finished, 'Of course, if you would prefer to take the responsibility on your own shoulders . . . '

The Adept smiled reservedly and without warmth. 'I wouldn't presume, Margrave. Naturally, I'll ensure that a message reaches the Castle; but of course these things take time, and time may not be on our side.'

Gant hunched his shoulders gloomily. 'Nevertheless, it seems to be our only hope, as all else has failed.' He glanced at his wife. 'I've heard tell that experiments are being made in using hunting birds as messengers in cases of emergency. If we could use such a method, we could send word to the High Initiate far faster than any man could ride.'

'I've heard something of it,' Hestor said cautiously. 'Falconers in Empty Province have been using birds, and the idea is also being tried in Wishet. But as to its reliability – '

'Damn it, surely it's worth the attempt?' Gant exploded, then with an effort brought his temper under control. 'Forgive me – but surely you can understand my feelings? The Lady Margravine is distracted with worry and grief – and if the Circle can't aid us, then there's nothing left!'

For a moment Hestor looked away, then seemed to steel himself and met the Margrave's gaze once more.

'You're quite right, of course, Margrave – I ask your

pardon if I've seemed doubtful or reluctant. I can't claim
to know how the Circle can help you . . . but there will
be a way. You have my assurance.'

Gant grunted. 'Then you'll inform the High Initiate?'

'With all possible speed.'

The Margravine sighed softly and her husband moved
across the room to pat her shoulder with stiff affection.
'There, my dear. You heard what the Adept said. We
have the Circle to help us. If any power in the world can
restore Drachea to us, they can.' He glanced at Hestor
again. 'Though the occasion won't be as festive as normal under the circumstances, we have a small family
gathering at dinner to mark the Margravine's birth-
anniversary. I'd consider it a pleasure if you and the
Lady would join us.'

Hestor bowed slightly. 'Thank you, Margrave, but I
think I'd be neglecting my duty if I didn't set the Circle's
investigation in train without any delay. I've promised to
escort the Lady Silve back to her Cot, and then I must be
on my way North.'

Privately, Gant was relieved by their refusal. The
anniversary meal would be an unhappy enough affair
without the presence of strangers to add further con-
straint. He rang for a servant to bring the visitors' horses
to the front of the house, and bade them a formal
farewell at the door. As they clattered away in the
direction of the drove-road, he watched them, frowning
against the low-angling Sun and wishing that he could
identify the new sense of unease that moved in him.
Something was wrong. The Adept's assurances had
been too glib, and he had the unshakable impression
that the two of them were concealing something from
him. Whether it directly concerned his son he couldn't
tell; but instinct told him that it boded ill.

The horses and their riders were out of sight, and a
stray cloud moved across the Sun's face, casting a grim
shadow over the grounds. Gant unclenched his hands,
which he had been holding unconsciously rigid, then
turned and, stooping like an old man, went back into the
house.

'I wish I'd not been forced to lie to him.' Hestor reined in to allow a lumbering wagon to pass on the narrow road. 'It sets a bad precedent.'

Lady Silve shook her head. 'You had no choice, *th*-Hestor.' The odd speech impediment that marred her words was a quirk she had had since childhood. 'We dared not, after all, *th*-tell him the truth.'

The Adept sighed through clenched teeth. 'So what am I to do? Send a message to the Star Peninsula that can't be delivered? I pity the Margrave, I feel for him – I have children of my own – but I've far more urgent matters to worry about than the disappearance of a feckless youth who's probably living wild with some whore not half a day's ride from here!'

Silve narrowed her eyes. 'That's not a sentiment that *th*-becomes you, Hestor.'

'No . . . no; I'm sorry; it was an unworthy thought. Put it down to the worry . . . I can't stop thinking of my own family at the Castle, and wondering what's become of them . . . what's become of them all.'

'There's still been no word?' she asked.

The Adept shook his head. 'Nothing. And with each day that passes I fear more and more that something's terribly wrong. I've been over it in my mind time and again and I can't find an answer that makes any sense. If Keridil had some intention of sealing the Castle off from the world, we'd have known of it. Even if he couldn't reveal the purpose, he'd have given warning! But this . . . ' He shook his head again, helplessly.

'Rumours are spreading rapidly,' Lady Silve said, her voice sombre. 'At first the speculation was *th*-confined to the Northern provinces, but now there are stories abroad *th*-everywhere. It won't be long before they reach the Margrave's ears.'

'And all the while we sit helplessly by and await word from those who returned to the Peninsula.' Hestor shivered. 'Part of me is afraid to hear the news they might bring, I'll willingly admit it.'

They rode on in silence for a few minutes before Silve

said diffidently, 'Do you have any – personal theories,
Hestor? As to what might have *th*-occurred at the
Castle?'

The Adept didn't reply at first and she wondered if
he'd heard the question. But as she was about to repeat
it, he suddenly said, 'No, Lady, I haven't. Or at least
. . . none that I dare allow to take root.'

She nodded, and made the Sign of Aeoris over her
breast. 'We must pray for guidance.'

'Guidance?' Hestor echoed. 'I'm not sure, Lady; I'm
not sure. Maybe we'd do better to pray to Aeoris for
deliverance.'

*   *   *   *   *

Cyllan lay on the wide bed in her room, fighting the
weariness that was trying to break down her defences. In
this timeless place such concepts as hunger and thirst
and tiredness were, she knew, illusory, but events were
taking their toll of her energy and she wished that she
could have simply closed her eyes and slept a dreamless,
untroubled sleep.

But in truth, she was afraid to rest. Disturbing and
unwanted thoughts were crowding into her mind, and
however hard she tried she couldn't banish them. On
their return from the library vault Drachea had hurried
away to his own chamber with his precious hoard of
books; she'd wished he would stay, but he had either not
understood her hints or chosen to ignore them, and had
left her alone.

Cyllan didn't want to be alone with her thoughts. She
needed a distraction to stop them from overtaking her
and gaining a painful, clawlike hold; she felt defenceless
against them, and reflected unhappily that even Tarod's
company would have been preferable to this solitude.

Tarod . . . she rolled over and sat up, angry and a
little frightened by the fact that her chain of consciousness had led inexorably back to its starting point.
Since she had awoken to find him here beside her she
had had no chance to analyse her thoughts and feelings,

but now they demanded attention. She had accused
Tarod of perpetrating the psychic horror that attacked
her in this room; he had sarcastically denied it, and –
albeit without good reason – Cyllan found herself
believing him.

Or was she a not altogether unwilling victim of self-
delusion? Drachea had accused her of prejudice, and
she was honest enough to admit that it would be an easy
enough trap to fall into. For many months she had
carefully schooled herself to the certainty that her path
and Tarod's would never cross again; their two brief
meetings had been meaningless coincidence, and to
hope for more – as, she admitted, she had done – was
childish and stupid. But now they *had* crossed, in circumstances which her wildest nightmares could never
have conjured; and all the old memories were clashing
painfully with the grim reality of the present. Tarod's
coldness, his sometime malevolence, the sheer power he
could command, appalled her . . . and then had come
Drachea's revelation.

She still couldn't believe it. Even with the High Initiate's own testimony before her, the thought that Tarod
was no man but a thing of Chaos was too terrible to face.
Those dark and ancient powers of evil were nothing
more than an ancestral memory to Cyllan; but the memory was deep-rooted, and somewhere, unimaginably far
back over the generations, were the ghosts of her clan
forefathers who had died fighting the monstrous forces
of the Old Ones. She had learned and believed – as
everyone learned and believed – that Chaos was dead.
Now she was confronted with one who, on the word of
the High Initiate himself, was the embodiment of that
evil, incarnated from the hell of the remote past.

*And, worst of all, one whom she had once thought she
could love* . . .

The one fact that she had been desperately avoiding,
shying away from at every turn, was suddenly coldly and
harshly clear in her mind, and the thought of it made her
freeze inwardly. If the accusations were true, then she
had fallen under the spell of a demonic power,

something so monstrous as to be almost beyond con-
ception. *If* the accusations were true . . .

Cyllan told herself that she dared not allow her mind
to follow that path. To weaken now, and to doubt, was
the way to damnation. She *had* to believe, or she'd be
lost.

Unhappiness and confusion were eating at her like a
disease, and her restlessness was a constant torment.
She rose, paced across the room and then back, not
knowing what she wanted, what she felt, what she could
do. To confide in Drachea would only make matters
worse; his interest in her well-being – as was becoming
abundantly clear – extended only so far as it affected his
own, with a small but patronising measure of common
humanity to mitigate. Wryly, she reflected that were it
not for the predicament which had thrown them forcibly
together, he would have considered her utterly beneath
his notice. Tarod's arrogance had at least some sub-
stance beyond accident of birth . . .

Abruptly furious with herself for making such com-
parisons, she swung round, clenching her fists in sheer
bitter frustration. She couldn't stay in this room, like
some fragile flower awaiting rescue by her paramour –
the idea, when applied to herself, made her want to
laugh aloud. Drachea might choose to study books as an
answer to their plight; she needed more direct and active
means. And immediately she thought of the vault, and
the silver door with its mystery.

That place had chilled her, and yet it had fascinated
her, too. Caution had thus far made her resist the lure of
returning, but the lure was there all the same. As if
something called, something that lay behind the door,
waiting . . .

She shivered. She had been enticed by such feelings
before, and wouldn't care to repeat the experiences
they'd brought. But she had to do something . . . and
her frustration was strong enough to overcome fear.

Suddenly decisive, Cyllan slipped out of her room into
the gloomy passage. Drachea's door was firmly shut,
and as she passed it she paused, listening; but no sound

came from within. Silent as a cat, Cyllan hurried away towards the stairs.

Strangely, she felt none of the nervousness she had anticipated as she descended the long flight of stairs to the library vault. Rather, she had a sense of returning home; an inexplicable *rightness* that baffled her. The vault was dark, the small door in the alcove as they had left it: cautiously she pushed it open, then stepped into the sloping passage. Her bare feet made no sound, and the only thing to break the utter quiet was the soft hush of her own breathing.

The silver door awaited her, glowing, but the glow seemed somehow softened. Quite why she had come to stand before it again Cyllan didn't know; it was locked, she couldn't enter the chamber beyond . . . yet it had seemed the right, the *only*, thing to do. And now her instinct was at work again, urging her to touch, to try, to dare . . .

Remembering the shock Drachea had received, Cyllan was reluctant to touch the peculiar metal surface; but knew she couldn't merely stand and stare. Slowly, she reached out . . .

There was no shock. Her palm came to rest on the door and it felt warm; unyielding, but almost alive. She drew breath, exerted a gentle strength, pushed –

Her head snapped back with a stunned reflex as an instantaneous and blinding flash of light slammed against her inner vision. *A star – a seven-rayed star –* then it was gone as shockingly as it had come, and she stared in astonishment as the silver door began, slowly and silently, to swing open.

There was light, an eerie, nebulous coruscation of mist, shifting and shimmering and deceiving the eye. Through it Cyllan thought she could see slender pillars that reached to an invisible ceiling, but they too seemed to move and change with the ever changing light. It was as though she had opened a door on to a fable-world, a place of miraculous strangeness and soul-tearing beauty; and she bit her lip hard against an irrational

surge of emotion. Slowly, not knowing if she dared
advance or if her presence would sully this silent perfec-
tion, she moved forward a pace, then another, until the
mists enveloped her, their light playing on her skin and
transforming her into some denizen of their own strange
dimension.

The Marble Hall . . . This could be no other place!
Awed, Cyllan advanced, gazing in wonderment at the
vast chamber which seemed to have no boundaries, at
the fascinating patterns of the jewel-hued mosaic floor.
It was a masterpiece, surpassing anything she could have
imagined – surely, she told herself, surely it could not
have been created by human hands!

She was so entranced by the undreamed-of beauties of
this magical place that all else was forgotten – until,
through the shimmering curtains of light, she saw something that jarred with the Hall's serenity. It loomed
black, angular and ugly out of the mist, and as she drew
nearer she saw that it was a great block of wood, roughly
the length and breadth of a man, that stood waist-high
like some crude altar. Pitted, scarred, clearly very
ancient, it was cruelly out of place among such beauty,
and something about it made Cyllan recoil. It seemed to
reek of decay and death and despair, and she skirted
widely round it, not wanting to move too close lest its
aura should touch her too.

And it was in changing her direction to avoid the black
block that she came face to face with the statues.

'*Aeoris!*' The oath was out before she could prevent it,
and Cyllan made the Sign before her heart in hasty
apology for such irreverence. Her eyes widened, barely
able to take in the sight that confronted her.

There were seven of them, towering figures which
rose out of the mist like something from a nightmare.
They were shaped like men, but gigantic; and the deceptive light playing and shifting over them gave a terrible
illusion of movement. They might at any moment have
stepped down from their stone plinths and advanced,
like giants, towards her.

But it *was* an illusion . . . they were statues, nothing

more. And yet, though she couldn't see them clearly, Cyllan felt a deep thrill of awed recognition. Seven statues . . . seven gods . . . this, then, was the most sacred sanctum, the Circle's own temple to Aeoris . . .

Fearing to commit a sacrilege by daring to look more closely at such holy artefacts, Cyllan was yet unable to resist moving nearer to the statues. Throughout the land she had seen many religious celebrations, bowed before many images of the White Lords; but never before had she been privileged to gaze upon the face of Aeoris in such an exalted place. She drew closer to the towering figures, staring up through the mists like a transfixed child, to see the carven features of the seven gods.

Disappointment filled her as she saw that the statues had no faces. The features of each one had been thoroughly and systematically hacked away until no detail remained, and the sight of such desecration shocked Cyllan to the core. But the statues were incredibly ancient – the black stone was worn and pitted with the ravages of countless centuries, and she realised suddenly that this sacrilege might have taken place even before the first Initiates made the Castle their stronghold. Astounded by her discovery, she peered up again at the towering figures –

And she stumbled back with a cry of shock.

Slowly, superimposed on the ruined and jagged stone, faces were forming, manifesting fully even as she looked. Those faces gazed impassively down on her, serene and immortal. But the serenity was shot through with malevolence; the features, though beautiful as only gods could be, sharp-etched and cruel; the eyes ice-cold and filled with a proud evil. These were not the faces of Aeoris and his holy brethren! These were the antithesis of Light, bringers of darkness and mayhem . . . *and she knew them!*

Cyllan's heart pounded agonisingly in her breast as she stared at the nearest of the statues – and she remembered a moment in Shu-Nhadek, just before the Warp had come shrieking through the town to snatch her and Drachea, when she had stared in fascinated horror at the grim, gaunt figure that beckoned like a nemesis from the street, outlined against the insane sky. *That face – she could never forget that face!*

Stunned by shock, yet unable to find the compulsion to turn her head, she looked at the second figure which stood beside the first. And what she saw made her slam a fist against her mouth to stop herself from crying out aloud. If the first face had been familiar to her, then the second was infinitely more so – and in one horrifying instant it confirmed everything the High Initiate's testimony had revealed, and swept away all possible doubt.

Cyllan turned, almost losing balance in her haste, and ran towards the silver door, now barely visible in the coruscating mist. Reaching it, she flung herself through and raced, sobbing for breath, up the steep slope to the vault. The vault door crashed behind her; she didn't hesitate, but stumbled over the scattered books towards the stairs –

In the gloom a dark shape moved, materialising out of the shadows. Powerful hands grasped her wrists, spun her around – and Cyllan came face to face with Tarod.

'*No!*' The word was a full-throated scream and, with the strength of panic, she twisted free and plunged towards the door. She had almost reached it when it slammed shut, and she cannoned into the unyielding wood with tremendous force. Tarod caught her as she reeled back, stunned, and Cyllan knew that she couldn't escape him. Sick with the dizzy aftermath of her collision, she could offer no further resistance as Tarod swung her to face him. Her back was pinned against the door now, and all she could do was turn her head aside, every muscle in her body rigid.

'*Don't touch me*,' she hissed through clenched teeth.

He didn't reply; neither did his grip slacken. Cyllan shut her eyes, not knowing what he'd do to her and aware that she was powerless to fight him. Fear and hate surged in her, but she was impotent.

'Cyllan . . . ' Tarod's voice was soft with menace. 'You will answer me, and you'll tell me the truth. *Where have you been?*'

She bit her lip until a bead of blood formed, shaking her head violently. She expected him to hurt her, but he didn't. Although the pressure of his fingers increased, he only said, almost gently, 'Tell me, Cyllan.'

Startled by the tone she looked at him – and saw the iron-hardness in his green eyes. He had no need to harm her physically. He could destroy her sanity with a flick of his fingers if he chose to, and they both knew it. She struggled with her tongue, knowing she was defeated but striving not to show weakness.

'I – ' The words came at last. 'Through the corridor . . . the silver door . . . '

'To the Marble Hall?'

'Yes . . . '

'And then?'

The green eyes still held hers, and she didn't dare lie. 'I'd thought the door was locked, but . . . it opened.'

Tarod ran his tongue slowly over his lower lip. 'Yes,' he said softly, almost to himself, 'I thought so . . . ' To Cyllan's surprise he released her arms and turned away, walking slowly across the vault towards the alcove. Watching him, she began to edge one hand towards the latch of the door at her back. If she could open it silently, she might –

'The door won't open,' Tarod said, without looking at her. 'It will stay closed until I release it.'

Her cheeks were afire with shame at her own naïvety when he turned to face her again. For a long moment he regarded her with detached interest, then he said,

'Why are you so afraid to answer my questions?'

'I'm not afraid.' She couldn't look at him; the memory of the statue's carved face was too strong.

'Ah, but you are. Why? Do you fear reprisal?' He smiled, though it wasn't a kindly smile. 'I *could* hurt you, if it suited me to do so, or perhaps if you angered me. But I'd prefer otherwise.'

The utter certainty that he could do precisely as he chose with her snapped Cyllan's self-control. She knew what he was; knew that she had nothing to lose, and

something awoke in her that made her fatalistically careless. If she was damned, then let the damnation be
complete – she could at least hold to what little pride she
had left.

Her voice suddenly stronger, she spat back defiantly,
'Would you? I doubt that!' She took a step towards him,
shaking. 'Why don't you destroy me, Tarod? I'm
nothing to you – I'm of no value!' One hand went to the
collar of the shirt she wore, and in a single, violent
movement she tore it, exposing her throat and the slight,
pale swell of her breasts. 'Isn't this how a sacrifice should
be prepared? You care nothing for human life – kill me!'

Tarod didn't move. Instead, the cool expression on
his face gave way to another smile, but this time there
was a faint trace of warmth in it. Quietly, he said,
'You're very courageous, Cyllan. But your courage is
misplaced. I don't intend to harm you; it would be
pointless, and I've no desire for it. So perhaps I care a
little more for human life than you think.' He came
towards her, and she stood rigid as he laid a hand lightly
on her breast where the shirt was ripped. 'I ask only one
thing of you – that you tell me what you found in the
Marble Hall.'

His touch was cool, but physical, human . . . Cyllan
suddenly felt confused as warring impressions clashed in
her head. She feared his wrath if he should discover what
she had seen – but fear of what he still might do if she
kept silent was stronger, and she whispered, 'The statues . . . '

'Ah . . . the statues.' Tarod nodded. 'Yes. And what
else?'

'There was a block of wood – a great black slab. I – it
was a repellent thing.' Her fear was receding now; he
seemed unmoved by the fact that she had seen those
sculptured monstrosities, and though his lack of reaction
puzzled her she was grateful for it. She had the temerity
to look up at him, and saw that his eyes were narrowed
and his expression set, as though mention of the block
had revived some dark thought.

'Repellent,' he repeated speculatively. 'I'm a little

surprised at your choice of words, but . . . they're apt
enough. And was there anything more?'

'No,' she said. 'Nothing.'

A pause. 'You're certain of that?'

She remembered the stone, and Drachea's theory that
it was hidden somewhere in the Marble Hall. She'd seen
no sign of it . . .

She nodded. 'Yes. I'm certain.'

Tarod tilted her face up, studied it intently, then
relaxed. 'Very well; I see you're telling me the truth.'
For some reason which Cyllan couldn't begin to guess at,
he seemed gratified by the fact, though it would have
been easy enough for him to wring the answer out of her
had she lied. He stood motionless a little longer, then his
hand moved from her breast to the torn fabric of her
shirt, and he folded it gently back over her.

'Cover yourself,' he said. 'And I'll hear no more talk
of sacrifice. Go back to Drachea, and tell him what
you've discovered.'

She frowned. 'Tell him? But – '

Tarod laughed, a harsh sound that contrasted sharply
with his previous manner. 'Then tell him or not, as you
please – it makes no difference to me! Drachea may like
to play his childish games, but he's no threat. If he were,
he'd no longer be alive.'

The words were casual enough, their meaning all too
clear. Cyllan had no answer; she merely nodded and
turned away. This time the door opened at a touch;
beyond, the long flight of stairs led up towards the
courtyard.

'I'll see you again,' Tarod said quietly as she set her
foot on the first step. Whether or not his words implied a
threat Cyllan didn't know, and didn't care to speculate.

When Cyllan was gone, Tarod stood staring down at the
scattered books around his feet. He felt sure that
Drachea had raided the library for a second time, but
neither knew nor cared what the young man might have
unearthed in his searches. Even the greatest rituals were

of little use in the hands of an amateur; Drachea was irrelevant – and Tarod had other matters on his mind.

He walked towards the narrow door set in its alcove, and quietly opened it. The comparatively brilliant light from the passage beyond flowed over him, giving a ghastly tinge to his already pale face, and though he was tempted to tread the familiar way to the Marble Hall once more, he resisted the temptation. He could gain nothing by it – the Hall was, as always, barred to him.

Yet Cyllan had been able to enter . . .

It was what Tarod had suspected and, in one sense, it was a hope fulfilled. Somewhere in that place – on the physical plane or not, he didn't know – lay the single clear jewel that was the focus of everything; and now he knew that he could use Cyllan, as he had intended, to find it and restore it to him. Yet the knowledge brought only a desolate satisfaction. With the stone, he would be again what Fate had made him; a being whose origins lay not with humanity, but with Chaos. The ancient powers would be restored; no man could gainsay him; and he could, if he chose, abandon all pretence of mortality to rise again to the heights which he had once, in immortal form, commanded.

Since the moment when he had broken through the final astral barrier to halt the Pendulum of Time, he had never once questioned that desire. It had been in him like a banked fire, only waiting for an opportunity to burst into flame. But now it seemed distant and unreal. The goal, suddenly so close, had lost its meaning.

Once, he recalled, he had renounced the Chaos stone with all the passion of which he had, then, been capable. He had pledged himself to destroy it, even if it meant his own destruction, and when the Circle turned against him he'd fought them, sublimating his loyalty as an Initiate to the greater loyalty he owed to Aeoris and the White Lords. Since losing the stone, and his humanity with it, he had forgotten that desperate pledge, but it was haunting him now where by rights it should be dead and buried.

For the first time since his final defeat of the Circle,

Tarod was beginning to question himself and his motives. He believed he had lost his humanity . . . but human emotions, far in the past and, he'd thought, unattainable, were calling to him again. Memories clamoured in his mind where there had been only cold intellect; a sensation that he recognised as pain constricted him. It was as though a window had opened, allowing him to look back on a bright, once treasured world that he could no longer reach, and for the first time those memories hurt.

He closed the door again, troubled and unsure whether the feeling within him was anger or sorrow. Briefly, when she had stood defiantly before him and challenged him to kill her, he had wanted to trust Cyllan with the full truth – but the old, ingrained cynicism held him back as he remembered Sashka, who had so manipulated his trust for her own purposes. Cyllan wasn't Sashka – the drover-girl, by comparison, was as transparent as a child, and even if she should prove duplicious she would still be no threat; yet a deep-rooted desire not to make the same mistake twice had stayed his tongue. That, and the certain knowledge that, were she to realise his true nature, she would turn against him as surely and as violently as the Circle had done. Though he refused to explore his reasons, he didn't want to count Cyllan as an enemy.

Tarod was unaccustomed to indecisiveness, but now he felt adrift. Feelings were moving him where previously there had been nothing; his path no longer seemed clear. For the first time he doubted his own motivation . . . and the doubt gave birth to the first faint stirrings of fear.

Very gently he closed the door in the alcove, shutting off all but a faint filtering glow of light from the Marble Hall that seeped under the old wood. With an effort he put all the unhappy thoughts out of his mind – it was a technique he knew well, and had used on many occasions. His face was a mask, as impassively unreadable as carved stone, but his green eyes were unquiet as he walked out of the library.

Chapter 7

'It's the final proof!' Drachea clasped Cyllan's shoulders and spun her round the room excitedly. 'It's all the evidence we need, Cyllan! Gods – to think that the Marble Hall should yield such a find. The stone must be there – it *must* be!'

Cyllan disentangled herself from his grasp, disquieted by his exuberance. 'Surely it's no cause for jubilation?' she said. 'It's proof that we're facing a power we can't hope to combat!'

Drachea dismissed her doubts with a careless wave. 'Tarod's not invincible. Without that jewel, as the High Initiate's testimony says, he can't call the forces of Chaos to his aid. And if *we* can find the stone, and restore it to the Circle – '

Cyllan laughed, a short, sharp bark with little humour in it. 'And how are we to do that?' she demanded. 'How are we to call back Time?'

Drachea smiled. 'It's not as impossible as you might think. I've been studying the books I brought from the library, and all the Circle's rites and rituals are there, in incredible detail. I'm convinced that I'll find the answer in one of those volumes.' His eyes lit up with a fanatical zeal. 'Just think, Cyllan – just think what might result if we can restore the Circle to the world, and deliver the perpetrator of this evil into their hands!'

His use of the word *we*, Cyllan knew, meant nothing – in his imagination Drachea saw himself as the Circle's sole saviour; and doubtless envisaged receiving all honour and glory as a result. He was a fool, she thought, if he believed that the path to such an achievement would be easy; yet he was brimming with confidence, already convinced that he'd succeed.

'Do you know,' he said, sobering a little when she didn't appear to share his excitement, 'that I discovered in one of those tomes the rite that the Circle must have intended to use to destroy Tarod.' Cyllan turned, and he went on, 'The wooden altar you saw – it's a very ancient artefact, rarely used. It's an execution block.'

Cyllan's stomach contracted, and she understood why the black wood slab had carried such an ugly aura. Unbidden, an image flashed through her mind of how a man might look, stretched out on that pitted surface, awaiting the final fall of the knife or sword . . . or something worse . . . and she shuddered.

'Yes – it's not a pleasant ceremony,' Drachea told her, with an edge of relish that she found repellent. 'And it's used only in the most extreme circumstances. Doubtless, when Tarod is in the Circle's hands once more, they'll conduct that rite where they failed before.'

She couldn't stop herself; the words were uttered before she realised it, and her voice was angry. 'And you find such a prospect *pleasing*?'

'Don't you?' Drachea frowned at her. 'This isn't a man we're dealing with – it's a denizen of Chaos! Damn it, would you rather see such a monster loose in the world?'

I'd rather not see anyone die so barbarically, Cyllan thought, but held her tongue. She was discomforted by the fact that some inner compulsion had made her come to Tarod's defence, but told herself it was nothing more than Drachea's ghoulishness which had offended her. Nonetheless, the thought of Tarod's fate if Drachea should succeed – no, if *she* and Drachea should succeed, for surely their cause was the same – chilled her to the marrow.

If Drachea was aware of her misgivings he chose to ignore them, too caught up in his own plans to heed anything else.

'We must return to the Marble Hall,' he said decisively, 'and find that jewel. And we'd be wise not to delay in what we have to do.' He stood up again, hugging himself. 'I still have the High Initiate's papers in my possession. If Tarod were to discover them, I don't care to speculate about how he might react. I think it might be prudent to return them as quickly as possible.' He glanced towards the door. 'Though the Gods know I'd feel a good deal happier if I were armed before making any further sorties in this place.'

'There must be weapons in the Castle,' Cyllan said, though she privately doubted that a blade would have any value against the dangers that lurked here. 'At the Inauguration festival there were tournaments – sword-fighting. I saw none of them, but I heard the tales. And Tarod used to carry a knife . . . '

Drachea gave her an odd look, faintly tinged with suspicion, but only said, 'Very well. Then you must find those weapons. Try the Castle stables – in Shu-Nhadek, the militia keep their arms close by their horses, and it's a sound enough principle. Bring me a sword, light but well balanced.' He paused. 'That is, if you know how to judge a good blade.'

Cyllan's eyes narrowed. Drachea had probably carried a sword only two or three times in his life, and then for ceremonial purposes. She had had a knife of her own, once; a wicked weapon with a curved blade and bone hilt. She had used it to slit open the face of one of her uncle's hirelings who'd thought he could take advantage of his master's drunken stupor to rape his niece and make his escape with three prize horses, and the man's yells had roused the entire camp. Kand Brialen had sent the would-be thief on his way with a broken arm and three cracked ribs – 'one for each good piece of horse-flesh' as he'd grimly put it – and had rewarded Cyllan's vigilance by giving her a quarter-gravine and selling her knife at the next town they reached.

She said, 'I can judge well enough, Drachea. And I'll take a dagger for myself if there's anything suitable to be found.'

He was slightly taken aback by her tone, but collected himself quickly with a shrug. 'Then let's not delay. I'll return the papers to their rightful place, and we'll meet again here when our errands are done.'

Drachea was unwilling to admit to feeling frightened as he headed down the long corridor that led to the High Initiate's rooms, but the sick pounding of his heart gave the lie to it. With Keridil Toln's and now Cyllan's revelations fresh in his mind, the thought of meeting Tarod with these incriminating documents in his possession was almost enough to send him bolting back to the sanctuary of his room. He wished he'd given his task to Cyllan and gone himself in search of weapons; but it was too late for regret. And surely, he told himself, trying to bolster his failing nerve, in all the vastness of the Castle the odds against encountering the Adept weighed strongly in his favour.

Part of the reasoning behind Drachea's decision to carry out this errand himself lay in the fact that he was growing more mistrustful of Cyllan. To begin with, he'd dismissed the obvious friction between them as nothing more than the natural outcome of the differences in their station – she was, after all, so far beneath him that in happier circumstances he wouldn't have associated with her at all – but now he wasn't so sure. She had met the Castle's dark master before; she seemed unwilling to condemn him for what he was – once or twice Drachea had deliberately tested her, and she'd leaped to Tarod's defence like a watchdog. When conflict finally came, as it must, he wondered whether she'd be so blinded to the truth that she wouldn't have the sense to fight on the side of justice.

Still, Cyllan was a minor consideration. In the final extreme she was expendable, and he for one wouldn't particularly mourn her loss. Any debt he owed her Drachea now considered repaid in full – had he not helped her, guided her and instructed her in everything since their unwarranted arrival here? If his plans, which were admittedly embryonic as yet, worked, then she'd do well to realise that his wisdom was superior to hers!

He had almost reached the end of the corridor, and unease gave way to relief as the High Initiate's door came in view. With the documents safely restored, Tarod could never discover that they had been disturbed and read; and any advantage, however trivial, was valuable.

He lifted the door-latch –

'Well, my friend. Your excursions grow bolder.'

Drachea spun round, jaw dropping in horror as he saw Tarod standing behind him.

The tall Adept stepped forward, smiling, though the smile didn't deceive Drachea. Tarod's green eyes were alight with an unholy fire, and Drachea knew that he was in a very dangerous mood.

'Such ambition doesn't become you, Drachea,' Tarod continued softly. 'It hints of a willingness to step into a dead man's shoes before the funeral has taken place.'

'I was – I merely intended – ' Drachea struggled to find an answer that might sound plausible, and Tarod watched his efforts with chilly detachment. He didn't know what had motivated him to seek out the young man for the sole purpose of tormenting him – it was a hollow and pointless pursuit and even his dislike of Drachea wasn't enough to justify it. But he had been brooding; the brooding had led to anger, and the anger desired an outlet. It was Drachea's ill fortune that he was to hand and that Tarod had no compunction about using him as a scapegoat.

But it seemed that Tarod's black mood had proved fortuitous – for he suddenly saw the sheaf of papers which Drachea was clumsily trying to hide. The topmost document bore the High Initiate's own seal . . .

The fire smouldering in Tarod's mind began to flicker into a blaze, and he stretched out his left hand. 'I think,' he said, 'that you'd do well to show me what you have there.'

Desperate, Drachea shook his head. 'It's nothing,' he replied carelessly, battling to keep himself from stammering.

'Then you'll indulge my whim to see it.' Tarod's voice was merciless.

Drachea tried to resist as the icy green eyes held his gaze locked, but he couldn't look away. Jerkily, and against his will, his hand came up, stretched out; and Tarod took the documents from him.

One glance at the sheaf confirmed his suspicions. *So Drachea knew . . . and doubtless Cyllan, too, had seen these pages. Little wonder she had been so afraid when he encountered her in the vault, with Keridil's testimony fresh in her mind . . .*

He looked at Drachea again. The Heir Margrave was shaking as though he had the ague, and the guilty terror in his eyes, the contempt his attitude aroused, disgusted Tarod.

'So,' he said softly, 'you consider yourself entitled to steal more than you can find in the library.'

White-faced, Drachea swallowed and dissembled weakly. 'Cyllan discovered them, not I . . . I – I didn't trouble to read them; I told her they were none of my concern . . . ' His voice trailed off as he saw Tarod's expression.

'You're a liar.' And, incensed by Drachea's shameless perfidy, Tarod felt something within him snap. His eyes fired with loathing; he flung the papers aside, raised his left hand, gestured once.

Something with the power of a horse's kick hurled Drachea off his feet, and he crashed against the High Initiate's door, which burst open. Sprawling across the threshold, Drachea tried in panic to struggle upright and run – but in doing so he caught Tarod's eye. Every muscle in his body locked rigid. He couldn't move, couldn't breathe; his mind fought against the inexorable will that held it, but he was helpless.

Tarod smiled, and the smile made Drachea want to scream. The gaunt face was changing, eyes narrowing, burning with an inhuman light, the black hair like a shadow of utter darkness. In an instant of terrified revelation Drachea saw what Cyllan had seen in the graven face of the statue – the malevolence, the knowledge, the sheer power that lay behind the mask. He made a sound deep in his throat; inarticulate, pleading. Tarod's smile widened, and the fingers of his hand curled as though outlining an invisible symbol.

The thrall that held Drachea broke, and he shrieked like a wounded animal, eyes starting out of their sockets and hands scrabbling for purchase on the floor. Tarod, seeing what he saw, acknowledged the nightmare with a laugh. The last time Drachea had crossed him, he had shown him but a brief glimpse of the horrors he could conjure if he chose. Now, the punishment was merciless.

'*No . . . n-no . . .*' It was the only word Drachea could form from a babbling, pleading stream of incoherence. He was crawling on hands and knees, as a mortally injured mouse might try to crawl away from a preying cat, and Tarod moved slowly, casually after him, holding the delusions and manipulating them so that Drachea's terrors deepened, pushing him towards the brink of insanity. He felt no true malice towards Drachea – contempt was too ingrained for that – and what he did now gave him no satisfaction. But something had moved him; a fury he couldn't contain. An *emotion* that demanded its due.

Drachea was sobbing, curling into a foetal huddle in the passage and seemingly trying to dig his nails into the wall, as though refuge lay that way. Tarod's hatred had reached its peak and, as abruptly as it had come, the rage was passing. He stared down at the hunched wreck at his feet. It would be so easy to kill him. A single movement, and it would be done . . . but there seemed no point. Better that Drachea lived on, and remembered . . .

He stepped back. The last time he had lost all self-control, a man *had* died, and hideously; but that, like so much else that plagued him, was in the past. He had no such motivations now.

Or did he?

The thought wasn't one he liked to live with, and when he looked at Drachea again he felt something close to remorse. Tarod turned on his heel and stalked away along the corridor towards the main doors. Behind him as he went he could hear the demented sobbing pleas diminishing in the distance, and the sound left a bitter taste.

The two swords and the light, slim-bladed dagger were all Cyllan had been able to find, but nonetheless she was pleased with her spoils. Drachea's theory that an armoury might lie next to the Castle stables had proved wrong, and after an unfruitful search she had taken to looking through individual rooms in the great building, where she had found what she needed. The experience of searching those chambers had been eerie; she felt like a desecrator as she rummaged among the personal belongings of men and women whose lives had been abruptly suspended and who now languished in a world beyond imagination, if they still existed at all; and it had taken all the self-will she could muster to begin the search. So many of the artefacts told their own poignant stories; a torn coat with a sewing needle and thread laid on it; two empty wine cups beside a rumpled bed; a sheaf of papers covered with simple drawings in a child's hand. It had been a sharp reminder that this Castle had once lived and breathed and rung to the sounds of its human inhabitants.

She had ignored, though with difficulty, the clothes that she found in some of the rooms. Gowns and cloaks in rich fabrics, graceful and decorative shoes that she knew would have fitted her, jewellery . . . the choice was almost endless, had she been able to ignore her conscience and steal them. But instead she had reluctantly set them aside, and her fantasies with them, and concentrated on the task at hand.

Her search had, thankfully, allowed her to stay on the upper floor of the Castle wing, where she knew there was less chance of encountering Tarod. She had taken two wrong turns on her way back towards her room, but the maze of passages was growing more familiar and there was little danger of becoming lost. She was crossing the broad landing where the main staircase ended when a faint sound caught her sharp ears, and she froze. Someone was moving; someone on the stairs . . .

Holding her breath, Cyllan inched forward, keeping close against the wall. The sounds seemed to have stopped, and no shadows moved to betray an approaching figure. Gaining confidence she crossed to peer over the balcony rail . . . .

The swords and dagger fell from her grasp, making an
echoing racket as they clattered across the floor. Cyllan
ran, flying down the stairs until she reached the figure
sprawled prone halfway down the flight.

Drachea wasn't quite unconscious, but the last dregs
of strength which had enabled him to crawl, inch by
painful inch, from the High Initiate's door had finally
run out. His hands were grasping feebly at the tread of
the next stair, the nails split and bloodied as though he
had been trying to claw his way through stone, and
palsied shudders racked his body.

'Drachea!' Cyllan tried to help him sit up, but he
couldn't rally. Appalled, she turned him over. His eyes
were tightly shut, face dead-white, and he seemed,
incredibly, to be trying to laugh, though no sound came
from between his bloodless lips.

Sweet Aeoris, what had happened to him? He couldn't
lie here – she had to get him to a bed! Crouching, Cyllan
hooked her hands under Drachea's arms and pulled with
all her strength. He moaned, but was too weak to struggle, and with a great effort Cyllan managed to drag his
limp weight to the top of the stairs. Bent double and
gasping for breath, she looked along the corridor. His
room was nearer . . . Taking a deep breath she lifted
Drachea again and struggled towards the distant door,
praying meanwhile that he wasn't physically damaged
and this unceremonious progress only making matters
even worse.

By the time she reached the chamber Drachea had
lost consciousness, which was a mercy. Her muscles
protested as she forced them into one last effort to lift
him on to the bed. She made him as comfortable as she
could, then studied him closely to see if she could find
any clue to what had happened.

Thankfully, there were no obvious signs of injury –
though Cyllan was no healer, and knew how easily she
might overlook some serious hurt. Nor could she even
begin to guess how this had come about . . . but a
terrible suspicion was eating at her mind.

She straightened, trying to quell the dread that filled

her. Whatever the truth, something had to be done for
Drachea, or he could die. And the only one she could
turn to might be the very one who was responsible for
bringing him to this condition.

She looked at him again, and knew she had no choice
but to ask Tarod's help. The worst he would do, surely
the worst he would do, was refuse . . .

Quickly, before courage could desert her, she ran out
of the room and back along the passage to the stairs. The
swords and dagger still lay where they'd fallen; she
hesitated, then snatched up the knife and thrust it into
her belt. She couldn't conceal it, but it gave her a little
confidence. Then she was running down the long staircase towards the Castle's main door.

The sight of the black steps winding up into utter darkness almost broke Cyllan's resolve when at last she stood
at the foot of the titanic Northern spire. She had seen the
dim light glowing in the narrow window at the summit,
and knew that Tarod must be there – but the thought of
climbing those endless stairs, through dark so intense
that it was almost tangible, was horrifying. She steeled
herself – it had to be done. Drachea needed help, and
she was his only ally.

And if Tarod refused to aid her? She'd thought of little
else as she crossed the courtyard, but amid all the doubt
and confusion was a spark of hope. Despite what she
knew, despite the terror she'd felt at their last meeting,
she thought she had, in the library, at last recognised a
shadow of Tarod as she had once known him, and she
clung tightly to that. He had treated her kindly, giving
the lie to those who had condemned him, and she prayed
that, if she could touch that same chord again, he would
help her now.

Or was she being a fool again? In her mind she could
hear Drachea's voice condemning her for her gullibility,
and hope gave way to uncertainty. If she was wrong . . .

She drew breath, squaring her shoulders. If she was
wrong, there was only one way to find out. She *had* to
try.

Determinedly ignoring the painful thumping of her heart, Cyllan set foot on the first stair.

It seemed that the black spiral would never end. Cyllan had climbed and climbed, trying not to falter but every now and again forced to stop, to rest aching muscles and regain her breath. The stops grew more frequent; her legs felt as though they were on fire, and the long struggle through the terrible, unchanging dark took on the proportions of a nightmare. She couldn't go back – she didn't know how many steps lay behind her, but they must have numbered thousands; the thought of giving in now and turning to face them all again was more than she could bear. And yet, though she prayed to reach her goal, the stairs still wound on and on, ever upward, with no reprieve.

Her foot slipped and she stumbled, sinking down on the cold black stone and sobbing with exhaustion. It *couldn't* be much further – unless she had unwittingly strayed into some twist of dimensions, some evil jest at her expense, the stairs must surely end somewhere . . . She pulled herself upright, hands pressed against the unforgiving wall, and willed her limbs to obey her. She couldn't falter now . . .

And, unexpectedly, Cyllan found that the seventh step she climbed was the last.

The unexpectedness of it shocked her out of her mesmerised state, and she reeled against the wall, having to exert all her remaining strength to keep her legs from buckling under her. She was on a dark, circular landing, and in the gloom could just discern the faint outlines of three doors. All were firmly closed, and Cyllan's flagging confidence fell still further. *If she were wrong, and Tarod wasn't here . . . or if he refused to help her . . .*

She swallowed back the thoughts, and stumbled towards the nearest of the three doors. But before her hand could reach it, the furthest opened, and a chilly light spilled out, silhouetting a tall figure on the threshold.

'Cyllan?' Tarod's voice was soft, faintly curious. 'What brings you here?'

She drew breath, but could hardly speak; the climb had finally taken its toll and she was exhausted. 'Drachea . . .' she whispered dazedly. 'He's ill . . . hurt . . . I came – I came for help . . .' Suddenly she swayed, and Tarod stepped forward, taking her arm.

'Drachea be damned – I think it's you who are in need of succour! Come; in here.'

She leaned against him, unable to support herself, and he led her gently through the door. The light, poor as it was, blinded Cyllan after the grim darkness on the stairs. Through its dazzle she had an impression of a small and overcrowded chamber, then Tarod was helping her to a couch, and gratefully she let her limbs give way until she was half sitting, half lying among its cushions. Gradually her vision adjusted, and her breath returned, until she was able to look at Tarod where he sat watching her.

'Are you recovered?' he asked.

'Yes . . . yes, well enough.' She met his gaze. 'Thank you.'

He inclined his head slightly. 'So Drachea is unwell, and you took it upon yourself to climb this great height to find me? You're very loyal, Cyllan. I hope our young Heir Margrave appreciates his friends!'

His tone stung her. 'Anyone would have done the same,' she said.

'I doubt that. What ails him?'

She shook her head. 'I don't know . . . I found him, lying on the main stairs. He was all but unconscious, and he – he was in a terrible condition! I don't know what brought him to that pass, but he was – his eyes; his hands – ' She struggled to find a way to explain, then stopped as she saw the expression on Tarod's face. He showed no sign of surprise, or even interest; and a faint, wry smile curved the corners of his mouth.

He saw her scrutiny, the dawning realisation in her eyes, and said evenly, 'Drachea has a habit of bringing his own misfortunes on himself. And if he's fool enough to steal what doesn't belong to him, he should anticipate the consequences.'

The gnawing suspicion flowered into sudden painful certainty in Cyllan's mind. Tarod must have caught Drachea as he tried to return the incriminating documents to the High Initiate's study . . . Slowly she got to her feet. 'You . . .' Her throat was constricted. 'You did that to him . . .'

Tarod looked back at her dispassionately. 'Yes. I did.'

A part of her had known; yet to hear Tarod admit the truth so carelessly was still shocking. Doubt and confusion were suddenly swept away, and in their place she felt only disgust.

'Gods!' She spat the word. 'You are *monstrous*!'

Tarod sighed. 'Oh, indeed. A callous monster, wreaking havoc at will with the minds and bodies of innocent victims.' There was a harsh light in his eyes. 'You understand nothing!'

'I understand,' she retorted, her voice shaking. 'I understand all too well what you are! To *tell* me, without qualm or conscience; to react as though it means *nothing*, to – to be *proud* of such a deed – '

'Proud?' He was on his feet so fast that she instinctively shrank back. 'Very well – I'll complete the picture for you, as you obviously know me so completely! I have no conscience, I have no ethic – I am what you see in your own mind, Cyllan. I like to bring torment to others for the pleasure it gives me; it's my sole purpose for living!' He took a grip on himself and added with tightly controlled ferocity, 'Does that satisfy you?'

He was challenging her, daring her to stand against him, and a sense of rebellion in Cyllan goaded her not to give way.

'Yes!' she flared back at him. 'It satisfies me, Tarod; for it proves to me that Drachea was right and I was wrong! You are *evil* – and I know from where your evil springs!' And she made the Sign of Aeoris, defiantly, in his face.

Drachea had told her . . . Swift as a cat, Tarod's hand came up and caught hold of her wrist. His own anger was rising, so rapidly that he was barely in control of it. She knew – and like all the others she had condemned out of hand, as he had known she must. Suddenly in his mind's eye another face supplanted Cyllan's; patrician, beautiful, limpid eyes hiding the calculating and self-centred heart beneath. He wanted to hurt the soul behind that face, take the retribution that was long overdue . . .

His vision cleared and he saw instead Cyllan's thin features and wide amber eyes. The beauty was gone; but not the pride. Cyllan had pride enough, but it was of a different order . . . and she had the courage to face him with what she knew, instead of wielding the blade from behind.

She was motionless, watching him and wary, ready to spring free at the smallest opportunity. Tarod gave her no opportunity. His hold on her wrist tightened until the pain showed in her face, but she made no sound. He could have snapped her arm; he could have killed her with one flick of his fingers . . .

'You think you know me,' he whispered savagely. 'But you're wrong, Cyllan. You're wrong!'

She twisted, trying to break free; he held her effortlessly, but had to battle to stem the tide of sheer, raw emotion that was rising in him. 'I'm not wrong!' Her voice was edged with pain, breath coming sharply. 'I know what you are!'

'Do you?'

'Yes! I saw the documents, Tarod – Drachea read them to me, and now I know why you took such a vicious retribution! You are a thing of *Chaos*!'

A thing of Chaos . . . Her words drove home, and the barriers which had been holding back the tide broke. Tarod smiled again, and this time the smile made Cyllan feel sick with terror. She had gone too far . . . he'd kill her; and a paralysis of fear locked her muscles rigid as she anticipated the final, fatal strike.

But it didn't come. Instead Tarod laughed as though at some private joke. 'Chaos,' he said softly. 'No, Cyllan; this time you're not wrong.' He drew her towards him, until her body pressed hard against him and he could feel the rapid pulse of her heart. 'But you are . . . misguided.' His free hand rose, pushed back

the pale hair from her face. Beads of sweat banded her
brow and now he could feel her trembling. There was
mayhem in his mind; he wanted to strike out, avenge
himself; and yet there was more, far more, behind the
compulsion.

'I'm no demon . . . ' he told her with soft menace.
'I'm man enough.' And before she could twist away, he
bent his face to hers and kissed her. It was a vicious kiss,
a taking and not an asking; and she fought back with a
strength that surprised him, writhing and clawing in his
grip. She was as lithe and sinuous as a cat, and her
ferocious determination struck an answering chord in
Tarod. His mouth found hers again, this time more
sensuously. He was reeling from the sensations that
were swamping him – vengeance was eclipsed by something far stronger and more urgent, and all thoughts of
Sashka were forgotten.

She broke free, breathless, and their gazes locked
briefly. Cyllan's amber eyes blazed – and then, so fast
that she almost caught Tarod unawares, she whipped a
dagger from her belt and brought it shearing up in a
vicious arc.

Acting on a reflex, Tarod swung her off balance as she
struck, and the blade flashed by an inch from his shoulder. His left hand locked on her right wrist and twisted it
until she choked out an involuntary cry; he pressed
once, with his thumb, and the knife spun from her grasp.

She glared at him, breath rasping in her throat. She
might be afraid, but she wasn't cowed; at the slightest
provocation he knew she'd fight him like a wild animal,
and the knowledge raised his adrenalin.

'You use a knife well,' he said, the words clipped by
the suffocating pounding of his heart. 'But I've been
fighting longer than you – and I know how to defend
myself!' He smiled, showing his teeth. 'Do you give me
best, Cyllan?'

She shook her head fiercely. '*No!*'

The green eyes that gazed into hers suddenly seemed
to take fire, and Cyllan felt her will draining away before
Tarod's implacable stare. She tried to resist, but she was

weakening – an inner voice reminded her that she was battling no ordinary mortal, and the fear came surging back . . . but mingled with it was an echo of the old feelings which she had thought banished, an overwhelming desire . . .

'Cyllan . . . ' Tarod's voice was sibilant, persuasive, smashing through her defences. 'Have I no warmth? No life?'

She tried to deny it, but the words wouldn't form. His hands on her skin were real, physical; and a long-dormant need within her answered with a power she couldn't combat. She gasped as his teeth grazed her shoulder and the shirt, already torn, fell away to expose her pale skin.

'Tarod . . . no – please, *no* . . . ' The protest was cut off as she staggered back under a gentle but irresistible pressure. She stumbled against the couch, fell; felt the weight and the strength of Tarod's body as he crushed her. This time when he kissed her she couldn't stop herself from responding. Terror was giving way to longing, and she could no longer fight him; no longer wished to fight him.

Tarod raised his head. The wild light in his eyes was suddenly muted by a look that Cyllan didn't dare try to interpret, and he shook his head, brushing a strand of his unruly black hair away from his face. The gesture was so human that confusion filled her again – whatever the Circle might say, whatever he might have done, he was surely no demon . . .

'You're brave,' he said softly, 'And you're honest . . . you fight fairly. I could defeat you easily, Cyllan, and you couldn't stand against my desire . . . but I won't. I still have some sense of honour . . . and you don't want to deny me. Do you?' His hands were light and cool on her skin, pushing aside the encumbering garments. '*Do you?*'

Against her will Cyllan's body was responding to him, racking her with a long-suppressed, aching longing that made her want to cry and scream, to thrust him away and yet hold him to her, all at once. A moan broke from

her throat, and involuntarily her lips formed a single
word.

   '*No* . . . '

She cried out at his hungry violence when he took her,
but he silenced her with his mouth on hers, making her
yield in spite of herself. And after the first resistance
there was pleasure as well as pain; a fierce, shuddering
release as her bare arms locked tightly around him, her
head thrown back and teeth drawing blood from her
lower lip. Once she fought him again; he quieted her and
she became pliant beneath him once more.

   At last, all desire satiated, Tarod let his hands move
slowly and gently over Cyllan's body, tracing the slight
curve of her breasts. She lay passive in his arms and her
eyes were tight shut, as though she was trying to deny the
truth. Tears that she stubbornly refused to shed sparkled
on her dark lashes, and a feeling that might have been
remorse awoke in Tarod.

   He spoke her name, and her eyes opened, reflecting a
mixture of uncertainty and accusation and shame. He
wanted to say more, but suddenly couldn't. Instead, he
raised his hand and made a gesture over her.

   Her eyes closed again and her breathing relaxed into
the light, even rhythm of sleep. He wanted no recrimina-
tions, not now . . . when her body relaxed and he knew
that her consciousness had slipped away, Tarod drew
her limp form towards him and kissed her, lightly, on
one pale cheek. Then he reluctantly released her, rose
and crossed the room to the narrow window, forcing
back the thoughts that threatened to take hold and
break through the barriers he had raised against their
onslaught.

Chapter 8

Cyllan woke to sense the uneven contours of the couch beneath her, and the rough texture of something that felt like an animal pelt covering her naked skin. Her body was filled with a devastating, fiery ache; her mouth felt bruised . . . and her stomach contracted as the realisation came home to her: *it hadn't been a dream* . . .

Apprehensively, she opened her eyes.

There was barely any light in the room, but in the dimness she could see Tarod seated in a chair. He had dressed, and a heavy black cloak was flung around his shoulders as though to keep out the cold. The high collar shadowed his features, but she thought that he was staring out of the window.

Cyllan's limbs began to shake as the full implications of what had happened went through her like a knife. Slowly, cautiously, she started to sit up, thinking to reach for the crumpled clothes that lay among the debris on the floor –

Tarod's head turned, and she froze. Mingled emotions tumbled through her mind as they looked at one another; then she saw the coldness in his green eyes, and her reactions coalesced into an icy rush of bitter shame. Tarod's passion was gone, as though it had never been; the barriers between them were up again, and his face was like stone. She had let him seduce her as though she were a simpleton . . . and all she had earned was his contempt.

Self-loathing swamped her, and with it a sick revulsion as she remembered what he was. But she still had a vestige of pride, and it came to her aid. Tossing her head back, she pushed away the blanket that covered her – it *was* fur, and rich fur, but she hardly noticed – and stood up. Tarod rose too, and Cyllan took a step back.

'Don't, Tarod.' Her voice was harsh. 'Don't come near me!'

He hesitated, then made a gesture towards the floor which she interpreted as careless. 'As you wish. But you might have need of your clothing.'

'It hardly matters now, does it?' She squared her thin shoulders, facing him defiantly. 'You've seen me, you've touched me; you've taken what you wanted from me. What have I left to hide from you?' To her fury, her voice was shaking with poorly suppressed emotion, and she knew she was on the verge of losing control.

Tarod said calmly, 'I took nothing that you were unwilling to give.'

'Ohh . . .' She turned away, hating him because he'd spoken no less than the truth. '*Damn* you! I came to you for help, and you – you – ' She couldn't say any more; her voice broke and it took every last ounce of her will power not to burst into tears. Crying, she told herself ferociously, was for children; she had learned long ago to suppress such emotion, and wouldn't allow it to best her now; especially not in the presence of a creature like Tarod. She covered her face with her hands, fighting the reaction with all her strength.

Tarod slipped his coat off and cast it round her shoulders. She didn't protest, but nor would she face him, only shook her head violently when he tried to turn her around. He watched her reflectively as she struggled to bring herself under control. Aware of her origins, he hadn't expected her to be virgin, and the knowledge that no man had ever lain with her before had disconcerted him. Yet she had chosen to give herself – and however bitterly she might regret it now, nothing could change that.

Cyllan had calmed at last, and savagely pushed her hair back out of her eyes. She stepped away from Tarod, then deliberately shrugged the cloak aside and let it fall. It was hard for her to gather her torn clothes and dress with any dignity, and he moved back to the window,

gazing out across the courtyard to give her what grace he
could. She tugged the ruined shirt across her breasts and
hesitated, looking at him. His face was an inscrutable
mask, eyes hooded and brooding, and any thought
Cyllan might have had of making a move towards him
died within her. She stared down at the knife he had
wrested from her hand . . .

'Take it, if it's of use to you,' Tarod said.

She glared at him, and let the dagger lie where it had
fallen, turning and walking towards the door. Hand
halfway to the latch, she paused.

'Will it open?' she asked icily. 'Or do you have some
further sport in mind?'

Tarod sighed, and the door swung noiselessly open
before Cyllan could touch it. She ignored a wild, irrational pang of hurt that he was prepared to let her go so
easily, and stepped out on to the dark landing. Then she
turned, looked back.

Tarod still watched her. 'It's a long way down to
the courtyard,' he said. 'I could make the descent
easier.'

For answer, Cyllan spat deliberately on the floor. 'I
want nothing from you!' she retorted ferociously. And
she was gone, her pale figure swallowed by the darkness
of the stairs.

She heard the echoing crash as the door above her
slammed, and the sound of it goaded her on, until she
was taking the stairs precariously fast, wanting only to
get away and not caring that she might fall and break her
neck. Suddenly the walls to either side of her warped;
the steps beneath her feet seemed to give way to a
dizzying emptiness, and she cried out involuntarily as
the blackness inverted into a dazzling white brilliance. It
lasted only the space of a single heartbeat – then she was
reeling against hard stone, and staring, shocked,
through the open door at the spire's foot.

Cyllan stumbled out into the Castle courtyard. *Damn*
Tarod – he'd had the last word, and she wished she could
have taken the knife again, struck him, stabbed him,
torn him apart . . .

But she had had her chance, and she'd failed. And what he took from her, she had given of her own volition.

She shut her eyes against the memory, pressing clenched fists to temples in a fruitless effort to blot out the small inner voice which accused her of being a hypocrite as well as a fool. Tarod had awoken a fundamental, animal need within her – she'd known it since their first meeting on the cliffs of West High Land, and though since then she had tried to deny and suppress it, it had never truly died. That echo of the past had finally proved strong enough to conquer the horrors of Tarod's true nature, and she had gone to him, yielded to him, like an infatuated child.

She wanted to kill him. However great a fool she had been, he had manipulated and preyed on her. If by destroying him she could free herself from guilt and self-torment and recrimination, then, she told herself, she would have no qualms. Drachea had known from the beginning how dangerous Tarod was; he had warned her –

Drachea. Cyllan came back to reality with a jolt, and realised with a cold fear that she had utterly forgotten Drachea in the mayhem of all that had happened. She had failed him; and he still lay in his bed, mortally ill, perhaps dying . . .

She began to run, racing towards the Castle's main doors and taking the shallow steps two at a time. If Drachea were to die – *no, don't think of that!* He *had* to live – she needed him, needed his determination now as never before, to keep the turmoil of her confusion at bay, and to help the clear, cold rage that she struggled to nurture shine through. Together they could defeat Tarod; they *must* defeat him, see justice done – he was evil, a creature of Chaos – he must be thwarted!

Cyllan repeated the silent litany in her head as she ran up the broad staircase to the Castle's living quarters. Heart pounding, she raced towards Drachea's room, flung herself against the door, and burst in.

Drachea was sitting on the bed. One of the swords which she had left on the landing lay at his feet; the other was gripped in his right hand, while his left moved slowly, almost hypnotically, up and down the length of the blade, polishing it with one of his sea-drenched and discarded garments.

Cyllan's heart turned over with relief, and she rushed forward. 'Drachea! Oh, you've recovered! Aeoris be thanked; I thought – '

He sprang to his feet, swinging the blade up in a wild, defensive gesture. Then the terror in his face gave way first to recognition, then to anger, and he snapped viciously,

'Where in all the Seven Hells have you *been*?'

Cyllan stared at him, astonished and chagrined. Drachea's face was dead white, and an obsessive, unhealthy light burned in his eyes. The hand that held the sword was trembling as he hissed again, 'I said, where have you *been*? You should have been here – I woke, and I was afraid, and I needed help, and you were *gone*! You abandoned me . . . '

'*Abandoned* you?' The accusation took her breath away, and her happiness at seeing him restored crumbled. 'I *found* you, Drachea – I found you on the stairs, unconscious, and I brought you here to sanctuary!'

'And then you left me to wake alone – '

'I was afraid you might die!' Cyllan told him savagely. 'I tried to find a way of helping you!'

Drachea's gaze raked her with a mingling of contempt and suspicion, then his mouth twisted into a travesty of a smile. 'Helping me – and what skills do you have that could combat what *he* did to my mind?'

'Tarod . . . ?' Her stomach tightened.

'Yes, Tarod!' Drachea turned and stalked away from her. 'While you were safely occupied elsewhere, he – attacked me. I didn't provoke him, but he turned on me and – ' He put a hand to his mouth, bit the knuckles. 'Gods, those nightmares . . . he conjured them out of *nothing*, he sent them against me, and I – I couldn't fight back. Not against that . . . *Scum*!' He drew a deep, heaving breath. 'He'll pay for it. I'll see him *annihilated*!'

Cyllan crossed the room to stand behind him, and
tentatively reached out a hand. She was struggling to
recapture the feelings she had clung to as she ran to find
Drachea, the sense of comradeship, of fighting a holy
war together; but it was slipping away from her grip.
Drachea's outburst had broken the spell; by turning on
her instead of welcoming her, he had struck her certainty and confidence a hard blow.

But, she told herself, he couldn't be held to blame.
She knew what Tarod was capable of, and she knew
Drachea's weaknesses. His ordeal must have been far
worse than her own; enough to unhinge the strongest
will. She had to help him, match his resolve with hers – it
was the only hope for them both.

She let her fingers come to rest on his arm; he shook
her off.

'I don't want your sympathy!' His tone was angrily hostile.

Cyllan bit back a retort, willed herself to be patient.
'I'm not offering sympathy, Drachea. I'm offering to
stand beside you against Tarod.' She smiled bitterly.
'For what little it might be worth.'

Drachea looked over his shoulder at her, suspicion
mingling with a sullen resentment in his look. 'Yes . . .'
he said. 'I don't know what your loyalty's worth, do I? I
don't know anything any more . . . how do I know that I
can trust you?' He swung round suddenly. 'You *say* you
went to find help – how do I know it's the truth? Where is
this help? What have you done for me?'

Cyllan gave a bark of harsh laughter, and put a hand
to her mouth. '*Done* for you?' she echoed. 'Drachea, if
you knew – if you knew what I tried to do, what happened – ' She took a grip on herself, her eyes alight with
all the anger and shame of the memory. 'I failed. Tarod
. . . would not help me.'

'You went to *him*?' Drachea's jaw dropped, and for a
moment she thought he'd launch himself at her in sheer
rage. Then, breathing hard, he hissed between his
clenched teeth, 'You treacherous *bitch*! So now you
consort behind my back with the very demon who
almost killed me!'

Astounded by such wanton injustice, Cyllan fired back without stopping to consider her words. 'How *dare* you say such a thing! Gods, when I think what I've been through for your sake – you're not the only one to have suffered at Tarod's hands!'

Drachea's lips curled into a sneer. 'You, suffer? You can't imagine what the word means! While you were telling pretty stories to your demon friend, I was helpless here, on the verge of death! *Traitor!*'

For a long, long moment Cyllan stared back at him, her face dead-white and every muscle rigid. Then she reached to her throat and pulled aside the ripped shirt, so that her neck and the swell of her breasts were revealed.

'Look at me, Drachea,' she said, her voice dangerously steady. 'Look closely, and you'll see what Tarod did to me. Maybe he didn't choose to assault my mind, not directly . . . but my body was a different matter!'

Drachea's angry gaze flickered to her pale skin. There were bruises, the marks of fingers, a livid red crescent where she had been bitten in the heat of passion . . . He moved closer, slowly . . . then his hand shot out and he hit her with all his strength across the face.

Unprepared for such an attack, Cyllan went down, and before she could scramble to her feet Drachea lashed out with one foot and kicked her as though she were a dog that had displeased its master.

'*Slut!*' he roared, hysterical. 'Lying, filthy, demon-spawned *whore!*'

Stunned, she couldn't even begin to protest before he kicked at her again. This time she had the presence of mind to roll clear, and Drachea snatched up the sword, brandishing it over her head. His eyes were starting out of their sockets, and Cyllan knew beyond all shadow of doubt that he'd lost his reason. Driven to the brink of madness by Tarod's sorcery, he sought an enemy on whom to avenge himself, and no power in the world could make him listen or understand.

She hunched into a tight ball against the wall, unable to escape, and appalled by the mania in Drachea's voice

as he demanded savagely, 'How many times have you
gone to his bed, harlot? How long have you been plotting with him against me? *Serpent!*' As he shrieked the
last word his arm swung wildly and the sword blade came
hurtling down, to strike the floor inches from her head
with a shuddering clash of metal.

'*Drachea!*' She screamed his name, trying to break
through the insane rage but knowing she stood no
chance of reaching him. He had regained his balance
and now held the sword in both hands, swaying. The tip
of the blade swung mesmerically before her; she tried to
hunch further back but the wall blocked her way.

'Serpent!' Drachea yelled again, his voice cracking.
'Demon! You've been in league with him all along! You
ensnared me, you lured me into this nightmare – *damn*
you! I'll *kill* you, you white-faced monstrosity!'

He raised his arms high, and the crimson light that
pervaded through the window seemed to drench the
sword blade in blood. Eyes widening with the hideous
foreknowledge of her own death, Cyllan flung herself
frantically to one side as the sword sheared down. The
breath burst from her lungs as she sprawled on the floor,
then she jack-knifed her body and made a convulsive
grab for the door. It was ajar; her momentum forced it
open and she rolled, trying to gain her feet before
Drachea could reach her. She heard a bellow like a
maddened, insensate bull, saw the blade whistling like a
giant fang, light stabbing along its length, tried to throw
herself clear – and pain exploded in her ribs as the point
of the sword bit through clothing and flesh.

She gave an animal shriek, eclipsing Drachea's triumphant howl. The sword came free with a fresh shock
of agony and she clasped a hand to her side, knowing
there must be blood and trying to stem it, but driven only
by a blind, terrified will to escape. Drachea bore down
on her again – she sensed rather than saw him – and,
rolling on to her back, she kicked out savagely with both
feet. By sheer fortuity the kick connected; she heard a
grunt and a thud, didn't stop to see what effect the
assault had had, but dragged herself to her feet and ran.

Before her lay the stairs, swimming and swaying through a grey fog of pain and shock. She knew she was weaving from side to side, wasting a valuable advantage, but she couldn't run in a straight line. Warm stickiness flowed over her hand, pulsing rhythmically with the pounding of her heart, and she tried to laugh aloud. She couldn't die – there was no Time here; her life couldn't bleed away without Time to help it . . .

Lucidity came back and she realised she was leaning heavily on the rail above the stair-well, laughing like a madwoman. A soft *ticking* sounded from the floor at her feet. Her blood, dripping from the wound Drachea had inflicted, sapping her strength . . .

'*Demon bitch!*' She heard the mad shouting behind her, echoed by the thud of running feet, and the shock brought her fully back to reality. She plunged on, reaching the stairs and almost pitching headlong down them before she could stop herself. A wild grab at the banister rail saved her, then she was half staggering and half falling towards the double doors that led to the court-yard. Drachea was behind her, and closing – she could hear his voice yelling for her to stop, and the sound of it goaded her on. Part of her mind, which seemed to observe from a misty distance, told her that flight was useless; that she'd merely prolong the inevitable. She could run only so far before she dropped from loss of blood. And then he'd move in, to finish her . . .

Cyllan forced the thought away and grimly stumbled on. The double doors lurched giddily before her, and as she ran out she lost her footing and fell down the steps into the courtyard. Struggling painfully to her feet she saw the crimson smears marring the stone behind her, leaving a trail that a child could follow, and desperation brought a wild hope.

Tarod . . . if she could reach Tarod . . .

Savagely she ignored the inner voice. Not Tarod, never Tarod . . . she couldn't, wouldn't . . .

A crash told her that Drachea had reached the doors, and she heard him laughing, certain of his success. Blindly she staggered towards the fountain, clinging to a

crazed idea that she might be able to break off some
delicate piece of the stone tracery and wield it as a
weapon against him. She cannoned into the fountain
basin, and the pain of colliding with solid stone took her
breath away so that she collapsed, clutching at an impassive carved fish as she fell. The running footsteps at her
back thudded closer, dinning in her ears; she twisted,
striking out with a rapidly weakening arm, spitting and
cursing a stream of drover's oaths in the face of her
nemesis, but knowing she was lost.

White light blazed beyond her tight-shut eyelids, and
hands gripped her. She screamed defiance, trying to
beat them off –

'Cyllan!'

He was going to slaughter her, and she fought him
with all her fast-waning strength, trying to kick, bite,
battle to the last.

'*Cyllan!*' The voice wasn't Drachea's – shocked, her
eyes snapped open and her body went rigid.

The grey fog clouded her vision still, but through it she
could see the raven's-wing shadow of his black hair, the
sharp-etched features, the green of his eyes. Cool fingers
touched her burning face and she heard Tarod say softly,
as though from a great distance,

'It's all right. You're safe . . . he can't reach you, he
can't touch you. You're safe with me, Cyllan . . . '

She tried to speak, but only choked as the pain within
her redoubled and swelled to a crescendo. Her hand
clawed convulsively and tangled in his hair; he clasped it
tightly, and his voice was more gentle than she had
believed possible.

'Peace, Cyllan. No more harm can come to you. Sleep
. . . I'll heal you. Sleep, now . . . '

The words were a balm, and she clung to them. His
hand still held hers, and she felt the throb of the pain
fading, fading, her senses like a hot tide receding away,
until a quiet, engulfing darkness overcame all else.

* * * * *

'*Drachea . . . No!*'

The words broke in harsh confusion from Cyllan's lips. She'd been dreaming, and in the dream Drachea had turned on her with the face of a devil, lunging towards her with a blade that glittered like molten silver against a blood-crimson background. She twisted convulsively and heard the soft thud of a cushion falling to the floor . . . then a powerful hand gripped her shoulder, pressing her back and gently yet firmly forcing her to quiescence. The knowledge that she wasn't alone with the nightmare eased her, and she felt her muscles slowly relaxing.

'Cyllan. The dream's gone. It's over; there's nothing to fear.'

In her half-waking state she'd expected Drachea's voice, and the unexpected yet familiar tone made her open her eyes in quick alarm.

She was in the room at the top of the spire, lying on the long couch. Tarod sat beside her, and his hand had moved to her brow, tracing lightly across her skin. She raised her own hand to clasp his fingers, a mute gesture of gratitude that brought a faint smile to his lips; then, still confused, tried to form words.

'I thought I was – ' Recollection came back then, and she drew in a violently sharp breath. 'Oh, Gods; *Drachea* – '

'Drachea tried to kill you,' Tarod told her, and the gentleness of his tone was belied by the cold anger in his eyes. 'It was fortunate that I found you before he could complete what he'd begun.'

The memory was crowding back, and she began to feel sick. 'Then the light – ' she whispered. 'It was you . . . ' She looked down at her own body. There was no pain now – she had only just realised the fact – and nor was there any trace of blood. The wound Drachea had inflicted had vanished as though it had never existed. Quickly she raised her gaze to meet Tarod's once more, uncomprehending, and he said quietly but wryly, 'Yes, it's more than any healer could have done. There are occasions when power such as mine has advantages.'

Cyllan swallowed, hard. 'Thank you . . . '

Tarod's instinct was to dismiss her thanks carelessly, but he checked himself. Such a reaction could easily be misconstrued, and he was anxious not to alienate her now. Instead he reached behind him to a table and picked up a cup, holding it out to her.

'Drink this,' he said, and smiled again, this time with a touch of humour. 'It won't fortify you, in a place where food and drink are irrelevant – but it'll warm you. And I imagine you've not tasted good wine since the High Initiate's inauguration!'

He was reminding her of their second meeting, when he had championed her against a cheating wine-seller, and tears sprang to Cyllan's eyes. She blinked them back, angry with herself for being moved, and took the cup. Over its rim, as she sipped, her amber eyes regarded him uncertainly, and at last she asked, 'Why did you save me?'

'Why?' He seemed surprised by the question, and she nodded.

'You owe me nothing. After we – parted – I thought – '

'That we were enemies?' Tarod finished the sentence for her. 'No, Cyllan. I feel no enmity towards you; in fact – ' He stopped, and a quick uncertainty flickered in his green eyes before he took a grip on himself again. Then he shook his head. 'You must judge me as you think fit. You've seen the High Initiate's documents for yourself, and for the most part Keridil presented the truth as he saw it.' His eyes narrowed. 'I can't deny what I am, and if you look on me as an enemy I can expect nothing better. But, demon or no, I saved your life because I wanted to . . . to protect you.' He shrugged. 'Perhaps that sounds glib. If it does, you must put your own interpretation on it.'

Demon or no . . . Cyllan detected the irony in his voice, and her throat tightened with an emotion she didn't dare allow to take hold. Whatever else he might be, Tarod was no demon . . . the term was more fitting to Drachea, who had turned on her, condemned her without a hearing and elected himself judge and executioner.

Cyllan had determined never to cry, least of all in Tarod's presence, but she had the terrible feeling that she was about to lose control and break down. Her ally had betrayed her; her enemy had saved her life – and the old feelings, which she had done all in her power to crush since arriving at the Castle, were fighting back to the surface.

Her hand started to shake and Tarod took the cup from her. He set it down, then gripped her fingers again, but gently this time.

'Why did Drachea try to kill you, Cyllan?' he asked.

She bit her lip. She didn't want to think about what had happened, but it had to be faced . . . and she had to tell the truth. She owed Tarod that, at least.

'He – he found out that I'd been here,' she said, so quietly that the words were barely audible. 'He was – was berating me for not being at his side when he began to recover from . . . ' She stopped, swallowed, continued with an effort. 'From what had happened to him. I was angry because his attitude was so callous, and I told him – told him – ' This time, she couldn't finish.

He began to understand. 'So he jumped to the conclusion that you were . . . shall we say, a willing victim?'

She nodded. The memory of Drachea's twisted face, his injustice, his cruelty, surged up from the dark corner of her mind to which she'd tried to banish it, and with it came a burning, bitter fury. Unable to stem it, she said, choking on the words, 'He called me a whore, and a serpent, and – '

And suddenly the barrier she'd been tightly holding on to broke. Cyllan covered her face with both hands and burst into tears as the pent emotion shattered her self-control. She felt Tarod's arms go round her and pressed herself against him, hiding her face in the black tangle of his hair. He said nothing, only held her, and the relief of being able to cry freely with no fear of rejection or contempt was like a cleansing balm.

Finally, the storm of weeping subsided. Tarod made no attempt to release her, and eventually it was she who disengaged herself from his arms, rising unsteadily to her feet and walking towards the window. She wiped her face with both hands, leaving smears on her cheeks, and said indistinctly, 'I'm sorry.'

'You've nothing to be sorry for. I've known many Adepts who'd weep at less provocation.'

She shook her head. 'No; I mean for more than that.' She wanted to look at him, to read the expression in his eyes, but didn't dare for fear of what she might see. She took a deep breath, aware that she must say what was in her heart, now or never. If she had misjudged Tarod then the mistake would hurt her badly. But she felt that she had nothing left to lose – and emotion was dictating what reason had finally been unable to suppress.

'I've done you a great injustice,' she said quietly. 'I believed that you were an enemy, not to be trusted, and I allied myself with Drachea because I believed – *thought* I believed – in the cause he espoused. He wants to destroy you. I thought he was right.' She laughed, her voice breaking. 'I call myself a seer, yet I couldn't see the truth before my own eyes. Or at least . . . I wouldn't acknowledge it. I thought Drachea's wisdom was greater than mine.'

'And now?' Tarod asked softly, when she didn't continue.

'Now . . . I don't know. Drachea thinks me a simpleton peasant, and perhaps he's right. But I can only judge by what I see, not by what I'm told.' The words were coming in a rush now, and with them was a growing fear that seemed to eat into her soul. She was gambling everything; if she lost, she couldn't live with herself. But instinct – and emotion – told her to put her trust in the gamble, and believe that, at very least, Tarod would understand.

'I wish,' she said, 'that I'd listened to my inner self. Because . . . I don't believe you're the demon they say you are. And I don't want to be your enemy.'

There was silence for a while. Then she heard a faint rustle as Tarod moved, and thought that he had come to stand behind her, though she didn't dare look round.

'You've read the High Initiate's testimony,' he said.

'No, I haven't. Drachea read it to me.' She smiled a smile that she didn't intend him to see. 'I can't read.'

There was no surprise in his voice, no amusement, no pity. He simply said levelly, 'I can't deny the truth of that document, Cyllan. I might challenge the interpretation, but the facts are real enough.'

She shrugged.

'Doesn't that repel you?'

'No. If those papers described a total stranger, then perhaps I'd condemn, because I knew no better. But they don't describe the man I met at West High Land, or the Adept who remembered me at the celebrations . . . or the man who saved my life.' She drew a breath. 'I thought I was afraid of you. But . . . I think I was more afraid of my own feelings.'

Tarod felt as though something were constricting his lungs and throat. Cyllan was almost silhouetted against the gloomy light from beyond the window, only a faint blood-red gleam tinting her pale hair, and he wanted to move towards her, touch her, hold her. Her hesitant confession had stunned him – yet he knew she'd spoken from the heart, willing to risk mockery or contempt. She'd trusted him, and he imagined that throughout her harsh life such trust had rarely been honoured. She was still uncertain – the set of her small shoulders gave away her determined resolve not to seem weak – but she had bared her soul. And he, though he was soulless and had thought himself incapable of feeling, was overtaken by a force he couldn't combat and didn't want to. Emotions moved in him like an implacable tide; hope, wistfulness, an aching longing to be able truly to live again. He had held the feelings back, afraid of what they might mean and what they could lead to. But he could no longer control them.

Cyllan laughed suddenly, chokingly. 'I still don't understand why,' she said.

'Why?'

'Why you saved my life.'

He stepped forward and laid his hands on her

shoulders. 'Don't you?' he said softly, and bent to kiss her upturned face. She responded eagerly, almost childlike – then her body tensed and she pulled away.

'Please, Tarod . . . don't. Not unless – unless you mean it.'

Tarod understood, and an image of Sashka as she had so often gazed at him, beautiful, hungry and inviting, came unbidden to his mind. He banished it. Sashka was dead; long dead for him . . .

'I mean it.' He drew her towards him, his mouth finding hers and his body responding to the warmth of her. 'I mean it, Cyllan . . . '

* * * * *

Desire was spent, but the emotion remained. They lay together on Tarod's couch, Cyllan's head resting in the crook of his arm. Neither had felt the need to speak, and now it seemed that Cyllan was asleep, her breathing light and regular.

Tarod watched her. He felt more at peace than he could ever remember, and yet the peace was touched by a sadness that he had, as yet, been unable to bring himself to face. He had been shocked by the feelings that this oddly courageous and loyal girl had aroused within him, but knew that there was nothing illusory or transitory about his love for her, or hers for him. And yet, despite the flowering of those feelings, he was aware of an emptiness at the core of his heart, a dark, emotionless shadow that marred his new-found happiness.

Could there be a future for them? Here, in this strange dimension where nothing ever changed, they could exist for eternity if they chose. But for a man without a soul, unable to give completely, it would be a hollow existence because he could never be truly fulfilled. Tarod wanted to be complete again; to know the pains and the joys of completion. Soulless, he was but half alive . . . and yet to regain his soul would be to face once more the full implication of his true nature . . .

He sighed, and Cyllan's eyes flickered open.

'Tarod?' Her fingers touched his arm lightly, sleepily, then she frowned. 'Something troubles you . . . '

She read him all too well. 'Idle thoughts,' he said.

'Tell me. Please.'

He drew her closer. 'I was thinking of the future.' He smiled, but not happily. 'Since Time was banished, I've existed here without caring about all that I'd left behind. But now . . . so much has changed. When I lost my soul, I thought I'd moved beyond humanity. I was wrong. And yet I'm a husk; a shell – there's a cold core within me that I can't break down. I can't give to you in the way that I once could have done; I can't love you with my soul, because I have no soul. And yet if I should try to turn back, and if I should succeed – '

'Tarod . . . ' Sensing his distress Cyllan tried to interrupt him, but he silenced her by placing a finger on her lips.

'No. It has to be said. You know what I've become, Cyllan. But do you know what I once was?'

An echo of the old fear crept into her eyes, and he felt as though a knife had twisted in his gut. She still didn't fully understand, and he was afraid that, when she did, she would be unable to face the truth without revulsion. But he couldn't keep it from her. She had been prepared to gamble – so must he.

'Once,' he said, 'I wore a ring. In the ring was a stone; a very beautiful gem. I learned that that gem was a focus of power, but I was ignorant of its true nature . . . until that nature was revealed to me by Yandros.'

'Yandros . . . ' The word sent an atavistic shiver through Cyllan, and she said tentatively. 'The testimony claimed that he was – is – a Lord of Chaos . . . '

'Yes.'

'And the stone . . . ' She knew the answer, but needed to hear it in his own words.

'The stone was the vehicle for my soul.' He ran his tongue over lips that were suddenly dry. 'It, too, is from the Chaos realm.'

She sat up, seemingly wrestling with some inner conflict – then turned abruptly to face him, reaching out to take his hand as her distress found voice.

'But you're no demon! You're of *this* world; you're human – '

'Cyllan – ' He squeezed her fingers, moved by her loyalty and yet finding it a bleak comfort. 'I'm not human. Not wholly. I never have been – though the Gods know it took me long enough to find that out.'

'Then what are you?'

Tarod shook his head. 'I don't know, Cyllan; I truly don't know. I have human feelings, human reactions; yet I also possess powers which no mortal man should be capable of wielding. The Circle say I'm a demon. And Yandros . . . ' his gaze flickered uncertainly to her face, 'Yandros called me "brother".'

Cyllan didn't speak, and when he looked at her again her head was bowed so that he couldn't see her face. Inwardly, she was struggling to assimilate all he had told her. She had expected him to deny the charges laid against him by the Circle; instead he admitted that, though slanted, they were in essence true. The idea that this man could be kin to a Lord of Chaos appalled her . . . and yet, no matter what every catechism she had learned since childhood might say, she couldn't reject him; couldn't turn against him for the sake of an abstract principle.

'If I were to regain the soul-stone,' Tarod said, 'The links with Chaos would be reforged. Yet without it I can't truly live, and I can't find the fulfilment I long for with you.' He smiled bleakly. 'Can you reconcile such a paradox?'

Cyllan looked at him. '*Is* it a paradox, Tarod? Whatever that stone might have made you, you're human enough! You were a high Adept, a servant of our gods, when you possessed your soul. You were no demon – why should that change if you regain it now?'

He laughed bitterly. 'The Circle would disagree.'

'Then damn the Circle! If they couldn't see the truth before their eyes, they were fools!'

He turned to regard her, unsure of himself. 'Do you really have so much faith in me, Cyllan?'

'Yes,' she told him simply.

The irony of her unquestioning loyalty, contrasted with the hostility he had met from those who had purported to be friends and peers of a lifetime's standing, was sobering. During his cold existence alone in the timeless Castle Tarod had turned his back on the old allegiance to the Lords of Order, for with the Circle's betrayal Order had failed him. But the stirrings of a rekindled humanity had brought back the love of his world. He wanted to be a part of that world again; and it was a world in which Yandros and his ilk played no part.

He looked down at the buckled base of the ring on his left hand. 'There could be dangers if the stone is recovered. It was the key to Yandros's plan to challenge the rule of Aeoris, and it could be that it would open the gateway . . . that Chaos could threaten the world once again.'

'You fought Chaos once before. Even the High Initiate admitted that. His papers said that you banished Yandros . . . '

'Nonetheless, Yandros doesn't accept defeat easily.' Tarod smiled thinly. 'As I know to my cost.'

Cyllan leaned forward and let her arms slip around him, moving closer until she was pressed warmly against him. 'I don't care about Yandros,' she said with determination. 'He's a shadow – and I'm not afraid of shadows. All that matters to me is that you've lost a part of yourself, and you want to regain it. That's what counts.'

Tarod gazed down at her, and one hand reached out to stroke her pale hair. 'Whatever that self might be? You don't fear that?'

'No.' She kissed him, and the kiss was fierce. 'I don't fear that.'

Chapter 9

Drachea's hand moved slowly, rhythmically back and forth along the length of the sword blade as he sat crouched over the weapon in one of the remotest of the Castle's many empty rooms. He had carefully wiped Cyllan's blood from the blade, but that wasn't enough; he needed to polish the steel until it shone blindingly, eradicate every possible trace of her. Purity, he told himself over and over again, with a twisted ferocity; the sword must be pure before it was fit for him to wield – he'd have no taint of the white-faced witch about him.

Memory of the frustration and fury he'd felt at being cheated of his victim brought a chilly sweat to Drachea's brow. Bearing down on Cyllan, certain of securing her death, he had been momentarily blinded by the shattering aurora of light that materialised around her from nowhere, and when its brief flash faded she had vanished. He had no doubt that Tarod was responsible, though whether his skills had been enough to keep her alive he didn't know. *If* she lived, then she was another adversary to be counted in his personal reckoning – but the scores he had to settle with both her and her demonic lover could wait awhile. He had more urgent matters at hand.

Drachea stopped polishing, studied the sword critically and, satisfied, laid it with something approaching reverence on the bed before rising and crossing to the window. During his search for a safe hideaway he had found new clothes that he felt were more fitting to his station both as heir to a Margravate and as champion of the Circle against their common enemy. Taking up a stance at the window, he flicked back the short, fur-trimmed cloak that covered dark green velvet jerkin and grey silk shirt and trousers, trying to glimpse his own reflection in the glass. The panes distorted the image and irritated him; he turned back and picked up the sword once more, hefting it and testing its balance. Not ideal – Cyllan had failed him there, as in so many other ways – but it would do. And he had found a knife for himself, which might prove a more useful weapon. The knife now hung in a sheath fastened to the belt at his waist; he slipped the sword through the adjacent loop, adjusted its angle at his hip and decided that he was ready.

Drachea had no illusions about his prospects if he should face and defy Tarod alone – his last experience at the Adept's hands had all but unhinged him, and nothing would induce him to repeat it. If Tarod was to be defeated, he would need help – and the only chance of securing that help lay in finding a way to reverse the spell which had stopped Time, and call the Circle back to the world. Then retribution would be his for the taking, and he would relish every sweet moment. If Cyllan lived she'd learn to regret her alliance with Chaos, and he smiled to himself, thinking of the satisfaction that forcing her to witness Tarod's final annihilation would give him.

But to relish his triumph now was premature – he had a long way to go before the victory. And the first step was to search for the Chaos stone, which could prove to be the most valuable weapon of all. With that in his grasp, he would be in a position to bargain with Tarod – a bargain that would be very much to his own advantage.

Drachea took a final glance around the room, wishing that he could have shared this moment with someone who would admire his courage and wish him well. No matter; he would in time receive the Circle's gratitude as their champion and saviour, and they would see to it that he had his just reward.

He left the chamber, closing the door quietly behind him, and set off towards the stairs.

* * * * *

'Cyllan.' Tarod laid his hands gently on her shoulders as she looked up at him. 'Are you sure you want to do this?'

She smiled, her face lighting. 'Yes, I'm sure.' She covered his left hand with her own, feeling the sharp contours of his broken ring against her palm. 'You can't enter the Marble Hall – but I can. And if the stone can be found, I'll find it.' She stood on tiptoe, drawing him down to kiss him. 'Trust me.'

'I do. But I'm uneasy.' His green eyes, unquiet, focused on a point beyond her. 'You persuaded me to show mercy to Drachea . . . I still think you were wrong.'

'No.' She shook her head emphatically, remembering how hard it had been to dissuade him from finding the young man and slaying him without a second thought. Why she felt a measure of compassion for Drachea she didn't know; he had betrayed her trust and, if their positions were reversed, would have had no hesitation in killing her. But mingled with her contempt was an element of pity; revenge played no part in her thinking, and to see Drachea die for no good reason would prey on her conscience.

Tarod felt differently. Drachea's treatment of Cyllan was in itself enough to provoke his quick temper, and he wanted nothing more than to blast him to damnation and have done. For her sake he had promised to stay his hand – but deep down he wondered if he might come to regret the promise.

'Drachea can do us no harm.' Cyllan said. 'He counts for nothing, Tarod. I'm not afraid of him.'

He hesitated, then smiled, though there was still a hint of doubt in his eyes. 'Go, then,' he told her. 'And if you need me, I'll hear you and be with you.' He kissed her, seeming reluctant to break away. 'The gods protect you.'

He watched the door close at her back, waited until he heard her light footfalls on the stairs, then closed his green eyes, concentrating briefly on the small exertion of power that would transport her to the foot of the titanic spire. When it was done, he turned back to his table and sat down. The single candle in its sconce stood among a clutter of books; he passed one hand over it, and the familiar green witchfire glowed into life. As it gained strength, casting a cold radiance across his gaunt features, Tarod gazed unblinkingly into the heart of the flame and tried to banish the uneasiness that lurked like a worm within him.

As she descended the stairs that wound down towards the library vault, Cyllan was keyed up with a mingling of excitement, anticipation and dread. She didn't fear the task that lay ahead of her, but knew that, if she was successful, the future would become unknown and perhaps perilous territory. With the soul-stone restored to him Tarod would again assume his true nature, and to stay in the timeless Castle wouldn't content him. He'd refused to admit the truth directly, but Cyllan believed that, when the stone was in his possession, he would use its power to call back Time to the dimension. The thought of what might ensue when he confronted the Circle again chilled her to the marrow; but she knew him well enough to realise he'd have it no other way. He couldn't exist in an unchanging eternity; he needed to *live*, and if living involved risk, he'd take the risk. She couldn't find it in her heart to argue with him, and yet the one fear which ate at her like a disease was the fear of losing him. Even with his soul restored, Tarod wasn't invincible; and if the Circle should prevail against him, she'd lose her own reason for existing.

The sudden and drastic changes in both herself and Tarod had happened so unexpectedly that Cyllan had had no chance even to try to question or understand them. Nor, if she was honest, did she wish to. At Drachea's behest she had convinced herself that Tarod was evil, an enemy to be mistrusted and thwarted, and she had fought against her own desires and instincts in an effort to reinforce that conviction. But she had never been at ease with it; and once the barriers between them finally broke down, the feelings she had tried to suppress had taken hold of her with a vengeance. Powerful emotions, long repressed, had found their focus in a man

who awoke in her a fierce desire, unquenchable love and
a loyalty that nothing could shake. Right or wrong she
had chosen her path, and no matter what the future
might bring she wouldn't turn from it.

She ran down the last few stairs of the flight and
pushed open the door that led to the library. The dim
vault was still and silent, and Cyllan paused on the
threshold, turning her mind to Tarod where he waited in
the spire. At once she felt an answering presence joining
with her and soothing her unease, and she was com-
forted by it. Whatever lay ahead, he'd be with her . . .

As she crossed the room towards the half-hidden door
which would lead her to the Marble Hall, the hem of her
skirt snagged on one of the scattered books which littered the floor, and she was forced to stop and free it.
She was unused to wearing clothes like these; for as long
as she could remember she'd had nothing but shirts and
trousers handed down from a cousin or, in recent years,
from one of the men in her uncle's drover-band. But
Tarod had told her that she deserved something better,
far better . . . and he had found, though the gods alone
knew from where, a dress of dark red silk which fitted
her as though it had been made for her alone. The feel of
the fabric fascinated her; the rustle as she moved, the
sensation of the silk swirling against her bare legs . . . and
when she wore it for him he had said she looked beautiful.
No one had ever paid her such a compliment before, yet
she didn't doubt Tarod's sincerity. To him she *was* beautiful, and the knowledge meant more to her than she could
express. Cyllan remembered his words, cherishing them,
as she reached the low door, opened it and gazed through
to the empty passage with its peculiar, silver-tinged light.
Then, gathering her courage, she started towards the
source of the light and the Marble Hall beyond.

Tarod's plan, as he had outlined it to her, was straight-
forward enough. Without the soul-stone he could do
nothing to reverse the forces which had halted the
Pendulum of Time and locked the Castle into this
strange non-dimension; yet the stone had been con-
signed to limbo along with the Castle's inhabitants. The

only way to resolve the paradox was to break through the barrier on one of the highest of the seven astral planes, and find the stone. If the stratagem worked – and Tarod admitted that he was uncertain of success – it could be brought back through dimensions, if the motivating power and will were strong enough. Tarod had the power, and the will, but the vital focus provided by the Marble Hall itself was denied to him through the quirk of fate which had shifted it fractionally out of synchronisation with the Castle when Time was banished. Soulless, he couldn't enter . . . but Cyllan could. And her innate psychic ability, Tarod believed, would be enough to enable him to succeed in his task using her as a medium.

Cyllan didn't pretend to understand the nature of the occult skill which Tarod would need to achieve his aim, but only prayed that she would be capable of doing what he wanted of her. He had warned her that there could be dangers but she had stubbornly dismissed them; she trusted him, wanted to help him, and she was resolved to play her part.

Now though, as she reached out to touch the dull silver door that stood between her and the Marble Hall, she was assailed by a chilly shiver of uncertainty. No one knew the true properties of this strange, illusion-haunted place; so much had been made clear in the High Initiate's papers, and Tarod had only confirmed it. If something were to go wrong with the plan, if some force that even Tarod hadn't bargained for were to manifest then no amount of foresight could predict the possible consequences. *Limbo* . . . Cyllan shuddered at the thought and all but withdrew her hand from the door.

Theres's no shame in being afraid, Tarod had told her. *Don't fight your fear, or pretend it doesn't exist.* He was right . . . the feeling, on the threshold of such an undertaking, was natural . . .

She took a deep breath, and touched her hand to the door. It swung open, and the shifting, shimmering mists enfolded her as she walked slowly into the Marble Hall.

Drachea stood in the shelter of the doorway, his gaze
roaming uneasily across the courtyard's vast expanse. It
seemed deserted, but it was impossible to be sure; the
crimson light played tricks with the eyes, and any one of
a thousand dense shadows might without warning move
and resolve into something other than shadow . . . He
glanced towards the summit of the Northern spire, and
thought he detected the faintest glimmer of light from a
high window; but again, it could easily be illusion.

He had arrived at the courtyard by a deliberately
tortuous route which finally brought him to an insignificant side entrance adjacent to the stables. If Tarod were
watching for him, the chances were that he'd mount his
vigil in sight of the main doors, which Drachea could see
standing open. If he kept to the deeper darkness, he
should be able to reach his goal with small risk of being
detected . . . and so, trying to quell the thumping of his
heart, he eased out into the shadow of the black wall and
began to edge his way along it. Nothing untoward happened – once he thought he glimpsed a blur of movement low down, as though something sentient had
detached itself from the foot of a buttress and slipped
snaking away across the flagstones; but it was nothing
more than his imagination, and at last he gained the
shelter of the colonnaded walkway. Here he could
merge easily with the gaunt silhouettes of the pillars, and
by moving with slow caution arrive at the door which led
to the library vault.

At the top of the vault stairs his determination almost
failed him as he realised that Tarod could be waiting for
him in the library, but Drachea forced himself not to
dwell on the idea. If he baulked now, seeing demons at
every turn, he might just as well return to his room and
wait for insanity or Tarod's vengeance – or both – to
claim him. The work must be begun, and he could gain
nothing by delaying.

Softly, though imagining every footfall to be as loud as
thunder, Drachea began to descend the stairs.

Cyllan stood at he head of the massive block of black

wood which lay at what was deemed to be the Marble Hall's exact centre. Her eyes were closed, and her lips moved silently in a fervent prayer to Aeoris for protection – though whether the god would see fit to grant it to her in the face of what she was about to do, she didn't like to speculate. Her stomach roiled with the sickness of nerves, and though instinct urged her to reach out and lay her hands on the block's surface, she couldn't bring herself to touch it. Passing by the seven defaced black statues, which loomed eerily out of the shrouding mist, she had faltered, and only by silently repeating the litany of Tarod's words to her could she force herself on. But she had come this far . . . for his sake, for both their sakes, she must look forward and not back.

The silence and stillness were absolute. Once she had imagined she had heard a distant sound like the muted chiming of a bell, and once an echo of soft laughter, almost beyond the threshold of human hearing, had seemed to shiver in the mist; but such illusions were gone now. The Hall itself seemed alive and waiting; she felt its tension like a physical presence. The mosaic floor was cold beneath her bare feet . . . she clasped her hands before her and struggled to quiet her mind, make herself receptive for contact with Tarod.

His presence in her subconscious mind came suddenly and powerfully. For an instant Cyllan glimpsed the darkened room at the top of the spire and seemed to see steady green eyes gazing into her own, lit with an intensity that frightened her. Then she sensed the guiding will that began to integrate with hers and to take control . . . breathing slowly, lightly, she reached out as though sleepwalking, and her hands came to rest on the pitted surface of the block. As they touched, a lurching sensation of vertigo struck up from far beneath the floor and she swayed, biting her tongue to stop herself crying out in alarm. The feeling passed, but she knew that, beyond her closed lids, something had changed. The tension was transmuting into a dreamlike sensation, as though she floated free of time and space. She wanted to open her eyes, but courage failed her. Whatever surrounded her now wasn't for mortal sight or mortal understanding, and the knowledge brought on something akin to panic. She flailed mentally, blindly seeking an anchor, and almost at once the other will touched her and held her, drawing her back from the terror. She felt Tarod's presence in her mind again, but it was a presence that transcended humanity, more powerful than anything she had ever known. For a moment her own will resisted through fear, but the presence soothed her, reassured her, and she let herself be eclipsed by it as Tarod drew her through the planes towards their mutual goal.

Sword drawn, Drachea stepped into the vault and picked his way carefully among the fallen books and manuscripts. At every other pace he turned quickly, the blade swinging up as though to block some assault from behind, but the precaution was needless. The library was empty.

And yet he had a conviction that not all was as it should have been. Something was awry, though he couldn't put a finger on the cause. Drachea was no psychic, but a glimmer of sensitivity warned him, even before he came across the low door in its alcove and found it standing wide open.

He stopped on the threshold, licking his lips uncertainly. This way lay the Marble Hall; the one place in all the Castle where, on his own admission, Tarod couldn't go. Yet the door gaped, suggesting that someone had recently come this way . . . and the Castle's only other inhabitant was Cyllan . . .

His previous unreasoning fear of the Marble Hall meant nothing in the face of this unexpected opportunity to settle the score. Drachea put the sword away, aware of its disadvantages in the confined space of the passage, and instead drew the short knife from its sheath. The blade glittered wickedly in the odd light, and he set off slowly, cautiously, towards the silver door.

First there was a terrible sensation of weight, as though the towering cliffs of West High Land were crushing her

beneath them . . . she resisted, urged by the will inter-
locked with her own, and abruptly the pressure gave way
to the balm of a cool, clear current which carried her like a
fish on its tide. She heard the eldritch song of the fanaani,
but it faded and instead she was being buffeted on a
laughing, capricious gale . . . which exploded into heat
that assailed her, burning, unquenchable. She seemed to
pass through fire, on the point of screaming until sud-
denly the searing pain was eclipsed by a voice that spoke
in her innermost consciousness, Slowly, *it seemed to say,*
Slowly . . . gently . . . I am with you . . .

And there was silence. She felt as though she hung
weightless and motionless amid nothing; yet there was a
disturbance in her mind, an unease, a fear . . . a sense
that below her, something waited . . . and the voice
spoke within her again and said, Look . . .

It was a black and silver world, with no colour to
relieve the austerity. Cyllan hung disembodied above a
floor where mosaics made a complex pattern, and she
looked down upon an extraordinary, motionless
tableau.

Some twenty or thirty men and women were ranged in a
circle, all heads turned towards one man in heavy, sombre
ceremonial garb, wearing a circlet that glittered coldly on
his head. His arms were outstretched, and in both hands he
held a massive, ugly sword which gave off a coruscation of
light that seemed to burn the air around it. The light
illuminated his powerful frame and a face which, though
young and handsome, was set in hard lines.

Cyllan felt a shaft of anger lance through her, and
knew it emanated from the part of the linked consciousness that was Tarod. She looked again, and saw
that the young man who held the sword stood before a
great block of black wood . . . and on the block was
another figure, tall, gaunt, face half hidden by a mane of
black hair. The tableau's still rigidity gave a macabre
twist to the attitude of extreme agony that racked the
victim on the block – then the fury flared into life again,
and Cyllan's mind recoiled in shock as she recognised
him.

The stone, Cyllan . . . find the stone . . . The voice
that spoke within her carried no overt emotion, but
Cyllan felt the savage thrust of pain that accompanied
the words. Momentarily she realised how Tarod must
feel at witnessing the scene of his own execution, but the
understanding was eclipsed by an urgent longing that
surged within their linked wills. Guided by Tarod, she
exerted her strength, seeking, hunting . . .

And then she saw it. It lay in the cupped hands of
another Initiate who stood at the foot of the block, and it
glowed with a cold inner life of its own. A single gem,
multifaceted and beautiful . . . the Chaos stone.

Take it, she heard Tarod's whispered command, and
something seemed to propel her forward and downward, so that her mind reached out to the still figures of
the tableau. The stone began to pulse, radiating seven
shafts of light that all but blinded her as she drew closer,
closer . . . and the presence in her mind prepared itself
for a last, single exertion of will. She knew that this was
the perilous moment; it would take all Tarod's skill to
link their shared consciousness with the soul-stone, and
snatch them back from this world of illusion and phantasm. She felt the power building within her, building
until she thought she couldn't contain it and would
shatter under its inexorable pressure . . . still it grew,
and the glowing stone blazed more fiercely than ever,
drawing her into itself like some terrible vortex . . .

A gigantic concussion smashed from every direction
at once, and Cyllan's scream of terror shattered into a
thousand echoes that dinned in her ears as she was
hurled from the dimension. Mind, body and soul split
asunder, the scream rang on and on – until with a titanic
crack the world returned.

She was sprawled across the execution block, all
breath knocked out of her lungs by the force of impact.
She tried to move, but her limbs had no strength and she
could only slide helplessly to the floor as her spinning
senses struggled to right themselves. At last, guided by
the feel of the cold marble beneath her, she gained a
small measure of orientation and by slow and painful

degrees was able to sit up. Her hands were clenched into fists and when she tried to unlock them she was racked by violent muscular spasms . . . but in her hand she felt something hard and cold and rounded . . .

'Tarod . . . ' She croaked his name aloud, trying to urge her will to meld once again with his, and almost sobbed with relief when she felt his mind reaching out to her. The presence was weakened by their shared ordeal; he had exerted all his strength in calling on the forces he'd summoned, and the contact was tenuous. Yet it was enough . . .

She projected the certainty she felt with all her remaining energy. *I have the stone . . .*

He was barely able to answer her, and Cyllan began to struggle upright. Gaining her feet, she was forced to lean over the block to balance herself and get her breath – and it was as she gasped air thankfully into her lungs, the Chaos stone still tightly gripped in her hand, that a glittering sliver of steel slid from behind her shoulder to hover a hairsbreadth from her throat, and a voice thick with triumphant savagery said,

'Thank you, Cyllan. You've solved my most pressing problem . . . '

Tarod slumped in the chair, his head thrown back and sweat gleaming on his face and hands. He was drained, and the strength he craved wouldn't return to him. To summon and use such power was taxing enough under any circumstances, but to do so at second hand, through the medium of another mind, had almost proved his undoing. Only by an iron control of his will had he been able to pull himself and Cyllan back from limbo, and now he felt as weak as a new-born child.

But it was done . . . The realisation lit a fire within him, though he hadn't the strength to rejoice. They had succeeded, and the stone had been retrieved from that netherworld . . .

He must go to Cyllan. In his present condition he had no power to bring her back to the spire, but he must go to her. With a tremendous effort Tarod forced himself to rise from the chair, and stood swaying as though drunk. And then, as he turned towards the door, something impinged on a deeper level of his consciousness.

Tarod . . .

He felt the first stirrings of concern, for he recognised the source of the voiceless, psychic call and its inflection told him something was wrong.

Tarod . . .

Fear. It was fear he sensed in the call she sent out to him; fear and an incoherent pleading. Drained as he was, he couldn't lock his mind completely with Cyllan's, but enough energy remained, fuelled now by alarm, for him to reach out psychically towards her. As he did, he heard her thoughts more clearly.

Tarod, I've failed you . . . I was wrong. I thought he could do us no harm . . .

The shock of her words struck his tired mind, and a terrible clarity brought home the truth to Tarod. He swung round to where the candle still burned with its sickly halo, and bent over the nacreous green flame. Distorted images danced before him; he willed them to focus, and saw her.

She knelt on the mosaic floor at Drachea's feet, both arms twisted viciously up behind her back. Drachea held the blade of a knife poised at her throat, in such a position that one incautious movement would sever the jugular vein. Her eyes were tight shut and Tarod saw blood on her lip where she had bitten into it.

A rage as he had never known before began to fill Tarod. The fury at Themila's death, which had led him to kill Rhiman Han, the bitterness of Sashka's betrayal, were nothing by comparison to the insanity of malevolence that consumed him now. He gasped, swaying back, then with one hand swept the candle, books and all other artefacts from the table-top. They smashed to the floor; the witchfire halo winked out, and blackness surged up in Tarod's mind, bringing with it a resurgence of power which he caught, focused, savagely directing it towards Drachea –

'*No!*' He yelled the word aloud in a desperate bid to

break his own concentration, and reeled back as the power-bolt disintegrated in his head. His magic was useless – without a willing medium he couldn't penetrate the barrier between himself and the Marble Hall, and to use Cyllan as a vehicle for this would be to kill her. He sucked air into his lungs, striving to calm himself and railing wildly against the realisation that he was trapped. He could do nothing to Drachea, and Drachea held Cyllan's life as hostage. Whatever the treacherous Heir Margrave wanted – and Tarod believed he knew the answer to that question – he had no choice but to comply. If he refused, Cyllan would die. And as he faced this final, terrible test, Tarod knew that no sacrifice would be too great to save her.

'So our mutual friend has heard you, and is aware of your plight.' Drachea smiled, speaking softly, and gave a vicious jerk to Cyllan's pinned arms that made her gasp with pain. 'No doubt he's aware, too, of what could become of his precious stone if he attempts to cross me!'

Cyllan didn't answer. She could make no move, knowing that Drachea held the knife-blade so close to her throat that the smallest slip would drive it deep, and the wound would be fatal;. She had felt Tarod's despair and fury as he realised what had happened, but now there was no presence in her mind at all. She prayed that he still had a reserve of power, that he could use it to blast Drachea, and cursed herself a thousand times for a fool. If she hadn't pleaded with Tarod to show leniency, Drachea would be dead . . .

Another cruel jerk at her arms brought her back to earth. 'Well?' Drachea demanded, his voice harsh in her ear. 'What does he say? What does he mean to do?'

Cyllan made an inarticulate noise and he withdrew the knife sufficiently to allow her to speak. 'I – don't know . . . ' she whispered.

'Liar!'

'No . . . it's the truth . . . '

Drachea laughed. 'Then perhaps your demon-lover

thinks less of you than you so fondly believe! Nonetheless, he values that pretty trinket in your hand. Release it, Cyllan.'

She clenched her fist. *'No . . .'*

'I said, *release it!'* The knife touched her neck and Cyllan realised she would achieve nothing by defiance. He could kill her and take the stone; she had nothing to gain by sacrificing herself.

The jewel fell to the floor with a small, cold clink and Drachea stared down at it, hardly able to believe his good fortune. It looked an ordinary enough bauble now; dull, lifeless, like a piece of glass. But he had seen the white-hot glare that sprang from Cyllan's outstretched hands as the thing materialised in his full sight, and he had felt the power pulsing from its heart. It was a deadly artefact – and the Circle would reward him well when he returned it into their rightful custody!

Drachea had entered the Marble Hall as the rite conducted by Tarod and Cyllan neared its climax. Cyllan was oblivious to her surroundings, and he had hidden himself behind one of the black statues, gambling that his presence would go undetected. He soon realised that Cyllan was acting as a medium for the dark sorcerer, and when he saw the soul-stone's radiance spilling from between her cupped fingers he knew what they had done, and a heady exultation filled him. Weak as she now was, Cyllan would be easy prey. Tarod couldn't enter the Hall . . . and with the Chaos-stone in his hand, Drachea would have an unassailable fortress from which to make his demands.

But as yet, he had had no chance to voice those demands. He had ordered Cyllan to make contact with Tarod, but although she swore she had done so, Tarod hadn't responded. Doubtless he considered her expendable – eventually he must come seeking the stone. And he wouldn't be inclined to risk the loss of his own soul for the sake of a simple bargain . . .

Drachea wondered if Tarod was planning some counter-move. The demon had great guile, and he felt uneasy with nothing to do but wait. Suddenly angry, he twisted

Cyllan's arm again, opening his mouth to voice a further threat if she didn't try to make contact again. But before he could speak, a new voice cut across the eerie quiet of the Marble Hall.

'*Drachea.*'

The tone was chilling, calm but terrible. Drachea started and all but lost his grip of Cyllan's arms; seeing a chance, albeit slender, she twisted in his grasp and tried to pull away, but before she could roll clear he had snatched at her and jerked her back, her head against his shoulder, the knife touching the flesh of her neck. Slowly, dragging his burden with him, Drachea turned around.

The coruscating mists had shivered apart as though a beam of light had cut through them, and the way to the silver door was unobscured. A single pace beyond the Marble Hall's threshold stood Tarod, mad-eyed, his left hand raised and pointing directly at Drachea.

Tarod said with unhuman malignance, 'Release her.'

For an instant Drachea baulked, then he remembered the Marble Hall's properties, and his face worked into a sneer. 'Release her?' he repeated mockingly. 'You may think me a fool, demon, but I'm not that gullible! I have the stone, and I have Cyllan. I will destroy either with impunity if you dare to give me orders again!'

Tarod's eyes blazed, and a dark aura flickered into life around him. 'You cannot destroy the Chaos stone, worm.'

'Perhaps not – but I can kill *her*!' Drachea jerked Cyllan violently – and saw fear in Tarod's look before he could disguise it. His own eyes lit with excitement as he realised that his adversary had revealed an unexpected weakness. Could it be that he had some care for Cyllan after all – or at least, that she was in some way vital to him?

Slowly, thoughtfully, Drachea ran his tongue over his lower lip. 'Let us say, Adept Tarod,' he went on, injecting a venomous contempt in the last two words, 'that there is something I want from you. Let us say that if you refuse to grant it, I will slit Cyllan's throat, and you may

watch her life-blood spill over this mosaic floor. What
would your answer to my request be?'

Tarod's face tightened and he responded savagely,
'Harm Cyllan in any way, and you won't merely die – I'll
send you to eternal torture!'

'Ah!' Drachea crowed delightedly. 'So the soulless
one has a flaw after all! What is Cyllan to you, Tarod,
that makes her so vital to your needs ? A whore's a
whore, after all – there are plenty better to choose from
in the world!'

Tarod's hand jerked up as though to release a furious
power-bolt, but Cyllan cried out, 'No! Tarod, he seeks
only to enrage you! Don't give him that satisfaction!'

Drachea swore and pulled viciously at her hair to
silence her, but Tarod knew she was right. Fury and fear
had taken him dangerously close to losing control; now,
with an effort, he collected his wits. If Cyllan was to be
saved, he had no business arguing with Drachea. There
was a bargain to be struck . . . and he knew what that
bargain must be.

The black aura flickered, faded as he stared at the
Heir Margrave and at Cyllan. The slightest move could
mean her death . . . he swallowed, his throat dry, and
he said to Drachea,

'What is it you want of me?'

Drachea grinned. 'Better! You begin to understand at
last. I'll spell it out clearly for you, demon. I have
Cyllan, and I have your soul-stone. If you want to save
Cyllan's life, you must use the stone, and call back Time
to this Castle!'

Cyllan twisted ferociously in Drachea's grip. 'Tarod,
no!' she shrieked. 'It would mean awakening the Circle
– you can't do it, not this way!'

Her eyes, wide and staring, met his, and she saw a
sadness and compassion in his green gaze that horrified
her with its implication. She tried to shake her head, but
the knife was too close. 'Tarod, no, *please* . . . '

He continued to look at her. 'I have no choice.'

'But you have! Let him kill me – it's better than the
alternative!'

'No!' The refusal was shockingly vehement, and Tarod raised his head to stare proudly, contemptuously at Drachea. 'I will do what needs to be done, Heir Margrave. And I congratulate you on your deviousness. My reckoning with you must wait!'

'Your reckoning will be with the High Initiate!' Drachea sneered. 'Save your pride for him, serpent!'

Tarod took a deep breath, fighting down his fury, and said calmly, 'Then give me the stone.'

'What?' Drachea was incredulous, then he laughed, a loud peal that rang and echoed clashingly through the Marble Hall. 'I gave up suckling at the teat many years ago, my friend! Until the Circle return, and you are safely bound, this stone stays with me!' He forced Cyllan forward until she crouched painfully with head bent, then with one foot shifted the Chaos stone, which still lay on the floor, into Tarod's view. 'You've already used this white-faced bitch as your medium. Use her again.'

It would take more strength than he possessed . . . he was still weakened by the force expended to call the stone out of limbo . . . Aloud, Tarod said, 'I can't.'

'You're lying! You've done it before!'

'Cyllan may not consent.'

'Damn you, then *make* her consent! It's a simple enough choice – either you do what I command, in the way I command it, or you watch her die! My patience has run out – make your decision!'

There was no other way open to him. If he refused to accede to Drachea's demands, the Heir Margrave would slit Cyllan's throat while Tarod stood helpless. And no matter what vengeance he took, nothing could ever compensate for her loss . . .

But Tarod knew that, weakened as he was by the forces he had used to call the Chaos stone out of limbo, he might not have the strength to do what Drachea wanted of him. This was no trifling magic, and if he failed, if his will broke, then the backlash of power could destroy Cyllan.

Yet she's damned already if you don't try . . .

The inner voice chilled him, for it spoke nothing less

than the truth. Tarod sighed. 'Very well, Drachea. I accept your terms.'

'Ha!' Drachea grinned, then leaned over to leer at Cyllan. 'It seems you can take comfort from your demon-friend's loyalty, bitch! And he thought I was the fool . . . '

Cyllan shut her eyes, wanting to blot out the image of Drachea's twisted, triumphant face. She *had* to stop Tarod somehow – it was better, far better, that she died and left him free, for the alternative was too appalling to consider. Desperately, she tried again to plead with him.

'Tarod . . . listen to me . . . '

'Quiet!' Drachea hissed.

'No! *Tarod!*' Her voice rose shrilly. 'I don't care what happens to me – let him use the knife, I don't care ! You mustn't do this, you *can't*!'

Drachea had twisted her around so that she couldn't see Tarod, but she heard his voice clearly enough, and it was implacable.

'There's no other way.' And as he spoke aloud, she heard other words, voiceless, echo in her mind. *Cyllan, if you love me, obey me in this!*

She summoned her mental resources. *I can't! The Circle will –*

Damn the Circle! I won't see you die . . .

I'll fight you . . .

You can't fight me. I'll do what I must do, and I'll use you in whatever ways I need to, to save your life!

There was venom in the last message, and Cyllan realised that nothing she could say or do would sway him. Tears began to trickle down her cheeks; tears of misery and defeat, and Drachea looked quickly up at Tarod. 'Is she subdued?' he demanded.

'She'll do what I ask of her,' Tarod told him curtly.

'Good. Then don't prevaricate – begin!'

Tarod bowed his head. To turn his mind from Cyllan's plight and concentrate on what must be done was a nightmare, but he forced himself to clear all extraneous thoughts from his mind. So much depended on his skill and remaining strength now . . . yet if he succeeded, he would be placing himself in a trap with jaws that could clamp ferociously on him. It was likely that Drachea would attempt to kill Cyllan the moment the rite was completed, and Tarod had to risk everything on the chance that, freed from the constraints put upon him by timelessness, he would be able to intervene before it was too late. *But if he failed . . .*

He spoke, hardly recognising his own voice. 'Let Cyllan kneel by the wooden plinth, and place the stone in her hands.'

Drachea spat. 'The stone stays where it is, and so does she!'

Tarod looked up, his eyes malevolent. 'Then there can be no raising of power. The procedures must be followed.'

The Heir Margrave flushed angrily, and looked about him. At his back the slab of black wood loomed out of the mist, and he dragged Cyllan towards it, kicking the Chaos stone along the floor as he went. Reaching the block he looked back at Tarod speculatively – then with a force that made her cry out, he wrenched Cyllan up on to the slab so that she lay staring at the invisible roof, her white throat exposed. Snatching the stone Drachea pressed it into her hands, then took up a stance over her and laid the blade of the knife lightly on her neck.

'I trust I make my intentions clear, demon,' he said to Tarod. 'If you attempt to trick me, however swift you are I'll cut her throat before you can touch me!' He smiled unpleasantly. 'When we play the game of Quarters at my home in Shu-Nhadek, both contestants know that to try to take advantage of such an impasse will gain them nothing.'

'We, too, play Quarters at the Castle,' Tarod replied. 'When impasse is reached, the game is at an end and there's no victor.'

'Then I'd suggest for Cyllan's sake that you don't attempt to change the rules.'

Tarod inclined his head. 'So be it.'

Lying on the unyielding, splintered wood of the block,

her eyes closed, Cyllan knew that they were lost. Tarod
had made his decision and had refused, foolhardily, to
sacrifice her. Now, she hadn't the will to defy him,
however much she might want to. He could overcome
any obstacles she put in his path, and she was helpless.

Inwardly she railed against the twist of Fate that had
brought them both to this. She should have let Tarod kill
Drachea . . . and she swore to herself that, if they both
lived – or if only she lived, which was too terrible a
thought to contemplate further – she wouldn't rest until
she had destroyed the Heir Margrave of Shu-Nhadek;
destroyed him and all he stood for. She hadn't thought
herself capable of such hate, but it burned in her now
like a black flame. And mingling with it suddenly came
the awareness of another mind, a raw emotion that
linked with hers and made her strong.

Tarod . . . She sent the mental call out softly and
heard his reply shape into silent words.

*Listen to me, love. I may not be strong enough – and to
conserve strength, I must act swiftly. Don't be afraid, and
don't resist me. Hold fast to the stone, let it guide you . . .
I'll be with you . . .*

His presence faded suddenly into a confusion of
images which resolved into a smoothness, a oneness,
like a dark, featureless sea. Cyllan felt her identity slipping away, and the stone in her hands seemed to pulse
hot, a living heart. She could still feel the touch of the
knife at her throat, but it was her only link with reality,
and a tenuous one. With a soft sigh she let her consciousness sink into the sea, merging with Tarod, with
the soul-stone, with infinity . . .

*It must be done quickly, for there would be no second
chance. Before, when he sought the Pendulum of Time,
he had travelled through the seven astral planes, gathering strength and will from each in turn, until at the last he
had cloaked himself in an iron strength that was sufficient
for his awesome task. But now there could be no such
precautions. There was but one way; savage and
instantaneous. And an ancient memory was unlocking*

deep within him, opening the doors that would take him to that brink . . .

Tarod reached out his will, and found the Chaos stone. It called him and he both loved it and loathed it; but he had to master it, or it would betray him. Every muscle in his body was locked rigid: all awareness of Cyllan, Drachea, the Marble Hall, faded away and was left far behind as he travelled onward and outward in spirit. The stone hung always ahead of him, just out of reach; he tried to breathe and found no air, and sweat soaked him as his hands clenched together into a sign which, in his human existence, he had all but forgotten.

It was drawing nearer . . . He felt its presence like some grim nemesis, and again reached his mind towards the stone, needing its power now at this crucial moment. An image flickered at the edge of awareness; darkness, rust, decay . . . he pursued it and it eluded him.

Darkness, rust, decay . . . remember what you once were . . .

And slowly, slowly, it materialised before him, a monstrous shadow amid dense, evil gloom. The shaft reared up into an unimaginable void, and the titanic bob hung still and lifeless, red-brown corrosion encroaching across its surface. The Pendulum, Time's arbiter in his own world, abandoned and rotting, a derelict hulk, frozen until the single bolt of power should wake it . . .

Tarod reached down, far down into the deepest recesses of his being. His strength was failing, the power of the stone slipping away from him – he must make the last summoning now, or be defeated. Drawing his psyche like an animal poising to spring, he felt a white-hot flowering at his heart as the force of the Chaos soul, momentarily freed from its crystal prison, flowed into him. For an instant he and the Pendulum were one – and Tarod flung himself forward with the full power of his will.

A high, thin shriek like a soul in torment split the darkness apart as the massive bob of the Pendulum gave under the forces that assailed it. The shaft quivered with a monstrous shock – and the Pendulum of Time swung forward, shattering the barrier between dimensions and hurtling into the world with a vast, clamouring boom that smashed Tarod back like flotsam against a tidal wave. Momentarily he glimpsed the tremendous bulk of the Pendulum bearing down on him, then it seemed to explode into a blinding, seven-rayed flash that blasted his senses. Walls rose from nowhere to meet him; he reeled, then his body crashed in a twisted contortion to the floor of the passage as all awareness was obliterated.

The scream that tore from Cyllan's throat was drowned by the awesome voice of the Pendulum, and the Marble Hall seemed to turn in on itself, the floor bucking and the walls shrieking a protest. She was flung from the block like a doll thrown by some giant, petulant child, and sprawled on the mosaic floor of the Hall with the reverberations of the great concussion still echoing in her head. Gasping like a stranded fish, she glimpsed through watering eyes the prone form of Drachea – then she was seized by a spasm of retching and doubled over as the muscles of her empty stomach contracted violently.

Tarod . . . Memory crawled to the surface of her mind at last. *Where was Tarod? Had they succeeded? And the stone* . . . Her hand clenched convulsively and she felt the sharp contours of the gem against her palm. In her confused state, all she knew was that she must reach Tarod, and she began to struggle upright –

'Ah, *no*, you bitch!'

Cyllan whipped round, and saw Drachea bearing down on her. He had recovered his senses more quickly than she, and was already on his feet, though unsteady. Horrified she started to run, heard footsteps at her back – and Drachea flung himself at her, bringing them both down with a jarring impact. Cyllan kicked out wildly, and a fist smashed across her face, stunning her; she slumped, and Drachea breathlessly grasped her shoulders as he got up, made to drag her back across the floor –

And stopped.

'*Aeoris!*' He dropped his burden and made the White God's sign over his heart. The robed figures – some twenty or thirty of them, women as well as men – who formed a circle around the black slab were all staring at him, their faces white and shocked and uncomprehending. One man, young and fair-haired, held a huge sword in both hands; now it fell from his fingers and clattered raucously on the marble floor as its wielder struggled to assimilate the sight that greeted him. A movement to one side alerted Drachea's attention and he was in time to see a much older man slide to the floor with a soft moan and lie motionless; then a woman began to scream, a long, wailing, featureless cry of hysteria.

Drachea and the fair-haired man continued to stare at each other, and all the words of triumphant greeting that Drachea had so carefully and frequently rehearsed died on his tongue. Then slowly, shakily, the fair-haired man moved round the block.

'What . . . ' He shook his head, dazed and unable to form the question.

Cyllan stirred. A livid bruise was spreading across her cheek where Drachea had hit her, and when she opened her eyes her vision wouldn't focus at first. Convulsively, she tried to move, and hands viciously pushed her down. She winced in protest – then realised that someone was staring at her. And as her sight cleared she found herself meeting the light brown, steady eyes of a man dressed in a sombre, funereal garb of purple and sapphire blue. Recollection dawned – she had seen that face, that garb, before, in the grisly tableau on the astral plane . . . and then she recognised the symbol at the man's shoulder; a double circle bisected by a lightning-flash. *Keridil Toln, High Initiate of the Circle – and Tarod's deadliest enemy* . . .

Drachea pushed sweat-dampened hair out of his eyes and made a creditable attempt at a bow in the fair-haired man's direction. 'Sir,' he said when he had breath enough, 'There's much explaining to be done, and I'd consider it my privilege. But . . . Aeoris be thanked for your safe return!'

Chapter 10

Keridil Toln stared at Drachea and Cyllan, stunned by the sudden and violent interruption of the Circle ritual. To him, it seemed that he had but a moment ago been standing before the execution block, ceremonial sword raised high above Tarod's head as he called down the White Flame of Aeoris to consume and finally damn the creature of Chaos. Then with no warning a colossal crash of thunder had split his mind, shattering the power he had built – and, reeling with the shock, he had opened his eyes to find his victim gone and two complete strangers fighting like wildcats on the floor of the Marble Hall. A combination of fury and fear of something beyond his comprehension filled him, and he snapped at Drachea, 'Who are you? And how in the name of all the gods did you get here?'

Drachea swallowed. 'Sir, there's no time for explanations now! Your enemy – the creature called Tarod – is at large, and must be found before he can wreak more havoc!'

Keridil's head snapped quickly round to look at the empty block. 'Tarod is behind this . . . ?'

Before Drachea could answer, Cyllan twisted in his grasp and cried out, 'No! He's lying, it isn't true! Listen to me – '

Drachea's bunched fist hit her hard on the side of the head and she collapsed to the floor. 'Quiet, you harlot!' Drachea spat. 'One more word from you and I'll kill you!'

Keridil's face darkened with anger, and he said furiously, 'I'll have no such behaviour here!'

Drachea stared down at Cyllan and said harshly,

'Even towards a woman in league with Chaos? This treacherous bitch is Tarod's paramour – and she has his soul-stone!'

'What?' The beginnings of comprehension dawned in Keridil's eyes and he moved to stand over Cyllan. 'Is this true, girl?'

Cyllan stared back with mute defiance, wishing that her mouth wasn't too dry to spit.

'She holds it in her left hand,' Drachea said, giving her a vicious shake. 'And there's only one way to make her give it up.' He touched the tip of the knife blade to Cyllan's neck.

'No.' Keridil raised a hand, forestalling him. 'I'll have no violence against her until I've heard the whole story.' His eyes met Drachea's again. 'You say Tarod is at large. Where is he?'

'I'm here, Keridil.'

Everyone turned, save for Cyllan who was held rigid with Drachea's blade still at her throat. Tarod walked slowly and unsteadily into the Marble Hall, barely able to stay on his feet. His sweat-soaked hair hung lank and his eyes were glazed with exhaustion; he had used the very last of his strength to call back Time, and its final draining had left him an empty husk.

Four men moved forward, weapons drawn, then hesitated, remembering how the sorcerer had dealt with such assaults before. Tarod smiled thinly and with an effort. 'Tell your friends they've nothing to fear, High Initiate.'

Keridil stared at him for a moment as though weighing his words. Then he said curtly, 'Bind him.'

One of the Adepts used the belt of his robe to tie Tarod's hands behind his back, then all four flanked him closely as he approached the gathering around the block, until at last he and Keridil stood facing one another.

Keridil said softly, 'So we failed to destroy you . . . I should have known you'd not admit defeat so easily.'

'Tarod, kill him!' Cyllan suddenly cried out. 'Kill him, before they – ' Her words choked off as Drachea

wrenched on her hair and raised his knife as though to
strike a death blow –

'No!' The harsh order came from Keridil, who swung
round and knocked the dagger out of Drachea's hand.
Cyllan tried to launch herself towards Tarod, but the
High Initiate caught her arm and dragged her back, his
other hand locking on her left wrist. He was taller and
heavier than Drachea, and she could only gasp a curse at
him as he tried to prize her fingers open.

'Let's see if the young man speaks the truth about this
girl . . . ' Keridil grunted as Cyllan ferociously resisted
him, then twisted her hand round so that he could get at it
more easily. Cyllan bit him with all her strength, drawing
blood, and two other Adepts stepped forward to pin her
while Keridil at last forced her clenched fingers to part.

The stone fell free, and Drachea pounced on it as
Cyllan shrieked a protest. He held it out to the High
Initiate, who handed the struggling girl into the safe
custody of the two Adepts before taking the stone – a
little gingerly, Drachea noticed – and weighing it in his
palm. His brown eyes looked with thoughtful speculation at the younger man for a moment, then he turned
his gaze once more to Tarod.

'We seem to have opened a veritable nest of vipers,'
he said evenly. 'But I think we hold the upper hand. We
have the Chaos stone – and Tarod, it would seem, is in
no condition to challenge us. Perhaps now someone will
explain to me what has happened here!'

Tarod said nothing, and Drachea stepped forward.
'Sir, I am Drachea Rannak, Heir Margrave of Shu
Province. I believe you are acquainted with my father,
Gant Ambaril Rannak . . . '

Keridil frowned. 'I know Gant . . . and you have his
look about you, I'll grant you that. But how, by all that's
sacred, did you come to be here?'

Drachea glared at Tarod. 'I've been held prisoner in
the Castle – just before the Spring Quarter-Day I was
brought here against my will – '

'*What?*' Keridil was incredulous. 'The Spring Quarter
Day is two months ahead of us – '

'No, sir! By now it could be two months or even two years past, for all I know!'

Keridil looked quickly at his fellow Adepts. Their faces were blank, and he said harshly, 'Explain yourself!'

Drachea took a deep breath. 'Time has been stopped. This Castle has had no true existence since the creature called Tarod used his demonic power to snatch it and all its inhabitants from the world and lock them in limbo.' He paused. 'I've seen the documents relating to his execution. He called on his Chaotic powers at the climax of your rite, and banished Time itself.'

Someone made a sound of shocked disbelief, and Keridil shook his head. 'No – I can't accept that such a thing's possible!'

'It's possible, Keridil.' Tarod spoke quietly, and when the High Initiate looked at him he saw a trace of the old malevolence in Tarod's smile. 'Did you think I'd meekly submit, at the last, to my own destruction?'

Keridil stared at him, and realised that he was telling the truth. The thought of such a titanic power in the hands of one man chilled him to the marrow, and he suppressed a shiver before turning back to Drachea.

'You say that Time here was halted – yet you and this woman found your way to the Castle. How?'

Drachea shook his head. 'I don't know, High Initiate – but I believe it was at *her* behest.' He pointed an accusing finger at Cyllan. 'She's a witch, a creature of Chaos herself – she duped me and lured me here, and since I arrived she's been plotting with that hellspawn against me and against all who stand for Light and Order.'

'Liar!' Cyllan spat. 'Traitor, betrayer!'

Keridil looked over his shoulder at her and said calmly, 'You'll have your turn to speak, girl. Until then, hold your tongue – or I'll cut it out.'

'She should die!' Drachea insisted vehemently. 'Isn't that the rightful fate of all Chaos's servants? She's a witch, a serpent – waste no time on her, High Initiate, kill her now!' His hand went to the sword at his hip.

'You've seen for yourself that she's in league with this demon – and after what they've done to me – '

'Touch Cyllan and I'll see you damned!' Tarod grated.

Keridil looked into Drachea's eyes and saw a feverish hunger for revenge. The young man was hot-headed; he had made his judgement and wanted to see it implemented. Cyllan's continued survival was of no personal interest to Keridil – and if she had indeed plotted with Tarod against the Circle, she deserved the severest penalty. But he wouldn't condone Drachea's idea of summary justice . . . and besides, Tarod's angry threat had given him a vital clue. Unlikely though it might seem, the girl was obviously important to him, and he was anxious to protect her – which placed the black-haired sorcerer at a singular disadvantage . . .

Drachea was launching into a further tirade against Cyllan, but a searing look from Keridil silenced him. The High Initiate crossed the floor to where Cyllan still fought her captors, and, taking a handful of her hair, tilted her head back until she was forced to look at him.

'It seems that Tarod sets great store by your safety,' he said, quite gently. 'We must see what we can do to accommodate his desire to protect you.'

'I don't want protection!' Cyllan fired back. 'I'm not afraid of dying, and I'm not afraid of you!'

'Brave words.' Keridil smiled. 'But we shall see how your courage faces up to your soul's damnation.'

His words provoked the response he hoped for. Tarod shook off the four men who held him and stepped forward. 'Harm her at your peril, High Initiate! If any hurt comes to Cyllan I swear I'll destroy you, destroy the Circle, destroy this Castle!'

The malign glitter was returning to his eyes, and Keridil guessed that he had regained some measure of strength. Not enough, yet, to make him dangerous; but nonetheless he'd be well advised to waste no time in sealing a bargain between them. He turned his back on Cyllan and walked with slow deliberation towards his adversary.

'Very well, Tarod. Your loyalty is to be commended,

and perhaps it can be used to the girl's advantage.'
His eyes hardened. 'Your fate is ordained. We have
the soul-stone, and we have the means whereby we
can finally see you annihilated. But you've already
proved yourself treacherous, and I intend to ensure
that you don't try to cheat us a second time.' He stroked
his chin, making a show of deliberation. 'The girl
will stay in the Castle, under close guard, while
preparations are made to repeat the ceremony which
failed tonight. If you submit to us, she won't be
harmed, and when you are dead she will be allowed to
go free. But if you attempt any treachery – just
one move which could be misconstrued – then I'll give
her to the Heir Margrave to take the vengeance he
craves.'

It was the same blackmail which Drachea had used to
force the return of Time, and Tarod's heart was bleak.
He knew Keridil well enough to realise that he'd have no
compunction in carrying out the threat – his was a cold,
calculated motivation, more dangerous than the personal score Drachea had to settle, and his choice was
painfully clear. If he agreed to Keridil's terms, he would
die; cruelly, agonisingly. And the Chaos stone would
remain in the world, a vehicle for Yandros's ambitions.
Yet if he did not, Cyllan's death would follow on the
instant.

He could carry out his threat; destroy Keridil and the
Circle, retrieve the stone and send them all to damnation. But he couldn't bring Cyllan back to life, and
without her there was no life worth the having. Damn
the world . . . he cared nothing for whatever evil might
threaten it if he allowed them to kill him. If Cyllan could
live, that was all that counted.

But Keridil had betrayed him once before . . . He
looked up, met the High Initiate's steady gaze.

'What safeguard do I have, Keridil? What guarantee
can you give that Cyllan will be treated kindly if I agree
to your demand?'

Keridil smiled reservedly. 'My word as High Initiate
of the Circle.'

The green eyes narrowed to slits. 'Your word is worth nothing!'

'Take it or leave it. You're in no position to barter – unless you'd prefer to see her die here and now?'

A sudden, violent scuffle broke out at Keridil's back, and he turned in time to see Cyllan wrestling with one of the Adepts. She was trying to wrench his short sword from its scabbard, and blood flowed from her palm where she'd cut it on the blade.

'Hold her!' Keridil snapped, furious as he realised what she was attempting. If she could have got her arm to the blade, she could have opened an artery and spilled her life-blood before anyone could stop her.

Cyllan fought as though demented, kicking and biting, but she was overpowered. One of the Adepts cut a length of fabric from his own cloak and bound her hand, and only when she was finally subdued did Keridil turn back to Tarod.

'Well?' he said. 'I'm awaiting your answer.'

There was nothing he could do but pray that Keridil would keep his word. The High Initiate had no personal grudge against Cyllan, and nothing to gain by harming her. It was a chance . . . and he had no choice but to take it.

Tarod nodded once, curtly. 'I agree.' Then his head came up and he regarded Keridil with a cold, cruel stare. 'But you must abide by your bargain to the letter. If any man lays hands on her against her will – '

'There'll be no abuse of her.' Keridil smiled unpleasantly. 'I doubt that any man living would want to bed with a servant of Chaos.'

Tarod ignored the jibe. 'And when I'm dead – ' He hesitated, hearing a stifled cry from Cyllan, 'she will be granted her freedom.' He looked at the girl. 'She has no power. She'll be no threat to you.'

'She will be released, unharmed.'

Tarod nodded again. 'I'll not clasp hands with you on the pact. But consider it sealed.'

Keridil let out a pent breath. For a moment he had wondered if Tarod's loyalty would waver in the face of the choice he had to make, but his first instinct had proved right. He gave silent thanks to Aeoris for the quixotic flaw in Tarod's character which would provoke him to sacrifice himself for the sake of a personal altruism – an admirable quality under some circumstances, but one which too often proved misguided. Yet as he turned away he was aware of a small worm of discomfort within himself that might have been a sense of shame. He dismissed it impatiently, then spoke to his fellow Adepts.

'There's nothing to gain from remaining here any longer. If our friend Drachea Rannak,' he bowed an acknowledgement in Drachea's direction, 'is right in what he has told us, we'll find the Castle in some disarray. There's much to put right, and a great deal of explaining to be done.' He gestured in Tarod's direction. 'Lock him up, and guard him heavily. I'll see about further precautions later.'

'And the girl?' one of the Adepts asked.

'Assign her a room, and see that she's comfortable. But have her watched.' Keridil turned to Drachea. 'Heir Margrave, if you would accompany us . . . ?'

Cyllan made no protest as the Adepts led her towards the silver door. Tarod stood motionless, watching her, and as she drew level with him she suddenly stopped and looked up.

'Tarod.' Her voice was frighteningly calm. 'I won't let this happen to you. I'm going to kill myself. I don't know how, but I'll find a way, I swear it. I'm not going to let you die for me.'

'No, Cyllan.' He tried to reach out to her, forgetting momentarily that his hands were bound behind him. 'You must live. For me.'

She shook her head violently. 'Without you, I'll have nothing to live *for*! I'll do it, Tarod. I don't want to stay in the world if it means . . . this.' She pulled her hand free from her guard's grip . . . embarrassed and uncertain, the man let it go . . . and touched his face gently. Tarod kissed her fingers, then turned his head away.

'She means it, Keridil.' His eyes were filled with pain.

'Stop her. You know what the alternative is.' And before Cyllan could speak again he walked away towards the vault beyond.

It was a strange procession that made its way up the winding stairs to the Castle courtyard. Keridil led, with Drachea hurrying eagerly at his heels, and behind them came Tarod under the close guard of four Adepts. Cyllan and her escort followed, while the remainder of the high-ranking Adepts brought up the rear.

As they approached the courtyard door, Cyllan felt a sense of foreboding at the prospect of what she might see. In a strange way she had come to love the Castle as she knew it; the eerie crimson light somehow befitted the ancient stone of its walls, and the stillness had a peace – albeit a dark, brooding peace – that was better suited to it than the bustle of human habitation. And there were memories here that brought tears to her eyes as she climbed the last few steps and emerged at last into the night.

The crimson glow had gone. In its place, a dense grey darkness hung over all; the pewter-green of a night sky lit by the reflection of one Moon, now setting below the high walls. A faint susurration caught her ears and she saw the glitter of water from the ornate fountain, catching and reflecting the dim starlight. The Castle stared down like a blind, indifferent beast, not a single lamp or torch showing in any of its myriad windows, and there was a smell of the sea on the night breeze.

Keridil drew a deep breath, tasting the air. 'Come,' he said quietly. 'There's an hour or more to go before dawn, by the feel of it. We'll gather in the hall.'

Silently they crossed the courtyard and mounted the steps to the main doors. As they walked through the Castle's corridors, footsteps echoing hollowly, Cyllan gazed about at her surroundings which had taken on a disturbing unfamiliarity. Every now and then she looked at Tarod, who walked ahead of her, and once she had tried to use her psychic skill to make mental contact with him, but he had not responded.

She felt bitter and miserable. With victory literally in their grasp they had been thwarted, and she blamed herself for the misplaced pity which had allowed Drachea Rannak to live. Now, nothing but an empty void lay ahead of her. But she would find a way to do what she had promised. And when she was dead, Tarod would be free to exact his revenge . . .

The doors of the dining-hall opened with a groan of protesting hinges, and Keridil surveyed the bare, deserted chamber. It shocked him deeply to see the Castle so empty and forlorn, and to assuage his uneasiness he became brisk.

'Rouse the servants, and have a fire lit,' he ordered. 'We'll send word to the kitchens for food to be prepared – oh, and if someone would be so good as to find my steward, Gyneth, I'll need him here.' He turned to regard Tarod. 'Find the securest place you can find for him, preferably on the lower levels where there are no windows. I'll finalise the arrangements later. And as for this girl . . . ' He stared at Cyllan thoughtfully for a few moments, then beckoned to her escort. 'Come with me.'

Cyllan looked back over her shoulder to see Tarod being hustled away through a side door before she was propelled up the stairs that led to the gallery above the vast fireplace. From the back of the gallery a small door led to another maze of passages and stairs, until finally they arrived at a narrow corridor on the Castle's highest floor. Keridil opened the door to a room at the far end, looked in and, satisfied, motioned for Cyllan's guards to bring her through.

The room was small, and sparsely though comfortably furnished. An alcove bed, a single upholstered chair, a small table, and heavy velvet curtains at the window. Underfoot were woven rugs, and Cyllan stood mute in the middle of the room, staring around.

Keridil crossed to the window and pulled the curtains back to reveal an iron mesh across the glass. Then he drew a knife from his belt and, with two quick strokes, severed the tasselled cords that hung from the curtains. Then he came to stand in front of Cyllan.

'Understand me,' he said, not unkindly. 'The window is barred, so that you can neither open it and jump out, nor break the glass and use it to slash your wrists. There are no curtain ropes by which you can hang yourself. And a lamp will be fixed at a point too high for you to reach, so don't think you can burn yourself to death either.'

Cyllan only glowered at him.

'Consider yourself a valued guest of the Circle,' Keridil went on. 'When we've done what must be done you'll be free to go, and if you choose to take your own life then, it's no concern of mine.' He paused before smiling in an attempt to thaw her ice-cold expression. 'Though I think it would be a tragic waste.'

'Think what you please,' Cyllan said venomously.

'I'll wish to talk to you when I've attended to some more urgent matters. I've yet to hear your side of this story, and I want to be fair.'

That brought a response. Cyllan laughed harshly. *'Fair?'* she echoed. 'You don't know the meaning of the word! Tarod has told me about you, High Initiate, and I want none of your idea of justice!'

Keridil sighed. 'Have it your own way. Perhaps in time you'll understand – I hope so. I feel no malice towards you, Cyllan – that is your name, isn't it? And I'll keep my side of the bargain I made with Tarod.'

She smiled unpleasantly. 'So will I.'

'I think not. Oh, you could try and starve yourself to death, true; but our physician, Grevard, has a few methods for dealing with such cases, and he can keep you alive and well whether you will it or no. So you'll live, and you'll prosper. If you understand and accept that now, we'll get along a good deal better.'

Cyllan walked to the window, shoulders hunched. 'I want to see Tarod.'

'That isn't possible.' Keridil returned to the door and spoke in a lowered voice to the two Adepts. 'Stay on guard outside until I can find someone to relieve you. Keep the door between yourselves and her unless there's some emergency – but whatever you do, don't let

her near your swords or she'll stab herself before anyone
can stop her.' He looked back at the small, defiant figure
by the window. 'She's a valuable hostage, although the
gods alone know how valuable she'll prove to be until it's
put to the test.' He clapped each man on the shoulder.
'Be vigilant.'

Cyllan heard the door close and lock from behind her,
and turned to find herself alone in the unlit room. Her
eyes had adjusted to the gloom, and she paced restlessly
around the chamber's perimeter, seeking something
which she could use to carry out her self-destructive
plan. She *wanted* to die; wanted to free Tarod from the
onus he had taken on himself – but Keridil had been
thorough, and there was nothing to hand. Even the bed
had no pillows, though she doubted if she could have
smothered herself anyway . . . she was thwarted.

At last, giving up the search, she moved to the bed and
sat down, clasping her hands in her lap and trying not to
let despair take hold of her. She wondered where they
had taken Tarod, how he fared, whether she would be
able to persuade them to let her see him, at least one last
time before . . . angrily she broke the dismal train of
thought. She wasn't going to admit defeat, not yet.
While he lived, there was still hope. And she'd find a
way to spark and fuel that hope . . . somehow, she'd
find it.

The words were brave – as Keridil had said – and yet
in the solitude of her prison they rang hollow. Cyllan
fought to keep them alive in her mind, but it was an
unequal struggle. And at last, giving in to the feelings
that lay buried far deeper within her, she began to cry,
softly, helplessly, as the first pale glimmer of dawn
showed beyond her window.

*   *   *   *   *

The dining-hall was a maelstrom of activity, gladdening
Drachea's heart as he sat, washed and refreshed and
replete from a good breakfast, at a bench near the huge
grate. A fire burned brightly, banishing the chill, and he

was surrounded by men and women who all morning had plied him with questions, praise and gratitude until he was giddy with their approbation.

A few paces from him, the High Initiate sat at a separate table with the senior members of the Council of Adepts – or at least, those who had survived their ordeal. It had been an unpleasant revelation to find that the return of Time had taken its toll. Seven of the Castle's older inhabitants, including the high Adept who had collapsed in the Marble Hall, were dead; their hearts incapable of withstanding the shock as the Pendulum had heralded its presence in their world like an earthquake. Others were in need of medical attention, and Drachea had glimpsed Grevard, the Castle's physician and by all accounts the most skilled of his kind in the world, harassed and weary, attending to one emergency after another, aided only by two assistants and a horse-faced, elderly woman in the white robes of a Sister of Aeoris.

An hour ago, a party from Shu Province had come thundering through the Maze that held the Castle aloof from all but the Initiated, and among their number had been a white-faced messenger from the Margrave himself, bringing a plea for the High Initiate's aid in finding his missing son and heir. Keridil had immediately despatched a rider to carry the good news to Shu-Nhadek, and imagined that the Circle could anticipate a personal visit from Gant Ambaril Rannak by return. The prospect didn't please him – he remembered Drachea's father as a fussy martinet, and with so much confusion to put to rights he could do without unnecessary interruption. But there were formalities that couldn't be avoided – Drachea must remain at the Castle at least until a full session of the Council of Adepts could be convened so that he could present his evidence in the proper manner. And, although he had to admit privately that he didn't entirely like the arrogant young man, Keridil acknowledged that Drachea was due some formal recognition of the service he had rendered.

He had now had the chance to hear the full story, at

least in outline, and it formed a disturbing picture. But
for Drachea's intervention. Tarod would have regained
possession of the soul-stone, and the thought of the
havoc he might have wreaked then was appalling. Now
though, Tarod was safely locked away in one of the
Castle's cellars, and as soon as Grevard had finished his
work and had a chance to rest, he'd be detailed to see to
it that the right precautions were taken.

Keridil pinched the bridge of his nose between forefinger and thumb as the papers before him blurred. He
badly needed sleep himself, but there could be no
respite yet. Messengers were arriving seemingly every
minute, and he was only just beginning to realise the
extent of the alarm that had been raised throughout the
land at the Circle's unexplained disappearance. Spring
was advancing; there had been plenty of time for
rumours to arise and grow, and it would take a
concentrated effort to spread the word that all was
now well. A report must be made to the High Margrave,
to the Matriarch of the Sisterhood; there were fears
and speculations to be allayed . . . the list seemed
endless and the prospect of completing the work
daunting.

But, somehow, it would be done . . . and Keridil was
warmed by the thought that, in his task, he'd have the
support of one person in particular. She sat near him
now, in a comfortable chair a little behind his, and when
he turned his head she smiled radiantly at him.

Sashka Veyyil looked as serene and as beautiful as she
had done at the moment when he had kissed her and left
to begin the rite that would send Tarod to destruction. In
a velvet gown with a fur-trimmed jacket over it to ward
off chill, and with her rich auburn hair carefully dressed
and ornamented, she was composed, self-assured, utterly the aristocrat, and Keridil felt proud of her. Time
and again Sashka was proving her worth to him . . . she
noted matters for his later attention, gave orders on his
behalf, fended off the constant flow of messengers from
the South. And later, when the work was done, she
would come to him in his private rooms and let him taste

again her pliant, hungry sweetness as she soothed away the ravages that the day wrought.

Sashka herself was intrigued with the turn events had taken. Listening as Drachea Rannak's story was told, she had at first been wide-eyed with disbelief – but Keridil had confirmed enough of the facts to convince her. She congratulated herself on her own strength of character in taking the return from Timelessness in her stride – despite the fact that her only experience of it had been the shock which had racked the entire Castle as the Pendulum broke through from limbo – and now was speculating on the realisation that Tarod was still alive. Once, when he was seventh-rank Adept of the Circle, she had been betrothed to him . . . but when the truth about him was revealed, she had thankfully had the wisdom and foresight to change her allegiance before any slur could be cast upon herself. And the gods had rewarded her by bringing her to the attention of a man whose rank Tarod could never have hoped to match; a man, moreover, whom she found far easier to cajole and persuade to her will. As the High Initiate's paramour she had an undreamed-of status . . . yet deep down something still rankled, and would continue to rankle while Tarod lived. She despised him, hated him . . . but she couldn't entirely forget him. And because of those feelings, she wanted him to suffer. Before, she had had the satisfaction of believing that he still loved her and yearned for her; but now it seemed that matters had taken a different turn. The young man from Shu-Nhadek had spoken of a girl from the Eastern Flatlands who had taken it into her head to champion Tarod's cause, and who was now shut away in the Castle. It would be interesting, Sashka thought, to find out a little more about her . . .

She leaned forward and touched Keridil lightly on the shoulder. He turned, smiling at her, and lifted her fingers to his lips to kiss them.

'You must be weary, love,' he said solicitously.

She shook her head. 'Not weary, no . . . but a little stiff with sitting for so long. Will you forgive me if I leave you for a while?'

'Of course.' He kissed her hand again. 'See if there's anything your mother and father are in need of. And convey to them my regards.'

'Of course.' She slid gracefully out through the narrow aisle between tables, and made her way at leisure along the length of the dining-hall. An elderly woman in a Sister's robes, passing by, gave her a withering look, but Sashka ignored the scrutiny. Sister Erminet Rowald had been one of her Seniors at the West High Land cot where she was officially a Novice, and was at no pains to hide her dislike of Sashka. Sashka cared nothing for the good opinion of Sister Erminet, considering her a shrivelled and frustrated harridan who vented her jealousy on those more fortunate than herself. And she had nothing to fear from the old woman, for if all went well, it was unlikely she would ever need to return to the cot to continue her studies.

Holding her head at an arrogant angle, she brushed past Sister Erminet, then glanced around the hall. Almost at once she saw her quarry seated among a group of younger Initiates whom he seemed to be regaling with a story. Drachea Rannak was a celebrity, but Sashka felt sure he could be persuaded to give her a little of his time . . .

She walked up to the table and said, 'Pardon me . . . '

Drachea looked up, and was startled to see the beautiful, patrician girl who all morning had sat beside the High Initiate smiling down at him. He didn't know her name or rank, but her face alone was enough to arouse his interest. He rose, and bowed.

'Madam. I'm afraid I haven't had the privilege of an introduction.'

His manners were impeccable . . . Sashka inclined her head. 'I am Sashka Veyyil, of Veyyil Saravin, Han Province.' She was gratified to see that the clan name was familiar to him. 'I believe you are Drachea Rannak, Heir Margrave of Shu?'

'At your service.'

The Initiates had also risen, and were watching the exchange with interest. Sashka turned her haughtiest expression on them.

'Gentlemen, the High Initiate has asked me to convey some information of a confidential nature to the Heir Margrave. If you would excuse us . . . ?'

The ploy was effective, and with expressions of courtesy they moved away, leaving Sashka and Drachea alone. She sat down, gesturing graciously for him to do likewise, and with no preamble said, 'I was most interested by your story, Drachea – may I call you Drachea?'

He flushed. 'I'd consider it an honour.'

'Thank you. I particularly wanted to know more about the girl whom you tell us was in league with Tarod.'

'Cyllan.' He didn't quite understand her; what possible interest could she have in Cyllan's well-being?

Sashka ignored his obvious puzzlement. 'Can you tell me something about her?' she asked sweetly. 'Her background, her past – I gather that she's from the Great Eastern Flatlands.'

Drachea studied his folded hands for a moment, then said with unexpected venom, 'Cyllan Anassan is nothing but an ignorant, gutter-bred slut who has yet to learn her place!'

Sashka raised her perfect eyebrows. 'Indeed? You are – vehement, Drachea.'

He smiled. 'Then I must crave your foregiveness. I have a personal score to settle with both that trull and her lover; memory of what I have suffered because of them makes me . . . indelicate in my expression of those feelings.'

She reached out and laid a hand on his arm. 'It must have been a great ordeal for you.'

Drachea's eyes burned eagerly. 'Yes . . .' *Gods, this girl was exquisite . . . a match for any man with the courage to try her . . .*

'You said,' Sashka went on, not removing her hand, 'that she was Tarod's lover.'

'Lover, paramour, harlot – ' Suddenly Drachea grinned wolfishly. 'Whichever term you choose, he was fool enough to sacrifice himself for her sake.'

'So he loves her . . . ?'

'Love? I don't know if a soulless vermin like Tarod can know the meaning of the word. But he made a pact for her safety with the High Initiate, so he values the little witch in some way.' He paused. 'May I venture to ask if you yourself knew Tarod?'

'Oh,' Sashka said carelessly, 'we all knew Tarod to some degree. I simply wanted to clarify one or two points that Keridil was unclear on.' She rose, amused by the haste with which he followed her example and gratified by his obvious anxiety to please her. 'Thank you, Drachea. You've been most helpful.'

The chances of being able to speak alone with her again were slim, Drachea knew, and so before she could turn away he said, keeping his voice casual, 'This room grows a little overbearing – perhaps you'll permit me to escort you into the fresh air for a while?'

She regarded him. 'Thank you, but no.'

'Then perhaps some refreshment?'

Sashka smiled sweetly. 'I think that to save embarrassment, Drachea, I should tell you that I am shortly to wed the High Initiate.'

She had flattened him and dismissed him with a single sentence, and as he began to stammer out an apology she gave him a small, almost amused bow and walked away. The boy must be arrogance itself if he thought he was worthy of her . . . he was well mannered and pleasant enough, but her prospects went far beyond a mere Margravate.

'Sashka!' A voice spoke behind her, and she turned to find her father, Frayn Veyyil Saravin, at her elbow.

'Father.' She kissed him. 'Is Mother rested?'

'Well rested, yes – she'll join us a little later.' He nodded in the direction of Drachea, who had sat down again disconsolately. 'I saw you talking with the Heir Margrave. He seems a very worthy young man.'

'I'm sure he is,' Sashka said disinterestedly.

Frayn pursed his lips. 'I hope you weren't rude to him. He looks downcast, and I know what your tongue can be like.'

'Oh, *Father*! Of course I wasn't rude. He made a

polite and proper advance, and I simply told him that I am betrothed to the High Initiate.'

Her father's jaw dropped. 'But you're not!'

'Keep your voice down; people are staring at us.'

His face purpled apoplectically and he repeated in a strangled whisper, 'But you're *not* betrothed!'

'Not officially yet, perhaps, but . . . ' Sashka shrugged. 'It's only a matter of time, Father. Would you therefore want me to squander myself in some dalliance with a provincial Margrave's son?'

Frayn frowned darkly. 'Sometimes, Sashka, your arrogance astonishes me! If Keridil hasn't yet asked for your hand – '

'But he will.' She planted a kiss squarely on her father's forehead to pacify him, then, turning, tossed her hair back. 'Sashka Veyyil Toln – it sits well on the tongue, don't you think? And don't try to tell me that it won't be the best alliance our clan has ever had!'

Frayn Veyyil Saravin sighed exasperatedly, but knew better than to argue with her. In truth he was deeply proud of what his daughter had achieved. He'd never felt easy with her original plan to marry that black-haired Adept; he'd always felt there was something wrong with the man, and his opinion had been vindicated. But the High Initiate was another matter. As a man of rank, Keridil was second only to the High Margrave himself; as an individual he was personable, trustworthy, had already proved himself a worthy successor to his sire, Jehrek. Frayn could hope for nothing better.

He caught his daughter's arm and squeezed it fondly. 'Then if you're so set in your own mind, Sashka – and I'm not about to gainsay you – take an old man's advice, and return to the High Initiate's side. That's a woman's proper place, and he'll appreciate you the more for it. Ask your mother if you doubt me.'

Sashka gave him one of her most beatific smiles, laced with a good measure of pity. 'Dear Father !' she said, and kissed him soundly again before moving quickly and gracefully away in the direction of the hall doors.

Chapter 11

Cyllan's face was white and pinched with strain as she walked between her two guards through the Castle's corridors. In the three days which had passed since her imprisonment she had seen no one, save the escorted servant who brought her food and returned after an interval to take away the untouched plate, and she had spent almost all her time sitting at the window of her room, gazing out over the courtyard in the vain hope of gaining some clue to Tarod's whereabouts.

She had to admit – though it rankled – that her captors had been scrupulous in keeping their part of the bargain for her life. No one had made any attempt to molest her; indeed, they'd treated her with punctilious courtesy, even kindness. She'd stonily rebuffed their efforts, ignoring the delicacies sent to tempt her and refusing to respond to any attempt at conversation. But she knew that this impasse couldn't last forever. Keridil Toln had anticipated and thwarted any effort she might make to kill herself; unless she found another way to break the deadlock, then the grim pact would be fulfilled, and Tarod would die while she remained a helpless hostage. And she had little time left . . .

She had tried to make mental contact with Tarod, but always her efforts failed, and she imagined that the Circle had taken precautions – perhaps by drugging him, perhaps by magical means – to prevent any communication. And so, with every other way she could think of barred to her, Cyllan had concluded that she had but one choice . . . to plead with the High Initiate for Tarod's life.

Knowing what she knew of the enmity between Keridil Toln and Tarod, and the reasons behind it, she felt that a mouse in the jaws of a cat would have a better chance of survival than she had of convincing the High Initiate to heed her. But when, on her third morning of captivity, two Initiates came to confer with the guards outside her door and then announced that she was to be brought before Keridil for an interview, she felt a spark of hope. She had nothing to lose by making her plea save her self-respect, and that counted for nothing.

And so she went with them willingly enough, her heart pounding with nervousness as at last they halted outside the door of the High Initiate's apartments.

'Come.' Keridil answered the knock crisply, and Cyllan was led in.

The room was lined with shelves crammed with papers, and dominated by a large table behind which Keridil Toln sat. Cyllan's spirits sank as she realised that, contrary to her hopes, he wasn't alone. Two elderly men flanked him, one fussing with a scroll, the other staring at her with something resembling distaste. Grevard, the Castle's physician, stood by the window, and on a chair nearby sat a girl of about Cyllan's own age; a patrician, beautiful yet cold-eyed girl with rich auburn hair. From Tarod's description Cyllan recognised Sashka Veyyil immediately, and forced herself not to react outwardly to her first sight of the woman who had been his chief betrayer.

'Cyllan.' The High Initiate's quiet voice broke into her angry thoughts and, dazedly, she turned to look at him. He smiled reassuringly. 'Please, sit down. There's nothing to fear.'

She gave him a withering glance, and seated herself in the chair he indicated.

Keridil clasped his hands and rested his chin on them. 'We want to give you the chance to tell your side of this unhappy story,' he went on. 'And I hope that you'll look on us not as enemies, but as friends. There's a great deal you don't yet know about the events that have led up to today, and it's the merest justice that you should under-stand fully.'

Cyllan stared back at him. 'Where is Tarod?'

Sashka Veyyil coughed delicately, and amusement flickered in her eyes. 'Tarod still lives,' Keridil said. 'And he has kept his side of the bargain we made. I hope we can persuade you to do the same.'

She ignored the remark. 'I want to see him.'

'I'm sorry; that's impossible. As I explained to you before –'

'Keridil . . . ' Sashka rose gracefully and came to stand at his back, her hands resting lightly on his shoulders. 'Please, let me intercede for this girl. Surely, under the circumstances, she can at least be permitted to see Tarod one last time before he dies?' She looked at Cyllan and her eyes were malicious.

'That's a kind thought, love.' The High Initiate was clearly unaware of any ulterior motive, and Cyllan wondered how he could be so blind to Sashka's duplicity. But if the patrician girl anticipated any reaction from Cyllan to her deliberate reminder of Tarod's impending fate, she was disappointed. Cyllan's expression remained stony. But inwardly the taunt was like a knife-thrust . . . and she knew she couldn't plead for Tarod's life in the presence of such an audience. Thought of Sashka's mockery, the cold hostility of the two old men, the physician's hawk-like scrutiny . . . she couldn't do it; the words would wither on her tongue, for her cause would be lost before she could begin.

Keridil glanced at Sashka, who had resumed her seat. 'We'll see what can be arranged . . . but there's time enough yet. I want to hear your story, Cyllan – and I want you to understand that we of the Circle are not your enemies. We want to help you, in any way that we can.'

The look he received for his well-intentioned remark was one of such searing contempt that it brought an involuntary flush to his face. Collecting himself, he tried again.

'Perhaps you'd begin by telling us how you came to the Castle? We've heard Drachea's side of the tale, of course, but – '

'Then you don't need mine,' Cyllan said.

'But we do. If justice is to be done – '

'Justice?' She laughed harshly, then: 'I have nothing to say to you.'

One of the elderly Councillors leaned across and cupped a hand to Keridil's ear. 'If this girl chooses to be difficult, High Initiate, I see little point in wasting time on her. We have, surely, all the information we need from the Rannak boy? And it must be said that any evidence she presents to us can at best be considered – ah – dubious.'

Keridil looked obliquely at Cyllan, who sat mutely defiant on the chair opposite him. Despite her allegiances he felt sympathy for her, and couldn't help but admire her steadfastness. He believed – and he didn't think it a rash assumption – that if she could be persuaded to speak at all, she'd speak the truth. And he wanted to hear what she might have to say.

He lowered his voice to a whisper. 'I take your point, Councillor Fosker, but I've a suspicion that the girl's reticence stems more from fear than hostility, and perhaps it's little wonder. With respect, I suggest that we'd have better hope of success if I were to interview her privately.'

The elderly Initiate looked at his fellow Councillor, who had overheard Keridil's words. The other man grunted. 'If the High Initiate thinks it wise . . . '

'I do.'

Fosker nodded. 'Very well. Though I must say I've little faith in the notion, Keridil.'

Keridil smiled thinly. 'I trust I can prove you wrong.'

Cyllan watched with wary suspicion as the two old men made a great fuss of escorting Sashka to the door. She had caught the flash of resentment in the girl's eyes when Keridil asked her to leave, but Sashka made no overt protest. When they were gone, Grevard levered himself up from his reclining posture against the wall.

'Do you wish me to leave, too?' he inquired.

Keridil inclined his head. 'I'd appreciate it, Grevard.'

The physician paused as he drew level with Cyllan,

and stared critically at her, eyes narrowed. 'I'll want to
see you again before much time has passed,' he told her
sternly, then looked at the High Initiate. 'She's not been
eating. We'll have to do something about that, if she's to
stay in good health. As soon as I've had a chance to catch
up on some sleep, I'll see to it.'

'Thank you.' Keridil watched until Grevard had
closed the door behind him, then sat back with a sigh. A
flask of wine and several cups stood near him on the
table; he poured two cups and set one in front of Cyllan.
She ignored it, and he said, 'You won't compromise
yourself by drinking wine with me, Cyllan. I need it, and
I don't doubt you do, too. Oh – and pay no heed to
Grevard's brusque manner; it's merely an affectation.
Now . . . do you feel a little better without a plethora of
strangers to stare at you?'

He smiled encouragingly, and a little of Cyllan's lost
confidence returned. He was attempting to bridge the
gulf between them, and if she could bring herself to
unbend towards him – or at least appear to – she might
stand a slender chance of winning a sympathetic
hearing.

She nodded, and picked up the cup. The wine was
light and crisp, and made her realise how thirsty and
hungry she had become. She drank more, and Keridil
nodded approval. 'That's better. If we can get along
without hostility, I think this will be a happier interview,
don't you?'

Cyllan stared down into her cup. 'I didn't ask for this
interview,' she said. 'And it's true that I've nothing to
tell you that you don't already know.'

'Maybe so. But I still want to hear the story from your
own lips. I want to be fair to you, Cyllan. You've done
nothing to harm the Circle, not directly; and it saddens
me to think that you consider me your enemy.'

The wine, on an empty stomach, was going quickly to
her head. Cyllan looked up, blinking, and found herself
voicing the thoughts she'd intended to keep to herself.
'But you're Tarod's enemy, High Initiate. That makes
you my enemy, also.'

'Not of necessity. If you only understood what lies behind this affair – '

'Oh, but I do. Tarod told me the whole story.' She paused. 'He also told me that you were once his closest friend.'

Keridil shifted uncomfortably. 'Yes, I was. But that was before I discovered the truth about him.'

'So you changed your allegiance without a second thought, and friendship and loyalty counted for nothing.' She smiled humourlessly. 'It's little wonder that Tarod is so bitter!'

The barb went home, and not for the first time Keridil felt echoes of shame.

Cyllan drained her cup and held it out for more. She was beginning to feel reckless, and although she knew the wine was dangerously loosening her tongue, she no longer cared. Keridil refilled her cup without comment, and she took another mouthful before setting it down.

'Tarod was loyal,' she said savagely. 'He was loyal to the Circle, and the Circle betrayed him.'

Keridil shook his head. 'You don't understand. Whatever Tarod told you, it's a twisted image of the facts.'

'Tarod isn't a liar!'

Keridil sighed. This was proving harder than he'd expected – he had hoped that by using reason he could persuade her round to his point of view, but the task was looking more hopeless with every moment. Cyllan had no thought for her own safety, no fear of reprisal – her loyalty to Tarod was ferocious, and the High Initiate realised that, however deluded she might be, she loved him. In the face of that, how could he make her accept that Tarod had to die?

'Cyllan.' He laid both hands on the table, palms down, in a conciliatory gesture. 'Please. You must listen to me, and try to see matters through my eyes.'

Anger flared in her look and she retorted, 'Must I, Keridil? You'll not see matters through mine – why should I make concessions where you refuse them?' She picked up her cup, drank again, beginning to feel giddy and a little sick. 'You hold me hostage while you make

preparations to murder Tarod. Yes, *murder*,' she added
as Keridil made to protest. 'It's nothing less than that!
He's never been tried for his supposed crimes – oh, I too
saw the documents! Instead, you simply condemn him to
death because it's *expedient!*' She spat the last word
viciously. 'If that's your justice, I want none of it!'

Keridil's mouth tightened as anger began to replace
the nagging guilt. 'As you're so ready to cry murder,' he
snapped back, 'then perhaps you'll spare a thought for
the fellow Initiate whom Tarod slaughtered in cold
blood, in this very room! Do you condone that?'

Cyllan smiled icily. 'Do you mean the man who killed
Themila Gan Lin?'

'That was an accident!' Keridil got up and paced
across the room, furious. The girl was twisting his every
word to her own advantage; he felt as though he were
the prisoner and she the inquisitor. Abruptly he turned
on his heel, pointing a finger at her. 'Your lover isn't
what you so fondly believe him to be. Damn it, he isn't
even *human!* Consorting with Chaos is a crime that
hasn't been heard of in this land for centuries, but you,
with your ridiculous romantic notions, have committed
that crime! The rightful punishment is death, and if it
wasn't for the fact that we need you as a safeguard, I'd –'
He stopped, realising that he was losing his temper, and
took a deep breath. 'No. I didn't mean that; I'm sorry.'

'You shouldn't be,' Cyllan replied, her eyes intense.
'Kill me. I don't care.'

He shook his head. 'I won't harm you. When Tarod is
dead, you'll go free with no stigma attached to you. I'll
keep my bargain – and the gods know I don't bear you
any personal ill will! But while you persist in this insane
determination to champion an evil-doer, I can't help
you, either.'

She turned her head away. 'I don't want your help. I
don't want anything from you – except Tarod's release.'

'You know that's impossible. One day, with Aeoris's
grace, perhaps you'll understand.'

The storm of rage was past now, leaving Cyllan
drained and weakened; and the wine was sapping her

will to fight. At this moment she would have gone down on her knees before the High Initiate and pleaded for Tarod's life, but she knew with a dismal certainty that it could avail her nothing. Keridil was implacable in both his hatred and his resolve, and nothing she could do or say would sway him. She felt despairing tears start in her eyes and struggled to hold them back, but Keridil saw the tell-tale glitter on her lashes. He moved towards her, knowing he couldn't comfort her and yet urged by an uneasy conscience to try, but was interrupted by a tentative knock at the door, which opened to reveal an elderly woman in the white robes of a Sister of Aeoris.

'Oh . . . forgive me, High Initiate.' Her bright, sharp eyes focused on Cyllan. 'I'm seeking Grevard, and I was told I'd find him here.'

Keridil forced himself, with an effort, not to snap at her. 'He was, Sister Erminet, but he's gone. Can I be of service?'

'It's simply that your captive should be attended to before he has a chance to recover from Grevard's last dosage,' the old woman told him briskly. Cyllan's head came up sharply and she stared at the Sister, receiving a frown in return. 'I understand it's a precaution that's better not neglected,' Sister Erminet went on. 'But if Grevard is occupied elsewhere, I'll gladly see to the matter myself.'

'Yes, yes.' Keridil was impatient, annoyed by the interruption and only thinking to rid himself of its perpetrator as quickly as possible. 'Please do as you think fit, Sister. Grevard will be grateful for your help.'

'Very well.' The old woman looked at Cyllan again, speculatively this time. The girl's face was frozen, as though she'd seen some ancestral ghost, and the snippets of hearsay she'd gleaned in the Castle over the past few days began to make a pattern in Erminet's mind. She pulled her gaze away, nodded with quick courtesy to the High Initiate, and went out.

Cyllan stared at the closed door until Keridil's hand on her shoulder startled her back to the moment. She

jerked away, her face venomous. 'She's going to Tarod
. . . where is he? What have you done with him?'

'He's safe, and he's well enough.' Keridil spoke
shortly.

'I want to see him!'

'And I've told you, you can't!' Sister Erminet's unwitting interruption had brought the High Initiate near the
end of his tether. 'Don't you think I've enough to do
without this miserable affair to contend with as well? I
brought you here in the hope that I could make you see
sense – I'm beginning to feel I'm wasting my time!'

Cyllan bit her lip hard to stop the tears. 'We disagree,
High Initiate, on what is sense and what is not. And if
you think you'll persuade me to change, you're wrong!'
She looked at him, accusation and contempt in her eyes.
'Unlike many others, I abide by my word of honour!'

Keridil's lips whitened and he strode to the door,
flinging it open and shouting for Cyllan's escort, who
were waiting a little further down the corridor. They
hastened in, and he made a dismissive gesture in
Cyllan's direction.

'Get the girl out of my sight,' the High Initiate said
coldly. 'She's had her chance – I'm wasting my time with
her!'

He wondered if Cyllan would have some last word,
even some plea, as she was led away. Even now he'd
help her if he could . . . but her face remained whitely,
icily expressionless, and she didn't so much as glance at
him. The door closed behind her and, angry and frustrated, Keridil lifted his own wine cup and drained its
contents in a single draught.

The steep stairs that led down to the Castle's cellar level
were uneven, and the unsteady light of Sister Erminet
Rowald's lantern made the way more tricky still,
especially with the added encumbrance of her bag of
herbs and philtres. She had, however, refused all offers
of help with her task, convincing Grevard that she could
quite well manage alone.

The physician had been thankful enough to have this

particular duty lifted from his shoulders, and his willingness suited Erminet's purpose perfectly. Past the wine
stores, he had told her; then the third cellar on the right.
A troublesome task, and a time-consuming one . . .
Erminet's nostrils caught the mingled smells of musty
casks, old, spilled wine, stale air and earth; and wryly
she wondered how any living being could be expected to
prosper in such unsavoury surroundings.

Reaching the bottom of the flight she set off briskly
along the dark, narrow passage. At her heels a small
silver-grey shape trotted, blending with the shadows,
and as she approached the third door Erminet paused to
look down at the cat which had followed her from the
main wing.

'Little Imp.' Affection softened the old woman's normally acerbic tone, and the cat raised its tail high.
'There'll be no tidbits for you down here!'

The cat uttered a self-satisfied chirrup in reply, and
ran on ahead. It was one of the numerous offspring of
Grevard's own pet which lived half wild in the Castle,
and for some inscrutable reason it had lately taken to
following Erminet wherever she went, attaching itself to
her like a familiar. Erminet was amused and gratified by
its partiality for her company; she had dubbed it the Imp
– not entirely in jest; many people mistrusted these
creatures' telepathic abilities – and, when no one was
about to observe, spoiled it with food from her own plate.

The cat, prompted by that same telepathic instinct
which enabled its kind to communicate in a primitive
way with human emotion and intent, stopped at the
appropriate door and looked at Erminet with inquiring
interest. The door was unguarded – Keridil had taken
more arcane precautions – and Erminet drew the key
Grevard had given her from her pouch. It turned stiffly
in the lock, and she entered the cellar beyond.

She couldn't see him at first. Her lantern-light was
poor, and the shadows played tricks with the eyes. But
as she turned from relocking the door carefully behind
her, a figure moved in the deeper darkness on the far
side of the chamber.

He was sitting on what looked like a pile of worn and discarded rugs, his back propped against the damp wall, and even in this dim light Sister Erminet could see the sardony in his green eyes. Grevard had been lax – the drugs he had administered had clearly worn off, leaving the captive in full possession of his faculties. But perhaps that could be to her advantage . . .

Tarod spoke suddenly. 'A Sister of Aeoris to administer to my needs. I'm honoured.'

Erminet sniffed. She had encountered this man – or demon, or whatever he was – before, under similar circumstances; and although they had crossed swords, she felt respect and a strong measure of sympathy for him. Heretical though the thought might be, the old Sister strongly disapproved of the kind of treachery which had brought Tarod to this pass, and disliked seeing a once proud individual so reduced. And she had stronger views still on the nature of girls like Sashka Veyyil . . .

'Adept Tarod.' She crossed the room towards him, aware that he hadn't as yet recognised her. 'I see Grevard's nostrums have done nothing to dull your tongue.'

The green eyes narrowed momentarily, then Tarod laughed a tired, throaty laugh. 'Well, well; Sister Erminet. I didn't expect this particular wheel to come full turn again.'

She set her bag down on the floor and stared at her patient. Gaunter than ever, unshaven, hair lank, clothes dirty . . . and the tell-tale lines of tremendous strain on his face. The sight of him affected her, and to combat such unwarranted feelings she was brusque as she said, 'You look no better for your respite.'

'Thank you. Did Grevard send you specifically to entertain me with your observations?'

'Grevard is too busy attending to what they tell me is the aftermath of your handiwork,' Erminet retorted. 'I've simply been detailed to see that you are, and remain, stupefied.' She frowned at him. 'It would appear that someone has been neglecting their duty.'

Tarod sighed. 'Perhaps they also tell you that I don't present a threat to anyone here, drugged or no.'

This was what Erminet had suspected, and it fitted with the slowly emerging picture. 'I heard some rumour of a bargain between you and the High Initiate,' she said, busying herself with the contents of her bag. 'But it sounded unlikely, and no one took the trouble to explain it to a withered old apple like me, so I dismissed it as nonsense.'

'It's true.' Tarod eyed the concoction she was preparing with distaste.

Erminet stopped her work and regarded him thoughtfully. 'Then I've misjudged you. I hadn't imagined you would accept defeat so easily.'

She saw the answering flicker of pain in his eyes, and the cat, which until now had sat peacefully washing itself, paused to give a little cry of protest as though its telepathic senses had picked up some powerful emotion. Then Tarod said curtly, 'I have my reasons, Sister.'

'Ah, yes . . . ' Erminet licked her lips. 'The girl . . . '

The sudden change in the atmosphere was palpable as Tarod sat upright, every muscle tense. 'You've seen Cyllan?'

She had expected a reaction, but not one so vehement; and to hide her surprise she feigned indifference. 'Cyllan; so that's her name. Yes, I've seen her, not an hour ago in fact. That is, if she's that frail-looking child with the pale hair and peculiar eyes.'

Tarod tensed visibly. 'Where is she?'

'Your anxiety betrays you, Adept.' Erminet eyed him with sour amusement, then abruptly relented. 'She was with the High Initiate, in his study – and yes, I recall the circumstances under which Sister-Novice Sashka Veyyil was granted a similar interview.' She remembered Cyllan's face, the agony of rage in her eyes; remembered, too, the argument on which she'd shamelessly eavesdropped before knocking at Keridil's door. 'You need have no fears there,' she added. 'Had the girl been armed, I imagine I'd have found the High Initiate with a knife through his heart.'

Tarod closed his eyes. 'Then she's alive, and she's well
. . . I thought Keridil might betray our pact . . . '

Erminet looked at him beadily. 'Your pact? How is
the girl involved in that?'

Tarod met her gaze, weighing her up in an attempt to
decide whether or not he should say more. This old
woman had tried to be kind to him once, in her peculiar
way; despite his contempt for Circle and Sisterhood, he
liked her – and, though in many ways the two women
were poles apart, something in her character reminded
him of Themila Gan Lin.

He said, softly, 'Cyllan is the crux of our pact, Sister.
She is a hostage against my good behaviour. If I should
fight against the fate the Circle has ordained for me,
Keridil will have her executed the moment I'm dead.'

Erminet was clearly shocked, and her customary sour-
ness gave way to sudden humanity. 'But she's no more
than a child! The High Initiate surely wouldn't – '

'She has consorted with me. Any Province Margrave
would hang her for less.'

That was true enough . . . no one, now, was in any doubt
as to Tarod's real nature, although in the privacy of the
cellar Erminet found it hard to believe she was talking with
a demon of Chaos. She should have been afraid of him, but
wasn't. To her, he seemed little more than a victim of
circumstance . . . and that was a condition she understood
all too well, even if the memory was forty years old . . .

'So you're prepared to die, in order to save her life . . . '
she said.

'Yes.'

Gods, she thought, was the age-old pattern repeating
itself yet again? She licked her dry lips. 'And when
you're gone?' she asked.

'Keridil has promised that she'll go free.' Tarod's eyes
darkened. 'I have no choice but to trust him. At least this
way she'll have a chance.'

Erminet doubted the wisdom of speaking what was in
her mind, but couldn't break her lifelong habit of brutal
honesty. 'Are you sure it's a worthwhile sacrifice,
Tarod? You were betrayed once . . . '

For a moment she thought he'd strike her, but the
anger in his eyes died and he only said, 'I'll not
be betrayed a second time, Sister Erminet. Not by
Cyllan.'

No . . . recalling again what she had overheard,
Erminet believed that he was right. She sat down, discarding her potions, and her face was suddenly drawn
with an uncomfortable mingling of confusion and pain.
Tarod's love for that strange little outland girl, his readi-
ness to lose his own life in order to save hers, moved her
deeply, awakening emotions which she'd thought gone
and forgotten. She sat motionless for what seemed a
long time, tormented by her thoughts, and only looked
up when Tarod's hand touched her arm.

He was smiling, faintly but kindly. 'Forty years ago,
you said, Sister. But you haven't forgotten what it is to
love, have you?'

The face of the youth, doubtless by now aged and
withered, as she was, who had spurned her and for love
of whom she had tried to kill herself, was suddenly sharp
and clear in Sister Erminet's inner eye. The cat ran up to
her and tried to climb on to her lap, making small sounds
of distress. Tarod stroked its head. 'I'm sorry. I
shouldn't have spoken.'

'Nonsense.' Erminet forced her voice to take on its
old brusqueness. 'Ghosts can't harm anyone . . . ' She
laughed, sharply and artificially. 'I haven't cried since I
entered the Sisterhood, and I'm not about to start now;
not for myself, at any rate.' She looked at him, her eyes
over-bright. 'But that doesn't stop me wishing there was
something I could do for you and that girl.'

Tarod leaned back. 'You could do something for me,'
he told her. 'If you will.'

'What's that?'

'See to it that she lives, and prospers.'

Erminet blinked. 'Should she not?'

'She's sworn to take her own life. She tried once,
when we were first captured, to stop the bargain being
made. I believe she'll try again, and I don't trust Keridil
to prevent her.' He hesitated. 'If you can do that for me,

Sister, you'll have my lifelong gratitude – ' He stopped, and laughed at the irony of his own words. 'No; that's worth little enough. Say instead, my thanks.'

It was a modest enough request; and if the High Initiate, or her own Senior, the Lady Kael Amion, disapproved, they might do as they pleased. The thought gave Erminet a *frisson* that was almost pleasant.

'I don't need your thanks,' she told Tarod. 'I'll do as you ask, because I don't want to see two lives wasted where one would suffice.' Abruptly she smiled. 'There; now you have a sour old woman's reasoning to comfort you.'

'You're not as sour as you like to pretend.'

'You've only seen my weaknesses. But you'll see my strengths unless you take this.' Bending, she picked up the concoction she had been mixing. 'Enough, Grevard says, to render you unconscious, so that the rest of us can sleep easy in our beds tonight.'

Sleep would be a blessing . . . its oblivion was far preferable to the long, solitary hours, the agony of waiting, of wondering. Tarod took the tiny silver cup. 'A bargain, then, Sister Erminet.'

'You're too fond of making bargains for your own good,' she said with an attempt at acid humour. 'But yes. I'll keep my promise.'

She watched as he drank the cup's contents, then took it from him and said, 'I'll speak to the girl. I'll tell her you still live – though whether she'll trust me, I can't predict. Were I in her place, I wouldn't believe a word anyone said to me.'

Tarod gazed thoughtfully into the middle distance for a few moments, then smiled wryly. 'Give her a message from me, Sister. Ask her if she remembers her first visit to the spire . . . and remind her that I took nothing she was unwilling to give.' His green eyes met Erminet's. 'She'll understand.'

His look made the old woman feel something akin to shame. She nodded, hiding behind a brisk defence. 'I'll tell her.'

Tarod leaned forward and kissed her brow. 'Thank you.'

Erminet smiled thinly. 'I never thought I'd live to be kissed by a demon from Chaos. That would have been a tale to tell my grandchildren, had I had them.'

The Imp, silent as a shadow, followed her out of the door. Tarod heard the key grate in the stiff lock, then tried to make himself comfortable as he waited for the drug to take effect. Although the cellar was almost pitch-black without Sister Erminet's lantern, he could see well in darkness. Not that there was any prospect worthy of attention . . .

He lay back, ignoring the irrational flicker of hope within himself. Hope was a pointless exercise. One old woman, however kindly her intentions, could do nothing beyond bearing a message; and during the stultified miasma of the days since his capture Tarod had consciously chosen to resign himself to what fate had decreed for him. He had quenched the fires of hatred and vengeance and fury, deliberately deadening all feeling and all thought of the future. If Cyllan were to survive, he could do nothing more.

His eyelids felt heavy, and he wondered if he would dream. If he did, likely as not they'd be fragmented dreams, meaningless; as everything else was meaningless now. Tarod closed his eyes. Briefly, in his inner vision, he thought he saw a many-faceted stone, glittering like a mocking eye, and from far away someone – or something – seemed to call his name with an odd urgency. Lapsing into narcotic-induced confusion he ignored the call, thrust it away. It faded and was gone, and he lay still in the silent darkness of the cellar.

Chapter 12

The Sun's last light had flared above the Castle wall in brief glory, and the first of the two Moons would soon show its pockmarked face in the East. Torches flickered in the courtyard; groups of people crossed the flagstones and an occasional burst of laughter drifted up to where Cyllan sat at her window staring out, unmoved, at the activity.

She was exhausted by her argument with Keridil Toln, dazed with the effects of the wine, and yet she couldn't sleep. She had had her one chance to plead for Tarod, however remote the hope of succeeding – and her temper had got the better of her. She'd failed him; and now it seemed there was no other path left.

Fury welled up in her, a bitter railing against the Circle's justice which could condemn one of their own to a terrible death without a qualm. The ceremony involved fire, Tarod had told her; a supernatural fire that burned more than flesh – abruptly Cyllan put a hand to her mouth, forcing back a sick spasm as hideous images sprang unbidden and unwanted into her mind. When the spasm faded she was shaking uncontrollably with the rage of impotence, and with a desperate fear that made her want to scream aloud. Tarod would die, while she sat by in this dismal room, helpless until she should be granted her freedom – and then it would be far too late.

But there was nothing she could do. Keridil had seen to it that she couldn't kill herself and thereby negate the bargain Tarod had made; Tarod would not abandon her as she had pleaded with him to do; the Circle was intractable. Her only choice, now, would be to go down on her knees and pray to Aeoris for a miracle.

211

But Aeoris was unlikely to take pity on one who interceded on behalf of Chaos. More likely the White Lord would rejoice at Tarod's destruction, and, not caring that the thought was blasphemous, Cyllan felt her anger focusing on the god himself. She'd find no help there – better to turn to Yandros, Lord of Chaos, who had claimed kinship with Tarod . . .

Yandros. The idea shocked her and chilled her blood. But surely Yandros, of all beings, wouldn't be willing to see Tarod die, if it was within his power to intervene?

She tried to dismiss the idea as insane. Tarod himself had rejected his links with Chaos, banished Yandros, and spoke of him as a deadly enemy. Yet, Cyllan reasoned, there could be no enemy deadlier than those who were bent on Tarod's annihilation. Perhaps Yandros couldn't aid her; perhaps he'd not choose to. But with every other door closed to her, she had nothing left to lose.

She rose, still shaking, and for a minute or two stared at the slowly rising Moon, which glared back like a malevolent eye. How could she reach out to such an entity as Yandros? The travelling Sisters who had cate-chised the children of her home village taught that Aeoris heard the most humble of petitions; that a pure heart and spirit was enough to ensure the great god's benevolence. Cyllan's heart and spirit were ablaze with a black flame of fury – and petitioning Chaos was a very different matter. By turning to Yandros, she would betray her fealty to the White Lords and damn herself in their eyes. But to reject any possibility that gave her even the most slender thread of hope was a greater betrayal still . . .

She lowered her gaze to look across the courtyard, beyond the splashes of torchlight and the groups of people, to the brooding bulk of the Castle's North spire where Tarod had had his eyrie. Her eyes misted as she thought of him, and she said softly, as though whispering to an intimate companion.

'*Tarod . . . forgive me. There's no other way left.*'

Turning, Cyllan sat down cross-legged on the floor.

By tradition all prayers to Aeoris were made while the supplicant faced the East. As Yandros was Aeoris's sworn enemy it seemed fitting that his petitioner should look to the West, and she quelled an instinctive sense of sacrilege as she set her back to the point of Sunrise. Closing her eyes, she tried to form an image in her mind, recalling the vision she had seen in the Marble Hall when the defaced statues had manifested their true origin to her. Sharp-etched features, beautiful but cruel; mouth smiling in mockery, eyes slanted and knowing . . . the picture wavered, eluding her. She concentrated harder, her breathing harsh and loud in the room's quiet, but still the image wouldn't form.

If only she had her stones . . . they would aid her, enable her to focus her mind and her desires. But her pouch lay somewhere in the Castle beyond her reach, and she didn't dare ask for it lest her motives should be suspected. Cyllan's eyes flickered open and she sighed. She was no sorceress – her skills were limited enough even with the precious pebbles; without them she could do nothing.

Then her gaze lit on a bowl which her jailers had earlier placed on the table. In an effort to tempt her appetite, and thus avoid the unpleasant necessity of calling on Grevard's services to force her to eat, Keridil had sent a dish of Prospect Province fruits from the Castle's precious supply. She had ignored them, despite their rarity and the fact that she had never been offered such delicacies in her life; but now she realised that the fruit would contain stones . . . and even a substitute might suffice if her own pebbles were unavailable.

Quickly she snatched the bowl from the table and broke one of the fruits apart. At its centre was a hard, wrinkled stone the size of her thumbnail . . . discarding the pulp, Cyllan set to work on the other fruits until she had a collection of some dozen seeds. Few enough, but they might be all she needed . . . She licked juice from her fingers – she was sorely tempted to eat one or two of the ruined fruits, but, having heard of the importance of fasting for magical rites, rejected the impulse – then wiped her palms on her skirt and gathered the stones into her hands.

This time, when she closed her eyes the darkness behind her lids was absolute. And moments later she felt the first prickling sensation at the back of her neck, suffusing through to her scalp. Quelling her excitement she focused her mind, feeling the rough, hard contours of the stones between locked fingers. Hardly aware of what she did, her lips formed a name, whispered it into silence.

'Yandros . . . '

Her hands were hot, blazing hot; the stones like ice by comparison . . . and a face was beginning to form in her inner eye, taking shape and life . . .

'Yandros . . . Yandros, hear me. Lord of Chaos, hear me . . . '

The room's stillness deepened and the air seemed to cloy around her, as though a vast, dark curtain had descended. Cyllan could feel her pulse pounding suffocatingly throughout her body; her hands burned, the stones burned . . .

'Yandros, Lord of Night, Master of Illusion, hear my prayer . . . ' The words were coming swiftly, unconsciously; she no longer chose them but they were suddenly there on her tongue, as though an ancient memory had awoken. 'Yandros, though you were banished, your servants still remember. Return to me, Master of Chaos, return from the realm of Night and aid me!'

It was as though the stones had caught fire in her hands. Cyllan cried out with pain and shock, and the fruit-seeds scattered across the floor as she flung them from her with a violent reflex, rocking back. And at the same moment a dull, echoing crack reverberated in her ears.

'Aeoris!' The oath, though inappropriate, was involuntary, and Cyllan's eyes snapped open.

The gloomy walls of her room surrounded her, unchanged. The stones lay on the floor, forming a random pattern which she couldn't even begin to interpret, and as the shock of their burning heat faded she realised miserably that she had failed. Yandros either could not or would not answer her call, and all she had experienced was the delusion of a fevered and desperate imagination.

She rose, ignoring the scattered stones, and walked to the window. The first Moon was high now – odd; for it seemed that only a few minutes had passed – and its scarred face, near full, mocked her chagrin. Down below in the courtyard the torches had been extinguished and the giant rectangle was empty.

Or was it? Cyllan looked again, and realised that there *were* figures in the court . . . but none of them was moving. Each stood like a statue, as though a single moment in their lives had been frozen and preserved. They looked faintly ridiculous, some with one foot raised in the act of walking, one with an arm held high in some extravagant, arrested gesture . . . and the fountain was no longer playing . . .

Instinct warned her in the split second before she heard the softly emphasised sound of a latch clicking behind her. She whirled round –

The outlines of a door which hung suspended in the middle of the room were flickering out of existence, vanishing even as she glimpsed them. He stood before her, and with a flowering of panic she realised that she faced something so far beyond humanity that the concept threatened her sanity. Tall, gaunt, gold hair flowing over his high shoulders, he could have been Tarod's twin – but for the fact that there was no trace of mortality in the beautiful, cruel features, that the smile on his lips made a mockery of human knowledge and ambition. His narrow, feline eyes were opalescent, their colour shifting and changing in the deceptive Moonlight.

Cyllan backed away until her spine jarred against the window-frame. She was struggling for breath, but there was no air to fill her lungs. The being – demon or god, whatever he might be termed – stepped with graceful ease towards her, and as he moved, the outlines of the room warped and twisted as though they and he could not exist in the same space. Cyllan sensed a vastness surrounding him, an alien dimension that clashed with the natural laws of this world. He was here, and yet not here – this was but one manifestation of an entirety whose essence, if once glimpsed, would send her screaming over the brink of madness. This was *Chaos* . . .

Propelled by a combination of terror, awe and a fearful reverence, Cyllan dropped to her knees. '*Yandros* . . .'

'Rise, Cyllan.' Yandros's voice was like silver, yet the mellifluence only thinly disguised an implacable menace. Shaking, she forced herself to obey, though all her instincts protested, and he walked slowly in a circle around her, his unhuman eyes critical and the small smile still playing on his lips. At last he stopped before her once more, and she felt his scrutiny like a physical pain as he gazed down at her.

'So you've chosen to damn yourself by calling on me.' Yandros spoke with careless amusement. 'I commend your courage. Or your foolishness.'

Cyllan shut her eyes tightly and reminded herself that Tarod had not feared this being. She had summoned Yandros of her own free will; if he proved a harsh master, she must take the consequences. With an effort she forced herself to speak.

'I had no choice. They mean to kill Tarod, and I can't help him.' Taking a grip on her fear she looked up into his ever changing eyes. 'You're my only hope.'

The Chaos Lord bowed sardonically. 'You compliment me. And why do you believe that it might be in my interests to save a pledged servant of Aeoris?'

He was challenging her to prove herself; as perverse as she might have anticipated . . . Cyllan licked dry lips. 'Because you once called Tarod "brother".'

Yandros continued to regard her for a few moments, and she didn't dare to imagine what he might be thinking. Then he stepped forward, and laid a hand on her head. She flinched inwardly from the cold touch of his fingers, feeling her stomach turn over, but forced herself not to give ground.

'And you are willing to jeopardise your very soul in

order to save him . . . that's a very noble sentiment, Cyllan.' The silver voice was disdainful still, but something akin to affection had crept into the tone. 'It would seem we chose well when we brought you to the Castle.'

Shocked, she stared at him uncomprehending. 'You – you *brought* me – ?'

Yandros laughed softly; a sound that made her shudder. 'Let's say we were instrumental in your arrival. Exiled we may be, but some of the forces that serve our cause still remain in this land.'

Suddenly she understood. 'The Warp . . . '

'As you say: the Warp. Even Aeoris and his corruption-ridden brothers couldn't entirely rid the world of their old enemy.' Yandros smiled. 'And when we also find a mortal willing to serve us, our ambitions begin to take form . . . and that pleases us.'

So she had been a dupe, a tool, manipulated by Chaos from the beginning . . . Cyllan began to feel sick at the thought of that implication and recalled what Tarod had told her of the Chaos Lord's machinations. Yandros wanted to challenge the rule of Order, to snatch the land back into the maelstrom from which Aeoris had saved it so many centuries ago. And he saw them both as pawns in the greater game.

But however evil Yandros might be, whatever the fate he planned for the world, Cyllan no longer cared. He alone could help her to save Tarod from annihilation, and no price was too great to pay for that.

The Chaos Lord regarded her, clearly aware of her thoughts. At last, almost gently, he said,

'What is it that you ask of Chaos, Cyllan?'

She took a deep breath. 'Help me to save Tarod's life!'

He inclined his head. 'And how would you envisage that I do it? Should I bring a legion of demons to raze the Castle and consign its inhabitants to the Seven Hells? Would you condone that, to save him?'

Cyllan met his searing gaze. 'If need be.'

'Ah; then you *are* worthy of Tarod.' To her astonishment she saw respect lurking beneath the amusement in Yandros's expression before his thin lips quirked downwards. 'But, much as the thought appeals to my sense of justice, it can't be done. We are in exile, Cyllan. Our powers in this world are a poor shadow of what they once were. I have been able to reach your mind and speak with you – but I can bring you no direct aid.' He smiled again, thinly. 'Only Tarod had the power to open the way to us, and he chose instead to break the pact we had made and turn his back on the old allegiance.'

Cyllan felt her throat constrict. Yandros's mercurial nature was twisting again, offering her hope one minute, despair the next. He had made no promise to help her . . . could it be that, even now, he'd refuse?

She said, her voice unsteady: 'I can't deny that. But I hope – I believe – that in spite of it, you won't abandon him now.'

Yandros's look was enigmatic. 'You place a childlike faith in our loyalty.'

'I have no other choice.'

The Chaos Lord considered. 'And if I am persuaded . . . what would you have me do?'

She had thought, and she saw only one way. 'Kill me,' she said harshly. 'Break the hold that the High Initiate has over Tarod. When I'm dead, there'll be nothing to stop him from taking revenge.' She hesitated, then her eyes met his and she added with heartfelt emphasis, '*Please* . . .'

'No.' Yandros held up a graceful hand, forestalling her protest. 'To free Tarod by destroying you would be a waste. I could do it – and would, if it served my purpose – but there are better ways, and you're of more use to us while you live. But understand this; if Tarod is also to live, you must serve us, and serve faithfully. Look at me.'

She had cast her gaze down, but now, at his bidding, looked up again. Yandros's eyes had turned black, and mirrored in them she saw images that made her recoil with a deep-buried, atavistic horror. *Havoc* – a wild, howling insanity of impossible colours, tormented shapes, shrieking faces – the stuff of Chaos itself, roiling from the implacable black eyes turned towards her, ready to explode upon the world in insane pandemonium.

'You see what you must pledge yourself to serve.' Yandros's voice was cruel, unrelenting. 'Make your choice!'

Panic seized her; the revulsion of a hundred generations who had sworn fealty to the peace of Order; the inherited memories of thousands who had died to wipe the plague of Chaos from the world; the horrors of eternal damnation. To ally herself to this being would be to betray all she had ever known . . . yet without Yandros, Tarod would die . . .

Slowly, shaking violently, Cyllan dropped to one knee before the Chaos Lord.

Yandros smiled. He had foreseen enough to confirm the judgement he had made in sending the Warp that had snatched this girl from her old life; in moving the fanaani, who owed no debt to Order, to save her from the sea; in manifesting a part of himself in answer to her call. And if she succeeded in her task, she alone would hold the key to Tarod's future . . . and the future of the Chaos realm. She would be a valuable servant . . .

'There can be no turning back,' he said softly, with satisfaction.

Cyllan didn't raise her head, but he saw her nod almost imperceptibly before she whispered, 'What must I do?'

'You must find the stone . . . and restore it to its rightful owner.'

She looked up quickly. 'How can I do that?'

'By using the cunning and the guile that have already stood you in good stead. We can help you – we have no power to intervene directly, but our . . . influence . . . may still be felt in the right quarters.' Abruptly the smile faded from his expression. 'It *must* be done, Cyllan. Only Tarod has the power to call us back to the world, and then only when the soul-stone is in his possession once more. But if the stone remains in the hands of these worms of Order, they'll not rest until its essence is bound and destroyed.' His proud, sinister face now held no

trace of kindness, but was cruelly venomous. 'If the
stone is destroyed, Tarod's soul will be destroyed with it.
And that is not what you want . . . is it, Cyllan?'

'No . . . ' she whispered.

Yandros raised a hand, pointing at her heart. 'Then, if
you desire him to live, I charge you to return the Chaos
stone into his keeping.' His eyes flashed with a white-hot
fire. 'Don't fail me – for if you do, you'll lose far more
than Tarod's life. Your own gods damned you when you
called on Chaos for aid; but if you fail Chaos now, your
soul will find no comfort in our realm!'

His tone struck to the marrow of her bones; a chill
certainty that brought back the horrifying images she
had seen in his eyes. She couldn't answer; she was too
appalled by the enormity of the bargain she had made.

Yandros seemed to relent a little and his eyes quieted,
strange colours moving once more in their slanting
depths. 'Do your work well, and you have nothing to
fear,' he said more softly. 'And don't think that you're
entirely alone. There is one here in the Castle who will
help you. When you meet that one, you'll know.'
Abruptly he caught her left hand, turning it palm up.
'You cannot summon me again, Cyllan. I've answered
you this once, and I can do no more. But I leave you with
my blessing.' And with a gesture that seemed to mock
human courtesy, he kissed her wrist.

It was as though a burning brand had been touched to
her arm. Cyllan screamed with pain, jerking violently
backwards – and as she fell, a fire-hot blast of air ripped
through the room with a muffled, thundering explosion.
The walls bulged out, tortured by a force they could
barely contain – Yandros vanished, and Cyllan slammed
back against the window before slumping in a dead faint
to the floor.

The servant who ran to fetch Keridil received a tongue-
lashing for his pains, but the High Initiate had no choice
but to leave the small celebration taking place in his
rooms and follow the man to the Castle's South wing. He
had cut off the garbled explanation, aware only that the

girl from the Eastern Flatlands had somehow managed to do herself some mischief in spite of his best precautions, and as he hastened towards her room he felt sick to his stomach at the thought of what might happen if she died. They could keep the news from Tarod easily enough, until the time came for his execution. But he wouldn't go willingly to destruction unless it was proved to him that she still lived and prospered. And if she did not . . .

Keridil swallowed back the bile of fear as he approached the locked door.

To his relief, his peremptory knock was answered by Grevard. The physician looked irritable rather than worried – surely a good sign, Keridil told himself nervously.

'Ah – Keridil.' The physician scowled at him. 'I told those damned fools there was no need to send for you!'

Keridil looked past him to the bed. Hard to make the girl's figure out; she seemed to be unconscious, and a white-robed woman whom he recognised as Sister Erminet Rowald was tending her, dogged by two servants who seemed to be more of a hindrance than a help.

'She's alive?' the High Initiate demanded tersely.

'Oh yes; she's alive.'

'What happened?'

Grevard shook his head. 'I don't know. We thought all possible precautions had been taken, but it seems we were wrong.' He nodded towards the bed. 'One of the servants found her huddled senseless in a corner when he brought her food. I thought at first she'd collapsed from malnourishment – you know how she's been refusing to eat – but I changed my mind when I saw her arm.'

'Her arm?'

The physician shrugged. 'Go and look at it for yourself.'

Frowning, Keridil crossed to the bed, nodding a brief acknowledgement to Sister Erminet as he drew near. Cyllan lay still and white-faced, and at first she seemed unmarked – until Keridil saw that the left sleeve of her dress had been rolled back, exposing a ferocious crimson mark that ran from her wrist almost to the elbow.

He looked quickly back over his shoulder at Grevard. 'That's a burn mark . . . '

'Precisely.' The physician grimaced. 'And if you can explain how she came to have fire in her hands, you're a better man that I am!'

'It's impossible. Unless she conjured it out of thin air – '

'Well, I've yet to hear a better theory. Does she have any power?'

Keridil mused, then shook his head. 'I doubt it. Besides, if she had a talent, the Sisterhood would have snapped her up years ago; isn't that right, Sister Erminet?'

The old herbalist eyed him enigmatically. 'Naturally, High Initiate.'

'Then if she didn't inflict it on herself, who could have . . . ' Keridil's voice trailed off as an unpleasant possibility occurred to him. *Tarod*. If the girl had somehow contacted him, persuaded him to break the bargain, he might have tried to use his power to kill her from a distance, in order to save himself. And almost succeeded . . .

He turned on his heel. 'Grevard, is that demon Tarod still under lock and key?'

'Of course.' The physician looked surprised.

'And have my instructions to keep him drugged been followed to the letter?'

Now Grevard looked affronted. 'If you're suggesting that I – '

'High Initiate.' Sister Erminet's voice cut in on Grevard's angry retort, and Keridil turned to see that she had straightened and was facing him, arms akimbo, like an admonishing tutor. 'The Adept Tarod is at this moment lying in his cell, oblivious to the activities of the world around him. I administered the narcotic with my own hands, and watched him drink it with my own eyes.'

Nonplussed, Keridil made a pacifying gesture. 'I'm sorry, Sister; I didn't mean to imply negligence. And Grevard – I apologise.'

The physician shook his head. 'It was a reasonable enough assumption under the circumstances.'

Again, Erminet spoke up. 'There is, of course, one other possibility,' she said indifferently. Both men stared at her and she continued. 'It may not be a burn mark at all. The stone of the walls is rough – if the girl really wanted to kill herself, she might have tried to graze her wrist to the point where the artery was severed.' She smiled pityingly. 'She couldn't have succeeded, of course, but who can fathom the reasoning of the desperate? And if she rubbed it hard enough, the grazing could produce a mark very akin to a burn.'

Grevard looked sceptical, but to Keridil the old woman's theory seemed as credible as any other. 'Thank you, Sister,' he said. 'You may well have solved our conundrum . . . but the question remains as to how we keep her from doing herself further harm. She can't be constantly watched – we haven't the servants to spare.'

'Perhaps I can be of use, High Initiate?' Erminet said, as though the idea had only just occurred to her. 'Grevard has little need of me now that his list of emergencies has been dealt with, yet he himself is still busy enough. It would be no hardship for me to divide my time between two patients.' She smiled ingenuously. 'I believe I could ensure that this girl doesn't have the opportunity for any further mischief.'

'I don't know.' Privately, Keridil wasn't taken with the idea; he had caught much of Sashka's dislike of the acerbic Erminet, although he had to admit that he could find no fault with her skills. 'I feel we've already imposed too much on your good offices, Sister, by detaining you at the Castle this long. You must surely have more vital work at your Cot?'

'Nothing that can't wait.' Erminet told him briskly. 'If truth be told, sir, I find great satisfaction in being in a place where I can *use* my skills rather than merely *teach* them. I feel that I am being of practical help.' She beamed at him.

Cornered, Keridil looked at the physician. 'Grevard?'

Grevard and Erminet had reached a tacit understanding

whilst they worked together, and the physician had developed a respect for the old woman. 'If the good Sister is willing to stay, I don't mind admitting that I'm grateful for her assistance. Especially with Tarod . . . ' His face tightened perceptibly. 'Don't take me wrong; I share the views of the entire Circle where he's concerned. But it isn't easy to face a man and prepare him for execution when I once knew him as a friend.'

Keridil's face remained impassive, though the physician's words went sharply home. 'Very well, then,' he said, making the best of it. 'If Sister Erminet is willing to take responsibility for both our prisoners, so be it.' He bowed to the old woman. 'Thank you, Sister.'

She cast her eyes down modestly. 'An honour, High Initiate.'

Grevard clapped Keridil on the shoulder. 'And now you can return to whatever tedious business was interrupted by this little drama!'

In the furore over Cyllan, he'd all but forgotten . . . Keridil's face broke into a broad grin. 'It was far from tedious, I assure you!'

'Ha!' Misinterpreting, Grevard burst out laughing. 'I should have known! Your cheeks are as red as a Sunset, my friend! Give the lady my personal apologies!'

Keridil held up both hands. 'Grevard, you've a mind like a cesspit!' Then his expression sobered, though he was still smiling. 'This news interrupted a celebration, and – you may as well be the first outside her clan to know, for the announcement will be public in the morning. Sashka Veyyil and I are to wed.'

Sister Erminet's head came up sharply, then as quickly she bent back to her patient. Grevard stared at Keridil in delighted astonishment for a few moments, before delivering a punch to the shoulder that almost sent the High Initiate to the floor.

'So you've finally asked her! Well done, Keridil, well done! There'll be a celebration as great as the Inauguration itself!'

Keridil flushed again. 'Thank you. I appreciate your good wishes.'

'You'll have the good wishes of the world, my friend, make no mistake. A beautiful girl; beautiful . . . and a just reward for you both after all that's happened. Your father would have been very happy.'

The two men headed towards the door, still talking, and Erminet paused to watch them go. Her bird-bright eyes were unfathomable, but one corner of her mouth was lifted in an expression that faintly suggested contempt.

Chapter 13

When Cyllan began to sweat and struggle in delirium, and scream out an alien-sounding name, Sister Erminet bustled the serving-woman sent to assist her out of the room, placating her with the assurance that this was only to be expected in such a case and she could cope perfectly well. Once alone with her patient, she turned to her collection of herbs and prepared a draught whilst listening intently to the panicked ramblings from the semi-conscious girl.

Yandros . . . she'd heard the name before somewhere, and recalled a connection with the condemned Adept. And that tied in with her suspicions concerning another apparently insignificant discovery she'd made in this room. A bowl of fruit which had been broken and pulped to no obvious purpose . . . and the fruit stones, scattered in an apparently random pattern on the floor. Stone-reading, she knew, was a form of geomancy peculiar to the East – so it seemed that the girl had been playing with fire, and – quite literally – had burned herself.

Cyllan's ranting had by now degenerated into wordless mumbles, and when Erminet looked at her again her eyelids were fluttering spasmodically. Consciousness was returning . . . good. The old woman carried her prepared draught to the bed, sat down and drew Cyllan's head forward.

'Here, now. Drink this; it'll unlock your muscles and calm your mind.' She held the cup to the girl's lips, watched with satisfaction as a good mouthful went down. 'That's the way . . . oh, Aeoris preserve us, girl, you're spluttering it everywhere; look at that mess!'

Cyllan had gagged on the drink, but Erminet's involuntarily sharp reprimand seemed to pierce her clouded mind. She batted feebly at the cup, then her eyes opened.

They looked at each other, Erminet curious, Cyllan hostile and wary. She had been dreaming monstrous dreams, haunted by Yandros's coldly sardonic face – and the shock of waking to find herself confronted by a Sister of Aeoris dismayed her.

'Well, are you simply going to stare at me as though I were your grandmother's ghost?' Erminet demanded. 'Or have you something to say for yourself?'

Cyllan lay back, but her gaze didn't leave the old woman's face. 'Who are you?' she demanded huskily.

'Sister Erminet Rowald. I see they don't teach good manners in the East,' Erminet retorted tartly.

Cyllan scowled. 'I didn't ask you to tend me.'

'Indeed not; but *someone* did, and so I'm here whether you like it or no.' She brandished the cup. 'Finish your drink.'

'No . . . you're trying to drug me.'

She was as perverse and obstinate as Tarod, Erminet thought, and sighed. 'It's nothing more than a simple restorative. Here; I'll show you. I don't doubt my need's greater than yours anyway!' She drank half the cup's remaining contents and held it out once more. 'Now are you satisfied?'

Dubiously, Cyllan took the cup from her and finished the draught. It tasted pleasant enough; spiced wine with a hint of honey and other, subtler flavours, and her stomach was glad of it. Erminet, meanwhile, had risen and crossed the room, her movements apparently casual, and was stirring something on the floor with one foot. Cyllan glanced at her – then felt her lungs constrict. *The stones* . . .

'The old Eastern geomancy,' Erminet said musingly. 'I'd thought the technique was all but dead.' And when Cyllan didn't reply, she smiled. 'So you're a seer, eh?'

'No!' The denial was too vehement, and Erminet saw fear in Cyllan's eyes.

'There's little point in denying the obvious, child, not when your guile doesn't extend to hiding the evidence!' Abruptly, and to Cyllan's surprise, her tone softened. 'Just be thankful that as yet I'm the only one to have divined your secret. The others all think you harmless enough, despite the protests of that spoiled little Margrave's son.'

'Drachea . . . ?' The word came involuntarily from Cyllan's lips; her hostility wavering in the face of puzzlement and a growing curiosity.

'Is that his name? Yes; the arrogant brat's still here, and no doubt his proud father and the entire brood will soon be on their way from the South to bask in his reflected glory.' Erminet's voice was acid, and Cyllan's confusion redoubled. Such harsh words, from a Sister of Aeoris? She didn't understand . . .

Suddenly Erminet came back to the bed and stood looking down at her. 'Who is Yandros?'

The change of tack caught Cyllan by surprise – as the Sister had intended – and she couldn't collect her wits in time to hide her chagrin. She swallowed. 'I've never heard the name.'

'Oho, you haven't! So unfamiliar it is to you that you called on it no more than a dozen times in your fever!' The old woman bent closer. 'You babbled a pretty parcel of words while you slept, girl. If I was a suspicious woman, I'd have sworn on my oath that they were a litany designed to call up something better left undisturbed!'

Oh, yes; the arrow had struck its target. Terror and guilt flickered in Cyllan's eyes before she could hide them. Then the peculiar amber gaze hardened.

'And if it was, Sister?' she replied venomously. 'Do you see a legion of demons ranged around the walls of this room? Do you see a supernatural army storming the Castle gates to my rescue? Whatever I might have tried, I *failed!*'

She was lying; Erminet knew it as surely as she knew the Sun would rise tomorrow. 'Did you?' she said softly. 'Or does that wound on your arm tell only half the story?'

Cyllan frowned, then looked quickly at her left wrist. The livid mark had been treated with a healing salve, but its ferocity was undiminished. She flexed her fingers and remembered Yandros's knowing, unhuman eyes as he bent to touch his lips to her wrist. Excitement and a sick fear churned in her – *then it was real; it had truly happened . . . Chaos had answered her summoning . . .*

Slowly she drew her arm close against herself, as though to protect the scar the Chaos Lord had inflicted from Sister Erminet's scrutiny. As odd, not quite rational smile distorted her mouth.

'Whatever story it tells or doesn't tell,' she whispered, 'you can't change it. Not you, not Keridil Toln; no one. It's too late.'

Erminet felt uneasy, and began to wonder if, in her determination to see justice done, she had made a grave error. She was in no doubt now that Tarod hadn't made a second mistake by putting his trust in this girl. She would do anything to save him, no matter what the consequences to herself or anyone else, and such single-minded devotion could be deadly. Tarod, they said, was of Chaos – an accusation he hadn't denied. If it was true, then it followed that he might have allies who also owed their existence to that same evil; allies who could be called upon in an hour of need . . .

She looked at Cyllan again and told herself that the idea was nonsensical. Chaos was dead – if Aeoris had failed in that task, her own Sisterhood would never have been created to keep faith with the memory of such a titanic victory. And the girl was no sorceress. She had a seeing talent, but that was all. It was love that drove her; and Sister Erminet empathised all too well with such a motivation.

And so she had to decide between duty and conscience. Stickler though she was, Erminet's code of honour was peculiarly personal – and whatever the High Initiate or her own Sisterhood might dictate, she had given her word on one matter, at least . . .

She met Cyllan's angry gaze once more, and said without any preamble, 'I have a message for you.'

The girl's defiance wavered, but she wouldn't allow herself to ask the question that lurked in her eyes.

Erminet licked her lips. 'He said to bid you remember your first visit to the spire . . . and that he took nothing you were unwilling to give.'

She knew there would be a reaction, but was unprepared for its nature. Cyllan froze, her mouth opening as though trying to speak – then her body heaved and she broke into agonised sobs, covering her face with both hands and crying as though her soul were tearing apart.

'Child!' Chagrin made Erminet forget her studied acerbity, and she put her arms around Cyllan's shoulders. 'Child, don't weep!'

Cyllan tried to push her away as a surge of fear and grief and desperate longing overtook her. She had tried to contain her emotions as best she could, knowing that they were the worst form of self-torment; but Tarod's words, so carelessly conveyed by this old woman, had brought back all the bitterness of the memories which, now, were all she had of him. Struggling to find an outlet, her feeling could only express itself in two helpless, futile and broken words.

'Oh, *gods* – '

Erminet cursed herself for not stopping to think of the effect her lover's message might have on Cyllan. A shared secret, a private jest between them – no wonder the girl wept at the ugly circumstances under which the message had been sent and delivered. She could easily have wept with her.

'Cyllan, listen to me!' Her fingers pressing on Cyllan's shoulders were rough, but she knew no other way to call her out of the depths of her misery. 'You must listen!'

Cyllan drew a great, heaving breath. Her hands dropped away from her face, and the eyes that stared into Erminet's were wild with loathing.

'Why should I listen to you?' she retaliated ferociously. 'You're no different from any of them! Tarod has never harmed you, but you'll stand by and nod your sage approval when they take him to the Marble Hall to kill him won't you?' She was shaking from head to foot, close to hysteria. 'And all the while you keep me locked in here, and I *love* him, and I can't do anything to stop this madness, and Tarod's going to *die!*'

Erminet, horribly moved by the outburst, gazed steadily back at her and said, 'Not if I can help it.'

Her words took a moment to register, but when they did Cyllan's face froze. '*What* . . . '?

'You heard me.' *Aeoris help me*, she thought, *what have I said*? She'd spoken on impulse, responding to the girl's distress and to a discomforting and growing sense of injustice in her own mind. When she left Tarod's cell she had been *angry* – partly with herself, partly with him for resigning himself to death so passively, but mostly with the uncontrolled chain of circumstances which had led to the condemnation of a young and vital life. Now she understood Tarod's reasoning, and pitied both his and Cyllan's plight. Romantic old fool that she was, she wanted to help them – and because of that quixotic urge, had let her tongue run away with her. But she wouldn't – *couldn't* – go back on her word.

She made as if to move back, but Cyllan's hand shot out and locked on her wrist. Behind the shocked immobility of her expression, Cyllan's thoughts were in a turmoil of stunned astonishment, disbelief and hope. This strange old woman had brought her a message which could only be from Tarod's own lips – and that must mean that Tarod trusted her. Sister Erminet didn't want him to die . . . and Yandros had said that help would come from within the Castle; that when it came she would recognise it . . .

'Sister – ' Cyllan's voice was hoarse with desperation. 'Please – can you help us?'

Erminet stood up, pulling her arm free and suddenly unsure of herself. 'I don't know . . . '

Cyllan twisted her hands together, hardly aware of what she was doing. Almost in a whisper, she pleaded, 'You have the key to this room. You could let me go free . . . '

'No.' Erminet took a deep breath. 'I want to help you.

The gods know why, but I've taken a liking to your Adept; I pity him, and I pity you. But it isn't easy – you must understand that. I can't simply let you slip away into the night. If it were to be known that I . . . ' she faltered. 'That my sympathies were – against the tide – I'd have no defence. And I value my life, albeit that I haven't many more years left to me.' A trace of her old tartness returned as she smiled. 'I've no wish to meet Aeoris just yet – at least, not with such a deed on my conscience.'

Cyllan subsided, fighting back her disappointment as she acknowledged that Erminet was right. Besides, freedom alone wasn't enough. She had to have the Chaos stone if she was to save Tarod and fulfil her pledge to Yandros.

She bowed her head nodding. 'I'm sorry, Sister. I thought – hoped . . . but I understand.' Through the curtain of her hair her expression was intense. 'Will you, then, answer me a question?'

'If I can.'

'There's a stone . . . Tarod used to wear it in a ring, and the High Initiate took it from him when he was first captured.'

Erminet remembered the gem. She had seen it on Tarod's hand at their earliest encounter; and rumour ran that it contained his soul . . .

'I know it,' she said cautiously.

'Do you know where it is now?'

A snatch of conversation, overheard as she went about her work in the early aftermath of Time's return . . . 'Yes . . . ' said Erminet.

Cyllan's eyes lit feverishly. 'Tell me!'

'Why is it so important?'

Cyllan hesitated, then decided that she had no choice but to tell Erminet at least a part of the truth. She remembered Yandros's words, and said softly, 'Because it must be returned to its rightful owner.'

If the tales concerning that gem were true, then to reunite it with its rightful owner could bring ruin on them all. Soulless, Tarod was formidable enough . . .

but with the stone in his possession he would be a far more deadly adversary. Erminet had to be sure of what she was doing. Chaos or no, that black-haired Adept was a man of honour. If he gave his word that no harm would come to the Castle through him, she would trust that promise. Not the girl, though – she'd use the stone against anyone, friend or enemy, who tried to thwart her. And however just her motive, Erminet couldn't take such a risk.

Aloud, she said, 'No. I won't tell you, Cyllan; not yet.' And as the girl began to protest she held up a firm hand. 'I said, *no*. I don't trust you, girl. And I don't intend to put my head on the execution block for your sake.' She turned and began to gather up her philtres. 'But I will see your Tarod again, and I'll speak with him. If – ' she swung round, wagging an admonishing finger, 'and *only* if he gives me his word that no harm will come to this Castle through any aid I might give you, then I'll reconsider what you've asked of me.' She gave Cyllan a grim but sympathetic little smile. 'I can do no more.'

It was so little . . . and yet it might be enough. Cyllan met Erminet's gaze, and hope flickered in her odd amber eyes.

The old woman smiled grimly. 'In the meantime, do you wish me to give him any word from you? I've been a go-between once; I might as well be one again. Besides, he's as suspicious as you are – if I don't bring him some word, he'll accuse me of keeping his message from you, and I could do without bearing the brunt of his temper.'

In spite of herself, Cyllan couldn't help returning the smile. 'Yes . . . say to him that the wound was quickly healed.'

' "The wound was quickly healed".' Erminet repeated the words to commit them to memory, then gave Cyllan an old-fashioned look. 'Another cryptic riddle! No wonder you two are so well suited; you're as bad as each other for intrigue. Not that I care what your private jests might mean . . . ' Then her expression softened. 'Don't worry child. I'll tell him.'

Cyllan nodded, and the look on her face tore at

Erminet's heart. 'Thank you, Sister,' she whispered almost inaudibly.

The tawny bird looked this way and that from its perch on the master falconer's arm, surveying its audience with something approaching disdain in its beady eyes. The falconer – a swarthy, hook-nosed native of Empty Province – leaned forward and whispered to the bird; it screeched in reply, extending its wings, then settled.

The falconer glanced at the High Initiate and smiled faintly. 'If your message is ready, sir . . . '

Keridil stepped forward out of the small crowd which had gathered in the Castle courtyard. In one hand he bore a single sheet of parchment rolled into a small, tight scroll. The falconer took it, and with a deft hand attached it to a looped thong that dangled from one of the bird's legs, ignoring its attempts to peck his fingers. His smile broadened to become a vulpine grin.

'Now we'll see if she's learned her lessons well.' He whispered to the bird again, and again the creature screeched, as though issuing a challenge to some unseen enemy. This time it extended its wings to the full, and a few of the crowd gasped in surprise at their span. The falconer flung his arm high; the bird sprang, the great wings cracking the air, and hung for a few moments hovering some ten feet above his head. Then with a speed that drew further astonished exclamations it hurled itself upwards, arrowing into the clear, cold sky until it was barely more than a dark speck against the blueness. It hovered again – then it was winging away South towards the mountains, vanishing in seconds beyond the high Castle wall.

A ripple of spontaneous applause broke out from the watchers, and Keridil clasped the falconer's gloved hand.

'An auspicious beginning, Faramor.'

The swarthy Northerner's face wasn't designed for expressing pleasure, and his answering smile was laced with embarrassment. 'She's a long way to fly yet, High Initiate. But if all goes as it should, the return bird should arrive by the time the Sun sets tomorrow.' He blinked as the tall, chestnut-haired girl who had stood at Keridil's side for the small ceremony stepped up and bestowed a dazzling if faintly condescending smile on him.

'And then it will be no time at all before the whole world has heard our good news.' She linked her arm in Keridil's possessively. 'Isn't that so, my love?'

Keridil covered her hand with his fingers and squeezed it. 'Certainly. You have our thanks, Faramor.'

As they moved away, the falconer was besieged by eager questioners – mostly from the ranks of the younger Initiates, Keridil noticed with amusement. Assuming that this early experiment succeeded, he thought, Faramor and his kind would have no shortage of apprentices to learn the new skill.

The idea of using birds as messengers was something that the High Initiate knew could prove to be a very valuable asset to the Circle. Falconers from Empty Province had been experimenting during his father's lifetime, trying to train the ferocious birds they normally used for hunting; but it had taken years and a great deal of patience for this first apparent success to be achieved. Now, Faramor's bird was winging its way towards Chaun, where – in theory, at least – another falconer would retrieve it and send his own bird back to the Castle with an acknowledgement of Keridil's message. From Chaun, he would also despatch other trained birds to other provinces to spread the news carried by Faramor's hawk. And if all went according to plan, the announcement of the High Initiate's betrothal to Sashka Veyyil would spread around the entire land in a matter of days, rather than the weeks that even relays of the fastest horsemen would need.

Keridil had chosen to broadcast this particular news mainly to please Sashka, but also – more pragmatically – because there could be no harm done if the experiment should fail. But he had high hopes, for although much depended on the birds' reliability, there was little else that could go wrong. Hawks had no natural predators,

and they flew far too high to stray within the range of any
irresponsible archer on the ground. If Faramor's faith in
the idea proved sound, it would mean an unimaginable
change in the ability of all manner of people to communicate at long distance. The Circle could reach its own
Initiates in far-off parts of the world; Sisterhood cots
could maintain closer contact with one another; Mar-
graves in need of aid or advice would no longer suffer the
frustration and sometimes the dangers of waiting . . .
the possibilities were more than impressive; they were
astounding.

It was an innovation, and one that was sorely needed.
In the aftermath of his father Jehrek's death, Keridil had
promised himself that he would make changes at the
Star Peninsula. The Circle had stagnated for too long,
losing touch with the realities of the world beyond these
Castle walls to become little more than nominal
upholders of the gods' laws, with a diminishing active
role in the land's affairs. They had become figureheads;
and the danger with figureheads was that they could all
too easily turn into anachronisms. It was time – high
time – that such a downhill tendency was stopped,
before it got out of hand –

And suddenly Keridil felt sick as he remembered
where he had heard such words before.

'You have no good reason to exist!' In his mind he
could hear the silver voice with its edge of shattering
malevolence; see the cruelly unhuman face with its ever
changing eyes . . . Yandros, Lord of Chaos, who had
stood among the ruined statues of the Marble Hall and
smiled with pitying disdain as Keridil tried to bind him
with the Seventh Exhortation and Banishment, the
Circle's highest rite against recalcitrant demons. He
might as well have tried to topple the Castle with his bare
hands . . . and yet he recalled, with a shudder, the
awesome power that Tarod had conjured so effortlessly;
power enough to send the Chaos Lord back whence he
came . . .

'Keridil?' Sashka was gazing at him and frowning.
'Are you unwell?'

He had stopped walking, he realised, and was sweating profusely. Those memories . . . they always seemed to ambush him when he least expected or wanted them. This was supposed to be a moment for celebration . . .

He took a deep breath. 'I'm fine, love. A chill, perhaps.'

'You should take better care of yourself.' Sashka, who was warmly wrapped in a fur-trimmed coat over her brocade gown, glanced up at the icily clear sky. 'It isn't Summer yet, but you haven't so much as a cloak about you.'

He laughed, grateful to her for dispelling the darkness at the back of his mind. 'You're not my wife yet!'

'I am in all but name.' Her answering smile was faintly lascivious. 'And I know some very pleasurable ways to warm you . . . '

Frayn Veyyil Saravin and his prim, rake-thin wife were crossing the courtyard to intercept them, and Keridil squeezed Sashka's hand in an admonitory warning. 'Hush! D'you want your parents to overhear us?'

Sashka smiled enigmatically. 'There are none so blind as those who don't find it in their interests to see!'

They walked on, as the small crowd began to disperse.

The celebration to mark the High Initiate's betrothal was to be an interim measure, a foretaste of the far greater festivities amid which the marriage itself would take place. Sashka wanted to wed as soon as practicality allowed, but for once Keridil had refused to indulge her, and at last, knowing when to exercise discretion, she had given way.

Keridil hadn't confided his reason for the postponement to her, but it was strong enough to override any other considerations. He wanted nothing more than to marry Sashka now – but if he did, he would be haunted by the spectre of Tarod, and that would be a hard ghost to banish. Although he had reconciled his conscience where his one-time friend was concerned, Keridil still had occasional nightmares, and the thought of going ahead with his marriage while Tarod still lived was something he couldn't face. The death-rite had to be prepared – the same gruesome ritual which had been thwarted before – and, as High Initiate, he couldn't escape the burden of carrying it out personally. It would be impossible to prepare for his own wedding with any pleasure while that prospect still hung over him . . . especially in view of Tarod's own past involvement with Sashka. But once Tarod was finally dead, the ugly taste would fade and he'd be free to look to the future. It wasn't guilt that motivated him, so Keridil told himself over and again – it was simply expedient common sense.

And despite the shadow of the pending execution, he was determined to enjoy the betrothal celebrations. In two days there would be a banquet at the Castle, at which the announcement would be officially ratified by the Council of Adepts. Sashka had sent a fast rider to her home in Han to fetch appropriate clothes and jewellery for the occasion, and Keridil would present to her the gold ring set with three huge emeralds that for centuries had been worn by the High Initiate's consort. Since his own mother had died giving him birth, the ring had been locked away in its carved wooden box among his father's possessions, and the thought that, after so many years, there would again be a consort to wear it had delighted the Circle, and the Council in particular.

There would, of course, be a good deal of disappointment mingling with the congratulations from certain quarters. Since he reached adolescence Keridil had been the focus of attention from every high-ranking clan with an eligible daughter in the land, and recently had come close – though unwillingly – to a match with the pretty but vacuous Inista Jair, from a wealthy and influential Chaun Province family. Jehrek Banamen Toln had approved of the liaison, Keridil had dreaded it; though had Sashka remained beyond his reach, he might well have wed Inista eventually for want of any happier option and because Jehrek had wished it.

But his father, he knew, would have approved of Sashka. Suitable though Inista Jair might have been as a daughter-elect, Sashka had the breeding and strength of character to fit her perfectly for an exalted position. Her beauty, her sophistication, her intelligence all promised to win her many friends. No clan could take insult at the thought that one of their own had been passed over for a less favourable candidate.

Sashka's parents had joined them by now, and as they reached the main doors Keridil excused himself and left the others to continue on into the Castle while he turned along the pillared walkway towards the library and the Marble Hall. Reaching the door that led down from the courtyard, he stood back to allow three servants, each dragging a heavily laden sack, to emerge. The staircase beyond was filthy with dust in which the prints of a myriad feet could be seen, and Keridil eyed the bulging sacks before speaking to the first of the three men.

'How's the work progressing?'

Sweating, the man straightened and touched a finger to his brow respectfully. 'Well, sir. Perhaps another three or four days, and it'll be complete.'

Thanks be to Aeoris, Keridil thought. He nodded, smiled, and moved on down the stairs. A few more days, and the seven black statues which had stood in the Marble Hall throughout the Circle's history would no longer exist . . . it chilled his blood to think that, for century upon century, the Initiates had believed those seven titanic figures to represent Aeoris and his six god-brethren, mutilated beyond recognition by the old race when they transferred their allegiance from Order to Chaos. That belief would have continued, had Yandros not revealed, with careless malice, that the revered images were those of Aeoris and his kin's seven dark counterparts – the old, sinister gods of Chaos, carved by their corrupt servants before the forces of Order sent them to oblivion. Keridil had ordered the destruction of the statues, and for two days now an army of the Circle's higher Adepts – who were the only people allowed, by ancient tradition, to set foot beyond the silver door – had been toiling to break up the huge figures, reducing them to rubble which servants then hauled from the Castle and threw over the edge of the stack into the sea. When the task was complete, a series of complicated rituals would be required to purify and rededicate the Marble Hall before the taint of Chaos could finally be eradicated.

As he approached the library, Keridil reflected bitterly that the legacy Tarod had left the Circle would take far longer to die than its perpetrator. Recent events had taught the Adepts that the centuries hadn't diminished the need for constant vigilance against the dark forces, and it had been a hard lesson. The peace that pervaded the Castle now was no more than a veneer; danger and turmoil still lurked beneath the surface, and would continue to haunt them until both Tarod and the stone were finally destroyed.

He entered the library vault, lost in his uneasy thoughts. A few Initiates sat in isolated corners, studying books or manuscripts, and muffled sounds drifted from the distant Marble Hall as the Adepts went about their work. Keridil headed towards the low door in the alcove – then started as someone plucked at his sleeve.

'High Initiate . . . ' Drachea was standing at his elbow, and Keridil tried to keep irritation from his expression as he stared down at the young man. Grateful though he was to Drachea for the service he had performed – and he couldn't deny that without him, the Castle's inhabitants would still be languishing in limbo – Keridil couldn't help a growing dislike for him. Drachea had begun to presume on the position in which he found himself; he dogged Keridil's footsteps, bombarded him with questions concerning his plans for Tarod and Cyllan, and was too ready at the least opportunity to offer his own opinion as to what should be done with them. Only two days ago Keridil had come close to losing his temper when the Heir Margrave had tried to insist that Cyllan, too, should face execution as soon as Tarod was despatched, arguing that a promise made to a demon had no validity and that the High Initiate would be right to break it for the sake of safety. Keridil, well aware that Drachea wanted personal revenge on the girl, had curtly reprimanded his temerity in questioning the High Initiate's judgement, and the young man had retired to his room to sulk.

Now though, the reprimand was apparently forgotten as Drachea said, 'High Initiate, I wonder if I might crave a few minutes of your time?'

Keridil sighed. 'I'm sorry, Drachea; I'm very busy –'

'I'll take no more than a moment, sir, I assure you! I've been wanting to speak to you before my father arrives from Shu Province, on a matter which is crucial to my own future.'

He was going to prove persistent . . . resignedly, Keridil waited for him to continue. Clasping his hands behind his back, Drachea said, 'As you know, sir, I am my father's eldest son, and therefore destined eventually to become Margrave of Shu. However, although I'm very sensible of my position and my duty, I have for some years felt that my aptitude lies in a different direction.'

Keridil stroked his own chin. 'Our duty doesn't always correspond to what we might desire, Drachea. Some of the responsibilities of my own position are ones I'd prefer not to have to shoulder, but – '

'Oh no; it's not the responsibility,' Drachea interrupted him. 'As I said, it's a question of *aptitude*. I'm sure that I could assume the Margravate without difficulty; but I feel that in doing so I'd be . . .' He hesitated, then smiled hopefully. 'Perhaps wasting a potential that could be put to better use.'

Keridil looked at him. 'You know your abilities better than I do, of course – I don't quite see how I can be of assistance to you.'

'Ah, but you can, High Initiate! In fact, there *is* no one else who has the authority to grant or refuse my request.' The young man drew himself up into a formal stance. 'I wish to ask, sir, that I might be considered as a candidate for the Circle.'

Keridil stared at him, astonished, then realised that he must have been a fool not to have anticipated this. Suddenly all Drachea's dogged persistence was explained – and, too, his anxiety to plead his case before the arrival of Gant Ambaril Rannak, his father. The Margrave, Keridil imagined, would not be pleased to hear of his son's ambitions – and the idea of Drachea qualifying as a Circle Initiate seemed more than a little far-fetched. Though psychic analysis wasn't his forte, Keridil was a shrewd enough judge of character to know that the young man stood little chance of passing even the lowest of the Circle's many inaugural tests. Drachea's motivation had far more to do with self-aggrandisement than with any desire to serve the gods; and Keridil also suspected that his mind wasn't stable enough to cope with the rigorous application needed to become an Initiate. He seemed to think that his position alone would qualify him for admission – and it would be a hard task to explain to him why this was not so.

Keridil couldn't face that task in his present mood: he had more important matters on his mind than one arrogant youth's presumption, and it would do Drachea no harm to remain in suspense for a while. Aloud, he said,

'That's not something to which I can give you an answer now, Drachea. As you've already admitted, you have responsibilities – and of course, your father would have to be consulted.' He smiled. 'I'd be failing in my own duty if I were to interfere in his plans for you without so much as a by-your-leave. And for a young man in your place, it's a change that can't be undertaken without a good deal of forethought.'

'I've thought about it, sir! In fact, I've thought about little else since I was a child.'

'Nonetheless, you must curb your impatience.' Aware that he'd have to offer the young man some sop, however small, if his own life wasn't to be made intolerable, Keridil added, 'When your father arrives, I'll discuss the matter with him. I'm sure he'll be agreeable to your at least being interviewed by the Council of Adepts.'

Drachea flushed with pleasure. 'Thank you, High Initiate!'

Keridil inclined his head. 'And now, if you'll excuse me . . . ' He moved towards the alcove door, but Drachea followed.

'Sir, I wonder if I might accompany you to the Marble Hall?' he asked eagerly. 'I'd enjoy the chance to witness the destruction of those monstrous idols!'

The High Initiate's face hardened. 'I'm sorry; that's not possible. The Marble Hall is closed to all but the higher Adepts.'

'But . . .' Drachea looked affronted. 'I hardly think such a rule applies in my case, sir. After all, it was in the Marble Hall that I helped you to – '

Keridil had had enough. Well aware that he was about to lose his self-control, he said sharply, 'One of the first lessons that a Circle candidate learns, Drachea, is not to question an order of the High Initiate.' He nodded curtly. 'I'll speak to your father, as I promised, but I can confer no further favours. Good day to you.'

He walked away towards the door, leaving Drachea staring after him with a mixture of chagrin and indignation on his face.

Chapter 14

Sister Erminet unlocked the door of Tarod's cell and paused on the threshold for a few moments to let her eyes adjust to the gloom before securing the door behind her.

'Adept . . . ?' Even as her vision improved there was no sign of him. Then she saw a tall, gaunt shadow leaning against the opposite wall.

Tarod raised a hand and ran his fingers idly over the dank stone surface. 'There was a window here once, by all accounts,' he said. 'You can feel the outlines of the mortar where a new stone was used to block it.'

His voice sounded flat, remote. Erminet advanced into the room. 'Doubtless it was filled in to protect the food stores against rats.'

He smiled thinly at her and examined a smear of dirt on his fingers before wiping his hand carelessly on his shirt. 'Doubtless.'

Looking at him as he moved to slump down on the heap of old sacks and rugs that was all this cell provided by way of a couch, Erminet judged that his will – or what remained of it – was rapidly fading. Despite their previous conversation, he seemed to have shrugged off all hope in the same careless way that he shrugged off the thought of his impending death. He was grimy, unshaven, and his mind seemed to match his physical state, giving her the uncomfortable feeling that, though for the first time she had something concrete to offer him, it might have come too late.

Tarod watched her as, too discomforted to say more, she busied herself with her now familiar bag of nostrums. Erminet was wrong in believing that he had lost hope; but since her visit of the previous day he had been savagely trying to crush the spark out of existence, telling himself that to believe in miracles was a thankless and fruitless exercise. The Sister might well have seen Cyllan, and might well have brought a response to his cryptic and very personal message; but beyond that there could be nothing. Even to convey the message had been a kind of cruelty; better if he'd given Cyllan the chance to forget him now, rather than prolong her suffering. And he, with the spark of hope firmly under control, would drink the narcotic potion Erminet gave him, and sleep away the hours, and move another day closer to dying . . . it didn't really seem to matter.

But the prospect of the death that awaited him triggered off another chain of thought. Instinct told him that something was afoot in the Castle, and though he had neither the will nor, in his present condition, the ability to discover its nature, imagination had led him to an all too obvious conclusion. And even without a soul, he was still human enough to dread it.

He said, hoping that his voice carried a convincing degree of bored disinterest, 'There seems to be a good deal of activity in the Castle.'

Erminet's bird-bright gaze fastened on his face. 'What would you know about that?'

He shrugged, perversely pleased by her surprise. 'My senses aren't dead yet.'

Her mouth pursed as though in disapproval. 'Well, they certainly don't lead you astray. There's all manner of upheaval – masonry being hurled around as though the whole place were being rebuilt, experiments with messenger birds . . . and of course preparations for the banquet following the High Initiate's announcement – ' she stopped.

'Announcement?'

Erminet scowled. She hadn't intended to let that slip . . . ' Of his betrothal,' she said with some reluctance.

'Betrothal.' Tarod's dark eyebrows lifted slightly. 'Ah. And need I ask who – '

'You need not. Sashka seems to think that the name of Veyyil Toln will suit her very well.' She watched him intently to see how he would react, but his face was impassive. Slowly, carelessly, he raised his hands and studied them, then touched the ruined silver base of the ring on his left index finger.

'A pity,' he said at last. 'Had circumstances been slightly different, it might have been amusing to kill her.'

Erminet was shocked by the unhuman detachment in his voice, and admonished uneasily, 'You shouldn't harbour such vengeful thoughts. They're unhealthy – and the little bitch isn't worth it.'

Tarod's green eyes met hers, coolly candid. 'I've no interest in revenge, Sister. It would simply be amusing; nothing more.' He smiled. 'As it is, I wish them joy of each other.'

'I wish I knew whether or not I could believe you.'

The smile widened slightly, but there was little humour in it. 'Does it matter? I'd have thought the consideration was academic.'

'It may not be,'

Even in the gloom the sudden awakening of a new light in Tarod's eyes was unmistakable. He leaned forward, and the hope which he thought he'd succeeded in stifling came surging up again. 'You've seen Cyllan – ' His voice was a harsh whisper.

Now or never . . . Erminet's conscience was horribly split between duty and instinct, but she'd known even before she came here that instinct would win.

'Yes, I saw the girl,' she said, dropping her own voice as if afraid of being overheard. 'I gave her your message. It made her cry, but I gave it to her nonetheless. And I made her a promise.'

Tarod waited silently for her to continue, and she cursed his ability to keep his feelings so firmly under control. He was making her task no easier . . .

'She wants the stone,' she went on at last. 'The stone from your ring . . . I wouldn't tell her where it's kept, because I don't trust her.'

'What do you mean?'

Erminet looked at him candidly. 'I mean that I don't trust her not to use any means at her disposal to free you. She'd kill the entire population of the Castle if she could, for your sake.'

Tarod laughed softly, and the old woman grimaced.

'Oh, I can sympathise with her feelings – but I won't be a party to any wrongdoing. I could release her, but she won't flee the Castle; not without the stone, and not without you. And if I tell her where the stone is hidden, she'll find it . . . and she'll use it.'

Still Tarod said nothing, and Erminet prompted uncomfortably, 'There's more to that stone than I know, isn't there? Perhaps more than anyone knows, save you . . .'

He sighed, the sound echoing oddly in the dark room. 'I've never denied what I am, Sister Erminet; nor have I denied the nature of the stone. Without it, I'm only half alive; yet it's more than a receptacle for . . . well, my spirit, for want of a better word.'

'Your soul?'

'If you like. Whether it's an evil gem or not depends on how you view such things. But the Circle can't control it, even with me gone.' He looked up at her, and his eyes burned intensely. 'Cyllan's right. I need it, if I'm to survive.'

It was what she had expected to hear, and Erminet nodded with some reluctance. 'Then I'll ask just one thing of you.'

'What is it?'

'Your word on a single question. Either you're a man of honour, or I'm a fool – and I think I've learned sound judgement in all my years. If Cyllan is released – escapes, shall we say – and she retrieves that stone and brings it to you . . . what will you do then?'

It was a question Tarod hadn't dared to ask himself during his imprisonment. Once, he had held an idealistic belief that the stone must be destroyed, even if it meant his own annihilation – but the humanity that was so paradoxically tied to the stone, and which had been lost with it, had wiped that slate clean. Cyllan had added her own influence, albeit one that he welcomed, and Tarod no longer knew what his ultimate goal would be. All he knew – and knew without a shadow of uncertainty – was that he wanted to live.

He lowered his gaze. 'I'd become what I once was. I'd be – complete.'

'Yes,' said Erminet. 'I know.' She wouldn't allow herself to ask for the assurance she needed. It must come from him, unprompted, or it would be worth nothing.

A long silence ensued. Then, at last, Tarod said, 'Vengeance would achieve nothing, Sister. I don't crave it – I like to think I'm above such emotions, even if that sounds like arrogance. If the stone was in my possession once more – ' Now he looked up again, and Erminet read a terrifying message in his eyes. *He could, if he chose, destroy the Castle and all who dwelt within its walls. He could erase them from the face of the earth, and laugh off any power short of that of Aeoris himself that tried to stop him. And that would only be the beginning . . .*

The fire faded from his look, and she let out her breath with a sharp exhalation. 'If the stone was in my possession,' Tarod said gently, 'Cyllan and I would leave the Star Peninsula, and neither you nor anyone else here would ever hear of us again.'

'And what would you leave behind you?'

'The Castle. The Circle. As they are, with not a soul harmed by my hand.'

Aware that she was at a crossroads, with no retreat offered to her, Erminet said, 'Do I have your word on that, as an Adept?'

'No.' He smiled. 'I'm no longer an Adept, Erminet. But you have *my* word.'

She twisted her hands together, licked her lips and wished that her throat wasn't so dry. 'That's good enough for me.'

'Then – '

Erminet didn't let him say what he'd been about to. 'I'll tell her where the gem is kept,' she said, so quietly that Tarod could barely hear her. 'And if I should forget to lock the door of her room behind me, when the

good people of the Castle are sound asleep in their beds
. . .'

He smiled. 'No one will ever know the truth.'

I hope not, Erminet thought, and nodded. 'There's a
banquet in two nights' time; it's probably the only safe
chance there'll be. She'll come to you then.'

He rose, but didn't approach her. 'I don't know what
to say to you. Thanks are so inadequate . . .'

'I want none. I've enough of a burden to carry without
your gratitude to add to it!' Erminet was near to tears
without knowing why, and to counteract the emotion
she raked him with a contemptuous glare. 'In the meantime, I'll bring you water to wash with, and a blade to
shave yourself. If you confront the girl looking as you do
now, she'll change her mind and I'll have risked myself
for nothing!'

It was the first time she had heard Tarod laugh unre-
servedly and wholeheartedly. When at last it subsided,
he said solemnly, 'I wouldn't have that, Sister. Not for
the world.'

Her cheeks reddened. 'So be it, then.' She glanced
down at her bag. 'I've prepared a further dose of the
drug that's supposed to keep you quiescent. I'll leave it
here – but I don't want to know whether you take it or
not.'

'If anyone chooses to visit me, they'll find me as
stupefied as ever.' Tarod smiled. 'You'll be seen to have
done your duty.'

Erminet nodded quickly. She poured the prepared
concoction, pressed the cup into his hands and made to
leave. At the door she paused. 'Ah . . . I all but forgot.
She said to tell you that the wound was quickly healed.'

'Yes. I thought she might say that . . . bless you,
Sister Erminet. I'll never forget what you've done.'

She returned the look almost sadly, he thought.
'Good fortune go with you, Tarod.'

He listened to the heavy key turning stiffly in the lock,
and to the sound of Erminet's footsteps diminishing
along the passage. When all was silent again he let out a
pent-up breath, and felt a new strength flowing through

him. He had hope where there had been nothing – hope of life, hope of a future. He could hardly yet believe it . . .

Sinking down on to the heaped rugs again, Tarod closed his green eyes and forced his muscles to relax, to ward off the excitement that threatened to overtake him. He must stay calm, expect nothing . . . the path from this moment to freedom was still a long and hazardous one, and rather than allow himself to indulge in speculation, he'd be better advised to conserve his energy lest some unforeseen trouble might occur. Even without the Chaos stone he had power, and the Circle's attempts to weaken him had had less effect than Keridil hoped – but he was by no means invincible. He must make contingency plans . . . and make them quickly.

Turning his head and opening his eyes again, he reached for the cup which Sister Erminet had left. For a moment he weighed it in his hand; then with slow deliberation he poured its contents on the floor. The liquid mingled with the detritus on the flagstones, forming a dark pool which gradually spread and faded as it soaked into the porous stone. If need be, he could put on a good enough show of stupefaction for the Circle . . . and he needed all his senses intact now.

Settling himself as comfortably as he could, and aware of the rapidity of his pulse which no amount of will could control, Tarod closed his eyes once more as his mind began to reach out tentatively towards the future.

Cyllan knew that some untoward event was taking place in the Castle. Watching from her window – there was little else to occupy her during the daylight hours – she had seen the bustle of activity increasing since early morning, and her first horrified thought had been to link it with the High Initiate's plans for Tarod's execution. But as the Spring day declined into a pleasant if chilly Sunset, it became obvious that this was a celebratory rather than a solemn occasion. People in their finest clothes converged on the main doors from all parts of the Castle, the tall windows of the main hall blazed with light, and as darkness fell she heard faint strains of music in the distance.

As the courtyard emptied, Cyllan left the window and sat on her bed, relieved from her immediate fear yet still fretting with impatience. It was three days since Sister Erminet had made her promise; three days during which the old woman had not been to visit her, and Cyllan's initial hope was fast turning to despair and anger. Surely, unless she was the victim of some complex scheme or joke, there should have been word by now? Several times during the agonising wait she had been tempted to try calling on Yandros a second time, but memory of his warning had stopped her. He had said he couldn't come to her again . . . she had no choice but to be patient. And to look to Aeoris for an answer to her prayers was hardly appropriate . . .

The music was louder now, and it irritated her; in her present predicament it seemed an intrusion and an insult. The Castle revelled while she waited, fear and uncertainty gnawing like rats at her stomach . . . it fuelled the anger that was growing inside her, made her want to strike out, yet gave her nothing to strike against. The tension she felt was almost unbearable – and when a key turned unexpectedly in the lock of her door, she jumped as though under the onslaught of a physical blow.

Sister Erminet came in. Her face was pale and taut, but she managed a quick, wry smile as she closed the door quietly at her back.

Cyllan sprang up from the bed. 'Sister – '

Erminet put a finger to her lips. 'Quiet, child. There's no one about, but no point in tempting the fates.'

Lowering her voice, Cyllan asked, 'What news do you have of Tarod?'

'He's well enough, if not exactly prospering.' Erminet paused, studying the girl's face. 'I gave him your reply to his message, and asked for his word on the safety of this Castle, as I said.'

'And . . . ?'

'He gave it.' Quickly, as though afraid of changing her

mind, Erminet unlooped one of the keys that hung from
her belt and held it out. 'This will unlock his door. I can't
take the risk of releasing him myself. And you'll find the
jewel in the High Initiate's study, locked away in a box
he keeps in his cupboard.' Her gaze wavered. 'There's a
banquet about to begin, to celebrate Keridil's betrothal
to Sashka Veyyil. I doubt if you'll ever have a better
opportunity to find the Castle deserted.'

Very slowly Cyllan reached out and took the key.
Then, catching Erminet completely by surprise, she suddenly and impulsively flung her arms round the old
woman's neck, hugging her tightly. She couldn't express
what she felt, but the mute gesture was far more eloquent
than any words. Flustered, Erminet extricated herself.

'Now, don't be so foolish!' she scolded, trying to cover
the fact that she was touched. 'You've a long way to go
yet, and this is no time to indulge in emotion.' She stood
back to study Cyllan critically. 'That gown, for example.
The colour's dangerously distinctive, and with your hair
it makes you too recognisable.'

Cyllan frowned down at herself. The dress was the
one that Tarod had given to her, and she didn't want to
relinquish it. 'They brought me fresh clothes,' she said.
'But I don't want them.'

Erminet, however, was adamant. 'Want or no, you'll
change your attire now, or look forward to being recaptured! Here.' She examined the garments which had
been left for Cyllan on Keridil's orders. 'This will do –
it's neutral enough.' She held up a dove-grey woollen
skirt with a darker long-sleeved top. For a moment
Cyllan seemed about to protest, then she shrugged her
thin shoulders and reluctantly slipped off the red gown.
While she changed, Erminet instructed her as to Tarod's
whereabouts and made her recite the directions twice
over to ensure she had memorised them, then finally
handed her a short black cloak with a hood.

'This will hide your hair well enough. Keep to the
shadows, and if anyone approaches you, walk the other
way as quickly as you can without drawing attention.
Are you ready?'

Cyllan nodded.

'Very well. I will leave first – I'm expected at the banquet, and there might be comment if I'm late. When all's quiet, make your way across the courtyard. It's unlit now; safer than the corridors.' She gave her charge one last look, then nodded. 'I wish you luck, child – even more for my sake than for yours. Aeoris help us all if you fail.'

Cyllan remembered her encounter with Yandros, and smiled. 'I won't fail, Sister Erminet.'

She stood back, watching as the old woman opened the door and peered out into the corridor. They exchanged a last glance, Erminet smiled conspiratorially, then she was gone. Cyllan waited, counting every painful heartbeat and hardly able to believe that what had happened wasn't a dream from which she would wake at any moment. Then, when she could hear no sound beyond the door, she crossed the room and slipped out into the passage. Erminet had disappeared towards the main stairs; Cyllan paused to pull the cloak's hood over her hair, then turned in the opposite direction towards a secondary flight which would, she had been told, lead her by a circuitous route to a side door of the courtyard.

And as Cyllan hastened away, the light of one of the wall-torches illuminated the rich velvet clothes and brilliant jewels of someone who stepped out of a side passage . . .

Sashka had been taking her time, despite her mother's pleas, in preparing for what was to be her triumphant night. She had changed her mind and her gown three times before finally deciding what to wear, then had spent an hour under the careful hands of a trusted servant while her hair was coiled and dressed. At last her parents had been forced to leave without her, and she had spent a few private and pleasant minutes luxuriating in anticipation of the evening. She would be the focus of all attention, elevated in a single night to a status that every eligible woman in every province would envy, and Sashka was determined to make the most of it. Let the guests await her arrival – she'd make that much more of an impression when she finally did grace them with her presence.

At last, judging the moment to be right, she rose and made to leave, scorning the proffered arm of her father's steward and telling him curtly to stay behind and mind his place. There would be a guard of honour waiting to escort her to the main hall; she needed no one else.

And so she had left her suite of rooms and walked at leisure towards the stairs. And, as she was about to emerge into the main corridor, Sister Erminet had walked briskly across her path.

Sashka instinctively drew back, irritated. She despised Sister Erminet, and the thought of having to walk with her and make at least an attempt to be civil soured her mood. Fortunately, however, the old woman hadn't seen her . . . so she waited until the quick footsteps had diminished before emerging into the corridor.

It was sheer chance which made her pause as she started towards the stairs, and look back over her shoulder. And she was just in time to see a small, cloaked and hooded figure turning out of one of the rooms at the far end and hurrying away.

Sashka frowned. Something about the figure struck a chord in her memory, but she couldn't place it. Yet . . . wasn't that the room where the Eastern girl, Tarod's little drover slut, was kept? Sashka's instinct for trouble assailed her, and she licked her lips speculatively. It was a ridiculous idea . . . but it would take only a moment to be sure.

Glancing about to make sure she was unobserved, she picked up her skirts and ran along the corridor.

The door from which both Sister Erminet and the mysterious figure must have emerged stood alone, and it was closed. Sashka grasped the latch-ring, turned it, pushed – and the door swung open.

The room was lit, but empty. Sashka's gaze took in an unmade bed, a plate of food, half eaten – and a red silk gown discarded over a chair. Remembering the one time she had seen Cyllan, when Keridil had tried and failed to talk some sense into her head, Sashka recognised the dress immediately, and her heart began to pound suffocatingly. *The slut had escaped – and Sister Erminet was implicated!*

A peculiar sense of elation filled Sashka. She could raise the alarm now, and within minutes Cyllan would be apprehended – but there might be more to gain by waiting a while. She felt certain that Cyllan's disappearance wasn't the result of a simple mistake on Erminet's part; the old woman was involved somehow in a deliberate plot, and Sashka felt certain that it might spring from a desire to spite her personally. Yet without direct evidence, she could prove nothing. Better, then, if she bided her time for just a little while, until she could trick Erminet into saying something that would damn her when she was confronted with the truth. The banquet would provide the perfect opportunity – it would also provide as many witnesses as anyone could desire – and she herself could secure the double triumph of ensuring Cyllan's apprehension, and exposing a traitor in their midst.

To aid and abet a minion of Chaos was a serious matter . . . Keridil could surely no longer argue in favour of clemency for the drover-girl, and the thought that Sister Erminet might well suffer alongside Cyllan gave Sashka a good deal of satisfaction. As for Tarod . . . his hopes of escape would be thwarted, and he'd die as Keridil intended. All in all, Sashka thought, a more than satisfactory solution . . .

She turned quickly out of the empty room, closing the door behind her, and made her way with unhurried grace towards the main stairs.

Gyneth Linto, Keridil's steward, leaned to pour wine into the two heavily ornamented silver cups that stood together at the high table. It was more than thirty years since these ancient chalices had been used to toast the betrothal or marriage of a High Initiate of the Circle, and Gyneth had insisted on taking personal charge of this duty, despite the fact that some might think it menial. A silence fell on the assembly as he completed his task with a flourish and stepped back. Keridil met Sashka's eyes and as one they raised the cups, touching the rims together as the entire gathering rose. Every gaze in the hall was upon them, and Sashka felt a thrill of excitement course through her as, slowly and clearly, Keridil spoke the formal words of the betrothal pledge.

'I call on Aeoris to witness this day that I, Keridil Toln, High Initiate of the Circle at the Star Peninsula, do pledge and bind to you, Sashka Veyyil of Han Province, to be protector and provider to you from the day of our marriage until my life's end.'

Sashka cast her eyes down, and her measured contralto carried through the hall. 'And that I, Sashka Veyyil, do pledge and bind to you, Keridil Toln, to be helpmeet and comforter to you, from the day of our marriage until my life's end.'

For a moment there was silence, as Keridil and Sashka each held their cup out to the other, and both drank from the other's chalice. It was a signal for the assembled guests to follow suit, and every man and woman raised their drinking vessels.

'Keridil and Sashka!' The toast was taken up, rippling through the hall in a swell of sound and interspersed with a few cheers from younger and bolder Initiates. Sashka's beautiful face smiled beneficence on the crowd, and the musicians in the high gallery began to play again now that the small ceremony was over, while servants hurried forward to begin serving food to the guests.

The feast was to be an informal affair. Since his father's death Keridil had, by slow and careful degrees, begun to make changes in much of the Circle's more esoteric practice. Remembering from his own childhood and adolescence the stultifying boredom of ceremonial banquets – endless speeches, hours spent stiff and uncomfortable on a hard bench, protocol demanding that he speak only to his nearest neighbours – he felt the use of too much ceremonial unnecessary, and was determined, as gently as possible, to persuade even the older

Adepts to his way of thinking. Tonight's celebration was the ideal opportunity – it was very much his personal festivity, had no direct link with Circle ritual, and he would offend no one by dispensing with the more familiar formal traditions. And so, as the guests began to eat, they also began to move and mingle around the hall, and the swell of conversation and laughter almost drowned out the subtle background of music. A steady stream of people made their way to the high table to offer congratulations to Keridil and Sashka, and among their number was Sister Erminet, who approached with a small group of Sisters who had arrived from West High Land that morning. Faramor the hawk-master's experiment had proved successful, and as a result Kael Amion, the elderly Senior at the West High Land cot, had sent a deputation of the women in her charge to the Castle to bring her personal good wishes.

Sashka disguised her amusement behind an artificial yawn as the Sisters approached. Erminet was smiling, but her eyes betrayed her, and Sashka believed she detected jealousy in their disdainful coldness. She forced down a desire to laugh. If all went well, Sister Erminet would have cause to regret her attitude before too long . . .

'High Initiate.' Erminet clasped Keridil's hand. 'A very gratifying occasion. On behalf of Lady Kael Amion and the Sisters of West High Land, may we offer warmest congratulations.'

Sashka gave Keridil a faintly pitying glance as she realised he was taken in by Erminet's unctuous manner. He thanked the old woman with great courtesy, and then Erminet turned to the girl at his side.

'My dear Sashka. This is a wonderful day for us all at the Cot – the Lady is very proud of you.'

Sashka smiled sweetly. 'Thank you, Sister; I'm very gratified by such praise.' Her voice oozed modesty, and Erminet nodded and made to move on. But before she had taken a step, Sashka added, as though the thought had just occurred to her, 'Oh – Sister Erminet . . . I don't wish to raise an unhappy subject, but . . . ' Her eyelashes flickered, though her gaze was steady, 'I gather that you are now in charge of both the prisoners held here at the Castle.'

Keridil frowned, surprised, but if Erminet was disconcerted she didn't show it. 'Yes,' she said evenly, 'I am.'

Sashka smiled again. 'It's just that . . . I'd so much appreciate your assurance that all's well and there's no danger of any trouble.' She reached out and took Keridil's hand. 'I'm sure the High Initiate will think me foolish, but I'd enjoy tonight so much more without the fear that something might go amiss.'

Erminet hesitated. She knew full well that Sashka had no fear of Tarod, Cyllan or any other living creature, but couldn't imagine what her motive for such an uncharacteristic question might be. Keridil, however, came unwittingly to her aid.

'My love, there's no need for any doubt,' he said, smiling fondly at Sashka. 'I understand your feelings in the circumstances, but I can give you my assurance, there's not the smallest chance of any threat to our happiness.' He looked up at the old woman. 'Isn't that so, Sister Erminet?'

Erminet inclined her head. 'Indeed, High Initiate.' She glanced at the auburn-haired girl. 'I looked in on the girl Cyllan not half an hour ago, and the Adept – the *former* Adept, I should say – a little earlier. Both are secure – in fact, the girl was sleeping when I left her. You have my assurance of that.'

Sashka smiled. 'Thank you, Sister. Your assurance is all we could ask.'

When Erminet and the other Sisters had moved on, Keridil said in Sashka's ear, 'It's not like you to be nervous, love. Why are you so troubled?'

She gave a little shrug. 'Ohh . . . perhaps I'm superstitious, Keridil. Forgive me – I'll be well enough now.'

'Sister Erminet's more than capable.'

'I know.' Sashka smiled sweetly at him in the way she knew could disarm him without a word spoken. 'Oh, I know.'

Cyllan heard the strains of dance music as she ran on silent feet through the maze of passages that permeated the Castle like a warren. In trying to avoid the main hall she had misjudged her own knowledge of the corridors, and had taken two wrong turnings before finally emerging uncomfortably close to the double doors that stood between her and the banquet.

Slipping into an alcove that masked her with its shadows, she stopped to catch her breath and get her bearings. Thus far, luck had been with her – she had encountered no one in the courtyard, and the one woman servant who had hurried past her as she crossed the entrance hall had paused only to bob a curtsey to the cloaked and hooded figure whom she had clearly taken for a late-arriving guest. But luck, Cyllan knew from bitter experience, had a habit of running out when least expected. If she was to fulfil her task, she must tread with the greatest of caution.

She had already made up her mind to steal the stone from the High Initiate's rooms before she made her way to the cellars where Tarod was imprisoned. In honesty, she had to admit that she would only feel safe when the jewel was in his hands; and while she might be no more than an anonymous figure to anyone she chanced to meet, he was known to the entire populus of the Castle and would be recognised immediately should he be seen.

The music, muffled beyond the heavy hall doors, was a light, lilting dance tune, underpinned by a murmur of many voices. The celebrations were at their height, and Cyllan dared waste no more time. Peering cautiously in both directions and seeing the corridor empty, she left her hiding place and hurried away in what she hoped was the direction of the High Initiate's apartments.

Her instincts proved true this time – and the outer door was unlocked. She suffered an agonising moment as she pushed the door fractionally open, half expecting to be challenged from within – but the suite of rooms was unlit and empty.

A box, locked in his cupboard, Sister Erminet had said

. . . Cyllan moved cautiously across the floor, skirting
the massive table that dominated the room, and found
the ornately carved cabinet a little to one side of the
fireplace. The handle refused to give when she turned it,
and swearing under her breath she began to search for
something that would force the lock. Her search was
hampered by the darkness, but she had nothing with
which to make a light even had she dared to. Groping
across the table she knocked over an inkstand which fell
with a crash, splattering its contents across table top and
floor. Cyllan froze, sweat breaking out on her skin, but
the noise brought no one to investigate, and after a
minute or so she resumed her hunt.

The table-top yielded nothing of any use, and it was
only when she turned her attention to the drawer set
beneath it that she found the knife. It was a wicked
blade, glinting like wet slate in the dimness as she drew it
from its sheath, but it would suffice well enough. There
was no time for finesse, and she gouged out the lock of
the cupboard in three fierce movements, wrenching the
door back and feeling inside for her quarry.

A glass bottle, a sheaf of papers . . . and the box.
Cyllan drew it out and put it on the floor, crouching over
it as she prised at the lid with her blade. Like the
cupboard it was locked, but it was made of soft pewter,
lead lined, and gave at her second attempt. She lifted the
lid . . . and stared with a chilling fascination at what
confronted her.

The Chaos stone lay alone in the box, and it glowed
with an inner light of its own; a cold, dim radiance that
spilled on to Cyllan's hands and turned them ghostly
grey. For a moment she baulked at the idea of touching
it – but then she gathered her courage, reached into the
box, and her fingers closed around the gem. An unnerving sense of elation filled her as she felt its hard contours
against her palm; her arm tingled and, just for a brief
instant, she felt a heady sense of power, as though some
unnameable force had flooded her mind from the stone's
depths. She took a grip on herself – she was by no means
triumphant yet, and jubilation must wait – and hastily

shut the box, putting it back in the cupboard and closing the ruined door as best she could. With the stone in her left hand she picked up the knife once more. She'd keep it, at least until both she and Tarod were safe . . .

Finding her way to the door, she bumped noisily against a chair, but again the noise was insufficient to raise an alarm. She waited until her heart stopped racing, then eased the door open . . .

The passage awaited her, seeming brilliant after the dark room. Cyllan stepped out –

And a figure moved across her path.

Cyllan's eyes widened in horror. She tried to dodge back into the High Initiate's apartments, but it was too late – he had seen her, stopped, recognised her as the hood fell back to betray her distinctive pale hair – and she found herself transfixed by the stunned stare of Drachea Rannak.

'No . . .' Cyllan croaked the word, her voice unrecognisable even to herself. 'No . . . Yandros, *no!*'

Drachea too had sworn aloud, and his hand went immediately to the short sword he had lately taken to carrying. He had slipped away from the banquet, bored and, he had to admit to himself, more than a little jealous of the High Initiate, and had been pacing moodily along the corridor at the very moment when, by sheer chance, Cyllan had emerged with her prize. Now he faced her, and as the initial shock which had frozen them both faded Cyllan saw realisation and alarm dawning in his eyes.

'Gods!' The sword rattled from its scabbard. 'You bitch, how did you – oh, *no!*' He brought the blade up in a wild, slashing movement as Cyllan made a desperate dive for freedom, and she reeled back against the wall to save herself from its shearing arc.

'Oh, no!' Drachea said again, harshly. 'Not this time, you demon – not this time!' And over his shoulder he yelled, '*Help! Servants, here – quickly!*'

The Chaos stone pulsed suddenly hot in Cyllan's hand, and a storm of bitter ferocity surged into life within her. *Drachea had thwarted her once; he had brought about Tarod's downfall – but not again! Never,*

never again! Like a vision seen in the instant of a bolt of
lightning her mind pictured Yandros's proud, sardonic
face, and his eyes seemed to reflect the colourless radiance of the gem –

Drachea started as her left hand came up, and a
sudden glare of light sprang from between her fingers.
On the verge of shouting the alarm again the words stuck
and died in his throat, and when he tried to draw breath
his lungs seemed to fill with ice. He swayed, staggered –
Cyllan took a pace forward, brandishing the stone like a
weapon, and her face illuminated by the gem's glare was
mad, insensate. Drachea tried again to yell out; his voice
broke in a cracking scream, and as the sound of it echoed
through the passage Cyllan sprang at him, the knife in
her right hand flashing up in a deadly stroke that took
Drachea in the stomach and sheared through to his
breastbone. His scream choked off into a bubbling howl
of pain and he doubled over, spinning around and
almost falling on his own sword. Seeing him down,
Cyllan's senses gave way to an explosion of rage and she
hurled herself on him a second time, the knife-blade
hurtling down and biting deep into his shoulder. She was
beyond all reason, driven by something she could
neither comprehend nor control; something that awoke
an insane, unhuman craving to kill, destroy, avenge –

A shriek that was neither her voice nor Drachea's cut
through the madness in her head, and she jumped back
as though jerked by a rope. Two servants, a man and a
woman, had come running in answer to Drachea's bel-
lowed summons, and had rounded the corner to be
confronted by the sight of what seemed to be a white-
faced demon, face and hands spattered with blood,
hacking with a gore-soaked knife at the struggling
Drachea. The woman fainted dead away and the man
stared at Cyllan, jaw gaping, gathered his breath to yell
at the top of his voice –

Sanity came back with a violent jolt. Drachea lay
between Cyllan's feet, dead or dying. The Chaos stone
was ice-cold in her left hand, the knife slick and slippery
in her right; her clothes a mess of new crimson stains . . .

Cyllan's stomach heaved, and, galvanised by nothing more than animal instinct, she turned and ran. The corridor veered crazily before her, and at her back, diminishing yet thundering like drums in her head, she heard the servant's high-pitched, frantic voice yelling a desperate alarm.

Chapter 15

The music from the gallery was loud enough to mask any commotion from beyond the heavy doors of the dining-hall, and from slow and formal set pieces the players had now progressed to lighter but more vigorous dance music. A few couples had taken the floor already, and the dancing would increase as the night wore on, continuing until the small hours when hot mulled wine and biscuits would be served before the revelry ended.

At first, Keridil didn't notice the two men who entered the hall and began to push their way urgently through the throng towards him. He was making conversation with Sashka's father, while at the same time privately reflecting on the success of the evening – and only when Sashka touched his arm and said, in an odd voice, 'Keridil . . . ' did he look up and see them approaching.

The looks on their faces were enough to tell him something was wrong, and as they reached him he rose to his feet. Curious onlookers strained to hear the brief, whispered conversation, but even Sashka was none the wiser when Keridil hurriedly proffered his apologies and strode out of the hall with the two men at his heels.

The servant who had raised the alarm was sitting with his back against the corridor wall, face hidden in his hands and shaking as though he had the palsy. A steward crouched beside him, speaking in low, urgent tones, while another man, grey-faced, was attempting to cover a body with his cloak and hide it from view. There was blood on the floor, on the wall, and spreading through the cloak in a dark, ugly stain.

'Wait.' Keridil spoke to the man as he was about to

cover the corpse's face. The servant drew back, and the High Initiate stared down at the victim.

He didn't need Grevard to tell him that Drachea was dead. The young man's eyes were half open and sightless, and blood still trickled from his mouth, though by the looks of it, Keridil reflected grimly, there must be little enough in his body left to be shed. Whoever had killed him must have attacked him as though possessed . . .

Feeling sick, he signed to the servant to cover the body once more, and turned to face the steward.

'Does anyone know who did this?' His voice was low and dangerous.

The steward got to his feet. 'Pirasyn here witnessed the whole thing, sir, and I think he recognised the killer. But it's hard to get any sense out of him.'

Keridil nodded and squatted on his haunches in front of the distressed man. 'Pirasyn. It's Keridil Toln. Listen to me – you *must* help us, if you can. Try to remember who it was you saw attacking the Heir Margrave.'

The man looked up and swallowed, and Keridil tried to smile reassuringly. 'He'll be apprehended, never fear. But we'll hunt him down all the quicker if you can identify him to me now.'

Pirasyn swallowed again, then shook his head. 'Not him . . . '

'Not whom?' Keridil was puzzled.

'*Him.*' the man repeated. 'Not him. *Her*. The girl – the one who aided the demon. White hair. Yellow eyes. And that *face* . . . ' He covered his eyes again and started to sob.

A liquid sensation clutched at Keridil's stomach and slowly he straightened up. *Cyllan?* It wasn't possible – she was safely locked up! He'd had Sister Erminet's own assurance not an hour since . . . But impossible or no, he also had Pirasyn's testimony . . . and a terrible intuition to add weight to it.

He swung round to the two men who had summoned him. 'Get up to the room where that girl's kept – check that she's still there. And *hurry*!'

They left at a run, and as their footfalls diminished
Sashka appeared from the direction of the main hall.
'Keridil? What's to do?'

He went to her, catching her by the shoulders and
halting her before she could see the carnage. 'Love, you
shouldn't have followed me.'

She gazed levelly back. 'When you're pulled from my
side by some obvious crisis, do you expect me to sit and
meekly await your return? I want to be of help – please,
tell me what's amiss.'

Keridil sighed. 'I didn't want to expose you to this, but
. . . Drachea Rannak has been murdered.'

Her lovely eyes widened in shock. '*Murdered?* Here,
outside your own apartments?'

The words brought him up short; it hadn't occurred to
him that there might be more than coincidence involved in
the location, but now he began to wonder. And if Pirasyn
had spoken the truth, there was one obvious motive . . .

He took a torch down from its bracket on the wall and
opened the door to his rooms – then Sashka heard a soft
oath escape his lips. She ran after him as he disappeared
inside, and found him staring at the detritus which
Cyllan had left. Spilled ink, scattered papers –

'Keridil, look!' she said harshly. 'The cupboard door –
the lock's been smashed!'

Keridil saw it, and ran across the room. He snatched
the pewter box from its shelf, and even before he opened
it the broken lid told him what he would find.

'It's gone,' he said.

'The stone . . . ?'

Keridil nodded. The mystery was beginning to piece
itself horribly together, and as Sashka peered into the
empty box he said softly, venomously, 'Cyllan . . . '

'What?'

Briefly, he told her what Pirasyn claimed to have seen.
She had never seen him so angry before, though he did
his best to control the rage in him, and she made no
attempt to mollify him. Rather, she thought, it would
serve her purpose the better if his fury could be chan-
nelled . . .

'Keridil,' she said as he was about to return to the corridor, 'Keridil, I was thinking . . .'

'What is it?' He was more curt than he had intended, but she seemed not to notice.

'About Sister Erminet . . . she told us that the girl was safely locked away. She gave us her word on it. I think she was lying to us.'

He frowned. 'I don't understand you. Whyever should Sister Erminet lie?'

'I don't know. But . . . well, I thought I must have been mistaken, but now I'm not sure.' And she told him of the hooded figure she had seen leaving Cyllan's room in Erminet's wake. As she related her story – though making no reference to the fact that she had checked the room herself – Keridil's jaw muscles tightened and his hands clenched.

'If she's in league with them . . . ' he said at last.

'It's possible. Isn't it possible?'

He was struggling to be fair, not to let anger cloud his judgement, but the evidence was hard to ignore. Sashka wasn't a liar . . . and Cyllan could surely not have escaped without help . . .

From outside the door he heard running footsteps, and a voice calling his name. Quickly he took Sashka's hand and led her out, in time to confront the two men he had sent to check on the girl. They were sweating and breathless, but their message was clear enough.

'She's gone sir! The room's been left unlocked!'

Keridil's mouth set in a narrow line. 'Very well. Organise as many searchers as you need, and make sure each one is armed. Tell them to gather in the dining-hall as soon as possible – we'll comb the Castle from end to end until she's found! I want the main gates guarded – oh, and set two men to watch that demonic lover of hers! It's ten to one he's behind this, and that she'll try to reach him. Whatever else happens, she mustn't succeed in that! Do you understand?'

'Yes, sir.'

'Then get about it, quickly!' And as they hastened

away he turned to Sashka, his face grave. 'I'm sorry that this has to ruin our celebration, love.'

She shook her head. 'It doesn't matter. The girl must be found – that's far more important. But . . . what about Sister Erminet?'

'Ah . . . yes. I wish I could be sure . . . '

Sashka nibbled at her lower lip. 'As yet, no one in the dining-hall knows what's amiss, Sister Erminet included. Perhaps if, before you break the news to them, she could be – invited to repeat her assurance?' She cast her gaze down. 'I know it's a devious thought, Keridil, but if we *do* have a viper in our midst, surely a little trickery is justified?'

She was right; and Keridil thanked the gods for her common sense. 'Very well. It's a shrewd suggestion, and we'll follow it. Though the gods know, I find it hard to credit that she should be a traitor.'

Sashka shrugged. 'Erminet was always unpredictable. At the Cot we lived in fear of her moods and fancies . . . and besides, we should remember that as well as guarding Cyllan, she's been responsible for tending to Tarod these last days.'

'You mean that she might be under his sway? I hardly think so – he's been kept drugged; I doubt if he can control his own mind, let alone influence another's.'

'We may have underestimated him.'

It was possible . . . and it could explain Erminet's perfidy.

'Well, there's only one way to be sure,' Keridil said. 'Let's return to our guests.'

Their entrance was greeted with relief and a great many curious questions. Keridil soothed anxieties with the promise of a full explanation, then sought out Sister Erminet, who – suspiciously, it now seemed to him – sat alone at a table and appeared disinterested in the furore.

'Sister Erminet.' He smiled as he approached her. 'I'm sorry to intrude on you with a medical matter, but – '

She looked up quickly, and he thought he detected relief on her face. 'Medical matter?' she said. 'Has someone been taken ill?'

'In a manner of speaking. It concerns one of your charges, and I'd like to clear up a little confusion.'

'Ah . . . ' said Erminet warily.

'The girl, Cyllan – I believe you said she was sleeping when you left her; is that correct?'

People were gathering round them . . . Erminet hesitated for a moment, and it was clear she was disconcerted. 'Did I? Perhaps so . . . yes, I believe she was.'

'And you did take care to lock the door behind you when you left?'

Now the old woman's face was unhealthily pale, but she rallied herself and smiled at him.

'Naturally, High Initiate. I have the key here at my waist, as always.' She held it up, but her hand wasn't quite steady. 'It never leaves my person.'

It was all Keridil needed. Leaning forward, he said softly, but ferociously. 'Then can you explain to me, Sister, how it was that Cyllan was able to leave her locked room, and commit cold-blooded murder in this Castle not fifteen minutes ago?'

The little colour that remained drained from Erminet's face, leaving it the shade of dried cement. She tried to rise, but her legs wouldn't support her, and her expression would have damned her without a word spoken.

'Oh, gods . . . she didn't . . . she couldn't have . . . ' She covered her mouth with one hand.

Keridil called forward two Initiates. 'Please conduct Sister Erminet Rowald to her room, and see that she doesn't leave until I send for her personally.' And to Erminet he added, 'I believe, Sister, that you have been guilty of an act which I would have thought unthinkable for one of your calling. I hope you'll prove me wrong, but I have very strong doubts. You'll have your chance to speak when Cyllan Anassan has been apprehended.' He nodded curtly to the old woman, and signed for the Initiates to lead her away. Shocked silence fell on the hall as they passed through the crowd to the door, then Keridil picked up an empty wine jug and banged it down hard on the table to call their attention. Every face in the vast room turned towards him.

'My friends,' Keridil said, the anger still tingeing his voice, 'I'm sorry to have to draw the evening's festivities to a premature close, but I have a very grave announcement to make, and I would appreciate the co-operation of every able-bodied man and woman here tonight.'

Beside him Sashka sank on to a convenient chair, her eyes cast down, and the faintest of smiles on her face.

* * * * *

She was lost. Her terrified, headlong flight from the scene of the grisly encounter with Drachea had taken her deep into an unlit and remote part of the Castle, where only endless black walls and silence confronted her. Blind instinct had led her down twisting flights of stairs and along narrow passages, until at last she was certain that her pursuers – if pursuit there had been – were left far behind. Then she stumbled to a halt, and collapsed exhausted to the cold stone floor.

Slowly the broken fragments of what had happened were beginning to form a coherent recollection, as the blankness of stark fear was succeeded by a peculiar calm. She had killed Drachea. In dark moments as she sat alone in her locked room she had often craved the chance to take vengeance on him, and her imagination had run riot. Now the fantasy had become reality, and the reality was bloody and ugly and shocking. Yet she couldn't feel remorse . . . her hatred of Drachea was too strong, the desire for retribution too great.

With an inward shiver she remembered the Chaos stone coming to life in her hand, the blazing glare of cold light that had transfixed Drachea where he stood. The stone had given her the opportunity she needed to strike – and it had also fed on her hatred, focusing it into a lust for destruction and mayhem that had eclipsed her reason and turned her into a savage assassin. The stone was quiescent now, nestling in her left hand. Her fingers ached from gripping it, and she had to prize them open in order to look at the gem where it lay in her palm. It seemed nothing more than a simple jewel, yet her flesh tingled as she felt an echo of the sensations it had awoken in her. She was beginning to understand Tarod's ambiguous feelings, part loathing and part need, towards it . . . he was right; it was a deadly gem. And now she realised why Yandros had agreed to aid her.

Quickly, half afraid that the stone might affect her further if she continued to hold it, she thrust the jewel into the bodice of her dress. Her hand came away smeared with crimson, and she realised that she was spattered from head to foot with Drachea's blood. The sight of it brought a lurch of physical revulsion and for a moment she thought she would be. sick; but the spasm passed as cold logic took over once more.

What was done was done, and right or wrong she didn't regret it. Drachea was dead – no one could survive such a savage attack – and she had kept her freedom, at least for the moment. But the hunt would already be up, and the chances were that her identity was known. She couldn't hope to evade capture for long while she remained in the Castle confines, and once she was caught there would be no second chance, and no reprieve this time. She would die, hanged or more likely beheaded, and Tarod would die too.

She had to reach him. She had to give him the Chaos stone, and plead with him to use it, if necessary, to save them both. Without his strength and power to aid them, the net would close and they'd be lost; they *needed* the stone, however deadly it might be.

Unsteadily Cyllan got to her feet, smoothing down her dress and ignoring the stains. The knife she tucked in her sleeve, unwilling to relinquish it lest she should need it again. Luck – and Yandros – had been with her once, but she dared not rely on them a second time. If she could keep to the Castle's unpopulated corridors until she found her way to the cellars where Tarod was imprisoned, well and good – but she would kill again if she had to, to reach her goal.

She pulled the hood of the short cloak up over her hair once more, and set off along the passage.

Cyllan had no way of telling how much time had passed before, at long last, she reached a place where steep stairs led down into the Castle's foundations, and knew she was close to her goal. From Sister Erminet's instruction she recognised the way to the storage cellars and began to hasten down the flight, until a sudden uneasy intuition made her pause. It might have been imagination, or a deceptive echo from somewhere, but she fancied she'd heard a sound from below, as though a foot had shuffled on stone. Holding her breath, and thankful for the dark clothes which helped her to merge with the shadows, she advanced a cautious pace, then another, until she reached the foot of the stairs. Here a narrow tunnel crossed her path, and, flattening herself against the dank wall, she peered round, holding the cloak hood close against her cheek.

Tarod was in the third cellar along, so Sister Erminet had said. And there, outside that very door, were two men. One leaned against the wall, hissing softly through his teeth while he whittled at a small piece of wood with the blade of a vicious-looking knife; the other sat gazing at the tunnel roof, seemingly lost in his private thoughts. But their apparent lack of attention was belied by the long-bladed, powerful sword that each bore at his hip. They had been set to guard the cell, and Cyllan knew that she had no hope of avoiding them should she try to reach Tarod.

Slowly and quietly she withdrew back into the darkness, her mouth dry with fear and anger. She was too late – the hunt was up for her, and she should have known that Keridil's first action would be to set a guard on Tarod's cell. They must by now have discovered that the Chaos stone was missing, and that would be enough to redouble their efforts to find her. Silently she cursed herself – by losing her way she had wasted precious time, and the High Initiate had thwarted her. Despair tied her stomach in knots of fury and frustration – she *had* to get word to Tarod somehow, let him know that she was free, for until he could be certain, he'd do nothing that might jeopardise her. But the chance was lost. She couldn't even reach one of the storerooms and hide there in the hope that the guard might change and Tarod be left unattended for a few minutes; the instant she stepped out from the stairs she'd be seen and apprehended. And she couldn't remain here, indecisive – she was too exposed; all it would take was one man to start down the stairs from above and she'd be trapped. And after what had happened to Drachea, they'd probably run her through without a second thought . . .

Wraithlike, she turned and crept away up the stairs, back in the direction from which she'd come. Her mind was gnawing frantically at her predicament, but she could see no possible answer. Yet she had to find a way – she *had* to . . .

A small shape moved across her path and she started violently, biting her tongue and almost losing her footing on the steep flight. The shape, too, paused, then raised its head and uttered a soft, querying cry. Cyllan's thundering pulse slowed as she recognised it for one of the telepathic cats that inhabited the Castle. She had already encountered two on her way here, felt their tentative probing into her mind. Their telepathy was a little like that of the aquatic fanaani, though of a lower order, and as she was about to move on past the creature Cyllan felt the delicate strands of its thoughts penetrating and mingling with her own. She hesitated – and suddenly, in her inner vision, she saw a blurred image of Sister Erminet's face. The cat mewed, urgency in its tone . . .

'What is it, little one?' Cyllan whispered, afraid that the echoes of her voice might carry to the tunnel below. 'What are you trying to tell me?'

She had bent down, and the cat reared on its hind legs, crying again. Cyllan's heart started to pound and she crouched, trying to steady her thoughts and open her mind to the creature's attempts to communicate.

'Tell me, little one,' she said softly. 'I'm listening . . .'

The Imp, Sister Erminet's adopted pet, knew that it had found the one it was seeking. It had left the old woman's room by its usual route, through the window and along a dizzying maze of incredibly narrow ledges to the ground, then, following instructions which it only barely comprehended, had headed for the cellars.

It was only the fact that the cat liked the Castle's underground rooms with their plethora of unexplored crannies and fascinating scents that had persuaded it to carry out the mission with which it had been entrusted – that, and the unmistakable urgency in its human friend's attempts to communicate. It had been curled asleep on her bed when she returned, and had resented being disturbed. But a combination of determination and blandishment had won through, and the cat's curiosity was aroused. The old woman wanted it to find someone, and the creature's mind formed a picture of another human, coloured grey and pale yellow, and of amber-hued eyes that were just a little like its own. And the cellars . . . it liked the cellars. And so when finally the old woman had refused to feed it, and refused to speak to it any more, it had reluctantly padded across the room, sprung up to the window-ledge, and slipped away into the night.

Now, it had found the object of its search, and immediately it sensed a mind with which it could communicate far more easily than it had ever done with Sister Erminet. And that mind needed help of a kind which, the cat understood smugly, it alone could give. A hand reached out towards it, stroking its hard little head, and the human began to project an image of someone the cat knew . . .

Cyllan didn't comprehend the cat's connection with Sister Erminet, but she understood enough of its nature to grasp at this slender hope as a drowning man might clutch a driftwood spar. She couldn't reach Tarod – but the animal could. No one would think to stop a cat if it passed by on some secret exploration. And if she could make it understand the message she wanted it to convey, and persuade it to find its way to Tarod, there was a chance – more than a chance, she prayed fervently – that Tarod would pick up enough of that message from the creature's strange, capricious mind to realise what was afoot.

She dropped to her knees and gazed into the cat's eyes, opening her thoughts to its mental scrutiny. It was curious; that was a good beginning. She projected an image of Tarod's face and saw its whiskers twitch with interest, then tried, though whether the cat could understand such human concepts she didn't know, to ingrain in it the idea that she was free.

'Tell him . . . ' She mouthed the words silently to reinforce her urgent thoughts. 'Tell him, little one. I am free. I am *free*!'

The Imp closed and opened its brilliant eyes in a long, slow blink. If the gesture meant anything, Cyllan couldn't interpret it. Then it uttered its peculiar little cry again, tail flicking – and before Cyllan could stop it or speak to it again it had turned and loped away, melting into the darkness, and was gone.

She sat back against the wall, not knowing what to think. She couldn't judge whether the cat had understood the message she had tried to instil into its mind; and if it had, whether it would choose to convey it or, with the perversity of its kind, would be distracted by some new interest and forget its mission. But she silently thanked Sister Erminet for her ingenuity and kindness in sending the creature to her. It was a slender chance, but it might succeed . . . and it was all the more imperative that she should find a hiding place where she would be safe until she knew whether the cat had reached Tarod with its message. If it did, he would find her. Somehow, he would find her . . .

The stairway was silent, the deep shadows still. Cyllan rose to her feet and began to climb again, alert for the smallest sound or sign of movement. If she could find a sanctuary before dawn broke she could wait in safety, at least for a while, and soon enough she would know. The waiting would be torment . . . but now, at least, the spark of hope had been rekindled.

Tarod woke from an uneasy sleep with the echo of a dream in his mind, and for a moment his senses were confused. Then, as his vision cleared, he remembered where he was.

He hadn't intended to let himself sleep . . . tonight was the night of the banquet, and Sister Erminet had told him that it was her one opportunity to release Cyllan. Yet there had been no word; and he surmised that by now the night must be well advanced. There were so many possible pitfalls in Erminet's plan that he feared something might have gone wrong, and the fear gave him a sharp, sick feeling in the pit of his stomach. Tense, he rose, flexing stiff muscles, and paced as far as the cell's confines would allow, railing against the lack of a window that prevented him from seeing the sky and judging the hour.

An empty cup stood on the floor – Erminet had maintained the charade of bringing him the regular dose of the drug ordered by Grevard, to avoid arousing suspicion – and in the gloom he kicked it over, so that it rolled noisily across the bare stone. As it came to rest, a hiss sounded from the shadows where the cup lay, and Tarod swung round, his green eyes narrowing. Something moved – and a small, silver-grey cat emerged from behind a pile of discarded sacks. Its coat was streaked with dust and there were cobwebs on its whiskers. It paused, then looked up at him and mewed what sounded like a resentful protest.

'Imp . . . ' Recognising the creature, Tarod spoke softly, squatting down and holding out a hand. The cat approached with caution and sniffed his fingers, then suffered him to brush the offending cobwebs from its face, shaking its head and sneezing. Then it sat down and, infuriatingly, began to wash itself.

Tarod watched it speculatively. Pitted though these ancient walls were with cracks and crevices, it was no mean feat for even such a small and agile animal to find its way through from the next cellar; and he suspected that the cat must have some ulterior motive for paying him a visit. In the past, he had had a way with most animals that enabled him to influence them; the most ill-tempered horse had been malleable to his will, and the telepathic cats – though less easy to command – were very receptive to his thoughts. Whether he still possessed those skills he didn't know . . . but he had already sensed an urgent imperative lurking in the cat's mind which, perversely, it was choosing to ignore, and he had no time to waste in waiting.

'Imp.' This time his voice was less cajoling, and the cat looked up quickly, pink tongue protruding slightly from its mouth. Tarod focused his mind, relieved to find that much of the old steel sharpness was there only waiting to be unlocked, and held the creature's gaze. Its slit pupils dilated to black orbs and he searched its alien consciousness, seeking the motivation which had brought it to him.

An image: distorted but recognisable . . . an old, wizened face that abruptly shifted and became younger, startlingly familiar. A pale nimbus that was the cat's concept of human hair; eyes with an amber-gold light to them . . . and a sensation; not a word, not even an idea, but a fundamental, primal emotion. Freedom. Freedom . . .

The cat was trying to tell him that Cyllan had escaped.

Tarod felt his pulse rate quickening until he could hear the rhythm of his own blood in his ears. If he had interpreted the creature's consciousness rightly, and if the message it brought was true, then why had Erminet sent the cat to tell him? His cell was unguarded, or so he believed – the old Sister had said that Cyllan would have the key and would come to him.

He straightened, uneasy. Something was wrong. Even if Erminet had secured Cyllan's release – and he didn't entirely trust the confused images in the cat's mind – something was preventing her from reaching him, and until he could be sure she was safe, he dared make no move. Moreover, without the soul-stone he was still vulnerable. Freed from the influence of the narcotic, he had regained his full wits and much of his former strength, but he didn't know how far his powers would extend. Certainly he was by no means the sorcerer he had once been . . .

He looked at the cat again. It hadn't resumed its interrupted wash, but was still staring at him, doubtless picking up the surge of emotion that was running through him. As their gazes met it yowled, loudly, and he crouched down again.

'Quiet, little Imp.' His hand reached out and caressed its head as he mentally calmed it. 'I understand you. But it isn't enough. I dare not – ' And he stopped, as a key grated in the lock of the cellar door.

The Imp hissed, and darted into a corner out of sight. Tarod turned, still half crouching, taken by surprise as hope and suspicion vied for precedence – then the door swung open and he was staring into the face of a burly man with an Initiate's badge at his shoulder.

'Aeoris!' The word broke out between the Initiate's clenched teeth. 'Brahen, here! This devil's supposed to be unconscious, but – '

He got no further. Tarod had no time to make a conscious decision, and instinct, coupled with a sudden, violent resurgence of the anger he had spent so many days trying to quell, took over. In one swift, fluid movement he was on his feet and his left hand came up in a gesture as familiar to him as breathing, summoning and focusing a power that swept from the depths of his consciousness like a striking Warp. Light glared crimson in the cell, throwing walls and roof and piled debris into stark and shocking relief, and as the bolt struck him the Initiate shrieked, his body a mad silhouette of flailing limbs in the bloody instant of the lightning flash. Darkness crashed down as the glare vanished, and Tarod had time to glimpse a huddled, motionless shape on the floor before a flare of poorer, natural light danced in the doorway as the second guard snatched up a torch and ran in from the passage.

By the flickering light of the brand he held, the surviving guard saw a sight which made his stomach churn in fear. His companion lay broken like a discarded doll by the cellar wall; while Tarod – who should by rights have been lying senseless on his pallet – stood like a dark angel of death, his eyes glittering and murder in his look.

Stunned, and incapable of thinking clearly or wisely, the guard brought his sword rattling out of its sheath. Tarod tensed like a hunting cat – he was unarmed, and the bolt of energy he'd conjured had sapped him; there was no time to rally himself for a second. Instead, he sprang.

The Initiate hadn't expected such an attack, and he brought his sword up clumsily, hampered by the blazing torch in his other hand. So fast that he had no time to react, Tarod's right hand shot out and snatched the torch from him; then with a savage swing of his arm he slashed the burning brand across the man's face. The guard howled in agony and spun around, dropping his sword and clapping both hands to his eyes. Tarod knew the blow had been enough to disable him, but the fury had taken hold and was unstoppable. He snatched up the sword – it was a heavy weapon, deadly in strong hands – and as the guard staggered yelling in a crazy zig-zag across the floor, Tarod swung the sword as a woodsman might swing an axe. A jarring shock ran through his arms and shoulders as the blade bit flesh and bone, and the Initiate's body crashed, decapitated, to the floor.

Tarod's breathing was harsh against a silence broken only by an unpleasant liquid sound as the corpse's blood drained away on to the flagstones. He let the sword drop with a clashing echo and backed towards the door, unmoved by the sight of the two dead men. At his feet the torch blazed sporadically; he stamped the flame out and darkness returned to cloak him.

He had broken his promise to Erminet. The thought occurred to him in a detached way, and he regretted it. Not the deaths of the two Initiates – he had no illusions about their willingness to kill him, if he hadn't struck first. But he had given his word that he would harm no one, and he didn't like the necessity of going against it.

Yet the thing was done . . . he'd gain no advantage by feeling remorse now. Quietly he moved out into the passage, closing the cellar door behind him. This place was too deep in the Castle's bowels for the guard's shouts to have been heard, and for the moment it seemed unlikely that he would encounter anyone else. Well and good; it gave him the time he needed. The fact that Keridil had set men to guard him where before there had been none proved that something had gone awry with Erminet's scheme, and he guessed that Cyllan's absence had been discovered and the alarm raised. Were the Circle still searching for her, or had she been recaptured? She was unfamiliar with the Castle's maze of rooms and corridors, and Tarod knew that she couldn't hope to evade a full-scale search for long. He had to find her – and, with or without the stone, he had to get her out of the Castle.

Erminet, he thought, was his best hope. If the hunt was up for her, Cyllan would be too frightened and too preoccupied for him to reach her mind and guide her. But Erminet might know her whereabouts.

Tarod knew every stick and stone of the Castle, and could make his way through it without encountering one of Keridil's search parties. He also, for the time being, had the advantage that as yet the Circle was unaware of his escape. If he could reach Erminet before the two dead guards were discovered, the odds in his favour would increase . . .

He started to move noiselessly away along the passage, then hesitated and, on an impulse, turned back and re-entered the cellar. The smell of blood made his nostrils flare as he stepped through the door; he avoided the headless corpse and moved to stand over the Initiate he had blasted. The man was dead enough, but the body relatively undamaged, and Tarod bent down to unfasten the hide cloak the guard had worn as a protection against the damp cold of the cellars. Beneath it, an Initiate's badge gleamed gold; he unpinned it and fastened it to his own shoulder, smiling faintly as he realised how long it had been since he wore a similar emblem. Then he cast the cloak around himself – it was hardly a disguise, but it made his black shirt and trousers a little less distinctive – and left the cell to its silence and the stench of death.

Chapter 16

Tarod emerged from the maze of passages below the Castle by a route known only to the more adventurous of those who had grown up within its confines. The courtyard was dark, but the Moons had set and in the East the stars were beginning to fade, telling him that dawn was little more than an hour away. For a moment he stayed hidden among the leaves of the overhanging vine which grew rampant over the ancient black walls, savouring the sweetness of clean air after his confinement. Then he cautiously moved out of the vine's shelter – and hastily stepped back again as a nearby door opened and three armed men came out. They passed by only three paces from where he stood motionless, but though he hoped to overhear something that would give him a clue to how Cyllan fared, they didn't speak. As soon as they were gone, Tarod moved away, keeping to the deep shadows. He didn't know where Erminet's room was located, or even if she would be there, but guessed that she would have been assigned one of the guest suites normally reserved for more senior Sisters in the East wing.

As he crossed the now empty courtyard towards a small door that led to another of the minor and little-used passages, he realised that there was indeed unprecedented activity in the Castle. Although lights blazed from the main hall there were no sounds of a celebration in progress, and the sporadic flicker of torches from various windows on the building's different levels suggested that many people were moving about. He smiled, faintly amused by the thought that Cyllan had caused such a furore and ruined Keridil's celebration, then, gaining the door, slipped inside and headed for a

flight of spiral stairs that would take him to the guest
wing.

It seemed that the search wasn't concentrated in this
section of the Castle; logical enough, as Keridil would
have no wish to alarm his guests unnecessarily, and
Tarod reached the corridor he wanted without encountering anyone. The Sisters' rooms were at the far end,
and the only way to reach them was to walk the length of
the lit passage in full view of any casual observer who
might emerge from one of the other suites. Tarod cast
the hide cloak back enough to expose the purloined
Initiate's badge, then, trying not to think of what he
might be forced to do if challenged, stepped out into the
corridor.

He was halfway along when a tell-tale gleam of light
from a side passage ahead made him stop in his tracks.
There was no chance to turn, nowhere to hide himself –
and a moment later a girl of some sixteen years or so
hurried out of the passage and, seeing him, squealed and
almost dropped the lantern she was carrying.

'Oh!' Her eyes widened as she stared up at him, then
her surprise matured into alarm as she recognised the
Initiate's badge. She tried to bow after the fashion of the
Sisters, but it was a clumsy and inexperienced attempt.

'Oh, sir – I beg your pardon! I was returning to Sister
Erminet; I wasn't neglecting my post, sir, but the Sister
very much wanted another light, and there was no one
else to send because they're all so busy searching . . . '
Her garbled apology tailed off under Tarod's steady
scrutiny and she blushed scarlet, stammering out, 'I'm
sorry, sir . . . '

Tarod had seen the gauzy white veil that covered the
girl's hair, and realised that she was a Novice in the
Sisterhood. He had never set eyes on her before . . .
and she hadn't recognised him. Aware that he might
turn this to his advantage, he nodded curtly. 'No one
would chastise you, Sister-Novice, for obeying the
orders of your senior . . . you are, I presume, under
Sister Erminet's tutelage at West High Land?'

'Well . . . I was to have been, sir. But of course, I

doubt if I will be now, after what's happened. I came with the party conveying the Lady's congratulations to the High Initiate.' Gaining confidence, she smiled at him shyly. 'I've only been a Novice for two months, sir, and I'm very grateful for such a privilege.'

After what had happened . . . Unwittingly, the girl had given away the truth, at least in outline. Tarod said, 'I'm glad you're sensible of it, Sister-Novice. But I hope you're also aware of your duty. You seem very young and inexperienced for such a responsible task.'

The girl reddened again. 'There was no one else, sir. What with the search for the prisoner who escaped . . . but I understand what I must do.' She looked up at him, hoping for approbation. 'I've not let anyone see the Sister without authority, as I was told.'

'Indeed. And what else were you told?'

Fortunately for him, the child was naïve enough to think that she was being tested. As though repeating a catechism, she said, 'Not to engage in conversation with the Sister, sir, on any matter other than her immediate needs. I . . . ' She hesitated. 'I was told she has betrayed the Sisterhood and the Circle, sir. And that she is to be questioned and possibly . . . tried.'

Gods; so they'd discovered what Erminet had done . . . Alarmed, but keeping his face expressionless, Tarod said. 'That's knowledge you should keep to yourself, Sister-Novice. I want to hear of no gossiping among the other girls, do you understand me?'

'Yes, sir.' The girl licked her lips nervously. 'Should I return to my post now?'

The child was easy enough to dupe; he could think of a way to get rid of her once he was face to face with Erminet. Aloud, Tarod said, 'You should; but I want to see for myself that the Sister is still where she should be. If all's well, count yourself lucky – and don't desert your duties again, whatever the reason!'

'No, sir. I'm sorry, sir . . . ' In an agony of shame and terror, the girl made another inept bow and hastened away along the passage, the lantern shaking in her hand. She stopped at the furthest door, fumbled inexpertly with a key, and at last persuaded it to turn in the lock. A soft glow spilled out, and Tarod gestured curtly for the Novice to remain where she was while he entered the room.

Erminet lay on her bed, asleep. Glancing over his shoulder to make sure that the girl hadn't misunderstood his order and followed him, Tarod crossed the room and bent over her, lifting her hand.

'Sister Erminet . . .'

There was no response, and the hand hung limp in his grasp. Intuition told Tarod the truth before he looked at her face. She was smiling, a small, secretive smile, and in a peculiar way she looked younger, the lines on her cheeks smoothed and her skin waxy. And on the table beside her bed stood several phials from her collection of potions, a wine flask, and an empty cup.

Tarod spun round, all caution forgotten, and his voiced barked out, '*Sister-Novice!*'

The girl ran in, alarmed by his tone. 'S-Sir . . . ?'

Tarod pointed to the small vanity table in one corner. 'Fetch that mirror! *Quickly!*'

She almost dropped it in her haste, and as she stumblingly approached Tarod snatched the glass from her hand and held it in front of Sister Erminet's face. The mirror's surface remained clear while he counted his own heartbeats; seven, eight, nine . . . He flung the mirror aside, hearing it smash on the floor, and the girl's squeak of fright fired him with contempt and loathing. He turned on her and, in a voice low and savage with grief, said, '*Do you know what you've done?*'

The girl was shaking like a leaf, one hand to her mouth. 'She isn't . . . she can't be, sir, I – I was only gone for a few minutes!'

'And a few minutes was enough! She's – she was a herbalist, a *skilled* herbalist! And you deserted her for long enough for her to take her own life!' He advanced towards her, hardly knowing what he was doing, and as he approached the girl gave a cry of distress, picked up her skirts and ran, darting out of the room like a frightened animal. Tarod stopped, listening to her running footsteps, his fists clenched at his sides so that the nails dug in to his palms. Then, shaking, he turned back to the bed.

'Erminet . . . ' He sat on the coverlet and took both her hands, as though his voice and his touch could bring her back to life. But her eyes remained closed, and the fixed little smile was frozen on her face.

She must have known what she was doing . . . and she must have chosen a drug that would act too quickly for anyone to save her. He took a shred of comfort from the thought that she must have felt no pain, but had died peacefully and by her own will. But that didn't change the cruel fact that she had died because of him.

Tears stung his eyes, and he squeezed the old woman's bloodless fingers until his grip all but crushed them. Erminet had been a true friend, putting aside duty for a more personal loyalty. And this was her reward . . . Her deception discovered, she had known what her fate would be if she was convicted of abetting him, and had chosen to do the Circle's work for them, to give herself the dignity of dying, if die she must, in her own way and in her own time. And her death, the cruel needlessness of it, fuelled Tarod's hatred of Keridil and the Circle, and their warped idea of justice. If he could avenge her – but she wouldn't want that. She had made him promise to harm no living soul in the Castle, and he had already broken that pledge by killing two men. There must be no more. He owed her that, at very least.

Tarod realised that some time had elapsed since the Novice had fled from the room, and knew that he must go, if he was to avoid being found when the girl returned with help. The Circle would understand quickly enough when she described the black-haired Adept she had met in the corridor, and the hunt would be redoubled as they sought him, too. He had little fear of recapture, but it would be a grim irony if Cyllan were found before he could reach her and Erminet had died in vain.

He folded the old Sister's hands across her breast, then bent to kiss her forehead gently. His left hand still

rested on hers – he raised it, then made a small gesture
over her heart. The gesture was a blessing, but no blessing that had ever been given by a servant of Aeoris.
Then he rose to his feet, and swiftly and silently left the
room.

The High Initiate received the news of Sister Erminet's
suicide with chagrin and distress – and also, reluctantly,
with the acknowledgement that her action was positive
proof of her guilt. But when he heard, from the tearful
Sister-Novice, of the mysterious Adept whom she had
encountered and who couldn't be found, the pieces of an
ugly puzzle fitted together all too well.

Of the four men despatched to check on Tarod, the
youngest was violently sick when he saw the carnage in
the cellar and the other three had difficulty controlling
their stomachs. Keridil heard their reports in the privacy
of his study, thankful that he had at last persuaded
Sashka to retire to her parents' suite until morning.
There could be no sleep for him – especially now that
Cyllan wasn't the only enemy they had to contend with –
but at least she had been spared this . . .

'I want the search intensified,' he told Taunan Cel
Ennas, who was the Circle's most experienced swords-
man, as they stepped out of the Castle's main entrance
and stood at the top of the sweeping steps in the sickly
first light of dawn. 'Double the guard on the gates, and
make sure they're not opened for any reason without my
authority.' He hunched his shoulders and stared about
him at the towering black walls, which seemed suddenly
oppressive. 'The gods know there are enough crannies
in this damned place for them to hide in. But we'll find
them, Taunan. We'll find them, if we have to take the
whole Castle apart stone by stone!'

Taunan sighed, pinching the bridge of his nose in an
attempt to clear his vision. Despite his tiredness he knew
Keridil was right; there could be no rest until their
quarry was run to earth. He only wished he could share
the High Initiate's certainty that they would succeed.

'It's easy to forget that we're not dealing with an

ordinary man, Keridil,' he replied wearily. 'Tarod has the cunning of Chaos, and a good many of its powers.'

'Not without the soul-stone,' Keridil reminded him. 'And we know that's in the girl's possession.'

Taunan grimaced. 'And if they should find each other before we find them . . . ?'

'We can't afford to let that happen. We *must* apprehend one of them – and I don't care which – before they have the chance to meet. If we fail in that, the gods alone know what the consequences might be.' Keridil squinted up at the lightening sky. 'I've called a meeting of the higher Adepts in an hour, to discuss what occult methods we can call on, but before that I – ' He stopped, his eyes narrowing.

'Keridil?'

The High Initiate took hold of Taunan's arm, and his voice was dry with unease when he spoke. 'Taunan . . . look . . . '

The older man followed his gaze. 'What is it? I don't – '

'Look to the North. And listen.'

Taunan sucked in a sharp breath as he understood, and stared beyond the towering bulk of the Northernmost spire. It seemed that another dawn was breaking in the far distance, challenging the true dawn in the East; the grey arc of the sky was tinged with a pale, sickly spectrum of colour that seemed to be shifting, moving, like a vast, dim, slowly turning beam of light. The wind was fresh in off the sea, but underlying its faint susurration was another sound, far off – a thin, unearthly wail as though, hundreds of miles out beyond the coast, a hurricane was raging and speeding in towards them.

The bands of colour in the sky were intensifying slowly but surely, and even as the two men watched a vivid slash of orange flickered across the heavens like a scar, followed by another, smaller streak of harsh blue.

'It's going to be a bad one . . . ' Keridil said quietly.

Taunan nodded, his throat dry. Even protected as they were by the Maze which held the Castle in a fractionally different dimension from the rest of the world, a

Warp was a terrifying experience; and Keridil was right;
the flickering colours in the sky presaged an abnormally
powerful storm. Taunan forced down the mind-numb-
ing terror of these weird and deadly phenomena which
he shared with every living man, woman and child, and
tried to smile.

'I'd defy even Tarod to try to flee the Castle during a
Warp.'

Keridil glanced at him in surprise, then his face
relaxed and he, too, smiled. 'You're right . . . and
perhaps it's the first time in history that the Warps have
been to our advantage!' He looked up again, and shivered. 'Come on. Let's go back inside. Advantageous it
might be, but that doesn't mean I want to watch it
coming.'

From her hiding place in a storeroom that adjoined the
Castle's stables Cyllan saw the first threatening changes
in the dawn sky, and felt the faint vibration beneath her
feet that presaged the onset of the storm. The thick
stone walls blotted out the sounds of the approaching
Warp, but couldn't protect her from the primordial fear
that turned her stomach to water as, through a narrow
window, she watched the bands of colour growing
stronger, marching out of the North. Sick with fright,
she crawled into a dark corner and pulled the cloak hood
over her head, but she couldn't escape; though sight of
the coming horror was blotted out, the vibration
increased until it seemed to permeate her bones and
beyond them to her soul.

She wished she had chosen another hiding place.
She'd tried to reach the North spire, thinking that perhaps Tarod, if he too was free, would look for her there,
but in trying she had almost run across one of the search
parties and only a chance piece of good luck and quick
thinking had saved her. She'd fled to the stable wing as
the nearest sanctuary, and since then hadn't dared to
emerge.

Now, even without the Warp to imprison her here, the
coming of dawn had made it too dangerous for her to

move. If anything the search seemed to have intensified, and though she hoped it might be a sign that Tarod had escaped, it did nothing to help her immediate predicament. He'd never think of searching here for her, and when a few minutes ago she had tried to focus her mind and reach him subconsciously, her own thoughts were too confused by fear of the Warp to allow her to concentrate.

A door at one end of the storeroom led directly to the stables themselves, and beyond it she could hear a restive stamping and snorting as the Castle's horses sensed the approaching horror. Cyllan left her corner and crept towards the door, reasoning that, now of all times, no one in their right mind would have need of a horse, and the company even of animals would be better than the terrors of solitude when the storm struck. She tried not to glance at the window as she went, but couldn't help seeing the strange play of sickly light over her hands and clothes. Swallowing the bile which rose in her throat and threatened to choke her, she pushed the door open a crack and peered through.

Tall, dim shapes moved in the gloom beyond; brown and grey and warm chestnut; one black with a wild, white eye. The nearest horse, a big bay, saw her and stamped back in its stall, ears flattened; she slipped through the door and approached it, speaking softly to pacify it. These Southern-stock beasts were more kindly tempered than the shaggy little Northern ponies she had ridden as a drover, and the bay quietened quickly under her hands, nudging at her as though grateful for human company. Cyllan passed down the line, talking to each animal in turn and glad of the chance to divert her mind from what was happening outside. At last the horses began to settle a little, and she reached the end of the line. Here straw bales for fresh bedding had been piled in a corner, and she sank down on them, pulling the cloak tightly around her body. She could do nothing but wait until the Warp had passed . . . shivering, she hunched deeper in to the straw and tried not to think about the storm.

The spectral bands of blue and orange and green that advanced across the sky were rapidly changing to dark, evil-looking shades of purple and livid brown when a man burst from the watchtower by the Castle gates and pelted head down across the courtyard. He took the wide steps three at a time, burst through the main doors just as a surprised servant was about to set the bars in place, and skidded to a halt, gasping for breath.

'Where's the High Initiate?'

The servant, nonplussed, gestured towards the dining-hall, and the man raced away.

Keridil was eating a hasty breakfast which his steward, Gyneth, had persuaded him to take, when the gateman came running in.

'Sir!' the man croaked, his lungs heaving, 'Riders! A party, coming across the causeway – '

'What?' Keridil got to his feet, pushing his plate away. 'Now, of all times? Damn it, the Warp's about to strike! Who are they?'

The gateman shook his head. 'Don't know, sir. But there's a herald with them, and a retinue – '

Keridil swore. He had enough to worry him without strangers needing sanctuary from the Warp at this last moment, but he could hardly leave them outside to face the coming horror. He turned on his heel and shouted at a servant who was putting up the hall's shutters.

'Leave that! Find Fin Tivan Bruall and tell him to get to the stables to take in new horses!' And to the gateman: 'Can you get them through in time, do you think?'

The man peered out at the dangerous sky. 'Just about, sir, if they don't fall foul of the Maze.'

'Pray they've been here before, then – and hurry!' The man left at a run, and Keridil followed, swallowing back his terror of stepping through the doors and seeing the Warp in its full spate. As he approached the entrance he could hear the high, screaming note that accompanied the storm, like damned souls howling in agony, and he shuddered before, taking a deep breath, he forced himself to walk out on to the steps.

The Castle gates were already opening, swinging

ponderously back with what seemed to Keridil agonising slowness. Overhead the sky raged and its insane colours tainted the walls and the flagstones, staining Keridil's skin so that he and the men who had followed him out looked like ghastly apparitions. The Warp would hit them within two or three minutes, and though in the Castle they were safe enough from its power, no reasoning on earth could stand against the sheer animal terror of being beneath one of the supernatural storms as it came shrieking overhead.

Now the gates were fully open, and he could see the approaching party. They had crossed the causeway from the mainland, but were having difficulty controlling their horses, which reared and plunged as the riders attempted to guide them across the darker patch of sward that marked the Maze. But at last the leading horse was through, and the others followed, kicked into a desperate gallop that brought them clattering and thundering under the great arch and into the courtyard.

Seven men – and three women. Keridil's heart sank as he recognised the tall, slightly stooped figure dismounting from the sweating iron-grey gelding while two Initiates ran to help him. Gant Ambaril Rannak, Margrave of Shu Province . . . Drachea's father.

He started down the steps, the Warp momentarily forgotten in the face of this unexpected and unwelcome arrival. But before he was halfway down, a commotion from the stables made him turn. Someone shouting, his bellow audible above the mindless yell of the storm – and a woman's high-pitched scream of protest.

'High Initiate!' The stentorian voice of Fin Tivan Bruall, the head horsemaster, was filled with triumph as he and one of his stable boys dragged a struggling, hooded figure towards the steps. 'We've got the murdering little bitch! We've got her!'

A howl from the sky, as though the Warp answered Fin's news with a furious protest of its own, drowned out all other sound, and Keridil swung his arm in an urgent gesture towards the main doors. 'Get those people inside! It's about to strike!'

The Margravine and her two maids were screaming in terror, their male companions faring little better. They stumbled up the steps, while several more Initiates braved their fears to take charge of the panicking horses as Fin and his boy dragged their captive towards Keridil. The High Initiate glimpsed Cyllan's bloodstained clothes and her stark white face, grotesquely distorted by the whirling spectrum reflecting from the sky, saw her mouth twist in a shrieking snarl though he couldn't hear the curse she spat at him. Then an instant later the sky turned blue-black, like a monstrous bruise, and red lightning spat across the heavens as the wail of the storm swelled to a howling crescendo.

'*Get to shelter!*' Keridil's cry was lost in the cacophony as a ferocious wind shrieked out of the North and the Warp came thundering overhead. Fin kept his wits sufficiently to hang on to Cyllan, hauling her bodily up the steps and cuffing her with a powerful fist when she started to struggle again. Keridil turned, started ahead of them – and stopped dead.

The voice of the Warp dinned in his ears, the insane sky blotting out the rising Sun and plunging the courtyard into chaotic darkness. But enough light flickered from the violent streaks of colour exploding across the face of the storm for him to see the tall, gaunt figure that barred his way to the doors. A tangle of wild black hair streamed in the gale, and the face, illuminated by a violent explosion of green and crimson overhead, was demonic. An appalling memory of Yandros, Lord of Chaos, smashed into Keridil's brain – this apparition was the Chaos lord's dark twin, and a hideous premonition of his own nemesis stunned him into immobility.

But if he was paralysed, Cyllan wasn't. She redoubled her efforts to escape Fin's grip, and her voice sounded shrilly above the Warp as she screamed, '*Tarod!*'

Her cry broke the thrall that held Keridil. He sprang back, darting down the steps to where Cyllan struggled, and snatched his sword out of its scabbard. Tarod came after him – then froze as Keridil stopped a pace from Cyllan, whose arms were now pinned by the horsemaster, and touched the point of his blade to her heart. The High Initiate's face was wild with fear of the storm and the fury aroused by this confrontation; Tarod knew that if he made a single untoward move, Keridil would run Cyllan through.

The other Initiates in the courtyard had by now realised what was afoot and, leaving one of their number to manage the Margrave's frightened horses as best as he could, came running to Keridil's aid. They were all armed, and Cyllan feared that without the stone Tarod couldn't hope to defeat them. She had to reach him – *had* to, whatever the risk –

Keridil was taken completely by surprise when, with a violence born of desperation, Cyllan brought one foot up and out in a savage kick that took him full in the stomach. He went down, losing his grip on the sword, and Cyllan twisted around to bite Fin Tivan Bruall's hand with all her strength. The horsemaster yelled and she kicked out again, backwards this time, breaking away from him. Her momentum sent her staggering down the steps; she turned with the agility of a cat as Tarod started towards her –

Three Initiates blocked her path, while two more ran at her from behind. Cyllan snarled like an animal, saw Tarod grappling with the first of her three assailants, and realised that the trap was closing around her. Over the shriek of the Warp she heard his voice.

'Cyllan, *go*! Run – get away from them!'

The High Initiate was on his feet, advancing – Cyllan turned and ran, hampered by her skirt and almost falling as she reached the foot of the steps. And suddenly she was in the midst of a group of milling, panicking horses, half of them running free while one young Initiate struggled to keep the others under control. A tall grey shape loomed across her path; she cannoned into the Margrave's gelding and reflexively clutched at a stirrup to stop herself from falling.

'Stop her!' She heard Keridil's yell behind her, and the gelding whinnied piercingly. Cyllan didn't pause to think – she reached up, gripped a handful of the animal's mane, and sprang. She landed half over the gelding's neck and frantically jack-knifed herself into the high-pommelled saddle, hanging on grimly as the beast reared in frightened protest.

'Tarod!' Her cry was lost in the cacophony overhead. 'Tarod!'

He saw her, but couldn't reach her; two men were attacking him and in the chaos he could barely defend himself, let alone spare time for any other consideration. His mind roiled – power was surging in him, fuelled by the insanity of the Warp, but it was wild, uncontrollable, he couldn't grasp it. He evaded a wildly swinging blade and his left hand locked on his assailant's wrist, twisting, crushing – he felt a bone snap, but the second Initiate was coming at him again

'*Tarod!*' Cyllan's cry this time was a shriek of alarm as Keridil, who had regained his own blade, ran at her with Fin and another man at his heels. The gelding reared again, almost unseating her, and snatching at the reins she pulled the animal into a side-stepping buck as the High Initiate lunged towards her. The blade missed her thigh by a hairsbreadth and instead sliced a shallow but ferocious gash along her mount's flank.

The gelding screamed. It arched its body, lashing out, then, panic stricken, it bolted. Sparks scattered from its hooves as it careered across the courtyard, instinct driving it to escape the Castle which it saw as the source of its terror. Cyllan crouched precariously in the saddle, hauling on the reins but to no avail – the horse was heading for the main gates, and the gatekeeper had deserted his post to help his fellows. The gates still stood part open, and the gelding galloped under the yawning arch, bolting straight for the sward and freedom.

Cyllan saw what lay ahead of her, saw the whirling chaos of black light and impossible colours that tore the world apart beyond the Maze. She glimpsed the tortured crags of the mountains twisting in on themselves, moulded by the Warp to hideous illusions, and in terror she flailed at the gelding, struggling to stop its headlong flight before it was too late.

The horse raced across the Maze – and the scream that tore from its throat as it emerged on the far side was shredded by a howling roar as the full force of the Warp hurtled at them like a monstrous tidal wave. Cyllan felt as though her body were being torn apart – darkness shot with livid silver fire erupted in her face, and agony smashed through every nerve before the world exploded in oblivion.

Keridil staggered to his feet, dazed by the force with which he'd hit the ground when he flung himself clear of the gelding's flailing hooves. As Fin Tivan Bruall ran to help him, he stared towards the gates and the maelstrom beyond, and his face was grey with shock.

'Aeoris . . . ' He made a sign over his heart. 'Fin, she – she – '

Fin didn't answer him. He was looking over his shoulder to the steps, and what he saw alarmed him. Tarod stood motionless near the top of the flight, and it was obvious from his rigid attitude that he, too, had seen Cyllan's appalling fate. One of his attackers lay at his feet, hunched and moving feebly. The other was backing slowly away down the steps, his sword half raised as though to protect himself from something no other man could see, and he was terrified.

Fin gripped Keridil's shoulder. 'High Initiate . . . '

Keridil turned, buffeted by the screaming wind, and his face tightened. Then he started to run, stumbling towards the frozen tableau on the steps. Taking their cue from him, the remaining swordsmen gathered their courage and closed in . . . then Tarod turned his head.

If he had ever been human, Keridil thought, his look now gave the lie to it. Tarod's face was demented, and his green eyes burned with an unholy light. His lips moved and he mouthed a word, though in the racket of the storm Keridil couldn't tell what that word was. Then he raised his left hand – and the High Initiate felt terror strike to the depths of his soul.

She was gone. Tarod fought against the knowledge, but

couldn't deny it; it had happened, and he'd been unable to prevent it. She was gone – the Warp had taken her, and hurled her into whatever unimaginable nightmare waited beyond its borders. She might be dead, or alive and trapped in some monstrous limbo . . . he had been so close to her, and again he'd lost her. And the grief that devoured him, far greater than the grief he'd known at Themila Gan Lin's death, or Erminet's, was the catalyst that finally woke the power in him to its full flood. Cyllan was gone, and all he could think of was revenge. For her sake he wanted to kill, ravage, destroy anything and everything in his path. And the focus of his blazing hatred was one man – his one-time friend. His betrayer. His enemy . . .

As he gazed like a transfixed animal into Tarod's eyes, Keridil felt Fin Tivan Bruall's presence at his side. It was small comfort.

'I tried to stop her.' He barely recognised his own voice.

The corners of Tarod's mouth lifted in contempt, but he stayed his hand. '*You tried to kill her.*'

'No—' And the protest died as Keridil realised Tarod wouldn't believe him. He had one chance, he thought; just one. Distract him long enough for the other Initiates to move in and take him unawares. It was a slender hope, and the thought of what Tarod might do if the gamble failed turned his stomach to water.

'We've both lost, Tarod,' he called above the gale. 'You see – she took the Chaos stone. So now your soul's gone forever . . . ' He licked his lips nervously. 'I don't think even you can prevail against us without that.'

Tarod's eyes narrowed to ferocious slits, and Keridil saw that the other men had, as he'd hoped, taken advantage of this brief respite to close in. One of them made a sudden clumsy move; Tarod's head snapped round –

'*Take him!*' the High Initiate yelled, goaded at the same moment by a sudden despairing premonition that his warning was too late. '*Take him, before –*'

His words cut violently off as a titanic flash of blood-red light exploded outwards from where Tarod stood. It coalesced into the form of a gigantic broadsword, twice the height of a man and glowing with a ferocious fire of its own, which Tarod held balanced in both hands as though it weighed nothing. One of the Initiates made an inarticulate noise and staggered back. Lit by the flaring glow of the supernatural sword Tarod's face was a mask of pure malevolence – then he swung on his heel and the blade shrieked in a whistling arc that cut down the two nearest swordsmen before they could jump clear. Blood spattered Tarod's face and arms as the two severed bodies pitched to the ground, and as he came face to face with Keridil once more, the incandescent sword glowing with a savage hunger in his hands, the High Initiate recoiled in sick horror. He had sent two Adepts to their deaths – the others now drew back, their gazes locked on the monstrous blade – and by the light spilling from the sword he saw his own nemesis in Tarod's unhuman eyes.

For a moment the howling thunder of the Warp seemed to abate, and in the comparative lull Keridil heard the slide of Tarod's foot on stone as he began, slowly, to advance. The blade pulsed, shimmered, blinding him – then without warning a blast of raw, uncontrolled power slammed into him like an invisible fist, knocking him backwards so that he sprawled on the flagstones. So fast that he had no time to react, Tarod sprang down the steps towards him – and as the daze cleared from his mind, Keridil found himself staring at the monstrous, glittering sword only inches from his face.

He bit hard into the flesh of his cheeks, willing himself not to give way to the panic that threatened to engulf him. The philosophers said that, when death stared him in the face, a man recalled the events of his life in a rapid flow of dreamlike images. Keridil had no such experience – his mind froze to a blank fugue and he could only stare helplessly at the blade and the silhouetted figure beyond.

From the corner of his eye he saw one of the surviving Initiates make a convulsive move in his direction, and he flung out one arm in a warning gesture.

'Stay back!' The man hesitated, then obeyed, and Keridil let his breath escape slowly between his teeth. When he spoke, he was surprised to find that his voice was steady.

'Get it over with.' The storm was rising again, but he knew his adversary heard him well enough. 'I'm not afraid of dying. Have done with it, Tarod.'

Tarod stared down at him. The sword in his hand didn't waver, but the madness in his mind was giving way to a clearer, colder reason. He could destroy Keridil. And if the blade once touched him, the High Initiate wouldn't merely die; for the sword was a lethal manifestation of the very essence of Chaos, a focus for the power that flowed through him. Keridil wouldn't merely die: he would be *annihilated*. It would be a just vengeance; a fitting retribution for Cyllan's fate . . . yet Tarod held back.

She might be living still. A Warp had brought her to this Castle; he himself had survived the hideous onslaught of such a storm when he was no more than a child. And if she *were* alive, he could find her . . .

To destroy Keridil would gain him nothing. Too many people had already died in this unhappy affair; to add one more to the toll would be a bitterly futile gesture, and a further betrayal of his oath to Sister Erminet. He didn't want revenge. Reason argued that the High Initiate wasn't wholly responsible for what had happened, and now that the insanity which had possessed him had passed, the desire for vengeance had gone with it. All that mattered was finding Cyllan.

Keridil's eyes widened in surprised confusion as Tarod raised the glowing, threatening blade until it no longer menaced him. He stared up at his enemy, suspicious and uncertain, not daring to acknowledge a spark of hope. Tarod gazed back, and the contempt in his green eyes was suddenly mingled with pity.

'No,' he said softly. 'I won't take your life, High Initiate. Enough blood has already been spilled here.' He renewed his grip on the sword and its brilliant corona flared up until Tarod stood wreathed in bloody light.

Overhead, the sky howled and spat a web of silver lightning high above the Castle spires, and Keridil felt a charge of energy jolt through him as the Warp renewed its fury.

'If Cyllan lives,' Tarod said, and despite the roar of the storm Keridil heard every word as clearly as though it were spoken within his skull, 'I'll find her. And if I do, I promise you that you'll hear no more of me.' He smiled thinly. 'Once, you refused to accept my word, and you betrayed my trust. I hope by now you've learned a lesson from that mistake.'

Keridil started to sit up, moving slowly, watching the blade in Tarod's hands. He didn't speak; his throat was too dry; but his eyes were venomous. Then Tarod raised his face to the screaming sky, as though communing with the storm's diabolical power. The Warp answered with a howling, shrieking crescendo, and Tarod's figure seemed suddenly to catch fire, black brilliance shot through with sparking silver blazing to life about him. The sky erupted in a rolling bawl of thunder, and an explosion of white light blasted the courtyard, making Keridil yell out in pain and terror as the colossal flash seared his eyes. He fell back, flinging an arm up to protect his face, struck the flagstones, sprawled –

There was silence. Dazed, Keridil lowered his arm, blinking at the dancing after-images which clouded his vision. Then, as his sight cleared, he realised with a fresh shock that the Warp was gone. The watery grey light of a natural dawn filled the courtyard; Eastwards the sky was streaked with the first faint rays of the morning Sun, while somewhere beyond the stack a seabird cried with a plaintive, mewing sound. And Tarod had vanished, as though he'd never existed.

Painfully, the High Initiate climbed to his feet. Every bone, every muscle, every fibre in his body ached; his limbs shook, and when a hand took hold of his arm he leaned gratefully against Fin Tivan Bruall's burly support. The horsemaster's face was pallid, his mouth set; Keridil looked beyond him at the ragged circle of Initiates who were approaching uncertainly.

'Keridil?' Taunan Cel Ennas was the first to speak. His gaze flicked to the bodies of the two men Tarod had killed, then he looked away quickly.

Keridil couldn't bring himself to look at the corpses. He said tightly, 'Have them covered and taken inside, Taunan.'

'What – ' the other man began to say, then changed his mind, shaking his head helplessly. The half-voiced question, *what happened?*, was too obvious, yet unanswerable. He turned and stumbled towards the steps.

Others were emerging from within the Castle now, and among them Keridil saw the anxious face of Drachea's father. *All this, and now he had to face explaining the death of the Margrave's son and heir* . . . He shook his head savagely to clear it, but a cold, angry bitterness remained. Behind him he heard a clatter of hoofs as the milling horses were recaptured and led away towards the stables, and – aside from the two dead men on the ground – the sheer normality of the scene made him feel sick. He should have ignored the demands of protocol and tradition; he should have shrugged off the opinions of those who insisted that he make a ceremony out of Tarod's death, and simply killed him without fuss or formality when he had the chance. Now, he had other deaths on his conscience. Drachea Rannak, Sister Erminet, the two guards in the cellar, two more here in the courtyard . . . He remembered the pledge Tarod had made before vanishing, and cold, cynical disgust filled him. He'd no more trust the word of that creature of Chaos than he'd trust a poisonous snake. While Tarod lived, the Circle and all it stood for were imperilled: he *had* to be destroyed. But how many more lives would be lost before this affair was finally over?

And Keridil's blood ran cold at the thought that followed: *if it ever would be over. If the Circle could prevail against Chaos* . . .

He had been moving towards the main doors, but abruptly he stopped. He felt steadier now, and his mind was as clear as a knife blade. Tarod had bested him – but Keridil's heart and soul craved retribution. And for the sake of the Circle, of the whole world, he'd take it or die in the attempt.

He looked up at the sky, which was brightening by the moment, and let the full flood of his bitterness and anger wash over him. He fingered the gold badge at his shoulder, the double circle with its diagonal lightning flash; and spoke so softly that the attendant Fin couldn't catch his words.

'I'll destroy you, Tarod,' Keridil whispered with savage intensity. 'By Aeoris and his six brethren, I swear I'll find you, and I'll destroy you. Wherever you are, however long it might take, I won't rest until I've erased your taint from the face of our world!'

As though in answer to the High Initiate's oath, the first vivid ray of the Sun touched the top of the Castle wall, casting a pool of light down to the courtyard. Keridil felt a peculiar sense of peace steal over him – the peace of knowing that he had spoken from his heart, and set himself on a right and just course which, come what may, he would see through to the end. He had the resources of an entire world at his hand; the power of the Circle and of the ancient gods it worshipped. Against such strengths, Chaos couldn't hope to triumph – and it was Keridil's sworn duty to see it crushed and destroyed.

They were watching him still, the silent little group in the doorway. Keridil hunched his shoulders, realising that he was cold. Then he began to walk purposefully up the wide, sweeping steps to meet them.